About the Author

Claudia loves to write about ordinary women who find themselves in extraordinary situations and to date, has written about three love affairs, five crazy mothers, two fractured sibling relationships, one cancelled wedding, a recovering alcoholic, two stately homes, one vicious stepmother and not forgetting countless failed 'goes' at online dating.

As a bestselling author, Claudia has published sixteen novels, four of her books have been optioned, two for movies and two for TV. Her books regularly reach number one in Ireland, they're widely translated, and in the UK, she's a *Sunday Times* bestseller.

In 2018, she published *The Secrets of Primrose Square* and the stage adaptation marks Claudia's debut as a playwright. During Covid lockdown, the book was one of the top ten downloaded books across all genres, both in Ireland and the UK.

Claudia is crazy excited about this, her next book, *The Fixer* and is particularly thrilled with the cover, which is so feck-off gorgeous, she wants to have it made into a t-shirt.

 @carrollclaudia

 @claudiacarrollbooks

The
FIXER

Claudia Carroll

ZAFFRE

First published in the UK in 2021
This paperback edition published in the UK in 2022 by
ZAFFRE
An imprint of Bonnier Books UK
4th Floor, Victoria House, Bloomsbury Square,
London WC1B 4DA
Owned by Bonnier Books
Sveavägen 56, Stockholm, Sweden

A CIP catalogue record for this book is
available from the British Library.

ISBN: 978–1–83877–394–6

Also available as an ebook and an audiobook

1 3 5 7 9 10 8 6 4 2

Typeset by IDSUK (Data Connection) Ltd
Printed and bound in Great Britain by Clays Ltd, Elcograf S.p.A.

MIX
Paper from
responsible sources
FSC® C018072

Zaffre is an imprint of Bonnier Books UK
www.bonnierbooks.co.uk

This book is warmly dedicated to Pat Moylan,
with love and thanks. For everything.

MONDAY

Chapter One

Meg

I'm standing two behind her in the crowded coffee shop. It's a grey, overcast morning, it's only gone 7 a.m. and pretty much everyone in the queue is in shite form.

No one is taking a blind bit of notice of me, which is just how I like it, so I shuffle up the queue, pretending to stare at my phone, while I do my thing.

Age: she's not much older than me, as it happens. Early thirties at a guess.

Appearance: tall, tall, tall and whippety-thin. Attractive. Dressed in Victoria Beckham jeans, with a shirt tucked in at the waist that I'd swear is Stella McCartney – this season's too. The hair is sun-streaked and light brown, worn long, loose and balayage-style. Expensive. High-maintenance. Nails are shellac, ruby red, and very recently done. One point of note; there's a tiny bruise on the upper left quadrant of her forehead. A fresh Botox jab, I'm guessing.

All of which point to one thing and one thing only; this is a woman who has absolutely no problem shelling out cash on herself. Clearly, she's gone and forked out on a brand-new wardrobe, with no expense spared. So I ask myself, why would anyone do that?

Because it's what you do when you're in a brand-new relationship. The heady early days when you do a major overhaul of your own look and when you can barely eat a cream cracker, on account of that intoxicating, infatuated, sick-to-the-stomach feeling you get when you think you're in love.

People are such idiots that way.

She orders an Americano, so I take this as my cue and dive in.

'Hey, it's so good to bump into you!' I beam brightly. 'Are you losing weight? You look so much thinner!'

Actually, she doesn't at all – there's no weight to lose. But this one's been banging on on Instagram about her weight loss goals for so long now, I suppose it's only polite to say something.

'Wow, thank you,' she beams back delightedly. She's called Nicole, by the way, and she only looks delighted that a complete stranger is showering her with compliments, at seven o'clock on a drizzly Monday morning.

'You're gluten-free and vegan now, aren't you?' I smile my biggest, brightest, most sincere smile. Utterly fake, of course, but you'd never know. It's a smile that says, *Look at me, I'm just like you. Trust me, I* know *you. No, really. Honestly, we've already met before, like,* loads *of times.* 'Because it, like, really shows. Look at your skin . . . glowing!'

#lifegoals #gettingthere #cleanliving.

At least that's what's plastered all over your Twitter feed, you oversharing moron. Don't you realise how easy you make it for people like me to get a handle on you?

And there it is. That dazed, slightly confused look on Nicole's face that might as well say, *Help!!! Where do I know this one from? School? College? She seems to know so much about me – why can't I place her?*

Nicole goes to pay for her order and when her back is turned, I surreptitiously tap at my phone. Bingo. Yet another photo on Instagram, that's been posted all of about twenty minutes ago. *God bless social media*, I think, as I do several thousand times a day, *for making my job such a doddle.*

Just for the laugh and to keep things interesting, I throw a little curveball into the conversation.

'Tell me, how's that new little puppy of yours getting on? Teddy, isn't it? Is he still weeing all over your kitchen floor?'

Because according to this photo, he is.

'Teddy?' Nicole says, looking baffled. 'You know about Teddy?'

'Isn't puppy training just the worst?' I chat away. 'I had nightmares with my little bichon frise. The farting is something else, even in public – the amount of apologising I've had to do to complete strangers.'

'Oh, *right*,' Nicole says. 'That must be where we know each other from – puppy-training class. So how is your . . . emm . . . Sorry, remind me what your dog is called again?'

'Fantôme,' I say, taking care not to let my fixed smile budge an inch. 'It's French.'

French for phantom, actually. Appropriate, given that the little fecker doesn't actually exist.

'Of course! Fantôme. Great name . . . he's a dote . . . that cute little face!'

Oooh, you're good. I'll say that much for you. You'll tell a barefaced lie, rather than admit you've never seen me before in the whole course of your life.

But then, aren't most people like that, I think, efficiently handing over my card to the barista and paying for my own decaf latte. Malleable, and easy to manipulate? You only have to bounce over, all friendly and bubbly, then flatter them about something – anything at all, really – because who on this earth doesn't like a nice compliment? The more you butter them up and act like you've met before, the more the other person ends up feeling like *they*'re the idiot for not being able to remember you in the first place.

And it's usually plain sailing from there on in. Or so I've always found.

'You know what else I find amazing about being a new dog owner?' I toss in lightly, scooping up my latte as the two of us fall naturally into step and leave the coffee shop together. Coincidentally, I appear to be heading down the street in the exact same direction as Nicole. Funny, that.

'Having a dog,' I chat away, as we weave in and out of other early-morning pedestrians, 'really is the most fabulous way to meet guys. The number of cuties I've had approach me when I'm out walking Fantôme . . . amazing!'

'Well . . . I'll have to take your word for that,' says Nicole, tight-lipped.

Oh will you now? I'll take that as neither a confirmation nor a denial of your relationship status. Which means this Nicole one is cautious and private. Useful to file away for future reference.

'You work just here, at Colchester Private, don't you?' I say, as we approach a dominating glass building, with imposing steps leading up to it and a lot of cool, architecty-looking chrome going on.

'Ehh . . . yeah, yeah I do,' says Nicole, looking puzzled as we get ready to go our separate ways. 'Wow, you must have an amazing memory. Because for the life of me, I don't remember telling you that.'

'It is easy to remember. I'm just across the road from you, as it happens,' I lie, nodding vaguely in the direction of a social media company's glitzy HQ, directly opposite.

'Wow! We certainly seem to have loads in common,' says Nicole, still looking politely confused, as swarms of her co-workers busily barge past her up the steps.

'Yeah – don't we just?' *You'd think that, wouldn't you?*

'It's just driving me nuts that I can't remember meeting you before,' she adds, shaking her head, completely baffled. 'Sorry . . . what did you say your name was again?'

I didn't.

'Meg. It's Meg.'

'Well, nice chatting to you, Meg, see you again soon!'

Oh, you have absolutely no idea, babes.

As Nicole sweeps off, Americano in hand, I stride briskly onwards, efficiently tapping notes into my phone as I walk.

Find out where I can hire a puppy. Or volunteer to walk a stranger's dog for about an hour a day – that's all I need.

Then, ever professional, I send a quick text update to my client.

Initial contact has been made.
So far, so good.

The response comes back instantly, but then this particular client isn't one to hang around.

6 weeks. That's all the time I'm prepared to pay for.
I expect results by then, or you can consider our
arrangement over.

Six weeks? I think, hailing a taxi to whisk me off to my next meeting. *Puh-lease. Gimme a decent challenge, would you?*

Chapter Two

Meg

'Now I don't want you to think that I'm, like, bitching or anything . . .'

'That was the furthest thing from my mind,' I purr down the phone, filching keys from the bottom of my handbag and letting myself in through the hall door of the penthouse apartment where, believe it or not, I happen to live.

Long story.

'. . . But he is really giving me a major pain in my hole,' says my client, who's called Denys, by the way, and who genuinely sounds like he's about to do time for someone. 'I mean . . . not that I'm being judgy or anything.'

'Of *course* you're not,' I say soothingly. But then two full years at this game have taught me that ruffled feathers need to be smoothed down and that the client is always, always right. No matter what the circumstances.

'Much more of this messing though, and I really will fucking kill him.'

'You're human,' I reply. 'And that's a perfectly natural reaction.'

'He was a good forty minutes late into work again this morning,' Denys grouses on. 'Eighth time this month – I shit you not. I mean, it's like this tosser thinks there's one rule for him and another rule for the rest of us.'

I'm just about to dump my bag and keys down on the hall table, but on hearing that, I stop dead in my tracks.

'So why not just fire this guy yourself?' I ask him, straight out. 'It certainly sounds like you have ample grounds to.'

'Ehh . . . don't you remember the name of the company I work for?' he sighs.

Course I remember, I remember everything.

'Cambridge Holdings,' I say.

'Correct. And this guy's full name is James *Cambridge*. That should tell you a lot.'

'Ahh.' OK, so now I'm beginning to see the full picture. 'You're a family-run business, then.'

'We certainly are. And just because this idiot's mother and his uncles and aunts founded the place and all have jammy seats on the board, he thinks he can just drift in and out as and when he pleases. Entitled little shit – pardon my language, but I'm really at the end of my rope here.'

'In that case, why don't *you* leave?' I ask, kicking off the trainers I've had on since early morning, heading for my bedroom and opening double doors that lead into a walk-in wardrobe.

'Because,' Denys says wearily, 'I actually *like* my job. In fact, I love it. I care about the work we do here and I know our company is helping to make the world a better place. I did a master's degree years ago, specifically so I could bring the right skill set to this organisation, and it's just beginning to pay dividends for me. So how do you think it feels that I have to shoulder this deadbeat, who doesn't care about his job and who's only there because he's got the right last name?'

'I take your point. It's certainly a delicate situation.'

'Now you see why I'm reaching out to you,' Denys says, as I do a lightning-quick scan through my wardrobe, where racks and racks of clothes, shoes and bags are neatly laid out. All colour-coded, naturally.

My job demands uniforms – lots of them. And no one, absolutely no one, barring the cleaning lady, is ever allowed in here – ever. Well, otherwise I'd have to fend off a list of annoying questions along the lines of, 'but how can a twenty-nine-year-old possibly afford all this?'

There's no way to explain it, really. Not without telling people what I do, which is out of the question. My own mother thinks I'm just flat-sitting for a colleague at work, and that's how I came to be living in such unheard-of, breath-taking luxury.

'Just don't get used to it,' Mum sniffed on the one and only occasion I let her inside the place. Big mistake, as it turned out. 'This wraparound balcony lark, and views over the docklands, and a spare bedroom? When I was your age, I was living in a bedsit with the one payphone in a hall-way and a two-bar electric heater with lumps of plastic coal on it. Whoever this owner is, they must be coming down with money.'

If my mother finds out the flat belongs to me, she'll think I'm out on the streets dealing drugs. Far better just to smile and keep my mouth shut. My situation is far too complicated to explain anyway – and particularly not to family. The fewer who know, the better.

Anyway, with AirPods efficiently clipped in my ears, I wriggle out of the jeans and jumper I've had on since early morning; my outfit for casually 'bumping into' my newest project, Nicole, in the coffee shop. Clothes that said, 'hey, I work in the tech industry, too – I could come to work in PJs and no one would give a shite'. That look might have been all very well and good for a 7 a.m. in Café Sol, but not for the lunchtime meeting that's ahead – not by a very long shot.

Carefully, I select a neatly tailored pencil skirt with a crisp white shirt and shimmy into the new outfit, while Denys keeps rabbiting into my ear.

'Anyway, you came very highly recommended,' he's saying. 'From a friend of a friend, if you're with me.'

'I understand,' I say, knowing precisely who this mutual connection is. My benefactress, the woman who set me up. But, of course, I'm far too discreet to let on. Discretion is the better part of valour, etcetera.

'And I know you're probably used to dealing with relationships of a far more . . . *intimate* nature than this,' Denys says.

At that, I allow myself a wry little smile. Over the past few years, I've earned the nickname The Fixer, because that's pretty much what I do. I fix your people problems – all of them. I'm pretty much entirely self-invented and, quite frankly, consider what I do for a living to be a kind of public service.

You've got someone in your life driving you nuts? I'll get rid of them for you. Gently and subtly, of course, using the time-honoured art of persuasion. Maybe you've got a partner who's cheating on you behind your back and you need this 'third party' to be airbrushed completely from the picture. Or an ex who won't leave you alone, or else a clingy former friend who won't take the hint that you're trying to shake off. So what to do? Send for The Fixer, of course. Hell, I've even dealt with a meddling mother-in-law who wouldn't back off a newly married couple, and if I can do that, I can do anything.

Two years now. That's how long I've been doing this. Two years of giving calm, dispassionate, discretional service. Two years of never getting it wrong, two years of completely smashing it. When hired, I immediately knuckle down to brass tacks, get on with the job in hand and get results, quickly and with an astonishing lack of fuss. Job done, game over.

You want to know the secret to my success?

When my work is done, everyone actually ends up far better off in the long run. Inconvenient 'third parties', whether professional or personal, are gently moved aside, so imperceptibly they barely even realise it's happening. Without fully grasping how, they often find themselves sidelined to different jobs in different companies, sometimes even in different countries, which, more often than not, work out far better for them. And the pure magic of it is, I always manage to convince them that it was entirely their own idea.

Not only that, but I'll always aim to guide them on to newer and far more suitable partners – critically, ones who are single and available this time. Ergo, my clients get what they paid for, cheating spouses are given their just deserts, and as I always make crystal clear – whether a client subsequently chooses to stick with or turf out an errant partner is entirely up to them.

True, when I first started out, I was merely doing a favour for a client of the company I worked for at the time, a lady whose husband was doing the dirt on her and who I just felt sorry for.

Back in the early days, as things started to take off for me, spouses were generally my stock-in-trade; men mostly. I'd get rid of mistresses, then deal with married, lying, scumbag cheaters as I saw fit.

But the trouble is, it turned out, I had such a talent for it that now I've evolved into something of an equal opportunities freelancer. Word about me seems to have spread like wildfire, and these days I'm as likely to be called in for a case just like this one, where a disgruntled employee needs to get rid of a deadbeat co-worker, as I am a romantic triangle – hence my wry smile.

'You see, I heard you were a woman who was good at fixing . . . undesirable situations, shall we say,' Denys adds.

Fixing undesirable situations. A delicate way of putting it, I think, phone in one hand as I touch up my lipstick with the other. An almost invisible nude shade – discreet. Unshowy. Perfect.

'But the reason I'm calling you in is that I've just been appointed project manager on a new venture for my company,'

Denys says. 'Which, as you can imagine, is big for me, huge. Career-making.'

'I can imagine.'

'And this tosser is just dragging my team down, constantly. Now, don't get me wrong, I wouldn't want anything, like, *bad* to happen to him – nothing like that.'

Jesus, what does this guy take me for anyway? An execution squad? The mafia?

'I just want you to get him . . . to move aside, if that's possible,' he clarifies. 'To another organisation. Preferably one that I never have to deal with. So that my team can get back to work and lazy-arse becomes someone else's problem. A big ask, I know, given that it's his family's company, but it's not like he gives a shite about them.'

There's a pause as I give myself a quick up and down in the full-length mirror in front of me.

Looking good. You know what? This works.

Just one more finishing touch, I think, dragging a comb through my hair, (shoulder-length, chestnut brown – utterly nondescript, ideal for my line of work). It's been hanging loosely around my shoulders since I left the flat at dawn, but now I slick it back into a neat, tidily low bun, with not a single stray hair loose. Glasses? I wonder, picking up a pair and testing them out. Too swotty? Trying too hard? Bit much, I think, putting them back into a drawer in the dressing table, which I keep specifically for props just like it.

If I say so myself, to look at me now, I'm utterly unrecognisable from the super-casual, almost studenty way I was dressed first thing this morning. Now I look like a slightly older, successful professional, a solicitor maybe, or a finance manager. But then, the last thing I'd ever want is to be recognised by someone I've worked on in the past. When it comes to appearance, in this line of work, the best thing you can be is a chameleon.

Finally happy that I'm wearing the right armour for what lies ahead, I step back out into the main, open-plan living area and sweep on through to my little study, immediately clicking on my laptop, so I can give the full focus of my attention to Denys and his dilemma.

'Right, then,' I say, briskly getting down to business. 'I'm going to need quite a few specifics from you. The sooner you can give me all the details, the sooner I can knuckle down to work.'

'Oh, it's such a relief to hear you say that,' Denys says wearily. 'Because if I have to look at this deadweight for one more second, I really will strangle him. I made the cardinal mistake of trusting this muppet with a pitch for the company, a new client we've been trying to land for months, and honestly, a child of ten would have done a better job . . .'

The bitching, I know of old, could go on for hours, so I cut him short. No rudeness intended, but I'm a busy woman and frankly, who has time for this?

'I'll need the guy's full name and date of birth,' I say briskly, 'his Twitter handle and a link to his Instagram account would be useful, if you have those, too. A home address is essential and any information about his personal life is a big bonus. Is he straight or gay? Single? In a relationship? Does he go to the gym? What does he like to do on his time off? The clearer a picture you can give me, the faster we get results.'

'Wow,' Denys says, a bit taken aback. 'That's a whole lot of information.'

'You want me to help you or not?'

'You really think you can?' he asks hesitantly.

'Trust me,' I tell him, allowing myself the luxury of a little smile. 'I've got a pretty good track record at this.'

But the truth is a bit more than that, actually. Because in this highly niche job which I've more or less created for myself, I've yet to fail.

Not once, not a single time.

Is it blowing my own trumpet to say that?

To be perfectly honest, I don't really care.

Chapter Three

Meg

I'm juggling multiple clients at the moment; I barely have time to go to the loo, never mind deliver the successful results everyone expects, and yet here I am, about to take on yet another.

A very, very big fish.

Far too big for me to even consider turning down.

Bang on the stroke of midday I arrive, punctual to the dot, for a meeting even I'm more than a little nervous about.

The constituency offices of Senator Katherine Sisk are right in the heart of Dublin's city centre, in an old Georgian building, easily identifiable by the posters plastered over every window screaming, 'Vote Katherine Sisk, Number 1!'

Godawful photo, I think, eyeing it up quickly as I buzz the intercom at the main door.

Katherine Sisk is a well-known, high-profile serving senator, famous for her liberal, left-wing views, who's up for re-election next week and who seems to be a shoo-in to top the polls. Popular and outspoken, she was one of the leading lights in the marriage equality and abortion referenda and is universally respected as a champion of women's rights.

In her poster, however, the woman looks every single day of her fifty-something years; her bullet-silver hair needs a right good cut and the forced smile on her face makes her look constipated.

Honestly, I think, brushing a crease out of my neat black coat and buzzing on the door again. Why is it that politicians end up looking like terrorists whenever they try to come across as being approachable and 'one of the people'? Haven't they anyone half-decent on hand to tell them the truth?

To my surprise, the mighty Katherine Sisk opens the office door herself. which is a bit like the Queen letting you in at the gates of Windsor Castle and asking you if you'd mind wiping your feet.

'Hi,' I smile brightly, reaching out to shake her hand. 'I'm Meg Monroe, it's good to meet you. Fabulous poster, by the way!'

That's the other thing; in my line of work, I've always found hypocrisy to be a particularly useful tool. Don't mind what anyone else says; having two faces really is the most wonderful asset.

'You're her?' Katherine asks, looking at me cautiously, then glancing up and down the street, almost as if she's afraid there might be a photographer lurking behind a wheelie bin who might jump out and pap her at any second. 'You're really her? The woman I spoke to on the phone?'

'That's me,' I say confidently.

'You're younger than I would have thought,' she says doubtfully. 'Considerably younger.'

You know what? There's no right answer to that, so I don't say anything at all. Instead, I just scan Katherine Sisk from head to foot and do my thing, instantly drawing conclusions.

Height: 5' 4", even in heels. Which, by the way, are tatty at the heel and scuffed at the toes.

Physique: a little on the curvy side. Her shirt is straining a little across her stomach – probably as a result of quite recent weight gain. She's been too busy to cook and been living off take out food lately, is my guess.

Clothing: plain black trouser suit. Reiss, but badly dated now, four years old, at least. Makes her look like she's on her way to a funeral.

Make-up: too heavy, too ageing. Concealer patted around the eyes, clearly intended to disguise too many late nights and a lack of sleep. Sadly, though, it has the opposite effect, and only makes her look even more worn out and exhausted.

'And you're sure no one knows you're here?' Katherine asks, keeping her voice good and low, so there's no danger of being overheard. 'I mean, no one knows we're meeting? Because . . . well, you know. Obvious reasons. In my line of work, you can't be too careful.'

'Of course not,' I reassure her, taking care to sound positive and upbeat – always the best way to win over any potential new client. If I inspire confidence – I know of old – that's half the battle.

'Right, then,' says Katherine uncertainly. 'I suppose you'd better come in. At least inside, we can have a bit of privacy.'

She's nervous, I think. *And twitchy.* A clear indication that the Good Lady Senator is slow to trust. Which, in my humble experience, only ever means one thing.

That someone close to her has betrayed her, in the very worst way, and at the very worst time imaginable.

Senator Katherine waves at me to follow her inside, on through the bowels of the constituency office, where it's busy and bustling, as election volunteers and campaign officials flit in and out of tiny, interconnected offices, most of them on their phones, everyone looking stressed and hassled. The main office is dominated by a TV streaming live news, and a besuited, bespectacled guy is studying it closely, drinking in the results of a poll that appears to put Katherine in a five-point lead over her immediate rivals.

'It's a head start,' he shrugs at Katherine, as she glides past. 'But that's all it is. I certainly wouldn't crack open the champagne just yet.'

'At least there's some good news over here,' an energetic-looking aide says from behind a desk, peeling an earbud out of her ear, while she juggles a phone, iPad and laptop all at the same time. This one looks early thirties at most and has a mane of wild, unruly red curls, so thick there's a biro perched on the top of her head that isn't budging.

'I've got *PrimeNews* on the line and it's a yes for tomorrow night.'

PrimeNews no less. Even Katherine stops in her tracks to absorb that particular nugget. *PrimeNews* is the single biggest late-night political talk show in Ireland; you're absolutely no one unless you've been grilled by its legendary host – and the more savagely, the better.

'What's the catch?' Katherine asks, folding her arms and frowning. 'Because with that shower, there's always a catch. I don't want to be the token woman on the panel, not like last time. It's got to be a fifty/fifty mix. Fairness and equality, that's the message we've got to keep hammering home, time and again.'

'The mix is gender-balanced,' this red-haired aide replies, 'plus they want you to discuss climate change, which can only be good for us – it's central to our whole message.'

'In that case, get straight back to them and tell them it's a very firm yes,' Katherine says decisively. 'And by the way, everyone, this is Meg.'

A few disinterested heads swivel in my direction and there's a couple of muttered 'hi's from around the room.

'Meg's a consultant,' says Katherine, 'and I just need to have a quick private word with her. If you'll excuse us for a few minutes.'

A consultant, I think, following Katherine into an empty office space, where there's boxes of campaign posters spilling out over every spare surface.

Well, I've certainly been called worse.

A lot worse.

*

'Forgive the mayhem,' Katherine tells me, closing the door firmly behind her, just as her mobile starts to ring. 'We've got exactly one week and counting till the election, so, as you can see, it's all hands to the pump.'

It's tiny and cramped in the office, but at least there's some semblance of privacy in here.

Katherine automatically clicks off her call, but no sooner has she done that, than her phone rings yet again.

'Oh, shoot,' she says, 'this one is vitally important – I have to take it, do you mind?'

Of course not, I wave silently.

'Yes, Minister, thank you for calling,' she says, sitting down behind her desk, putting on her reading glasses and bringing up some kind of document on the screen in front of her. 'Not yet, but we are moving forward on it . . . let me just double-check those figures for you . . .'

I seize the chance to have a quick scan around the place, just so I can piece together a bit more information on Katherine and her campaign, which doesn't take too long. But then, it never does. I also use the time to run a few preliminary Google searches on my own phone, and by the time Katherine winds up her call, I'm prepped, primed and ready to go.

'You're a busy woman,' I say, pacing around a bit and thinking aloud. Walking and talking always works best for me. Besides, who has time to sit still? The last time I can remember sitting down was back in 2017. 'So, let me save us both a lot of time. It's got to be your husband, surely? Well, clearly it's him, because why else would you need to see me?'

Katherine winces and there's a tight little pause before she nods yes. But that's all it takes; I'm already well ahead of her.

'Say no more, I understand,' I tell her, efficiently tapping away on my phone. 'You're up for re-election and any kind of scandal that would detract from your message would be hugely damaging to you. Plus, you're a mum.'

I throw a curt nod in the direction of some of the Sisk family photos dotted on the desk opposite. 'Two kids, one in college, and one in senior school, by the look of it. Do they have any inkling about this? Rows, arguments at home, anything like that?'

'No . . . not at all,' Katherine says hesitantly, clearly not used to being with someone who takes the lead.

'Good,' I say, warming to my theme. 'Then let's keep it that way. Your kids don't need to know about this any more than the general public does. Your family life is strictly off limits, and my job is to make sure it stays that way.'

'Go on,' says Katherine, taking off her glasses, swivelling in her chair and listening intently.

'If you want my help,' I say, pacing and thinking and thinking and pacing, 'then you have to do exactly as I tell you. First and foremost, you absolutely must *not* blame yourself for this in any way. If your husband is offside, then I'll deal with him, quickly and, above all, discreetly. But be warned: as soon as I'm done, then you, Senator, will have some pretty big decisions to make. You might subsequently choose to separate and start afresh, or you might decide to take your husband back, go for counselling, and put it all behind you. How you decide to live your private life in the future is, of course, your own business and no one else's.'

'So . . . how do you propose to . . . ?' Katherine asks, looking a bit confuddled, but I'm already clicking away on my phone, miles ahead of her.

'Your husband is Philip Sisk, he works for an environmental consultancy start-up, he's active on your campaign, and he's a stay-at-home dad too. At least, according to what I can glean online. Nice family photo, by the way,' I add, holding up a feature that had appeared in a recent Saturday weekend spread. A group shot of the whole Sisk clan, even though the two teenage daughters look like they had to be nailed to the sofa to pose for the picture, and everyone's smile is strained.

But then, aren't they always in these 'casual, at home' shots?

My eye falls on a particularly ugly shot of Katherine, dressed in an uncomfortable, ill-fitting cocktail dress, leaning up against her already set dining table, pretending to light a candle, as if it were Christmas Day. Jesus. Do people really fall for this crap?

'Philip is working on your re-election,' I say, still walking the room and thinking out loud. 'Therefore, my guess is he's out and about at all hours of the day and night, covering your whole constituency, just like you. So it doesn't take Sherlock Holmes to figure out that he was thrown into the company of someone who works equally long and crazy hours. Someone on your team, for instance. Possibly even someone in this very office.'

At that, I stop dead in my tracks.

'Maybe even someone who's here right now.'

Got it in one. Katherine flushes hotly and that's all the confirmation I need.

'There's no possible way you can have known that . . .' she stumbles to say, but I'm already over at the glass wall that separates Katherine's private office from the main campaign HQ outside, scanning through it and taking careful note.

'Curly, red-haired woman who had two phones on the go when I came in?' My eye quickly falls onto that distinctive mane of red hair.

Not a huge stretch either; this particular aide is young, pretty, she clearly isn't wearing a wedding ring and she has the banjaxed look of someone who works twenty-four/seven. Or at least, who claims that she does.

A curt nod from Katherine.

'I'm more or less certain,' Katherine says quietly, starting to sound genuinely upset now. 'I'm not stupid, I've suspected for a long time. Phil takes calls and disappears out of the house at all hours, then tells me it's about the campaign. At first I believed him, mainly because I wanted to . . . but then . . . then . . .'

Her voice cracks and I almost feel the first stirrings of sympathy for her.

Almost.

I don't indulge it though – because that's the golden rule. You don't get close – you never get close. These people aren't my friends, they're my clients.

I got close once before, and it turned out badly. For all involved. Never again.

Self-pity, I've always found, helps nothing and hinders much. Cold clear-sightedness is what sorts out messy, emotional situations. In confidential talks like this, I always have to be the strong one, the dominatrix, the bossy-pants. Clients might not like it, but in the end, they'll thank me.

'You need to be fully upfront with me about everything,' I tell Katherine. 'Remember, I'm here to fix this, but I can only do that if you're a hundred per cent honest with me. At all times.'

'Oh Christ, this is a nightmare . . .' she sighs, fumbling up her wrist for a tissue as her eyes begin to tear up. 'It's just the bloody cliché of it, that's what gets me more than anything. Phil and I have a life together, a good life, or so I thought . . . and now this? At quite literally the worst time imaginable. With a general election in less than a week.'

'Just stick to the facts,' I tell her coolly, folding my arms. 'That'll do me for now.'

'OK . . .' Katherine says, making an effort to compose herself. 'So I caught him out in more than a few barefaced lies. He'd tell me he was out doing door-to-door canvassing, but I subsequently discovered he was with *her* the whole time. Dog-walking is another great excuse of his, but I know right well that poor Mycroft, the family Lab, is being walked no further than *her* front door.'

'Did you check the call record on his mobile phone bill? GPS on his phone and car?'

She nods a tight little yes.

'Good. At least you're thinking straight. You'd be amazed at the number of clients who don't.'

'I even managed to get my hands on his credit card statement too,' Katherine goes on, 'and there it was – all the proof anyone would need. Bastard even took her away on a weekend to a five-star spa retreat down the country. I don't know what annoyed me more – that he did it in the first place, or that he was stupid enough to pay with a card, so there was a paper trail.'

'Did you confront him with it?'

'You bet I did,' says Katherine, in a barely audible voice. 'And, of course, he denied, denied, denied everything. Then he blamed the campaign, then came out with a load of horse dung about how I'm so focused on re-election, I've lost the run of myself and was throwing out baseless accusations willy-nilly.'

'Gaslighting you, in other words?'

'Precisely.'

I nod and listen and drink it all in and take a moment to think, *for fuck's sake, why are people so bloody stupid? So careless of other people's feelings? What's the point of being in a relationship in the first place, if you're only going to shit all over the other person and humiliate them in the worst way imaginable? And, in this case, fuck up their career in the process.* No, I can't let that happen. Not on my watch.

I've been at this game for two years now and it still makes me boil with hot, irrational anger, every single time. I park it though, just like I've schooled myself to. Because that's the only thing to be done with feelings that run too high. And I thank my lucky stars that I'm far too smart to bother getting into a relationship in the first place. Curious thing I've observed about people in love; they invariably turn into a shower of self-absorbed, self-sabotaging lunatics.

Someone should really run a scientific study on the subject.

'You just leave Philip to me,' I say to Katherine, taking control again. 'Dealing with cheaters is all part of the service.'

I could have added that this is actually the single best part of the job, the bit I'd gladly do for free. The Almighty Come-uppance, I've termed it. Making sure the punishment aptly fits the crime. Giving the Philip Sisks of this world all the retribution and humiliation they so richly deserve. Like a cross between some kind of karmic angel of retaliation and the Terminator.

Christ knows, I've every good reason to enjoy it.

'What do you plan to do with him?' Katherine asks, frowning worriedly over her glasses. 'Nothing that upsets my girls, I hope?'

'Your daughters will never know a thing,' I reassure her. 'But for now, my first task is to get his mistress clean out of the picture and make sure she'll never bother you again. I'm going to need her full name, plus any other personal details you can give me. Anything. Trust me, I'll need whatever you've got.'

'She's called Jess Butler,' Katherine says, taking care to keep her voice good and low. 'She's thirty-four years old and she's been on my team for over a year now. And I've been so torn about whether to let her go or not. On the one hand, she's my PR and I'm desperately dependent on her, but on the other, having to look at her day in and day out is just too much to bear right now. How can she do it?' Katherine's voice starts to sound choked with frustration. 'How can she sit there and let me pay her wages and work hard to get me re-elected, and all the time she's shagging my husband behind my back?'

'Letting Jess go now is the very worst thing you could possibly do,' I say to her, horrified. 'Whatever she's done, she deserves fifty per cent of the blame, and no more. She is, after all, a single woman, whereas your husband is still very much a married man. *He*'s the one that made the commitment, *he*'s the one that made promises to you.'

'Are you suggesting that Jess keeps working on my team?' Katherine says, clearly not used to being told what to do.

'I'm not suggesting anything. I'm telling you straight out that if you want my help, then that's exactly what you *have* to do.'

'But . . . but . . . I am human, you know,' Katherine says, in a pitifully quiet voice. 'Have you any idea how it is for me, seeing her and Philip supposedly working together every time I come into the office?'

'From now on, Jess is my problem, not yours,' I tell her crisply. 'Besides, changing your team this close to the election would be a huge mistake, and that's before we even discuss my strategy to fix this. In the meantime, you have to try and detach yourself from the whole thing.'

Katherine rests her head back wearily against her chair and looks utterly defeated.

Which I take as my cue to toughen her up a bit.

'Come on,' I say, in a tone that brooks no contradiction. 'You're a politician, you don't need me to tell you to go out there and smile and act like everything is hunky-dory, even at a time like this. There's an old saying: don't get emotional, get even. We need to keep Jess close to hand, because that's the best possible way for me to get to work on her. You need to get re-elected and I need to clean up the mess. Jess Butler, you said?'

Within milliseconds, I'm on my phone searching for Jess Butler's Twitter handle and Instagram account – social media is always a good place to start.

'Don't make the mistake of thinking that I'm being a complete doormat here,' Katherine says, trying to claw back a bit of pride, while I'm busily scrolling. 'Because I'm ready to throw Philip out over this and have done with him. I'm a feminist first and last, that's the platform I stand on. It's unbelievably hard for any woman to work in public life in the first place – and to think that all this could be derailed, just because my husband is a lying arse who can't keep his dick to himself? If it wasn't for the election being so close . . .'

'Your job,' I tell her again, still glued to my phone, 'is to focus on your campaign and get re-elected. So you can start right now by telling Jess that you've drafted me in to help you out a bit, and that she and I are going to be working closely together in the next week.

'And now, if you'll excuse me . . .' I say abruptly, ready to go, as Katherine looks up at me dumbly, like she's just witnessed a tornado up close, 'my job is to take out the trash.'

On my way out of the office, I spot Jess's distinctive coppery mane of curly hair and make a point of 'casually' passing by her desk.

'Didn't get a chance to say hi properly,' I say to her, all warm and friendly, instantly switching character and persona, which is not the easiest thing to do, but then I've had a lot of practice.

'Because I'm actually hoping I might get to join the team soon,' I add. All smiles. All charm. 'My interview with Katherine went well just now, so fingers crossed!'

Jess is on the phone but gives a quick thumbs up sign and waves to indicate she's on a call she can't get off. Meanwhile, I grab the chance to really have a good look at the woman, doing what I always do. My thing, in other words.

Features: pale, white, freckly Irish skin, but you'd never know it underneath all that fake tan.

Hair: appears to be a natural red, but up close, it's actually not at all. Impeccably maintained though – where does she find the time to go to a hairdresser? Curls are wild and free falling past her shoulders. Overall effect? Sexy. Beguiling. Like she was out till all hours last night and didn't even get a chance to run a brush through it on her way into work.

Dress sense: boho chic. Floral dress, Penney's. There's a cropped denim jacket over the back of her chair – Zara, about two years old, at a rough guess.

Handbag: overstuffed and lying wide open by the desk. A phone charger is clearly visible at the top of it and, interestingly, a second phone, tucked into a discreet corner.

Only drug dealers or people having affairs ever have two phones, I know of old, making a mental note to try to get my paws on that phone as soon as I get a reasonable chance.

'I'm locking down *PrimeNews*,' Jess mouths at me. 'Just on hold.'

'No worries,' I beam back brightly. 'I'll leave you to it. And if things go my way, hopefully I'll be seeing you again soon. Very soon.'

'Best of luck,' Jess hisses.

Oh, luck has nothing to do with it, I think, mind like ice as a game plan slowly begins to form. But, outwardly, I smile at Jess. I even wave a friendly little goodbye.

I'm just about to leave, when, next thing, the office door bursts wide open and the man himself breezes in, weighed down with a clatter of heavy-looking boxes. The root cause of all of Katherine's pain and humiliation. It's him all right, I think, coldly drinking him in. The raven–black hair so unnaturally dark it can only be dyed, the tall, wiry build, the slight stoop, almost as if to compensate for being so tall and lean.

Definitely no mistaking him. Philip Sisk himself.

There's a woman in the office inside, I think; *a good woman. A woman who's working hard, and doing her best to make life a little easier for others. And right now, that woman is a shaky, vulnerable mess. All because of you, you prick, with your roving bloody eye.*

A familiar hot surge of bile begins to bubble up inside me as Philip inches his way through the door, boxes balanced precariously, one on top of the other.

I try to squeeze my way past him, fake-sincerely saying, 'Oops! Excuse me, sorry! Am I in your way?'

Then Philip trips.

This may have been deliberate on my part. I may well have purposely stuck my foot out, so he'd fall over.

Then again, maybe I didn't.

'Bugger, shit, poo and bollocks,' Philip swears, losing his balance and landing flat on his arse, as three of the boxes slip from the top-heavy pile he's balancing and go flying, scattering dozens and dozens of fliers with Katherine's photo emblazoned on them all over the floor. 'Feck's sake, somebody give me a hand, will you?'

Quick as a flash, I switch personality, instantly diving down on my hands and knees to help.

'I'm *so* sorry,' I say, flashing an angelic smile. 'Did I bump into you?'

'Lazy man's load,' Philip says, as the two of us scoop up everything we can and put the fliers back into neat, tidy piles. 'Serves me right.'

Then, realising that I'm fresh new meat, he stands up to his full height and instantly sticks out his hand to introduce himself.

'Well, hello there,' he says, towering over me, eyeing me up and down appreciatively, in a way that, frankly, makes me want to gag.

I shake hands with him, noticing how hot and clammy his skin is.

You're on high alert, I think. Pupils dilated, face flushed – give me enough time, and I could probably take his pulse.

'I'm Philip Sisk,' he grins, his manner easy and charming, a man who introduces himself to the masses a thousand times a day. 'And you are?'

'Meg Monroe. I've been drafted in to help Katherine. And Jess too, of course.'

At that, I turn around and give a little wave in Jess's direction. But Jess doesn't acknowledge me, or Philip either for that matter. Instead she acts like she hadn't even noticed that Philip's arrived. The only person in the office who didn't look up, not even when he fell.

Stupid girl, giving herself away like that. Why are idiots having illicit affairs so fucking thick? Don't they realise how easy they are to spot? They're the only ones who ignore each other to the point of rudeness, whenever there's other people present.

'Very nice to meet you, Meg,' Philip smiles. 'Good to have you on board – and welcome to the team.'

'That's kind of you,' I answer as politely as I can, my smile hardening, growing slow and calculating.

Then, to cheer myself up, I think of the furies of hell that are about to be unleashed on him, and whaddya know?

My smile grows even wider.

Chapter Four

Meg

Same day, yet another case.

Told you I'm in demand.

'You're so good to drive me.'

'Hey, what are friends for?' I smile from behind the steering wheel.

'I never even knew you had a car.'

I don't, actually, I think, eyes trained dead ahead on the road in front of me. I hired the car especially for this, but, of course, that's hardly something I'm about to divulge.

'Fuck's sake,' says my companion, who goes by the self-invented name of Bella Bumble, and who describes herself as an 'online creator and style queen'. Which, as far as I can see, effectively means Bella somehow manages to get paid for lounging around in her pyjamas all day, while posing for highly filtered Instagram shots, then boring her legions of followers with her 'hashtag perfect' life. Hashtag 'blessed'.

Hashtag vomit, more like.

Right now, Bella's flicking away at her waist-length, ash blonde hair extensions, fiddling with her phone and double-checking her make-up in the visor mirror so much, it's started to become grating.

'I'm nervous and I shouldn't be nervous,' she says. 'I mean, like . . . what the *hell* have I got to be nervous about?'

I judge it best to say nothing.

'I mean, *he*'s the one who should be nervous, not me,' she says, working herself up into a right state. 'He should be in bits right now. He should be on total tenterhooks, wondering if I'll even show up or not. After last time.'

'I know,' I say absent-mindedly, indicating into the lane for Dublin airport.

'It's just that . . . well, we've had weekends away together before and it's never exactly been a barrel of laughs for me, if I'm being honest . . .'

'I thought as much.'

'I mean . . . he says he's leaving his wife and all that . . . but . . . sure that's what they all say, isn't it?'

I continue to stay silent.

'And the last time we did this, it was, like, seriously *sick*. I mean, every time his phone rang, he nearly had a coronary. Every single time. Total passion-killer, if you know what I'm saying.'

'I hear you,' I say quietly.

'Then there's the way he keeps talking about his kids,' Bella says, jumpy and tense as she checks her make-up for about the twentieth time. 'How young they are and how much he misses them. I mean, for fuck's sake, I ask you! We get so little time together as it is, you know. So, is it, like, selfish of me not to want to listen to how his daughter, who he thinks is the next Mozart by the way, is able to play all the verses of "Let it Go" in her Grade 2 piano exams? If you ask me, he's the one who's being selfish, the way he goes on about his family all the time. I put up with a lot, you know, Meg. An awful lot.'

I just nod and focus on the road ahead, instinct telling me this is by far the best course of action.

'His little boy is only six and he acts like he's the next Lionel Messi. I mean . . . honestly . . . I shit you not. Nothing against kids, but when you don't have any, it's, like . . . SO boring.'

Again, no response from me. Just the sound of an ambulance siren, as we grind to a halt, stuck in rush-hour traffic.

'Meg, you're very quiet. Do you think I'm mad to do this? I mean, tell me honestly, do you think I'm mad? Come on, we're friends, you can say what you really think.'

'I think you're possibly having second thoughts,' I say calmly, sensing that the conversation is finally beginning to shift in the right direction.

'Tell me the truth. Do you think he's ever going to leave her?'

At that, I suck in my cheeks.

'You really want to know what I think?'

'I really want to know,' says Bella jumpily. 'Definitely. Maybe. No, definitely. Go on. For fuck's sake, just tell me.'

'Well, here's what I don't get,' I say, careful to sound like I'm genuinely puzzled. 'Your boyfriend has two kids, a mortgage and a cat and a dog. And then there's his wife, who he doesn't seem to have any problem cheating on and lying to. So maybe he'll break up with her and maybe he won't. But what you have to ask yourself is – is this really what you're settling for? A forty-one-year-old man who cycles around in Lycra and who works as a security guard and who doesn't tip properly when you're out and who hides you away from the world and who lies like it's second nature? Someone who doesn't know the meaning of the word commitment and brings a *lot* of baggage with him? Do you really need me to go on?'

'I know, I hear you,' Bella says doubtfully.

'Good.'

'And you're right about the Lycra – he just doesn't have the arse for it. I've told him, like, loads of times, but he never listens to me.'

'You know what's the worst part of all this?' I tell her, gently pushing my case, sensing I'm close to victory.

'Go on, tell me. As my friend. My best friend.'

God love you if you think I'm your best friend. This one is quite insecure enough, thanks very much, without the thoughts that her 'best friend' is actually being paid and paid handsomely to be in her life.

'OK then,' I tell her, judging that the time is right and indicating to pull over onto the hard shoulder so she and I can talk eye-to-eye. 'In that case, here it is.'

I take a deep breath and brace myself for a good, stout lie. But at this stage in the game, it feels like I was born to fake sincerity.

'Just look at you, Bella, you're *fabulous*,' I say. 'Not only are you jaw-droppingly gorgeous, but you're beautiful on the inside too. Where it really counts.'

'Thanks very much,' Bella says, like this is nothing less than her due. 'That's the eyelash extensions. They make me look like a Disney princess. Everyone says so.'

'You're . . . kind and . . . friendly and super-successful . . . and you've got a fantastic job and you're living your best life,' I say, digging deep to lavish on the compliments. 'The only thing dragging you down and holding you back is that you fell in love with someone unavailable. So ask yourself – is this really what you're prepared to settle for? Don't you think you deserve so much better?'

'I didn't know he wasn't free when we met,' Bella says sulkily, putting her two feet up on the dashboard – in a brand-new hire car. The gesture annoys me irrationally, but I let it go. Bigger fish to fry, etcetera.

'Yeah, but you do *now*, don't you?' I say. 'Just think of his wife—'

'Oh God, do you have to remind me about her? I've already got a stress rash on my chest from all this.'

'What did you say her name was again?' I ask, all faux innocence.

'Rebecca,' Bella sighs reluctantly.

'Then think of Rebecca. Because the chances are she's not whatever he's telling you she is. Chances are she's just like you and me. If you could see Rebecca now, I bet she's normal. Ordinary. I bet she's a woman, doing her best, just trying her best to get by. If you met her, you might even like her. The only thing she did wrong in her life was to hook up with a commitment-phobic . . .'

Git, I wonder if I should say?

'Arsehole,' Bella says for me.

'If you *do* go ahead with this weekend,' I caution, 'then that's your call. Your choice. Look, here I am, even driving you to the airport, in good faith.'

'But . . . ?' says Bella, wavering.

'But I think you're having doubts.'

Because I took great care to put them there.

'And as long as you're having doubts,' I go on, 'then this weekend is going to be miserable for you. Totally shit.'

'So . . . what are you saying?' Bella asks, biting her lip.

'I'm saying how about I turn the car around? How about if you don't turn up for your flight?'

'You mean . . . just, like, leave him standing at the departure gate, waiting for me?'

'Just like Rick at the end of *Casablanca*,' I say, guessing that Bella's too buck stupid to get the movie reference, but still.

'You mean . . . without even texting him or anything?'

'Why would you bother?' I reply coolly. 'What about all the times he's let you down at the last minute, because something came up with one of his kids? Doesn't he deserve payback for that?'

'Yeah, well . . .' says Bella, wavering. 'There's been plenty of last-minute cancellations all right. And it would certainly serve him right for taking me for granted so many times.' She pauses. 'He took a sickie off work today and all, just so we could go to Paris for the night. And he paid for the flights, even though they were only Ryanair cheapies. He'd be raging.'

'You could always post a load of photos on Instagram from where I'm taking you,' I tell her, with a cheeky little half-wink, indicating to turn the car around and blanking out the cacophony of car horns blaring from behind. 'He'd be sure to see them and they'd drive him mad.'

'Where do you wanna go?' she asks, curious.

'To the Dylan bar in town.'

Because it's your favourite. It's your home from home, your comfort zone.

'Come on, Bella, what do you say? I'll buy you a glass of fizz and you can send him the pic of you being your gorgeous and fabulous self, drinking it? Maybe even surrounded by a few hotties' – I cringe at using her vernacular – 'like . . . born in the same decade as you, for starters?'

*

Exactly one hour later, that's precisely what she and I are doing. One glass leads to two and, pretty soon, Bella's way too sozzled to even notice that while she's knocking back the drinks, I'm carefully staying sober.

'Get him to send you a photo of him waiting at the departure gate,' I suggest wickedly. 'For the laugh.'

'Brilliant idea!' says Bella tipsily, bashing away on her phone.

The photo comes through almost instantaneously, along with a caption from her highly irate, abandoned boyfriend that reads, 'Where the hell are you? It's the final call for the flight!'

'Hilarious!' Bella squeals, tittering happily as the photo pings through.

'Forward it on to me, will you?' I say casually. 'Just . . . you know, for the lols.'

She does as she's told, and barely bats an eyelid when I slip off to the loo, with my own phone discreetly tucked down my bra.

I think about Cheater Man, currently standing at the airport in a hot temper.

Took a sick day off work today, did you? Yeah, right. Good luck with that, sunshine.

Without a second thought, I log into a fake email address and forward the photo on to the security company that Cheater Man works for. A highly incriminating photo too, of him with a backpack at his feet, standing in front of a Ryanair priority check-in queue, with '*last call – Paris*' writ large on a monitor behind him. Absolutely no mistaking where he is, no grey area here, thanks very much.

And it serves the lying fucker right. Best of luck to him explaining that to his line manager when he goes back to work. Sickie, my arse.

Then I send a second text – but this time to his wife Rebecca, who is, of course, my client here.

Mission accomplished, it reads simply. **Even managed to teach him a lesson he won't forget.**

I sign off as I always do whenever I secure a great result.

Game over. Game won.

Then – an odd thing. Automatically, I go to check my messages, now that I'm well away from my companion's incessant, self-indulgent, vacuous stream of chatter. In the privacy of the ladies' loos, I glance through everything, emails, voice messages and texts, noticing that there's quite a few missed calls, all from the same number.

A new client, maybe? Someone who's heard about the 'special services' I can offer? Well, if it is, I think, with no false modesty, they'll be lucky if I'm able to take them on. I'm out the door with clients and there's only one of me to go around. This job demands quality time; you certainly can't cut corners or short-change people. An assistant, I think with a wry little smile – that's what I really need. A PA, who I can trust and delegate to.

Then I listen to the first of my voice messages, and suddenly I'm not smiling anymore.

No. Just no.

No, no, no, no, no.

The voicemail is fuzzy and indistinct, with whooshing, windy background noise that all but drowns out the message, which keeps cutting out on me anyway. Just like a call from overseas, from a country with a particularly shit signal. But the voice is familiar. Scarily, terrifyingly familiar.

And there's one word that rings out loud and clear. 'Dublin'.

Now a cold clutch of fear grips me and my breath will only come in short, stabbing gulps.

Dublin. Dublin. I definitely heard the word Dublin.

Which can't possibly be right. There has to be some kind of mistake. I rarely make mistakes, but, as my nan always says, what's seldom is wonderful.

I must have misheard. That's all there is to it. It's a rubbish signal, there's loads of background noise from the bar. There's no way this person is back in town again – in a million years, that's the last thing that would ever happen. Didn't I make good and sure of that?

At that more steadying, soothing thought, I start to breathe again. Pulse rate lowers. I glance in the mirror to check my pupils have gone back to normal size.

It's OK, I tell myself. *It was a simple, straightforward voice from the past, nothing more. We've spoken before and we will do again. But there's nothing to concern me. Nothing that can rebound on me. After all, it's not like anyone can turn up on my doorstep and derail everything now, is it?*

Calmer now, I switch the phone off and stride out of the ladies' loos, to rejoin a pleasantly pissed Bella.

Fixing a bright smile on my face, I hop back up on the bar stool.

'So, come on, what do you say?' I beam at her. 'One more for the road? My twist?'

'Oh Meg,' Bella slurs back. 'You're like . . . *so* cool and amazing . . . You wanna know something? I honestly think you're the best friend I ever had.'

Chapter Five

Meg

Finally, finally, finally, I sense now is the optimum time to leave Bella at the bar, as she seems to have hit on the Holy Grail, in that she's chatting to a reasonably normal guy who seems to be a) single, b) straight and c) interested in her particular line of 'take no prisoners' full-on flirtation. Seizing this as my cue to beat a retreat, I say my goodbyes, abandon my hire car and nab a passing taxi.

Hard to believe, but my day still isn't over. I give the address to the driver, strap myself into the back seat of the car, then relax, and for the first time all day allow myself to rest, close my eyes and breathe. I've been on the go, go, go ever since dawn, but instead of flagging and crawling home to the sofa and Netflix, I have to steel myself for one final task of the evening.

This isn't just any old job though; this is a regular appointment of sorts, one I half look forward to and half dread, never knowing quite what to expect. Sometimes it goes brilliantly, sometimes it's so disastrous it puts me in bad form for days on end.

But this is partly what I work so hard for.

My job certainly comes with perks of sorts. Nights exactly like this one, I think, snapping my eyes back open again. Ten seconds of rest; frankly that's all I've time for.

Then I flip open a tiny glass compact mirror that comes everywhere with me and do a quick make-up touch-up. Next, I whip off the little black jacket I've been wearing, shove it into my bag, then peel off the tight-fitting Stella McCartney black T-shirt I have on underneath that, till I'm left sitting in the back of the taxi in my bra and very little else. Not giving a toss what the driver might think, I shimmy out of the sexy, clubby-looking, short black skirt I've been wearing, and fumble around the bottom of my handbag for a neat, pretty, floral dress I'd taken particular care to pack there.

'Ah Jaysus, love, what are you doing?' says the driver, staring at the goings-on in his rear-view mirror, horrified. 'Some kind of a strip tease? Now, behave yourself – none of that carry-on. Do you hear me?'

I totally blank him though, as, in one quick, practised move, I pull it over my head and downwards, where it almost reaches to my ankles. I scoop up my hair, which has been hanging loosely around my shoulders beach-wave style, then expertly clip it up into a tidy little bun, before double-checking how it all looks in the compact mirror.

Good. Better. My 'hot-to-trot, cocktail bar' look is completely banished and now, in a maxi cotton dress, buttoned up to the neck and with a neat little belt nipping at my waist, I look demure. I look fresh and innocent. I look like a good girl, a hard-working girl. A primary school teacher maybe, or a librarian. But then looking perfect for whatever role I'm required to play, no matter what hour of the day, or night, is all part and parcel of my USP, isn't it?

I should have been an actress. I'm that bloody good at this.

'I've got a dashcam here you know, love,' the driver gripes at me, 'any more of that stripping-off lark, and I'll report you. Do you hear me?'

I don't even waste my breath answering. Instead, I sit back and allow myself the luxury of letting my thoughts wander for a moment.

The way things are going, I think smugly, I won't need to take cheek from taxi drivers for much longer. Another six months of this and I'll be able to afford a car and a driver. Easily.

My taxi arrives at the narrow streets of a 1940s housing estate in one of the rougher parts of town; the type of area where you grip your handbag extra tightly to you before venturing out on your own. The type of area where you wouldn't dream of chatting on your phone while walking down the streets, lest it be whipped out of your hand by a passing mugger on a bike. The type of area where you'd be reluctant to leave a new car parked on the kerb, for fear it wouldn't be there when you got back.

The type of area where I'm from, as it happens.

'You sure this is the right address?' says the taxi driver, carefully inching his car around a mattress and a mound of stuffed bin liners that have been abandoned slap bang in the middle of the street.

'Just keep going,' I tell him, 'it's directly after the bookies and before you come to the chipper.'

The driver looks warily to the left and right, where a gang of teenage lads are all sitting on a graffiti-covered wall, drinking cans and smoking a spliff. A drug deal seems to be happening right beside them, and everyone pretends not to see. The minute they notice the taxi though, the lads are straight over, smelling fresh blood, clustering around it and banging on the roof, boisterously wolf-whistling and catcalling and basically trying to intimidate the living shite out of us.

Automatically, the taxi driver clicks on the car's central locking, but I don't bat an eyelid. I'm well used to this carry-on; I've seen a lot worse.

I completely blank the gang as the car inches past and calmly direct the driver to the right house, telling him to pull over outside number forty-seven. It's a nondescript, *Coronation Street*-style, Victorian two-up two-down red-brick bang in the middle of a row of terraced houses exactly like it, all of which are in varying states of disrepair/squalor. Number forty-seven at least, however, has a few half-hearted window boxes outside of it and a fresh lick of paint on the woodwork, in stark contrast to the house beside it, with its cracked windows and a boarded-up front door. The house opposite has graffiti sprayed on it that reads, 'Scanger luves Bex. Up the IRA'.

Delightful.

'You sure you want to get out here, love?' the driver asks, looking worriedly back at me in the rear-view mirror. 'Looks a bit dodgy, if you ask me.'

'This is it, thanks,' I tell him, briskly handing over a few crisp, fresh notes and waving at him to keep the change.

Then I step out of the car, glance the house up and down and steel myself.

Home sweet home. Back to the loving bosom of my family, where doubtless they'll have the red carpet out, a warm welcome and a yummy home-cooked dinner waiting for me.

As if.

I ring on the doorbell and wait. Meanwhile, a gang of young kids come weaving dangerously down the street like a swarm of wasps on bikes, those city bikes that you hire by the hour, and which undoubtedly have been nicked.

One boy spots me as I wait on the pavement and immediately pulls up his bike on the kerb opposite.

'Hey, you!' he yells over. 'I *know* you!'

'Shouldn't you be home in bed?' I throw back at him. It's a fine summery night, but still, it's close to 10 p.m., and this kid looks no older than about eight or nine.

'Piss off, you, I'll go home when I feel like it.'

I roll my eyes and turn back to knock on the door again.

'I definitely know you,' the kid insists, as his mates cluster around him. 'You're mental Maddie MacMadser's granddaughter, aren't you?'

'Your granny is a right nutjob!' another kid yells. 'She went for a walk in her nightie the other day and said we all had to get to a bomb shelter quick, before Hitler came to get us!'

'Nutcase, nutcase, mentaler!' the others all start to chant, circling around on their bikes like a mini-plague of locusts.

I could do a lot of things here. I could tell the lot of them to piss off, but I don't. I could cross the street and throttle them, but don't bother doing that either. Instead, I sigh and pull out my door key to let myself in, seeing as how no one inside the house is going to bother their arse.

'*Now* I remember your name!' the first kid taunts me. 'You're Megan MacKenzie, aren't you?'

This time, I turn to face him, looking him straight in the eye with an icy stare that's calculated to stop a charging rhino in its tracks.

'I used to be.'

*

'Oh, it's you, Megan,' my mum says flatly, opening her eyes and waking up from the peaceful snooze she'd been having in front of the telly, when she hears me letting myself in. 'I forgot it was your night to call.'

'Sorry I'm late,' I say, taking in the state of the room at a glance. It's neat as a pin and all the utilities are brand spanking new, but other than that – it's a pretty dark, dismal open-plan kitchen, really, with a tiny sofa and TV at one end, which Mum's now crashed out in front of, as she so often does at the end of a long day's work.

I have a good, long look at her.

Face: Mum is in her early fifties, but if I didn't know that, I'd give her at least a decade older, mainly thanks to her twenty-a-day cigarette habit and the fact that she works out of doors in all weathers, selling flowers at a street stall right in the heart of town. She's thin, far too thin. Lost at least another pound since I was last here. Clearly living off the fags and little else.

Dress: her work clothes – jeans and a warm fleece. Both ill-fitting and much the worse for wear.

Jesus, I think, momentarily frustrated. *I give the woman money – lots of it. What the hell is she spending it on, if not herself and Nan?*

There are a few empty beer tins shoved under the sofa though; I can still see them poking out, along with the tabs from said cans. That, and a telltale splodge on the rug (recent stain visible, thanks very much), tells me all I need to know. Clearly Mum heard my key in the lock and hastily went to hide away all trace that she's had a few too many tonight.

Right then. Mystery solved. So that's where my money has been going.

Some kind of reality show is on TV and the sound of a contestant mangling a song from *The Greatest Showman* is blaring out. In fact, the only bright spots in the whole room are the bunches of tulips in a myriad of colours that seem to be dotted all over the place, in just about any available container. Vases, jam jars, even the teapot is being used for the overflow of flowers.

'So how are things, Mum?' I ask her, standing at the edge of the sofa. Not that I need an answer. One glance tells me everything.

'Total shite,' she yawns, barely able to keep her eyes open. 'Couldn't shift the last of the tulips, even though I was almost giving them away. Been at the flower market since six this morning. Banjaxed now. Never even heard you at the front door.'

'Go on back to sleep then,' I tell her, already peppering to get away, if the truth be told. 'I'll run upstairs to see Nan.'

'Sit down for two minutes first, will you? You're making me nervous standing there.'

'Can't. Sorry. No time. How has Nan been this week?'

'Got out twice when I wasn't here. Once in her nightie. Bridie across the street had a right job getting her home. She kept saying there was going to be an air raid any minute.'

Worse, in other words. A whole lot worse.

'Did you bring me anything?' Mum asks, suddenly perking up.

'Of course I did. Same as I do every week.'

With that, I reach for my bag, unzip it, whip out a neat white envelope and hand it over.

'How much this time?' she says, with a spark in her eye.

'Two thousand,' I tell her, leaving the envelope on the coffee table in front of her.

If I was expecting thanks, though, I'm left disappointed.

'Thought you'd be pleased, Mum.'

'Well, at least you remembered to bring cash,' she sniffs. 'Cheques are no good to me. A cheque from someone called Meg Monroe? Sure, what use is that? Who's this Meg Monroe when she's at home?'

'It's the name I go by now,' I sigh. 'As you know perfectly well.'

'Well, you'll always be Megan MacKenzie in this house.'

There's a tense pause, but I'm not rising to the bait. Not again.

'Anyway, you've enough cash there for this month's mortgage,' I tell her, making to leave. 'I'll bring more next week. And in the meantime—'

'Yeah, but where's all this cash coming from, that's what I'd like to know,' she interrupts, looking flatly over at me.

'I've told you a thousand times. I have a new job, a great job. I'm in waste management now and I'm working hard and the money is good. So good, in fact, that you and Nan—'

'If you're going to suggest your Nan and I move out of here again . . .' Mum says, with a warning note I know well in her voice.

'The offer is still on the table,' I tell her, calmly folding my arms and facing her. 'You know I can find you somewhere a lot better to live than here. Somewhere safer, for a start. Somewhere where you don't have to witness a drug deal every time you go out to buy a carton of milk.'

Mum shakes her head stubbornly and sits up, reaching across the table in front of her for her cigarettes and a lighter.

'I'll never leave this house and you know it, missy,' she says firmly. 'Just because you're ashamed of the place, with your fancy new accent, and your new name, and your expensive clothes, doesn't mean that I am. Your nan loves this house and it's where she and your grandad raised their family, and if that's good enough for them, then it should be good enough for you too. With your notions and your flashy job, and your ridiculous, invented new name. *Megan.*'

I don't rise to the bait. Instead, I leave the room without another word so I can get upstairs to see my nan. Pointless having the same roundabout argument with my mother, time and again. Best thing, I know of old, is to get in and get the hell out as fast as I possibly can.

'What does a job in waste management even mean?' Mum calls up the stairs after me. 'A posh way of saying you put out bins?'

I keep my cool and will myself not to give a smart answer back. Instead, I knock gently on Nan's bedroom door and let myself in.

'Heard all that, loud and clear,' Nan says, sitting bolt upright in bed, rollers wobbling in her snow-white hair, with a flowery, old-fashioned bedspread tucked around her, surrounded by magazines with articles in them about gardening and how to knit the perfect egg cosy. 'You're not in the door two minutes, and already you and your mother are at each other's throats. What are the pair of you like? You need your heads banging together, if you ask me.'

I bend down to kiss her lightly on the forehead, inhaling the deep, comforting smell of lavender talc that I always associate with Nan.

'How are you, Megan?' Nan twinkles up at me. 'Stand there till I have a good look at you.'

I do as I'm told, grateful that Nan seems a little bit more like herself this evening.

'Lovely dress,' Nan smiles. 'You look nice. Like one of those girls who give out the free samples in Marks and Spencer. The kind of girl that any fella would be glad to bring home. Do you have a boyfriend, love?'

'Nan!' I say to her, faux annoyed. 'Why would I want a boyfriend?'

Why would anyone want a boyfriend? Who has the time, for starters?

'Because that's what people do,' Nan replies, frowning. 'You never have boyfriends. Why are you always single?'

I instantly change the subject. 'I brought you some Werther's Originals, Nan. Would you like one?'

'Stupid question, course I want a Werther's Original,' she says as I delve into the bowels of my bag and produce five value packs I picked up for her earlier. But then it would be a hardy soul who dared cross the threshold of this house without a good supply of Werther's Originals for Nan.

'Anyway, pay no attention to your mum,' Nan says, gratefully taking the stack of sweets and ripping open the first pack her bony little hand lights on. 'I know she's in a right nark tonight, but it's only because your dad went to see her at the flower market earlier.'

Just at the mention of his name, I swear I can feel my spine stiffen.

'What the hell did that gobshite want?' I ask icily.

'What do you think?' Nan replies, taking out her dentures, and leaving them on top of a magazine with Prue Leith on the cover before popping a sweet into her mouth. 'To talk about you, of course. Said he's been trying to track you down for ages now, but you've changed address again and he can't get a hold of you.'

I rub at my temples as my head begins to pound.

'Worthless fucking tosser . . .' I mutter, but there's absolutely nothing wrong with Nan's hearing.

'You watch your language,' she says sternly.

'Sorry, Nan.'

'Your mum and I are allowed to call him a fucking tosser, but you're his daughter and you're not. Anyway, he says his youngest kid is going to be ten next week, and he's having a party for her. Chocolate fountains, bouncy castles, the whole works. Wants you to go. Says she's your half-sister and you can't keep on ignoring her and the half-brother and your stepmother forever.'

'Oh, can't I, Nan?' I say, starting to pace the room, just to calm down a bit. 'Just watch me.'

At that, I think back to my own tenth birthday party. My dad faithfully promising to take me to McDonald's, and then to the movies. I was all excited and had even dressed up for the day in my brand-new party dress. It's not even like the whole day would have cost the fucker that much, I think; the price of a kid's meal, a bucket of popcorn and the movie tickets?

But the arsehole couldn't even get that much right. Instead, he left me waiting on the front step outside the house till it got dark and cold, with not even a phone call to cancel – nothing. Eventually, Nan came out and coaxed me back inside, with the promise of Häagen-Dazs and Fanta and all the telly I wanted.

Still, though, it hurt then and it still stings now.

'You're only narky because your dad is far better to his new family than he ever was to you, that's all that's wrong with you,' Nan nods sagely. 'There was a family just like that on breakfast telly this morning. Deadbeat Dads, they called it. Eejits who were louses to their first family, but as soon as they remarried and had kids with a new partner, sure it was nothing but trips to Disneyland and private schools and brand-new mobile phones all the way.'

No, actually, I think, as an old familiar fury rises up inside me. *No, that's not it at all. The only reason I'm annoyed is because I'd gladly sort out the likes of my father in about two seconds flat, if only I was allowed. I do this kind of thing for a living now and astonishingly satisfying it is too. And, in his particular case, it would be a fucking pleasure.*

Just then my phone rings out loud and clear, distracting me. But when I glance down at the phone to see who it is, my stomach instantly withers.

No, no, no, no. Another clatter of missed calls from the very same number as earlier.

Which means this is no coincidence. Which means this could be *bad*.

Not again, not now, just NO.

A brand-new sensation washes over me. Guilt, maybe? A long-abandoned conscience finally niggling at me?

If so, it feels exactly like heartburn.

'Who's that ringing you at this hour?' Nan says, as I click it off and try to put it out of my mind.

'No one. Nothing important. Just work.'

'Funny, isn't it?' Nan says, looking beadily at me. 'How many people want their bins collected at ten o'clock at night?'

'Never you mind who it was, Nan,' I say briskly, determined to get the most out of the tiny chink of quality time I spend with her. Particularly when she actually seems well this evening. Coherent, even.

'Now, how about another nice Werther's Original, and you can tell me all your news since last week?'

'Oh well, I'm glad you asked, because loads has happened since you were here last,' Nan says, sitting up in the bed and smiling brightly. 'The main bit of news is that Edward the Eighth has abdicated to marry this skinny malink called Wallis Simpson. She's American and she's twice divorced. Or so Queen Mary was telling me, when she rang just now . . .'

I sigh and settle in for what I know is going to be a long, long evening.

Chapter Six

Harriet

Airport arrivals hall

'It's absolutely wonderful you're home, pet! Your dad and I missed you so much. And I know the twins did too, in their own way. Even though the pair of them wanted to sell all your stuff on eBay, because they were so sure you were never coming back from Africa at all.'

'Oh, Mam, it's so great to hear your voice!' Harriet says, loving that she can just call her mother and get through instantly, without going through all the palaver of trying to find Wi-Fi in the back arse of Mombasa, Kenya, just so she could Skype or make a WhatsApp call.

'I wish you'd given us a bit of warning though,' her mam says. 'You remember I'm over in New York all week for this big conference? Well, your dad came with me too – sure, you know how he can never resist a freebie at a nice hotel that someone else is paying for. But, my God, we wouldn't have dreamt of going away if we'd known you were coming home, pet! Not in a million years.'

'I wanted to surprise you, Mam,' Harriet beams, so thrilled to be home that she doesn't even mind the never-ending queue at passport control she's stuck in. Probably the only person in the whole arrivals hall who looks all happy and glowing and 'lit from within'. As opposed to pissed off and stressed, like anyone halfway normal.

'Your dad will be so happy you're back, too,' her mam chatters away. 'You're always so good at refereeing arguments when the boys are around. And there have certainly been plenty of them since you left, let me tell you. With this double wedding, honest to God, my nerves are shot.'

'I can't wait till I see you, so I can hear all about it,' says Harriet, as the queue inches forward by another half-degree.

Her twin brothers, Jack and Terry, have been double-dating two best friends for years now, and then both couples got engaged on New Year's Eve, with a double wedding in the planning ever since. In fact, that's one of the reasons Harriet flew home so early; the twins are having their stag night in Dublin this weekend, and there's no way on earth she's going to miss out on all the fun.

One of the reasons she's come home, but by no means the main one. 'It's so weird to be back, Mam,' Harriet smiles, struggling with the backpack that has been strapped to her aching shoulders and hauling it off her, dumping it on the floor in the passport hall. 'Cold weather for one thing – and no mosquitoes. And just hearing all the accents from home after so long – it's incredible. All I need now is a big feed of Tayto crisps and McCambridge's brown bread and chocolate Kimberleys and then I'll really believe I'm back!'

'We've so much to catch up on,' her mam says, slightly wafting in and out of phone coverage. 'Your dad and I will be home in a few days, so we can have a lovely family reunion then.

So exciting! I'm delighted you're home, pet. It's going to be a lovely fresh start for you, wait and see. After all of that . . . well, you know. Unpleasantness, I suppose. After everything that happened last year. Oh . . . you know what I'm trying to say here.'

There's a tiny, strained pause before Harriet answers.

'Well, for better or for worse, I'm back to stay now, Mam,' she says quietly, as an airport announcement in the background almost drowns her out. 'Onwards and upwards, and all that.'

'Do you know what?' her mam replies. 'It's so wonderful to hear you say that, love. Just wonderful. Bigger and better things ahead for you, wait till you see. No more running away!'

No, Harriet thinks. *No; I'm done with running away, that's for certain.*

'So will I send one of the twins up to the airport to collect you? Although, mind you, I wouldn't put it past the pair of them to be out on the tear with their mates. Yet *again*. Honestly, they're acting like this stag night malarkey is a month-long event, and the whole town should be out buying them free drinks.'

'Don't do any such thing!' Harriet insists. 'Sure, it would take the twins the guts of three hours to drive to the airport – I wouldn't ask anyone to do that.'

'But you can't stay in a miserable old airport hotel on your first night home,' her mam says, worriedly. 'That would be awful.'

'Who said anything about a hotel?' Harriet smiles, as the passport queue lurches forward again. Directly ahead of her in the queue a woman is struggling with a buggy with an unruly toddler strapped into it, crying and cranky on account of the late hour. The little boy flings his toy tractor out of the buggy, hurling it down on to the floor in a tantrum, and Harriet immediately bends down to help.

'Actually, I was going to stay with a friend,' she beams happily. 'You remember Meg Monroe? Course you do, everyone remembers Meg!'

Chapter Seven

Meg

It's late, late, late when I'm finally in the back of a taxi, rolling home after that duty visit to my family. I'm shattered at the tail end of another exhilaratingly insane Day in the Life and so looking forward to a well-deserved snooze. Out of force of habit more than anything else, I whip out my phone to double-check it. Well, as I'm sure you've gathered by now, this gig requires me to be on call twenty-four/seven. A bit like an emergency paramedic, I think, with a self-satisfied little smile.

Two seconds later and I'm certainly not smiling anymore.

Because there it is, again. Yet more missed calls from that same unfamiliar number. Except this time, I know for certain it's her. Which means so far she's rung dozens of times, left two voice messages and a countless string of rambling text messages.

Jesus, Jesus, Jesus.

And now my breath will only come staccato-style and I'm sweating. Me, who never breaks a sweat – ever.

I catch a tiny glimpse of one text before instantly punching delete.

Meg, need to talk, where are you? I have a HUGE surprise for you – please return my calls!

You see? I think, kicking myself crossly. *This is what happens when you break your own rules. This is what happens when you let someone in. This is what you risk when you let your guard down, when you get too close.*

The very fact she's back means that . . . potentially . . . worst-case scenario . . . I don't allow myself to finish that thought though. Instead, I sit back against the car seat and try to breathe nice and regularly, like they teach you on mindfulness apps. *In for two and out for four, in for two and out for four . . .*

I remind myself that she can't find me. She doesn't have a clue where I'm living now, and thank God for it. I can just ghost her – then with any luck, she'll assume I've changed my number.

I tell myself I've actually done this particular person a favour. A very big favour, as it happens. And OK, so maybe I had to be a teeny bit cruel to be kind, but hey, that's the way the world works and you could sink or swim – your choice entirely.

Brain pounding, I pay the taxi driver, then let myself in through the communal door in the hallway where it's so late, even the concierge is off duty. Stepping into the lift, I give my throbbing temples a comforting little rub.

The lift doors glide gracefully open on the penthouse floor.

And suddenly, I'm shocked wide awake, blood whooshing most unpleasantly through my ears.

What. The. Actual. Fuck?

There's a tight little ball of a person, right outside my apartment door. Fast sleep, and with a wheelie bag and a tatty old rucksack beside her, as if she's planning to stay.

So she found me, then. Somehow. Some way. She tracked me down to my home, the very last place I'd ever want her to know about.

I will myself to stay cool. Regroup. I'm good at weaselling out of things, and I'm pretty sure I can deal with this too.

'Wake up,' I hiss at her, bending down to give this unwanted guest a good poke in the shoulders.

Next thing, a pair of eyes open drowsily and the silky fair head of waist-length hair that had been sprawled out on a rolled-up puffa jacket begins to stir.

'Meg, there you are!' she says, blinking up at me – a Disney princess stirring to life – utterly vomit-making. 'You're back . . . finally! I've been calling you and calling you and waiting for you to come home all night. So, here I am, and I'm back! Surprise!'

'How did you find me?' I ask, still shell-shocked. Still trying to focus on breathing and not give myself away by screaming right into her face, Edvard Munch-style.

'I went to your old address,' she smiles sleepily, 'but the new tenants there had never heard of you. I got lucky, though – I ran into one of your old neighbours and she remembered forwarding you on a package a few months ago. She kept the address in case there was more post you might need. Wasn't that just the luckiest thing? So here I am – after all this time!'

I seem to have lost the power of speech. I think on my feet for a living and now all I can do is stand there, staring mutely down at her. Pretty, pretty, pretty, so pretty I want to punch her on her big, blonde, stupid head.

'I'm so pleased to see you, Meg,' she warbles on, getting teary the more she talks. 'It's just so good to be home! I never thought I could be as homesick as I was. I missed so much about home, my family and the twins and you . . . and, of course, I know you're probably furious with me because I haven't been in touch as much as I should, but you've no idea what it was like out in Kenya . . . the broadband was practically non-existent . . . Oh, and I've so much to tell you, Meg! You won't believe what's been going on since we last spoke . . . you're the only one I can really talk to, I didn't even want to tell my mam what's really been going on . . .'

She's here. She's at my home. No one comes into my home, my sanctuary. This is my very worst nightmare manifested.

I can't even think about what to do, I can't seem to think straight at all.

'I'm just so happy to see you, Meg,' she says, in a shaky little voice that cracks with real feeling, as she rises to her feet and gives me a big, warm bear hug. 'And I didn't want to go to a hotel tonight – so I've come to stay with you. That's OK, isn't it? I mean, I so badly need to talk to you and you are my best friend.

'Meg? *Meg*? Why has your face gone a funny colour?'

TUESDAY

Chapter Eight

Meg

Harriet Waters, that's her name. Christ Almighty, right now I'm cursing the very day I first heard it. Two full years ago now, I think, tossing and thrashing about in the bed, while Miss Unwanted House Guest luxuriates on my brand-new cream sofa in the living room.

'Wow, Meg, you really live here?' Harriet had gushed, her tears forgotten, as soon as I'd reluctantly let her inside the apartment late last night. 'How can you afford all this? It's fabulous! Out of this world . . . Oh my actual God, check out that view!'

Have you any idea how disastrous this is for me, I wanted to snap back at her, but, of course, politeness and profession-alism prevailed, and I didn't. Instead, I thrust a spare duvet at Harriet, made up a bed on the sofa for her and slammed my own bedroom door firmly behind me.

Now? Really, did this have to be happening now? When I'm working myself to the bone and everything is going so swimmingly?

Another two years, that's what I'd given myself, before I could finally afford to cash in my chips, quit what I'm doing and start enjoying life for a change. Maybe even start building normal, ordinary, trusting relationships, with normal, ordinary people for a change. To be perfectly honest, I've been ducking and diving, manipulating and cajoling for so long now, I've almost forgotten what it feels like to function as a normal human being in the world.

And now this? This is *not* supposed to happen. Once I'm hired to get someone out of the picture, they're pretty much supposed to feck off into the sunset forever. Not much to ask for, surely?

Yet, here she is. On my sofa. In my apartment. Blissfully unaware that I've been paid an astonishingly hefty sum to make sure a situation exactly like this never, *ever* happens.

For one sickening moment, I think of the client who hired me to take care of Harriet Waters in the first place. Or rather, the client's family, because this lot are a bit like the Kennedys – there's an awful lot of them and you'd be hard-pressed to say which of them was the most intimidating.

What would they say if they knew she'd come back? I'm not a woman to be easily shaken, but they can be a terrifyingly scary bunch. Supposing, I think, as my stomach clenches and an icy-cold clutch of fear takes hold, that this got back to them?

Because any halfwit could see at a glance how unwelcome and unwanted Harriet Waters was in these people's lives. It may have sounded cruel, but Harriet was pretty much unmissed when I eventually did encourage her to step aside. Or, to be more precise, to accept a job offer overseas – good and distant enough that the family in question would never be troubled by her again.

So why the feck couldn't Harriet have just known where she wasn't wanted and stayed well away? And, more importantly, how am I going to get rid of her a second time?

I pass a shitty, sleepless night, but whether I like it or not, I've got no choice but to abandon Harriet the following morning and get on with my day. It's physically causing me chest pain to have to leave her alone in my flat, but then, what else am I supposed to do?

I've a 7 a.m. rendezvous with my new 'friend' Nicole, the one I only began to work on yesterday morning. Nicole, who works for a huge social media company, who's obsessed with clean living and who litters her own Twitter feed with hashtags like '#kindnessmatters' and '#womenlookingoutforwomen'.

Yet the same Nicole is also sneakily seeing a guy in work fifteen years her senior, with a wife and four dependent kids. So what about 'kindness mattering' and 'women looking out for women' now, I wonder?

Hashtag hypocrite, more like.

Course, all this is before I even get started on her married boyfriend, a forty-something estate agent with pockmarked skin and absolutely no neck at all, who's shortly about to get a royal comeuppance I hope he'll remember for a very, very long time to come. The how and wherefore, I'll focus on later – that's the fun part, thanks very much.

Right now, I've got a job to get on with, so that's exactly what I do. First task? To airbrush this Nicole one completely out of the picture. I'm actually pretty pleased with the progress I made at our first meeting yesterday – Nicole and I bonded over a shared love of dogs, even though I don't actually own a dog. Even though I don't particularly like dogs.

That, however, is a mere minor detail. The critical factor is that I've managed to convince Nicole that we've got loads in common and could potentially be pals. But then, manipulating people into thinking what I want them to think is kind of my forte.

As ever, I've done my homework inside out and up and down again. For starters, I know Nicole is an early riser. I also know that she's a regular at a pre-work flow yoga class in town at 7 a.m. – you only have to look at her non-stop Twitter and Instagram feeds to see the proof of that.

Looking forward to my new gym class at Crush Fitness tomorrow! #Lifegoals #yogabody #worthgettingoutofbedfor #cleanliving

Honestly, I think, sighing at just how piss-easy this is. It's like some people intentionally leave a virtual trail of breadcrumbs after them.

So, come hell or high water, I've got to be there for this 7 a.m. class, even if I do have an unwanted house guest who I have to abandon in my apartment, completely unsupervised and snoring her head off on my sofa. Like a time bomb just waiting to explode.

But whether I like it or not, this is a God-sent opportunity for a trust-building exercise with Nicole, and the early days, as I know well, are utterly critical in a delicate game like this. As far as Nicole is concerned, I have to simultaneously be everywhere and anywhere, and God knows, that takes consummate skill. Nicole has to be pleasantly surprised to see me again so soon, she has to enjoy the chats with me, and, most importantly of all, she has to slowly find herself growing to think of me as a friend. Besides, I think. Given the stress I'm under, a nice, soothing, early-morning yoga practice actually isn't the worst idea in the world.

I arrive just in time for the class, take careful note of where Nicole is (right up the front, fully clad in Lululemon, in the throes of a downward dog) and position myself close by, rolling out my mat and joining in. Close, but not too close. It never does to arouse suspicion that you're some kind of stalker at this early stage in the game.

The class goes on. There's nothing but the sound of deep breathing, along with a few grunts from a woman opposite, which gives me precious time to think.

The breathing gets deeper. A guy opposite farts and looks mortified. Slowly, everyone begins to look more and more relaxed.

'And now . . .' intones the class instructor, sounding as ethereal as a woodland sprite, 'let's all go into our child's pose, let's take a moment to tune out the stresses of the morning and let's allow our thoughts and cares to float away, like a fluffy pink cloud . . .'

Fluffy pink cloud, my arse, I think, correctly holding the perfect pose as my stressed mind whirrs into overdrive.

Harriet Waters.

Jesus Christ, what the hell did I ever do to deserve Harriet Waters back in my life?

Two years ago

So how did it all start? Simply enough, as it happened.

With a recommendation, actually – I can only guess from a satisfied client who was kind enough to spread good word of mouth.

At the time, I'd been working as a humble legal secretary at Sloan Curtis, a highly regarded law firm that specialised in family law cases, separation agreements, divorces, that sort of thing. 'Third party' acrimonious cases. Messy and emotional cases.

Right up my alley, in other words.

And OK, so I may not have had a law degree like the rest of my colleagues; in fact, back then, my job was considered rock bottom in the pecking order and, boy oh boy, did my senior colleagues never let me forget it. But I was quick and smart and eager to learn. So I paid close attention during all those long, gruelling hours sitting in on conference meetings patiently taking notes, while soon-to-be-divorced spouses listed off every 'irreconcilable difference' they could possibly use against their ex.

My heart actually cracked when I saw partners who'd invested everything into deeply committed marriages lose it all, when one or the other partner strayed. Believe it or not, back then I really did have a heart that could crack. But then this, you see, was very much my area of expertise. Oh, I knew all about married cheats who shat all over the lives of those they were supposed to love and look after, thanks very much. I knew first-hand the damage it caused. I could have written a fecking thesis on the subject.

*

So I handed over the Kleenex to our clients and doled out cups of coffee, listening carefully to what they were saying and, more importantly, to what they *weren't* saying, which, naturally, was of far more interest.

And the most astonishing thing of all? In all my time working at that firm, I never once came across a single deserted party who actually *wanted* to get divorced. Rather, I saw spouses who still loved their partners deeply, who'd been left devastated by their affairs and who couldn't accept it was now all about to come to a crushing end in an office block, with a bunch of strangers in suits dangling Mont Blanc pens and saying, 'Just sign here, here and here, please.'

Yet the guilty parties, men mostly, all seemed to be waltzing away with it scot-free, I thought, simmering angrily at the back of the conference room. Which was hardly fair, now was it? What about a minor little thing called equality? Surely the very least these cheating feckers deserved was to be taught a lesson they'd never, ever forget?

Then, out of the blue, I spotted a job opportunity.

It all began in the ladies' loos of Sloan Curtis, one rainy Thursday afternoon. I was rushing back to man the reception desk, but couldn't fail to notice a client of the firm's, a tall, well-groomed lady, desperately trying to compose herself as she patted concealer around her red-rimmed eyes.

'Bad meeting?' I asked her politely.

'The worst,' came the sniffled response.

I sighed deeply as she dried her hands. I knew the ins and outs of her case and didn't want to patronise the woman with useless platitudes like, 'it'll get better', or, 'you'll be fine'. Nor did I want to tell the truth, which was that this woman's soon-to-be ex would probably go on to have a pretty great life with his new partner and be a far better dad to a second family than he ever was the first time around. All while those he'd left behind had to look on and suck it up and piece their lives back together again as best they could.

At least, certainly if my own bitter experience was anything to go by.

'It will all be over soon enough,' was what I did say.

'You don't understand,' this elegant, graceful lady replied through the tears. 'No one does. You see, I had a great marriage, and all was well until *she* came along.'

I nodded sympathetically, but the sad thing was, ever since I started working at the firm, I'd pretty much seen this so many times before I could practically write the script. *Cheating spouse going through a midlife crisis meets a younger version of his wife and thinks he'll dodge death by starting all over again with a newer, younger, shinier family.* The cliché of it almost made me want to vomit.

But that's when this particular lady surprised me.

'I get it,' she confided, 'my husband is an unscrupulous cheat and everyone says I'm so much better off without him. But what they don't get is that I still love him. We have kids together – we have a home, mutual friends, we have a *life*. I've invested blood, sweat and tears into this marriage and now some twenty-four-year-old waltzes along and threatens it all? Everything I've devoted my life to? If someone could just make her disappear, help him to see what he's already got, remind him of how happy we've been, it would be the answer to my prayers.'

At that, my mind went to work. An idea began to germinate and once it took hold, it wouldn't budge. Because maybe, just maybe, there was some way *I* could be of help here.

Turned out the mistress was called Amy and she was around my own age too. Right there, that gave me a huge advantage. She and I were both young, we spoke the same language. So, what's to stop me tracking this Amy down via social media? I thought, my mind beginning to race. Couldn't I find out where she worked, ate, drank, lived, hung out, who her friends were and who her friends' friends were, for good measure? Couldn't I inveigle myself into her life and, in time, maybe become a pal? And using the gentle art of persuasion, couldn't I then encourage my new-found friend to dump this married loser she was wasting her time on?

And now that I'd thought of it, why not go a bit further? What about this client's husband? This lying-arsed, two-faced, hypocritical git, whoever he was? Was it fair that he just walked free? If I say so myself, I've always enjoyed getting creative when punishing idiots like these, so couldn't I teach him a thing or two about what happened to love cheats just like him?

Given my background, I certainly had the motivation. In fact, I only wished someone had been there for me when my own dad shattered our little family and went cavorting off with someone new. Wouldn't I have loved a karmic angel of retribution to have come along back then and taught my father a lesson he'd never forget?

I could do it, I thought. *I'd relish it. Without false modesty, I'd actually be pretty good at it.*

My client would get back the life she craved, the young girlfriend, whoever she was, would stop wasting her time on a married man, and who knows, I might just be able to earn a nice few quid extra on the side.

Win-win.

Unsurprisingly, my plan worked beautifully and my 'career' snowballed from there. Good word of mouth about me seemed to circle upwards and upwards, in the way that these things do. That's until the happy day when my name was duly passed on to none other than Mr and Mrs Frederick de Courcey, figureheads of probably one of the wealthiest and certainly the most powerful families in the country.

Think of the Rockefellers. Now think of the Windsors. Now the Gateses. Now combine all their lovely, lovely dosh and imagine it in the hands of one single family, and you'll have some idea of the unimaginable levels of wealth and privilege the de Courceys operate at.

To give you just a brief, potted history, the de Courcey fortune all began with the first Frederick de Courcey, just after the First World War, when, against all better advice, he invested his family inheritance into what was considered then the riskiest and most insane business model going. None other than aviation.

Back in 1919, young Frederick de Courcey was royally mocked for believing that a single aeroplane had the power to fly the North Atlantic with an engine the approximate size of a hairdryer. But to everyone's astonishment, not least the print media of the day, Frederick was actually proven correct.

The Second World War subsequently saw him grow the business so that not just the military, but also the rich and powerful could fly from London to New York, non-stop. Of course, long-haul flights like that were only open to the mon-eyed elite of the day, not forgetting the fact that the whole palaver took over eighteen hours in total. But it certainly didn't seem to put them off, and the money kept rolling in.

The post-war period saw the family fortunes explode, and with the rise of cheaper commercial air travel in the 1960s, soon they were one of the richest families in the world. Then, when Frederick de Courcey the Second took over, he made sure that the family airline, now called Connair, was at the forefront of the whole low-cost, budget airlines movement. You know the deal: flights that you paid a fiver for, but that flew you to an airstrip in the middle of nowhere, often upwards from 100 miles from your final destination.

The lower the airfares went, the more passengers queued around the block for them and, over subsequent decades, the company's tentacles grew like buddleia, so there was barely a single airport on the globe where you didn't get to see the shiny orange Connair logo screaming back at you.

Now, of course, the de Courcey wealth was so unfathomably, breathtakingly, mind-bogglingly vast, that it would take actuaries working round the clock to make a rough stab at calculating it.

Son and heir to the dynasty, I knew well, was Frederick the Third, thirty-two years of age, an only child and pretty much everything the gossip columns and tabloids would have him be. Good-looking, intelligent, charming and a bit of a magnet to the ladies, there was rarely a day when 'Freddie 3', as he'd been dubbed, wasn't splashed far and wide in the media, generally on the arm of an ever-changing array of girlfriends. All stunning, all fabulously successful in their own right, thanks very much, and of course, it went without saying, all jaw-droppingly magazine-cover, Instagram-gorgeous.

So when I first got the summons, over two years ago, to the de Courcey mansion, I could take a good, educated guess as to what the problem was. Or rather, *who* the problem was.

Initially, however, I'd thought it was some kind of joke when the secretary of a private secretary first got in touch. The email and follow-up phone calls were discreet and to the point; my presence was requested at a meeting in one of the family's many, many homes dotted around the globe. This particular residence was outside of Dublin, almost hidden away in the secluded privacy of a working stud farm that only ever seemed to produce Grand National winners and Derby champions. The de Courceys were winners through and through, and wouldn't have stood for any less.

A car was sent to take me there, with a driver who point-blank refused to engage, so that by the time we pitched up at the first of several security checkpoints leading to the private house, even a hardened veteran like me, who'd never experienced nerves in the entire course of my life, actually found myself getting antsy.

The whole set-up was calculated to intimidate, with all kinds of nonsensical requests to bring photo ID and a lanyard pass, just for the privilege of a ten-minute meeting with person or persons unknown – I still hadn't been briefed as to who it was that actually wanted to speak to me in the first place. The information restrictions were Kremlin-like.

The de Courcey house itself was a huge Palladian-style mansion, so beautifully preserved and lovingly maintained, it would put you in mind of *Brideshead Revisited*. An exquisitely maintained driveway that seemed to go on for miles swept you to the portico at the main entrance, with a flight of a dozen stone steps that whisked you from there up to the front door. Which was opened before I even got to ring the doorbell. Which in turn meant there were CCTV cameras discreetly all over the place, so they quite literally could see you coming.

An actual butler opened the door and was the first person who spoke to me by name. 'Ms Monroe. Come this way, please. You're expected in the library.'

'Thank you,' I said, drinking in the spectacle of the double-height hallway, with its stone lions guarding the cantilevered, gilt-edged staircase that seemed to sweep upwards to the sky.

Although why anyone bothered to use the stairs in this house was beyond me; there was a discreet lift with white marbled doors right beside it.

I was guided on through to the library, which would have put Hogwarts to shame. Leather-bound books dominated mahogany bookcases that stretched right up to the ceiling, which must have been over twenty feet high. So high, in fact, that there was a balcony at an upper level, all the better to reach whatever first edition you wanted to get your clammy paws on. Although, I thought wryly, they probably made you handle everything in here with disposable cotton gloves, a bit like they did with Ancient Egyptian finds in the National Museum.

Silence; just the muted ticking of a clock from somewhere.

Feeling on edge, a bit like Pip about to meet Miss Havisham, I whipped my phone out of my bag. I was pretty well prepped for this meeting, but no harm in brushing up on a few facts while I waited.

No signal. Nothing, not a sausage. I was just about to try switching the phone off, then on again, when a whispery, papery-thin voice from behind startled me.

'You'll find there's no data coverage inside of the property, Miss Monroe. The entire house is firewalled and only those with a personal password have access to Wi-Fi. For security reasons, I hope you understand.'

I jumped and turned around to see an old, old lady in a wheelchair, who appeared to have glided in noiselessly and who was now directly behind me.

I scanned her up and down and did my thing.

Appearance: she looked about a hundred and three, with snow-white hair so fine that you could see her scalp clearly through it, wearing a pussy-bow blouse and with a plaid checked blanket covering her legs and knees.

Features: her hands were bony and liver-spotted, with heavy, oversized rings on what seemed like every single finger. In fact, the rings were so hefty-looking, they appeared to be the only thing weighing this wisp of a woman down.

Jeez, I thought, taking in a diamond the size of a small egg on her hand. Pawn that alone and you'd have the price of a town house in Dublin 4. Easily.

'Good morning,' said the old lady, holding out a wizened hand, which I shook very, very gently. This one was so frail-looking that a firmer handshake might have landed her in the A&E.

'And apologies for all the secrecy in getting you here,' she added, in a soft-spoken tone with an accent that could have been from anywhere. East Coast American? The Hamptons, maybe? Posh English? It was impossible to tell.

'But you come highly recommended from a close personal friend of mine, you see,' she went on, 'and I think it's just possible that you might be able to help our family in what, I'm afraid, is a most delicate matter.'

I felt my confidence surge at that, but then dealing with 'delicate matters' was something I was fast gaining experience with.

'I'm Ellen de Courcey,' this old, old lady said with a steely smile. 'And, as you can probably guess, I'm here to talk to you about my grandson, Frederick Junior.'

'I thought as much,' I nodded.

'Won't you sit down, please? So we can talk properly.'

She wheeled noiselessly over to a vast sofa and coffee table and waved at a Trafalgar chair by an other, ormolu coffee table for me to sit down and make myself comfortable. Then she must have given some invisible command, because the butler glided back into the room like he was on castors, laden down with a tea tray. Without asking, he poured tea into chintzy pink floral teacups and passed a cup over to me, automatically assuming I'd love nothing more than a watery Earl Grey.

'You must understand, Miss Monroe,' Ellen de Courcey said, with the stiff, old-fashioned manners of someone straight out of an Edith Wharton novel, 'that my grandson is everything to my husband and me. Everything.'

I nodded, but then I'd done my research thoroughly and you didn't need to look far to see why. Freddie Junior's parents had separated many years before his father had passed away from alcohol poisoning – it had been headline news at the time and Freddie Junior would only have been ten or eleven years old back then. His mum, meanwhile, had remarried a leading cosmetic surgeon in New York, and if the tabloids were anything to go by, she was now about to sign up for a second series of a reality TV show in the US, where her two teenage daughters, along with the second husband, appeared front and centre stage. Freddie Junior was now pretty much all his doting grandparents had, and vice versa.

'Frederick Junior has always lived his own life, of course,' Mrs de Courcey said, faffing between a slice of lemon or milk, 'but we've always been in loco parentis to him, you see. Great things are expected of him. A lot rests on his shoulders. It's long been the dearest wish of his grandfather and I that he would, in time, take the helm of the family business, and steer it into the future. Whereupon he might even have children of his own to pass it all on to. Naturally, as his closest relations, Frederick's well-being is our top priority. We want him to be happy. But it goes without saying, we also want him to be happy with the *right* person. Ideally, we're looking for a good, sensible Kate Middleton sort. Polite. Respectful. And, above all, trustworthy. Her Majesty must bless the day that a rock-solid young lady like Kate Middleton came into all their lives.'

Yeah right, I thought, my mind working fast. You want Frederick to be happy – but with someone of your choosing, as far as I can see.

'And the sad thing is,' Mrs de Courcey sighed wistfully, 'that Frederick Junior always had such lovely girlfriends in his life. Beautiful, successful young ladies from good, solid families, most of whom we knew socially. Girls who'd been to the right schools and who had desirable careers. His grandfather and I would have been overjoyed to see him settle down with any of them. But he's been such a rogue, you know! Constantly overlapping one girlfriend with another, till it almost made one's head swim.'

I nodded, knowing exactly what she meant. But then tabloid banner headlines like 'Love Cheat Freddie Strikes Again!' weren't all that uncommon.

I can help you there, I thought, calmly looking across at my hostess. *You've certainly sent for the right woman. For no extra charge, I can even scare him monogamous, if that's what you want.*

'But one in particular stood out,' Ellen de Courcey went on, in that whispery, Jackie Kennedy-esque little voice. 'A most delightful young lady, a doctor, you know, studying to be a consultant, if you don't mind. Always convenient to have a medic in the family, you know. But then, just when I began to relax and think all would be well, and that we might even hear news of an engagement . . .'

There was a brief hiatus as she paused to take a delicate sip of tea, so I took advantage.

'If I may, Mrs de Courcey,' I interrupted, 'I think I can possibly second-guess the rest.'

After all, you wouldn't need to be Sherlock Holmes to see what was coming here. Clearly, this Freddie Junior had been happily dating the consultant-to-be, only to fall in with some gold-digging wannabe who was only after him for his money. Someone Grandma and Grandpa heartily disapproved of and wanted to see the back of, ASAP.

'Frederick is seeing someone and you'd prefer it if she was out of the picture?' I offered tentatively.

'Her name is . . . Harriet Waters,' said Mrs de Courcey disdainfully. 'And I know it must be quite serious between them, because Frederick appears to have changed since he met her. He's no longer playing the field as he's always done. Instead, all he can talk about is Harriet this, Harriet that, insisting that his grandfather and I actually *meet* her, if you can believe that. So I'm prepared to pay you a very vast sum of money to remove this person from our lives. If you'd be so kind, please,' she added, almost as if this was already a done deal.

As if this was ever easy. As if what I did wasn't a potential minefield of duplicity and manipulation and, when necessary, coercion. As if she was politely asking me to take out the trash, then wash my hands thoroughly afterwards.

'Can you give me any information about her?' I asked, quickly getting down to brass tacks. 'The more I have to go on, the faster I can get you results, you understand.'

There was a disgusted sniff from Mrs de Courcey and she held a delicate tissue to her nose, as if she was driving past a stinky pig farm.

'Oh my dear,' she said faintly. 'The worst. The very worst imaginable. And Frederick is so very young and susceptible, you see. He's . . . perhaps not the most . . . intellectual person you've ever met . . .'

Which, I knew, was effectively code for, 'he's not the brightest bulb on the tree'. I nodded along, remembering only too well the tabloid nickname for this Freddie de Courcey. Tim Nice-But-Dim.

'So his grandfather and I have a clear duty of care to steer him in the right direction, you understand.'

Jesus Christ, I thought. Just what exactly had Freddie Junior got himself into? And how bad could his girlfriend possibly be? A drug user? A reoffender, just out of women's prison on bail? A porn star? I racked my brains, unable to imagine just how undesirable she could be, whoever she was.

'You must brace yourself,' Mrs de Courcey continued.

Then she told me.

Then silence. Just the ticking of a discreet clock in the background and the clink of Mrs de Courcey's china cup against a silver spoon, as she took a tiny, delicate sip of tea.

I tried not to react, but must have betrayed myself a little, because two beady old-lady eyes instantly lit on me, sharp as Sabatier knives.

'You perhaps think that I'm being a little too harsh?' she asked, peering at me over her teacup. 'Too judgemental? Perhaps even snobbish?'

'No . . . not in the least . . .' I tried to say, but for an elderly lady of such advanced years, the old matriarch was considerably ahead of me.

'I am most relieved to hear it.'

More silence.

'You must make allowances for my advanced years, Miss Monroe, because, on occasion, I can be a tad forgetful,' Mrs de Courcey said after a lengthy pause. 'As you already know, you and I have a mutual connection in common.'

'That's right,' I nodded, purposely not saying the name.

'And I happen to know from this mutual connection of ours,' she went on, ringing a tiny silver bell beside her, 'that you're seeking to set yourself up in business. I'm a little uncertain as to your exact job description . . .'

'I'm a fixer,' I said confidently. 'I make your people problems go away. And that's it, that's what I do.'

'Very successfully, too, according to what I've heard,' she replied.

'Well . . . thank you.'

'However,' she went on, 'in order to succeed, you will need clients, won't you? Lots of them. High-end people too, well connected, with enough money to make your chosen vocation lucrative. Am I right?'

I nodded.

'Which is where I can help. You do this for me, and I will personally set you up in business. I'll refer everyone I know to you – discreetly, of course. If you manage to fix my own particular "people problem", as you refer to it, I will make certain you have such an abundance of clients that you never need to look back.'

I looked over at her, dumbstruck at the carrot that was being dangled in front of me. I thought of the sheer amount of people this woman would know, the level of society she operated in, the *money* I could make . . .

'And there's something else too,' Mrs de Courcey said, calmly and coolly. 'You are, I understand from this same mutual acquaintance, flat-hunting at the moment, I believe is the common parlance. And that, in time, you ultimately wish to purchase your own home. Is that not correct?'

'Well, yes,' I said, not quite sure where this was going.

Just then, the butler appeared once more, silent as the grave and carrying what looked very much like an estate agent's prospectus. Brand new, glossy and shiny – the kind that I occasionally flicked through for property porn but knew that anything in it, on my humble salary as a legal secretary at a law firm, was for evermore out of reach.

'If you'd be so kind as to peruse this,' Mrs de Courcey said, as the butler handed over the brochure.

Puzzled, I did as I was told, and it almost took my breath away. These apartments were in the swishest, most out-of-my-league part of the city; the whole development was brand new and still under construction, but I knew that even a broom cupboard in one of them would go for a sky-high price.

Why was I being shown this? This was nothing more than a tantalising glimpse into a pipe dream and frankly, I thought, a big waste of everyone's time.

'You're thinking you could never afford something like this,' Mrs de Courcey said softly, reading my thoughts. 'But supposing you could?'

'It's out of the question,' I replied, firmly putting the brochure on the coffee table, refusing to annoy myself anymore by looking at it.

'Oh, but nothing is out of the question, my dear. Our entire family fortune is founded on that very principle. Call this a "sweetener", as my husband says, to seal our little arrangement. Meanwhile, I suggest you check out the penthouse. Doesn't the two-bedroomed have the most heavenly view?'

Chapter Nine

Harriet

It is a very peculiar thing, Harriet thinks, *when your best friend seems less than happy to have you back in her life again.*

But why is Meg acting so *weirdly*, she wonders, as she steps outside onto the wraparound balcony in Meg's flat, pulls Meg's dressing gown tightly around her, cradling a cup of coffee made from Meg's Nespresso machine, plonking down on one of Meg's elegant grey rattan armchairs and staring out over the city docklands, shimmering below her in the midsummer heat – the very same view Meg got to look at every day of the week.

It made no sense on any level. She and Meg had been as thick as thieves; they were inseparable, they were like sisters, and had been ever since the day they'd first met.

This was a notoriously hard city to crack, and for Harriet, moving to Dublin in the first place had been the most challenging and intimidating thing she had ever done. She'd come from a small town down the country where everyone talked to everyone else and where the dogs on the street knew your business better than they knew their own.

But living here was so different, it was tougher, less forgiving for a start; everyone was so busy and on the make all the time. For Harriet's first few months here, she barely talked to anyone at all. Her whole life involved getting up, leaving the tiny little shoebox of a spare room she was lodging in, courtesy of her Auntie Mai, then shuffling into work and straight back home again afterwards, walking past pubs and bars full of people having a far better time than her.

Of course she had a few friends from home and college working in the city too, and while it was fun whenever they met up, nights like that were very few and far between. Everyone was either too broke or too busy, so a snatched bite to eat after work and a movie every so often was about the best they could do. Meanwhile, Harriet's old set of pals were still back home, texting her, Skyping her and almost cracking her resolve by telling her, 'We all miss you so much! When are you coming back home?'

But Harriet was determined. Her job was more than just a job to her; so much more than that. It was a vocation, a way of life, a mission statement. She knew, of course, that there were sneers and put-downs from some people about what she did for a living. She worked for the HQ of a big charity organisation, and, as part of her job, had been seconded to manage a small charity shop that was so run-down, even the locals had nicknamed it Dead Old Lady Dresses.

'Really?' she was asked on one ill-advised Tinder date she went on, when she'd first moved to Dublin. 'That's what you work at? That's actually your chosen profession?'

'Yes, but that's not all I do,' she'd smiled shyly. 'I volunteer for the Samaritans two nights a week and I work for Amnesty at the weekends. We all live such first world lives here, we have a responsibility to give something back don't you think? Even if it's just your time?'

'Hmmm,' her date said hesitantly, 'but just to make sure I got this right – your day job is working at a CRAP store? Voluntarily?'

Never was a charity shop more aptly named; its full title was Charity Resale And Purchasing. CRAP for short.

'That's right,' she said.

'But isn't that more like something prisoners are forced to do on community service?'

Then he looked at her very, very weirdly, slowly taking a small step back from the crowded bar where they'd managed to nab two stools together.

'Jesus,' he added hastily, 'don't tell me you're out on probation?'

Hurtful remarks like that were par for the course for Harriet. It was something she'd never got used to, and she'd been working at CRAP for almost four years now. Promoted to Regional Sales Manager and everything, not that fancy titles held much appeal for her.

'Climbing the career ladder now, I see,' her dad had joked when he'd first heard about her promotion. 'You see, love? I knew all this altruistic shite about helping the less well off was just a business plan for you. Good to see that it's beginning to pay off and that you're finally making a few quid out of it.'

'It's not that big a deal, really, Dad,' she'd blushed, 'I'm the only one in the store most of the time, and my boss Mona only gave me a fancy title because she thought it would anchor me to the job.'

'You're too honest, Harriet,' her mam had chipped in. 'That's your trouble. Why can't you just blow your own trumpet for a bit? I'll certainly be bragging to them all in Kelly's Hotel tonight that my daughter was just made Regional Manager. It's not too shabby, now, is it?'

Harriet had let it go – what was the point in arguing? Her parents were comfortably off, both still working and working hard, too, and they couldn't see why their youngest daughter, scrap of a thing that she was, could possibly want to devote her whole life to the voluntary sector. No more than anyone else could.

So, Harriet would do what she always did, whenever people were less than kind or encouraging about what she did for a living. She regrouped. She went for long, bracing walks on the beach. And she reminded herself why she was doing this in the first place.

To help those less well off. To try, in her own small way, to make the world a better place. And above all, to charge the maximum amount possible for ancient, knackered pairs of nun's knickers, and first-generation car phones that didn't work and that were the approximate size and weight of a brick.

*

Harriet could never be quite certain when Meg Monroe had first bounced into her life; it all seemed to happen so easily and organically. It was about two years ago now, when Meg just took to calling into the shop daily, then sometimes twice a day for the chats. She lived locally, she'd claimed, in one of the old cottage houses across the street that she was trying to renovate from scratch. Meg had got it at a knock-down rent, she'd said, but the downside was that the elderly man who owned it had died there, and had been a lifelong hoarder.

So it seemed like every single day without fail, sometimes twice a day, Harriet would see Meg's small, neat silhouette in the window lugging yet another bag load of cast-offs and chipped china dogs and magazines that were so yellowing and frayed, Princess Diana was still alive in them.

The two had become buddies from the get-go, but then, Harriet had been starved of friendship and it was just so easy to get pally with someone like Meg. She was so much fun and light-hearted and easy to chat to. Harriet would offer her cups of tea and Jaffa Cakes whenever she dropped by and, pretty soon, Meg started popping in for chats in the evening, just as Harriet was closing up. Before long, they took to slipping into a local pizzeria after work to share a few cheesy margarita slices between them.

The two swapped phone numbers, and in no time they were doing more and more together, though always on a low-rent budget. She and Meg only ever went to the cheapest restaurants, and split a starter between them. And even at that, it was always for an early bird. If they were out drinking, they only ever ordered soft drinks and made them last for a good two hours, topping their glasses up with discreet

plastic bottles filled with supermarket vodka, to much messing and stifled giggles from the pair of them.

Sunday strolls in the park became a regular thing for them,
and they'd sit on a park bench, sip coffee from a flask to save
money and chat about whatever gossip there was from the
night before. It got to the stage where there wasn't a free outdoor movie the girls didn't know about, or a cheapie sample
sale that they weren't at the top of the queue for.

All the best fun imaginable, and nothing that cost any
money. But then, you didn't need money to have a good time
with someone like Meg; even sitting on the top deck of a bus
with her was an adventure. In a very short space of time,
they'd become inseparable. They were Thelma and Louise.
They were Tina Fey and Amy Poehler. Patsy and Edina from
Absolutely Fabulous. They were each other's closest, most
trusted mate. Harriet had even gone and bought Meg a mug
from the charity shop that said, *Bestest Friends Forever*. It
was chipped at the rim and it cost seventy-five cents, but,
feck the expense, Harriet thought, *I'm buying it anyway*.

Months passed and it got to the stage where there was
very, very little that Harriet hadn't confided in Meg about
her private life. Including a certain someone who she'd just
met, but who was turning into someone . . . well, someone
very, very special, as a matter of fact.

Meg had been all ears when Harriet had first told her
about Freddie de Courcey. Full of thoughts, full of wise
advice, full of helpful suggestions. The two even met, many
times, and got on brilliantly. In fact, Meg had been amazing
about Freddie from day one. She always seemed to be there

when Harriet needed her, to steer her, to advise her and then, in time, to pick her up off the floor when things started going belly-up.

Which they did, spectacularly.

But Meg had been by her side, through every single day of it. She'd been like a cross between a guardian angel and a wise, calm relationship counsellor during one of the very lowest ebbs in Harriet's life. More than that, in fact. Meg was actually the one who'd warned her off Freddie in the first place, on the grounds that it was never going to work out anyway, mainly because he was seeing someone else. Oh, Meg had all the cold, clear evidence, the online photos of Freddie and his medical consultant, a woman so intimidatingly successful, it was almost scary.

What would I ever have done without Meg? Harriet often wondered, when she was at her most upset and vulnerable.

Back then, Meg had turned out to be such a stalwart friend. And yet, just look how things seemed to have changed. Now, when Harriet had come back after a full year abroad, Meg seemed so frosty and unwelcoming. Almost as if she wanted Harriet gone. Was it really possible that the foundations of their friendship had shifted, in such a short amount of time? No matter what way Harriet looked at it, it made absolutely no sense to her.

As soon as she was up, showered and dressed, she called Meg's number, just to talk. It didn't matter what about. All she wanted was to hear her pal's voice. It was late when she'd arrived here the previous night; maybe Meg was just tired. Maybe that was it.

But Meg practically bites the nose off her.

'Please, Harriet, I'm trying to *work* here, will you stop calling me?'

There was no mistaking it; Meg had been borderline rude. Why in God's name was she acting the way she was?

Harriet thought about it, then worried about it, then texted her again a little while later. Just a lightning-quick message, to make sure she wasn't imagining things.

Didn't mean to disturb you. Guess you're having a stressful day, sending love.

The brusque reply came back almost immediately.

I'll be back later and will drop you off wherever you need to be.

No, Harriet thought, when she read it.
Definitely not imagining things.

Chapter Ten

Meg

Guessing you're having a stressful day, sending love.

I'm in the middle of doing one of my super-fast costume changes in the back of a taxi, but I only have to glance at the message and I can physically feel my blood pressure spike to danger levels.

The worst part is that it's all my own fault for letting Harriet into my life in the first place. I've no one but myself to blame for allowing us to get close. Not that I've got anything against Harriet per se; sure, she's a little naive and excitable, but she's a good and kind person and her heart's in the right place. In a parallel life, maybe we'd even have become proper friends. Not that I'd know all that much about friendship.

But this isn't a parallel life, is it? This is reality and, right now, I need her to cop herself on, realise that she's majorly in the way and bugger off into the sunset, long before Ellen de Courcey ever gets wind of the fact that she's back. I need to leave emotion out of it, park my conscience at the door and airbrush her clean out of the picture.

It's a problem. It's a massive headache for me, and just thoughts of Harriet being there in my flat, all alone and possibly snooping through my private business, actually makes me burst a blood vessel in my eye. Thank you, hypertension.

There's nothing I want more than to turn this taxi around, head home and sort this out once and for all. Can't though, can I? It's my first day on the Katherine Sisk job, probably the biggest and most lucrative gig I've had all year, and how would it look if I just didn't turn up?

With little choice in the matter, I have to put the whole Harriet situation to the back of my mind for now, regroup and keep going.

In a few deft, practised moves, I've shimmied out of my Lululemon leggings and into a neat little shift dress from LK Bennett, along with a pair of nude pumps I'd pre-packed in my gym bag. But then, preparation, I've always found, is key. I check my face in a compact make-up mirror, dab on a hint of mascara with a light dusting of powder, and once I've scraped my hair up into a neat chignon, I take one quick, final check in the mirror before I'm good to go.

Yes, this look works. I'm in uniform. Looking utterly unrecognisable from the sweaty, tousle-haired mess I needed to be at yoga class earlier.

Which at least is something.

I pay the taxi driver, tip him overgenerously because he let me change in peace, then step briskly out of the cab and into Katherine Sisk's constituency office, where I've 'volunteered' to help out with the upcoming election campaign.

First job on the list? To work closely with Jess Butler, Senator Katherine's campaign PR manager, not to mention her husband's girlfriend, in a bid to gain her trust and hopefully grow closer to her. Grow closer to her, that is, before gently persuading her to move aside, so I can really go to town on Philip Sisk and his little extramarital dalliance.

Not that this would be my usual modus operandi – far from it. Normally, I get to know my targets socially first, and that strategy has never failed me. But how are you supposed to get to know a team who work twenty-four/seven on a politician's re-election campaign? The only way is by joining that team and working alongside them. So that's precisely what I plan to do.

Half an hour in, though, and I realise this isn't nearly as piss-easy as it usually is. Ordinarily, I'd study your life, follow your digital trail – and, make no mistake, everyone leaves a digital trail – then I'd find a foolproof chink in your day, so I can slowly wriggle my way inside. I'd find out where you go for coffee, hang out in the evenings, go drinking with your buddies, or if there's some kind of evening class you go to regularly maybe?

But this? This is more like actual, well, *work* really. No sooner am I in the door to a few quick 'good mornings' from the rest of the team and a knowing nod from Katherine Sisk than I'm hurled straight in at the deep end.

'Now everyone, listen up,' says Katherine, looking tense and stressed as she addresses the entire office. 'You all remember Meg, I hope, and as it's her first day here, I want you all to show her the ropes. And be nice to her! Got it? Good.'

And with that, she just whisks out of the room and straight on to another meeting, effectively abandoning me to the sharks. No sign of Philip Sisk either, but that's OK, I figure. His girlfriend first; him later. Never any harm to save the best for last, is it?

'Right then, let's crack on with it,' says Jess, swivelling her chair around to face me and shoving a biro up into her thick red mane of hair, as she juggles two phones at the same time. 'So Katherine is on *PrimeNews* tonight at 7 p.m., and I need to get fully prepped for that. In the meantime, though, here's a list of campaign donors you need to contact immediately. I know you're new and all that, but this should be straight-forward enough.'

With that, she shoves a printout at me that runs to eleven pages, all double-sided.

Look at you, I think. *So bossy and important.* How the feck did this one find the time for an affair, never mind the energy?

'But . . . I thought maybe you and I could grab a coffee or something, before we start work?' I offer hopefully. 'Just so we can chat about what's actually involved in the campaign? We're going to be working side by side, and the election is so soon, shouldn't we at least get to know each other first?'

But Jess isn't even listening. She's already on to her next call.

'Yes, Senator Sisk needs a car to take her to Channel Seven studios for 6 p.m. at the latest, with full approval on all questions in advance, please. You can get your producer on the line and I'll confirm it all with her. Yes, I'll hold . . . and no, I most certainly will not take no for an answer.'

'Where do I sit?' I ask, looking around at the chaotic office, with posters strewn on every surface, several TVs on in the background all showing major competing news channels, and everyone looking busy and under pressure, to the point of having coronaries.

Someone must overhear me though, because just then a chair on wheels is shoved in my direction, which I automatically catch with my foot.

When I look up, there's the same bespectacled guy who'd been at the office the previous day too, glued to his phone, talking about stats and percentage of number one preferences to God knows who. He's dressed in a suit, as if he's about to go on TV himself, but is baggy-eyed and looks as exhausted as everyone else. Jeez, did they pull all-nighters in here, or what? I grab the office chair and give him a grateful thumbs up sign.

He covers the phone with his hand for a moment and catches my eye.

'We all look a lot busier than we are, really,' he hisses across at me. 'Remember, this gig is about one thing and one thing only. Getting that little X beside Katherine's name in the polling booth next week. And that's it.'

'I'll bear that in mind,' I mutter under my breath, sitting down and studying the list that's been thrust at me.

'So what do I say when someone answers the phone?' I ask Jess, who's ended her call and is back to bashing away at her computer as if her life depends on it. 'What are the key points I need to hit?'

No response.

'Jess?' I repeat. 'Did you hear me?'

'I already told you,' Jess snaps back, utterly focused on the screen in front of her. 'You contact everyone on the sheet and discuss campaign donations. I thought you'd have at least started by now.'

So, not only are you having an affair with your employer's husband behind her back, I think, smiling benignly, while my mind stays icy, icy-cold. *But you're rude and dismissive with it. Well, your days are so numbered, babe.*

Maybe this gig won't be as bad as I'd initially feared. Maybe it'll actually be a fucking pleasure to take this one down in flames.

'No problem,' I beam back, nice as pie. 'And I'm sorry to be a pain. First-day blues, you know how it is! You'll have to let me buy you lunch to thank you for being so patient with me.'

'Did you just say *lunch*?' says Jess, looking up over her computer screen. 'Are you having a laugh? How about we get Katherine re-elected first, then worry about lunch afterwards?'

'Absolutely. Let's never forget, you're the boss.'

Chapter Eleven

Harriet

Mid-morning, and Harriet is getting bored and restless, pacing about the flat, not quite knowing what to do with herself. So far, she's made brekkie, lunch, coffee, herbal tea and watched a shedload of daytime TV, anything just to kill a few hours. She is utterly unused to not working, and now that she's home again, she's found herself desperately missing Dead Old Lady Dresses and all the eccentric characters who'd drop in and out to her all day for chats. And still, if the truth be told, she's puzzling over what the hell had got into her one-time best friend, Meg.

Harriet hasn't been on social media in months, but with absolutely nothing else to do, she takes a quick photo of the cityscape view from Meg's balcony, which looks so shimmery and gorgeous in the warm summer sun, then posts it on Instagram. She captions it,

So happy to be back in Dublin! #realBarrystea
#nomosquitoes #theresnoplacelikehome

Then she sits back on Meg's rattan sofa out on the balcony and scrolls down through the comments. In a matter of minutes, there are loads. Mostly from her old school pals down home, all dying to know when she is coming to see them. 'So we can arrange the biggest welcome home party that Ballyroan has ever seen!' as her future sister-in-law-to-be posted.

But then there is one comment that makes her heart stop. From @freddiedecourcey.

Him. Most definitely him.

Welcome home, Harriet. Can I call you?

Instantly, she drops the phone, as if she's just been electrocuted.

Ohgodohgodohgod, she thinks, her heart rate soaring as she gets up and goes inside and paces around a bit.

This isn't the first time she's heard from Freddie either. There were a few – more than a few, to tell the truth – stray texts and a couple of late-night phone calls from him when she was away. 'Just wondering how you're doing. When you're home, maybe we can meet up?' To date, she'd stonewalled him, ignored his messages and not returned his calls.

And that, she tells herself, *is exactly what I'm going to do now, too.*

Certainly not till she at least gets to talk the whole thing through properly with Meg, because if there was one thing Meg never did, it was give bad advice. After all, the reasons why Freddie and Harriet broke up in the first place are still very much there, aren't they?

Do nothing, she tells herself. *Do absolutely nothing. Wait to talk to Meg properly, get advice.* Meg had been right a year ago when all of Harriet's deepest, darkest suspicions about Freddie had turned out to be entirely correct. He was out of her league, Meg had told her, and wasn't she right?

'You're well in over your head with a guy like him,' she'd said; Harriet could still remember every word vividly. Meg had gently talked her through it all, no detail spared. 'I hate having to tell you this,' she'd said reluctantly, 'but sometimes you have to be cruel to be kind, and I wouldn't be a true pal unless I told you what everyone else seems to know. Fact is, Freddie is still seeing an old girlfriend behind your back, someone else far more suited to him, certainly as far as that snotty family of his are concerned.'

Harriet could still remember how she'd felt on being told that her intuition was completely on the money. And worst of all was that Meg was right; there was no chance in hell that his family would ever, ever have accepted the likes of her. She knew it, they knew it, the dogs on the street seemed to know it. Yadda, yadda, yadda – Harriet had heard it all, and nothing has changed since she's been away over the last year. Not a single thing.

God, but she was a misguided moron to have read anything into Freddie getting back in contact with her. He was just so well mannered and polite – he was kind and considerate like that to everyone, not just her. He'd been to a public school, for God's sake. You couldn't fault his manners. Well, except for the whole sleeping with someone else behind her back thing. Besides, he's probably figured enough time has passed between them for it to be OK to get in touch, 'as friends'.

He just feels a bit guilty about how it all came to a crashing halt between us, she thinks. He probably wants to make sure that she isn't sobbing herself to sleep at night, in a tea towel bought at the charity shop for twenty cents.

She and Freddie have been apart now for almost one whole year. Well, three hundred and fifty-two days, to be exact. And for every single one of those days, Harriet has thought about him and wondered how he is, and even though she tried her very hardest to throw herself into her new job abroad, and even though it killed her to keep ignoring his messages and stonewalling him, absolutely nothing would stop the feeling that there was a great slab of stone right where her heart used to be.

Abruptly, she stands up.

Distractions. She needs distractions, badly. She checks the time difference in New York, figures it's early morning over there, and tries calling her parents.

Her dad answers, yawning sleepily down the phone.

'Harriet, love,' he says. 'It's so good to hear your voice – we missed you so much! I can't wait to see you when we're home this Thursday – and neither can your mam.'

'I hope I didn't wake you up, Dad?' Harriet says apologetically, although she can clearly hear the sound of the TV on, as a weatherman gives out the forecast for the Tri-state area and predicts thundery downpours for the whole of Manhattan.

'Not at all,' her dad says sounding as clear as if he is actually in the room with Harriet, and not thousands of miles away. 'Your mam is already up and showered and dressed and giving out yards because Macy's on Herald Square doesn't open for another two hours.'

'I never said that!' Harriet hears her mam insisting loudly in the background. 'I'm only up and dressed because I have to go to a major veterinary conference and work hard all day, to keep you in the manner to which you're accustomed, you roaring eejit!'

'In fact, you're not even our first caller today, Harriet, love,' her dad says wryly. 'Your two brothers already woke us up at six this morning, New York time, with, I'm not joking you, a list the length of their arm of stuff for us to bring home for their stag night. Oh, you'd want to hear the kind of shite they were after: inflatable willies and latex crap and all that bollock-ology. They've a right fecking cheek, the pair of them.'

'Give me that phone,' Harriet's mam says, grabbing it from him, as Harriet smiles at all their affectionate squabbling. She's missed all this so much more than she realised. 'And for God's sake,' her mam says, 'if you're going to cut your toenails, can you please do it in the bathroom? No, not you, Harriet, love. I was talking to your dad. So how are you feeling today, pet? Not too jet-lagged, I hope?'

'Did the boys really ask you to bring back sex toys?' Harriet asks, making herself another Nespresso from Meg's fancy machine and sitting up onto a stool at the kitchen island, loving the chance to catch up on all the family gossip.

'They certainly did, and the pair of them got a right lash of my tongue, I can tell you,' her mam says in a brisk, no-nonsense tone. 'Can you imagine us going through customs with all that sleazy tat in our suitcases? Honestly. If we were stopped and searched, I'd never hold my head up high again.'

'And how are the brides-to-be?'

Jack and Terry were engaged to two lovely girls who work together in the same hair salon, and all four first met during a charity fundraiser a few years ago, when the lads agreed to shave their full heads of hair off for a cancer awareness stunt. That made page twelve in the local paper, the twin engagements had made page five, and everyone was hoping the actual double wedding might be a page one story, come the big day.

'Well,' her mother harrumphs, 'all I can say is, Kate Middleton and Meghan Markle have absolutely nothing on that pair. Honestly, all they're short of doing is ringing up the Archbishop of Canterbury and asking him for a loan of Westminster Abbey for the ceremony. The money this wedding is costing!'

'Really?' says Harriet, all ears.

'Don't get me started,' her mother groans. '"Oh, your presence is the greatest gift we can possibly ask for," Alisha says, the last time I was with her getting my highlights done. "So all we're asking is that our guests make a little contribution towards our special day. Just whatever you feel you can afford – but just to make it nice and easy for you, there's a bank giro attached to the bottom of each individual invitation. My own parents have given us two thousand quid each, just to give you a rough guideline." Well, I won't repeat to you what your father said to me afterwards.'

'"What a load of bollocks!" I believe were my exact words,' she hears her dad shout in the background.

'Two *thousand*?' Harriet says, nearly falling off her stool in shock.

'I know,' her mam says. 'Do they think we're on the rich list, or something? Or from a family like that de Courcey fella you used to go out with?'

But Harriet doesn't answer and just goes very quiet instead.

Suddenly the whole mood, which was so light and jovial, seems to shift.

'Oh, I'm so sorry, pet,' her mam says, sensing the change in atmosphere. 'I didn't mean to upset you. I just hoped that a bit of time away would have given you some perspective on all that. All in the past now, though, isn't it? Don't get me wrong, that Freddie sounded like a perfectly nice fella, but I always felt you were a bit of a mismatch. Your backgrounds were so different, you might as well have come from different planets. He went to one of those posh public schools, for God's sake. And do you remember how the twins used to slag him off for coming out with things like, "golly gosh" and "blimey" the whole time?'

'He's been in touch again, Mam,' Harriet blurts out. Can't stop herself, but then, she tells her mam everything. 'Since before I came back, actually. Just as a friend, I'm sure. Nothing more.'

'*Really?*' her mother says, using an entire octave in that single word and loading it with about three different meanings. Opera singers at the Met have got absolutely nothing on Harriet's mother.

'It's all cool, Mam, honestly,' Harriet rushes to reassure her. 'You don't need to worry. Really. It's only a few messages and texts, that's all.'

'Whenever anyone tells me not to worry,' her mam says very, very slowly, 'then I automatically worry twice as much.'

'So you're staying at your friend Meg's?' her dad says, grabbing the phone back and thankfully changing the subject.

'*I'm* in the middle of a conversation with her,' her mam says, snatching the phone right back again as a hissed conversation between the two of them ensues. 'Now kindly go back into the bathroom and finish your toenails.'

'I already finished them, now it's my turn for the phone—'

'Did you wash your hands?'

'Course I did, now let me talk to Harriet!' Then more movement and muffled conversation. 'Sorry about that,' her dad says, finally getting hold of the phone. 'I just wanted to say that it's great your pal Meg is putting you up till we get home. Good on you, love. Save yourself a few quid. Unlike this bloody stag night – the whole thing is costing me a right packet. I'm telling you, it'll be a miracle if I don't end up on parish relief, this wedding is costing so much.'

'Hand me back that phone,' her mam says crossly, 'and for the love of God, stop grousing about money for two minutes, will you? Now Harriet, love, I really do need to go. The conference is starting shortly, but you can tell me everything that's been going on with that de Courcey fella as soon as we're back home. We're so excited to see you. And I know your brothers will be too—'

'Even though they're acting like a right pair of gobshites with their three-day wedding extravaganza and their joint stag night, and don't get me started on the two wannabe Kardashians they're marrying,' her dad grumbles good-heartedly, grabbing the phone again. 'They want a rehearsal dinner the night before the wedding. Rehearse what, I says? Sure we already know how to use knives and forks, thanks very much.'

'For God's sake, I'm *trying* to talk to her,' her mam says, to much grunting and moaning from her dad, as the phone is snatched back from him yet again.

'I really can't wait to see you guys,' Harriet smiles. 'And in the meantime, it's lovely to be here with Meg. You'd want to see the place she's living in . . .'

'I'm very fond of that girl,' her mam says approvingly, and Harriet can almost hear the smile in her mother's voice. 'Always came across like a young one with her head screwed on right. And she was so kind to you, love. Remember when that Freddie fella started messing around on you? She was a real pal to you then, wasn't she?'

'She certainly was, yes,' Harriet agrees.

'She was good enough to tell you the truth, Harriet,' her mother says. 'When plenty of other friends would have been only too delighted to see you hanging out with a rich kid like that, to see what they could get out of it for themselves.'

'I know, Mam,' Harriet says quietly. 'I remember very well.'

'Then when the Kenya trip came up, wasn't it Meg who helped you pack your bags? And even drove you to the air-port, if I remember right?'

'She did, Mam. She was a dote.'

'And now you just arrive on her doorstep and she takes you in? Now that's a true-blue friend, pet. You mark my words.'

I hope you're right Mam, Harriet thinks. *I hope to God you're right.*

*

As the day wears on, and with nothing better to do with herself, Harriet wanders around the wraparound balcony, gazing down on views that stretch all the way over the docklands, probably the coolest and most expensive quarter of town. It's high summer, the day's getting hotter by the minute, and all she can see five floors beneath her at street level are hipster-y coffee shops, high-end boutiques and the very same trendy farmers' markets that she and Meg once used to snigger at because they were so grossly overpriced.

'Three fifty for a coffee?' Harriet used to say. 'Are they for real? And did you see the heads of broccoli that they're charging two eighty for? Sure that's half the price down home!'

'Ahh, but don't forget the missing ingredient,' Meg smiled, 'the designer mud that's caked onto the sides of it. That's what these ones with more money than sense are prepared to fork out for.'

'There's farmers down home would give you that for free – cow dung isn't an extra luxury there!' Harriet had said, and the two fell about laughing. She still remembers the day so well; it had been mild and sunny and they'd taken a stroll around the whole dockland area, just to have a sneaky peek at the luxury homes and flats that they could never afford.

And now, here's Meg, actually living in one. And living on her own too, as far as Harriet can see, even though this apartment is vast and could house a whole family, easily. Although, mind you, to call a place like this an apartment is a massive understatement. This is more like a millionaire's crash pad – it has all the bells and whistles, everything you could possibly imagine.

How much money has this cost whoever owns it? It is unfathomable to Harriet, whose earthly goods could all be contained in a small backpack and a few black bin liners. She's been working abroad on a charity programme for the past twelve months, and has come back with little more than a big red sunburnt face, a collection of mosquito bites and a shocking case of diarrhoea. Yet in the meantime, Meg seems to have gone from being as broke as Harriet to living the life of a multimillionaire. What on earth has happened in the meantime? Is she out dealing drugs in her spare time, or what?

Harriet picks up her coffee cup, slides open the balcony doors and goes back inside the apartment, whistling as she wanders from the staggeringly huge living area and on into the master bedroom. Not that she's deliberately snooping or anything, but still. There are an awful lot of things she can't help noticing. That the dressing table in the main bedroom is stuffed full with all of Meg's things, for one; her face creams, the special make-up she wears so many signs that she's been staying here for a long, long time. Then, in the kitchen, there is the special gluten-free cereal that Meg eats in a neatly labelled container. Not only that, but post addressed to Meg has been laid out on the hall table.

The evidence is starting to stack up, and it all points to one thing. Meg is lying about this place. She has to be. She told Harriet she was only here on a lucky Airbnb, but that just doesn't hold up.

Next thing, parcels from DHL arrive at the door, and the delivery guy asks Harriet to sign for them.

'So what's in them?' she asks curiously.

'Looks like dresses to me,' comes the shrugged response. 'When they're over a certain price band, the VAT goes up, so that's why I need you to sign for them.'

After he's gone, Harriet examines the customs declarations on the outside of the boxes. Two dresses from Marni, a pair of trousers from Comme des Garçons and a pair of boots from Russell and Bromley. At even the roughest calculation, that has to be well over a thousand quid's worth of lovely new things, right there.

A thousand quid, Harriet thinks, in total and utter shock. An insane amount of money.

Which makes no sense on any level, because Meg never, ever used to have a single spare bean for clothes at all. So how come she's suddenly living the life of a multimillionaire? And how could she afford it? A win on the lottery, maybe? An inheritance from a wealthy relative?

Just then, a text pings through on Harriet's phone. Meg, again.

This time her message is short, sweet and very much to the point.

Hi Harriet. I'm so sorry I can't ask you to stay on any longer. I'm very happy to help you pack up and get home though. Will even drive you there myself.

So now Harriet isn't wondering about her erstwhile pal Meg anymore.

At this stage, she's starting to be a little suspicious of her.

Chapter Twelve

Meg

Ever the hypocrite, I've spent most of the day smiling and being perfectly polite to Jess's pale, pinched little face. It's almost killing me, but so far, I've successfully managed to be sweetness and light around her, all while dreaming up new and novel ways of getting her far, far away from her married boyfriend, where she wouldn't be a bother to anyone anymore. Like the North Pole, I think, as Jess beavers away at the desk beside me. Or the Arctic Circle at the very least.

Just then, Senator Katherine herself bounds into the office, fresh from a meeting with the Department of the Environment, her presence instantly sending an electric current of energy through the whole team. Trailing behind her is her husband Philip, laden down with a tray of fresh pastries and croissants for everyone. The differences in their personalities, right down to the way they greet the room, couldn't be more striking.

'Hi everyone, so sorry to be late, my last meeting ran way over . . .' Katherine says apologetically, not even stopping to take off her coat, as that guy, the bespectacled, besuited one who's forever banging on about percentage points is straight over to her, bringing her up to speed on what's happened since she left.

Philip, on the other hand, acts like a late arrival at a cocktail party.

'Well, hello there!' he grins broadly at the room, with an eye that lingers on Jess's slim frame just a degree too long.

Don't think I don't notice, Philip, because I do.

'Brought some reinforcements for the troops,' he says. 'Gotta have a carb hit at this hour of the afternoon, don't you?'

A few of the team thank him and wander over to help themselves to pastries and Danishes, except for Jess, who stays resolutely at her desk, face buried in her computer.

But Philip is straight over to her.

'Can't tempt you?' he says, waving the tray under her nose. 'Some seriously hot-looking buns here.'

Oh Christ, I think, overhearing everything. Did he really just come out with a line like that, and right in front of his wife?

Jess looks up at him, teasingly playing with the ends of her long, scraggy red hair.

'I'm sugar-free right now,' she says. 'So can you please just stop trying to tempt me? In work?'

'So how about if I leave something here for you in case you change your mind *after* work?' Philip smirks back at her.

He's talking about cakes and yet he's not talking about cakes, and it's vomit-inducing and he's doing it all right under his wife's nose, I think furiously. In her office, where she works.

I will bury him. I will really fucking make him suffer for this.

Meanwhile, a memory surfaces right at the very back of my mind. Inconvenient and unwanted, just like always.

'Why wasn't Dad there today, Mum?'

'I'm sure he was just working late again, love,' Mum had replied tightly. 'We all have to work, you know how it is.'

'But he missed my school Christmas concert.'

I'd been playing the piano at the show, the youngest in the whole school who'd been chosen to perform. I'd spent weeks practising, I'd memorised every single note of 'Oh Holy Night' and even sang along to it too. My whole school had clapped, my headmistress called me a little prodigy, and I'd never felt so happy and proud.

'Never mind,' Mum had said. 'I'm sure he'll be there next time you play.'

To this day, I can still recall, in ultra-HD, the muffled row I heard my parents having later on that night, when they thought I was tucked up in bed and fast asleep.

'What kind of an arsehole lets a six-year-old girl down, Charlie?' Mum had said, loud enough that her voice carried up the stairs. 'You couldn't even do that much for her? And now you can't even come up with a decent excuse as to where you've been all night?'

'Will you shut up nagging me?' Dad had snarled back. 'I said I was covering for one of the lads in work, and that's where I was. Call Micko if you don't believe me.'

'Do you know what, Charlie? I might do just that. The stink of perfume off you! Do you think I'm stupid, or what?

The way you keep sneaking off to make phone calls at night? The way you're never here anymore? All that dosh gone out of our joint account?'

'*You're paranoid . . . would you listen to yourself . . .*'

'*Don't you dare attempt to twist this around so it's my fault!*'

I mentally discipline myself not to go any further. Instead, I stand tall and remind myself of exactly why I've gone into this business in the first place. To right wrongs. To bring justice to anyone who has ever felt they've been shafted. And to sort out every single bloody cheater who as much as *dares* to cross my path. So Philip Sisk had better watch out, hadn't he?

Chapter Thirteen

Harriet

'I saw your post online.'

'Oh. You did?'

'You're back in town?'

'Yes. Just. I mean, only since last night.'

'So I just thought I'd call to say . . . well . . . welcome home, really.'

'Thank you. That's . . . kind of you.'

'And how was Africa? Kenya, wasn't it?'

'Well . . . it was . . .' Harriet fumbles about for the right words. She could have said 'fulfilling'. She could have said 'humbling'. Instead, she comes out with, 'I'm covered in mosquito bites and still not over the desperate bout of diarrhoea I got on the way home.'

But she could swear she can hear him smiling.

'I'm awfully glad I called,' he says, sounding warmer now. More like himself.

'Really?'

'You know I am. It's always lovely to hear your voice. It's been such a dreadfully long time, hasn't it?'

A pause – an awkward one. It worries Harriet a bit, because she and Freddie never used to run out of things to say to each other. Never.

'So . . . how have you been?'

'So how are things with you?' he asks, at exactly the same time.

They both snigger nervously, and that seems to break the ice a bit more.

'Oh God, this is really weird, isn't it?' he says. For the first time, Harriet notices that it's noisy wherever he's calling her from. Where is he anyway, the airport, she wonders?

'This is beyond weird.'

'I mean, you and me . . .'

'Used to be able to chat all night!'

'How are your family?' he asks politely, but then Freddie was unfailingly polite. Well brought up, as Harriet's mother would have said.

'Good.' She doesn't know what else to say. So she fills the dead air with what is effectively white noise. 'Mam's at a veterinary conference in New York this week, and Dad went with her for the freebie trip.'

'And they're both well?'

'Oh, in great form! Mam finally got to do surgery for kneecap dislocation on a three-year-old Labrador just a few weeks ago. Medial patella luxation, you call it. Dream come true for her – she's wanted to do an operation like that for years. She's the envy of the whole local vet community.'

'And walking normally again?' he asks, over the swelling background noise.

'Mammy always walked great, thanks very much.'

'No, I meant the Labrador.'

'Oh,' says Harriet, cursing herself. 'Yeah. Grand, thanks.'

'And your father?'

'He got a nice bit of news too. His gooseberry jam got second runner-up at the Summer Farmers' Market last month, and now he's thinking of selling it online under some artisan-y name. He reckons people will pay double if you slap the label "organic" on anything these days.'

Mother of God, she thinks. Did those words really come out of her mouth? A Labrador's kneecap and gooseberry jam?

'Wonderful, that's wonderful to hear,' Freddie says automatically, as the background noise wherever he is intensifies. It sounds wild and windy, like he's on the tarmac of a runway; but then you could never be too sure with Freddie, either of where he was, or of what was going on in his life. Once he'd called her from Maui where he'd been sent on Connair business, but she'd completely misheard, and could have sworn he was calling her from Mallow.

'And your brothers are well too, I hope? Jack and Terry?'

The twins are the only members of Harriet's family who Freddie has actually met. When Harriet had first introduced Freddie to the twins, miracle of miracles, they'd all actually cracked along together a storm. Freddie had grown up an only child, reared by his grandparents in a house that sounded terrifying, more like a palace, really, and he seemed to enjoy the loose banter and all the slagging and teasing that went on in a normal, functional family.

'Everyone is grand, thanks,' Harriet says, not really wanting to get into the fact that Jack and Terry are planning a big double wedding.

Weddings. Marriage. Not a great topic to get on to with the man who's broken your heart.

Silence; just the wind whooshing down the phone line. Harriet knows better than to ask about Freddie's own parents; his father had passed away years ago, drugs and booze had got the better of him, irony of ironies, while on his way to a spiritual retreat in Red Feather Lakes, Colorado, where he was planning to dry out. And one of the big pluses of volunteering in Kenya for the past year for Harriet was that she had no Wi-Fi. Which meant she wasn't even tempted to look at the US-based reality TV show which Freddie's mother now guest-starred in, along with her new husband and their two teenage daughters, who'd all become YouTube sensations and who were never off all the gossipy magazine covers these days.

'Where to, sir?' she could have sworn she heard a driver asking Freddie in the background. Harriet doesn't know how to fill the pause, so there are whole chasms left unsaid.

How's your girlfriend, she could have said.

Are you still happy with her? Is she still making you happy?

Is she still studying to be a medical consultant? While probably discovering a cure for cancer, and catwalk modelling in her spare time, by the skinny-arse look of her?

She didn't though.

'The signal is terrible here—' Freddie has just begun to say. 'I'll call you back . . . that OK?'

But then the phone goes dead before she can answer. Of course he isn't going to ring her back, Harriet thinks dejectedly. He could be anywhere, for one thing. In Singapore or Bali or Rio de Janeiro. He might even be with *her*, for all she knows.

And what does she think she is doing anyway, letting him back into her life again? Yes, Freddie was nice to her, of course he was nice to her, but then Freddie was nice to everyone. Freddie was nice to the man who came to zap bugs in their family mansion, and the driver who seems to be at his beck and call twenty-four/seven. Freddie is unfailingly polite. It means nothing. It means less than nothing.

Overwhelmed with sadness, Harriet automatically does what she always does; she goes to pick up the phone to her very best friend.

But then puts it straight back down again. Sure what's the point?

Chapter Fourteen

Meg

The TV studio is packed and buzzing. Everywhere you look, crew are faffing around with running orders and clipboards, as the camera crew expertly manoeuvre three hulking cameras and studio monitors into position.

Daniel Rourke, the *PrimeNews* host, is sitting importantly behind a huge oak desk flicking through a batch of cue cards and radiating gravitas, as the election candidates are positioned nervously at podiums on either side of him, evenly spaced out along the studio set. The backdrop is Dublin city illuminated at night, and it all looks very intimidating and highbrow.

Tensions are running high. The candidates know a biggie like this so close to polling day is make or break for them, and the nerves are palpable.

Meanwhile, Katherine is bundled into a huddle with both myself and Jess, getting all the last-minute tips and pointers she can possibly cram in. The only person notable by his absence is Philip, who's apparently staying home to 'work on his online consultancy business'.

Hope he enjoys it while it lasts, I think but of course, say nothing out loud.

'Well? How do I look?' Katherine asks, for about the fourth time.

'Utterly fabulous!' says Jess sycophantically. 'You look fresh and well-rested, and your outfit is bang on-trend without being ostentatious.'

'You need more work, actually,' I tell her, at exactly the same time.

Katherine's head swivels around to me, as the hassled-looking floor manager taps at his watch and almost yells time.

'Places everyone, please! Two minutes till we're live!'

'I'd lose the pussy bow for a start,' I tell her crisply, 'it makes you look like Margaret Thatcher, which is never a good thing. And who did that to your hair? It's too stiff and lacquered, puts years on you. May I?' I ask, stepping forward, whipping the bow scarf off from around Katherine's neck, then running my fingers through her bouffant hair and scrunching away at the rock-hardness of the hairspray till it begins to look softer and less terrifying.

'Better?' Katherine asks, peppering with nerves.

'Ten years gone off you, instantly,' I reassure her. 'Now you look more approachable. Nicer. The kind of representative I'd feel comfortable picking up the phone to.'

'Good to know someone around here will tell me the truth,' Katherine says, with a sidelong glance at Jess.

Then I escort her over the mound of cables and wires that are strewn all across the studio floor and into her position behind the podium, as Jess glares daggers at me.

'Sorry,' Katherine mutters under her breath. 'Some digs are just too hard to resist.'

A sound technician comes over to Katherine and is just checking her radio mike, when there's a voice from directly behind.

'Wait up a second! I'm here, and I have it!'

I swivel around to see that guy, whatshisname from the constituency office. Tall fella, dark hair, wears glasses. He's out of breath and panting, like he's sprinted all the way here.

'Talk about cutting it fine,' Katherine chides him, taking the papers and casting a quick glance down at them. Then, softening a little, she adds, 'Thank you.'

'No cabs to be had,' he says, gasping for air. 'Anyway, I rewrote your opening address to camera, so now we're kicking right off with your internet safety proposals for kids – that's a key message, so we need to hammer it in there first, because that's what voters at home will remember.'

'But what about the autocue for my summation?' says Katherine, starting to panic, as a floor manager waves at her to get into position behind the podium, along with the other five candidates.

'Already fed into it,' this guy says, finally having caught his breath. 'What, do you think I'd just shove you out on live TV with an unprepared opening monologue? Come on, this isn't my first rodeo.'

'Places, people, please, we're about to go live!' the floor manager barks, as Katherine stands in position, along with the others.

The familiar theme tune to *PrimeNews* booms out on the studio floor as the lights beam up to their fullest and brightest. I automatically move to the shadows at the back of the studio, where I'm well out of everyone's way, but still close enough to hear Katherine's performance. I'm also close, but not too close, to where Jess sits alone on an empty chair, utterly absorbed by her phone.

'Hello, good evening and welcome,' the booming, authoritative voice of Daniel Rourke comes bouncing off the walls, as the studio goes scarily still and silent.

This is Daniel Rourke's arena now; he has one of those voices that when he speaks, you listen. He's the kind of heavyweight news anchor and veteran griller of politicians that government ministers quake in fear at; a broadcaster whose silver-haired authority makes those in public office respect and fear him in equal measure. When Princess Diana died, people were so shocked, they said they only really believed it was true when Daniel Rourke told them so, live on *PrimeNews*.

So just imagine what he'd say and do with Katherine live on air if her private life ever blows up in public, I think, almost able to hear him grilling her. '*But wasn't your partner's infidelity a huge source of distraction to you, as a serving Senator and member of government?*' – exactly the kind of question that a man would *never* be asked, I fume quietly. Katherine's team would spin it, of course, and who knew? There'd doubtlessly be public sympathy for her, given that she's completely blameless in the matter.

And still, and still. These are exactly the kinds of things that distract voters and distort your message so close to an election. Katherine's instinct is absolutely on the money: Jess has to be airbrushed out of the picture and the affair has to end, good and fast, so the fallout can be dealt with – *after* she's won the election.

'I have with me the five leading candidates for the upcoming elections,' Daniel Rourke is saying, 'but only one of them is going home with the job. So who will it be? Up to you, the voting public, when polls open.

'Tonight, here's how it's going to work,' Daniel says smoothly, as the camera cuts into tight close-ups of the five candidates, all of whom have fake smiles plastered onto their sweaty faces. 'Each candidate will open with a direct address to you at home, for three minutes precisely. Then, it's gloves off and may the best man – or woman – win. Right then, to begin, we'll go to the representative for the south-east constituency, Councillor Toby Callaghan . . .'

'Somebody should have put a dab of powder on Callaghan's face before he went on camera,' whispers that guy, the one who'd just dashed in with a rewritten opening speech for Katherine. 'Look at him, he's sweating more than Nixon ever did. Makes him look shifty. Like he's got something to be nervous about.'

But I'm distracted and only half listening to him.

Toby Callaghan. A European minister based in Brussels who's had a stellar career spanning several decades and who now has his eye on a seat in the Senate. A big shot. In this election, the man to beat. For God's sake, all you have to do is take a look at the size of the entourage he has with him tonight; whereas Katherine just has two people with her – three if you count whatshisname. Callaghan has a team of half a dozen stringing along after him.

'Ehh . . . hello? Earth to Meg?'

Whatshisname is still trying to catch my attention, but I'm too busy scanning the back of the room, assessing exactly who's there with Callaghan, weighing things up, gauging the lie of the land. Doing my thing, in other words.

I get the spark of an idea, consider it, then decide. *Maybe*, I think. Just maybe. It's a very, very long shot, but with the clock ticking to the election, it's still worth a try.

'Are you even listening to me?' says whatshisname, but I'm already busy on my phone, tap, tap, tapping away, barely even looking up at him. Checking, double-checking everything. Who exactly is on Callaghan's team, from his campaign manager (easy to find; she has a Twitter handle and is almost overactive on Instagram too), to his election advisor; an older man, dishevelled and exhausted-looking in a crumpled suit, seventies at a guess and annoyingly with absolutely no social media presence. I don't let that deter me though, and a few quick Google searches tell me exactly who the guy is and more to the point, what he's doing at the back of the TV studio, arms folded and with his eyes glued to his candidate, like an expert trainer watching a racehorse out on a field. I work super-speedily, fingers flying, just as Katherine takes her turn to talk to camera.

'I said, I see Katherine is crashing and burning up there,' whatshisname says drily. 'Not that it's any reason for you to look up from your phone. I mean, God forbid we should have your undivided attention, or anything.'

'Hmm,' I mutter, wishing he'd kindly just bugger off and leave me alone. Bingo. I discover via an online news article that the older man I've been googling is actually Callaghan's brother, who's been steering his career for decades. Interesting.

'You don't even know my name, do you?' whatshisname persists, puncturing my concentration.

At that, I look sharply up from my phone, locking eyes with him.

'No,' he shrugs back at me, 'I thought not. It's Billy, by the way. Not that you remember, I don't expect you to. I mean, why would you bother?'

So this time, I look at him properly. Normally, I'm pretty good at assessing people; and sometimes so accurate, it would frighten you. I scrutinise them up and down and down and up again and, purely based on what I see, I can get the full measure of a person in a matter of seconds. At school, it became almost like my signature party piece, and at the law firm where I worked as a legal secretary, people used to joke that I should do it on a TV show like *Britain's Got Talent*.

I pause, take a breath and do my thing.

'Your full name is Billy Kingston,' I say, observing him keenly this time. 'And your car is clearly giving you trouble. You've recently moved house, but it's a hell of a commute in and out to work every day. And you came back from holiday about two to three weeks ago, but where you went, I can't tell. Although it was somewhere south of the Equator, that's for certain.'

Now I really have his attention, as he gapes back, stunned.

'Wow,' he says, shaking his head in shock. 'I mean . . . *wow*. How did you do that? How can you have known? You're not hacking into my emails or anything, are you?'

'That would be telling,' I shrug, going back to my phone.

'Meg?' Billy says, his mouth hanging open and still looking mystified. 'Meg Monroe? Who the hell *are* you, anyway?'

Chapter Fifteen

Harriet

Harriet has just opened the hall door at Meg's apartment, and there he is. Just standing in front of her. Unchanged. A few more lines around the eyes and an awful lot more freckles than she remembers, but otherwise, the very same Freddie. His strawberry-blond hair is cut shorter now; it looks tighter and neater than when they first met, like the corporate world is finally beginning to suck him up.

But some old Freddie touches persist; like the fact he's obviously just cycled here; he is dressed in chinos and a light blue shirt, but he's perspiring a bit and has his bike helmet tucked under his arm.

'Hi,' he smiles, a little self-consciously. And there it is, that wide-open, wonky, freckly grin that makes him look so adorable.

'Hello again,' Harriet says, completely flustered.

'Good to see you, Harriet,' he adds, 'I really do mean it. Honestly.'

'Come in,' she smiles, holding the door open for him. 'Meg isn't here just now . . . but I'm sure she'd have no problem with you being here. Something to drink?'

'So your friend actually lives here?'

'Yes,' says Harriet nervously. 'At least, I'm pretty sure she does.'

'On her own?'

'I think so. Something else, isn't it?'

'It most certainly is,' Freddie says, dumping his bike helmet and walking around the open-plan living area, with the sunken coffee table and snow-white cushy sofas neatly dotted in front of a cinema-sized plasma screen TV. There's a little pause as he shoves his hands in his pockets and walks around, whistling as he surveys the place up and down.

'Wow,' he says. 'I mean . . . *wow*.'

'Oh, come on,' Harriet teases. 'Yes, it's a huge apartment, but I'm sure it would comfortably fit into your granny's broom cupboard.'

'Yeah . . . but still,' Freddie says, by the balcony now, peering out over the edge. 'Would you look at that? I can almost see cruise ships on the harbour from here. Isn't it breathtaking?'

Harriet can't help smiling. That has always been one of the most endearing things about Freddie. His childlike enthusiasm for absolutely everything.

'I actually know this building,' he smiles.

'Really?'

'My grandparents own the construction company that built this whole development. Isn't that funny? Wow, wish I lived here myself!'

'Me and all,' Harriet says.

'And your chum Meg has all this to herself?'

'Looks like it.'

'The same Meg who used to go into bars and order a tonic water, then top it up with plastic bottles of gin she'd have hidden in her handbag? That Meg?' he asks, his bright blue eyes totally focused on her.

'That's her all right.'

'Golly. There's people out there making six-figure salaries who couldn't afford this place. I mean . . . who *is* she, anyway?'

Harriet has no answer for that. So, she changes the subject instead.

'You met her a few times,' she says helpfully. 'Do you remember?'

'Yes, yes, absolutely,' Freddie says, running his fingers through his thick red hair, in a gesture that Harriet once used to find so adorably dotey. 'We first met . . . outside that place where you used to work, wasn't it? That shop, with the most dreadfully unfortunate acronym.'

'CRAP,' she offers helpfully. 'Stands for Charitable Resales And Purchasing.'

'Quite right, absolutely,' Freddie nods politely. 'Yes, it's all coming back to me now. Where you and I first met too, do you remember?'

Did Harriet remember? Did she what?

Two years ago

It had been a blisteringly hot summer's day, and Harriet was pretty new to working at this branch of the charity shop. Doris, an elderly lady who lived locally, had just dropped in, more for a cuppa tea and a chat than to actually buy anything. Instantly realising that this lovely old lady really just wanted a bit of company more than anything else, Harriet dropped everything and sat Doris down on a knackered old brown sofa with the foam spilling out at the corners.

'Pension day,' Doris was saying. 'So I thought I'd treat myself to something nice. A few paperback novels, or something like that maybe. Nothing with any smut in it, mind you. The last book I bought here had a funny title and it was all about tying people up and smacking them on the arse. BDSM, I think it was called, or some funny load of initials like that. My Jacko read a bit of it and he got so excited, he had to take a double dose of blood pressure tablets and have a little lie-down. I was terrified it might start giving him ideas.'

'No problem,' Harriet had smiled. 'In fact, the nuns from that convent close by dropped off a shedload of stuff earlier.

You enjoy your cuppa tea, Doris, and let me sift through it all and see what you might like.'

'Nothing religious either, mind you,' Doris said warningly. 'I'd nearly rather all the M&S stuff than some aul book about the Vatican, or something.'

Freddie had slipped into the shop without Harriet even noticing. As it happened, she was trying to haul down a heavy box piled on top of yet another cardboard box, which in turn was piled high to the ceiling; all part of the stash the elderly nuns had dropped off earlier that day. She had no stepladder and was balanced precariously on top of a broken microwave, half afraid that the whole pyramid might come crashing down on top of her, when a voice came from directly beneath her.

'Golly, that's high. Perhaps I can assist?'

She looked down and there he was. Freddie, dressed in cycling shorts with the red hair standing up on end and a heavy-looking backpack strapped to him, smiling up at her and instantly reaching to help.

Harriet didn't know what she was more surprised at. That this guy was under the age of eighty, unlike ninety-five per cent of her clientele, or that he actually came out with things like 'golly' and 'can I assist?'

'He's nice, isn't he?' Doris had said, talking exactly as if he wasn't there. 'Go on, Harriet, offer him a Jaffa Cake.'

'Thanks so much,' Harriet flushed at him, as Freddie lifted down a stuffed cardboard box full of books. 'Is there something I can help you with?'

'More supplies for you,' he'd grinned back, pulling at his backpack and showing her what was inside.

Harriet peered in, and couldn't believe what she was seeing.

'Mother of God, a posh coffee maker that uses those capsule pod yokes?' she'd said, looking back down at him in shock. 'Sure that's worth a fortune! And it's all brand-new-looking.'

'There's more,' he'd said, rummaging further down into the backpack and whipping out a perfectly good iPad, a mobile phone and a NutriBullet. 'All right to leave it here? If it's of any use to you, that is?'

'Are you joking me?' Harriet replied. 'Sure you could sell this stuff on eBay and make a nice few quid for yourself! The NutriBullet looks like it's hardly even been used.'

'Oh, that's quite all right,' he grinned delightedly. 'Happy to drop stuff off here, if it's no trouble. Hate to be a bother, but my girlfriend wants to get rid of it all, and I wasn't quite sure what else to do with it.'

'Girlfriend?' Doris piped up from the sofa she was plonked down on.

'Oops! Sorry. Meant to say *sort of* girlfriend. Bit of women trouble, you know how it is. Anyway, she insists on dividing up all our things, and I have no need for it, so there's going to be an awful lot more where this came from.'

'Well, you're very polite, I'll give you that,' said Doris, eyeing him beadily up and down. 'Come back any time, always happy to see young ones with more money than sense dropping off perfectly good stuff in here. More bargains for me.'

'Rightio,' said Freddie, as Harriet looked at him, dumbfounded. 'Well, I'd best be on my way. Nice to meet you . . . emm . . .'

'Harriet,' she said, amazed that there was someone on the planet outside of Hugh Grant who actually said 'rightio'.

'Delighted,' he'd said, shaking her hand politely. 'And I'm Freddie, by the way. Freddie Miller.'

'Freddie,' Harriet nodded, noticing how silky-smooth his hand felt. Like this guy actually used moisturiser. Or that he'd never done a day's work in his life.

'Well, best be off,' Freddie grinned, 'but don't worry, I'll be back soon with lots more supplies for you. And next time, I'll bring the Jaffa Cakes,' he added, with a respectful little nod to Doris before he left, clanging the shop door behind him.

'Well, he seemed nice, didn't he?' Harriet had said, trying to sound casual as she scooped up everything he'd dumped off and hauled it over to the shop counter.

'Very nice,' Doris said, greedily taking another biscuit out of the box and stuffing it into her mouth. 'Out of his fucking mind, but still.'

Chapter Sixteen

Meg

'Meg? I'd like a word. In my dressing room. Now, please.'

Katherine has just come off air as the *PrimeNews* TV show wraps, and is in absolutely no mood to be trifled with.

Not good. This is not good at all.

'Well, that was certainly a strong, solid interview,' Billy is saying to her, walking and talking directly behind her as we all troop down the tiny corridor that leads out of the studio, with the other candidates trailing after us, engrossed in frantic post-mortems with their teams of advisors. 'You were hit with a lot of curveballs and I thought you dealt with them pretty smoothly. You made absolute mincemeat of Senator Callaghan – you rang rings around him. You should be well pleased here, Katherine – I know I am.'

'Hmm,' is the only distracted response he gets.

'Katherine,' Billy persists, in a lighter vein. 'I want you to stop walking and take a good look at me. Because I'm smiling. And I never smile, ever. Certainly not slap bang in the middle of a campaign. We could be looking at as much as a three per cent lead in the polls from tomorrow.'

Jess is in tow too, of course, banging on about social media and how dominant the debate has been across pretty much every platform.

'You're trending on Twitter,' she's saying, barely glancing up from her phone. 'Actually, you're trending twice over. There's even a hashtag *#katherineforpresident*. Early print media is all on your side too, which is beyond price for us—'

Katherine gets as far as her dressing room door, then stops dead in her tracks and turns to face us all. 'I know you need to talk to me,' she says, sounding tense and tight and not at all like a woman who's just nailed a major national debate with a bulldog of an interrogator. 'And we will, believe me. But just for now, I need a quick private word with Meg. If you'll excuse us, please.'

'Well, that's her for the chop,' Jess mutters under her breath, although I catch it loud and clear. I don't respond though, just stay cool, do as I'm told, and step into the cramped little dressing room that barely holds a single chair in front of a dressing table, surrounded by garish fluorescent light bulbs.

Katherine bangs the door tightly behind her and rounds in on me. 'You saw what happened out there tonight? Live on camera?' she says, in a low voice so there's no danger of this being overheard. 'You're the only one who knows what's really going on in my private life, so you're the only one I can trust to tell me the truth.'

'Yes, of course I did, I saw everything,' I say. 'But Senator, it went well for you. Exceptionally well. I've got the live

stream on my phone, if you don't believe me. I thought you'd
at least be pleased with the reaction you got. You stormed.
You were *fabulous*. Callaghan floundered out there, but you
really owned it tonight.'

'For a smart woman,' Katherine says tightly, folding her
arms and pointing at my phone, 'you're entirely missing the
point. Don't you get it? Don't you see the bigger picture
here?'

I don't want to inflame her by saying, 'Get what, exactly?
What is your problem?' Instead, I bring up the interview on
the screen of my phone, hold it out in front of her and fast
forward to the final third of it, when Daniel Rourke, acting
more like a ringmaster at a circus than a seasoned heavyweight TV presenter, gets onto the subject of 'the future – if
elected'.

'That's it,' Katherine nods, looking down at my screen.
'Let it play out. I want to gauge exactly how bad it is.'

'Turning first to you,' Daniel Rourke says smoothly on
the recording, addressing Senator Callaghan, a burly, portly
man in his late sixties. 'If elected, there would naturally be an
understandable interest in your private life. It's reasonable to
expect a degree of press scrutiny – it's unavoidable for anyone in the public eye. So would you care to elaborate for us
now on your own personal situation, please?'

'No, I most certainly would not,' Callaghan booms back
at him. 'As I have previously stated on numerous occasions,
my private life is entirely out of bounds. The public are
far too sensible to be interested in any such nonsense. Next
question, please.'

But Daniel doesn't give up so easily. 'Could that possibly have anything to do with the fact that you're twice divorced, you won't even admit to the wider media how many children you have, and you're currently in a relationship with your press secretary?'

Callaghan huffs and puffs as the camera instantly cuts to Katherine, who appears cool and composed in stark comparison.

'Same question to you, Senator Sisk,' Daniel Rourke says.

There's a tiny, telling pause before she answers.

'Well, nothing to see here,' she manages to smile back at the host. 'I'm a happily married woman, and my husband and I will be celebrating twenty-two years of marriage later this year. We have two wonderful daughters, both teenagers now, and I'm proud to say I've been a working mum for all of their lives.'

'So would you say your family's support is essential to you, in the work you do?' Daniel needles at her. 'Your entire platform, after all, is one of family values, is it not?'

'Family first,' she replies clearly. Then, as if trying to ram the point home, she adds, 'Family, all the way. That's what it's all about, really, isn't it? My own family are everything to me, and they always will be. I understand how tough it is for working mothers out there, because, hey, I'm one too. It's not easy, is it? So I want voters to know that I'm here to do everything I can to support them—'

'You can stop the video right there,' Katherine says over my shoulder. 'I've seen all I need to.'

'Never mind about voting you into power,' I tell her, 'after that performance, they really should give you an Oscar.'

Katherine slumps down into the tiny seat and looks exhausted enough to cry.

'You gave a great answer,' I say, reassuringly.

'You may well know all about how to get rid of people,' she says wearily, 'but you know sweet damn all about politics. Don't you get it? Don't you see how I've just set myself up for the most spectacular fall? I painted my home life as being perfectly normal and happy. I basically said my whole campaign and strategy is based on good, old-fashioned family values. How do you imagine the press will respond if and when they discover that's far from the truth? And that my own husband is shagging one of my team behind my back?'

There's a loud knocking at the door, which we both ignore.

'If you're concerned that gossip about your private life will leak to the media,' I say calmly, 'I promise, you don't need to be. I'll have everything sorted for you, long before the election. I did only begin working for you yesterday,' I remind her, gently but firmly. 'And as I explained to you then, these things don't happen overnight.'

But Katherine is beyond listening.

'I can't do it,' she says, turning to face the dressing room mirror. 'I just don't think I can take one more unendurable minute of this. I have to go out there and face the public and the press and smile and act like my family life is tickety-boo, thanks very much. And then I have to go home and look at Philip and listen to all the lies he comes up with when he says he's going out canvassing door to door for me, when I know he's really meeting up with her. It's too much. Do you hear me? It's just too much to bear.'

She's crying. There's no mistaking it, the woman is shedding real, actual tears. The same woman who'd been grilled up, down and sideways on live TV for the past sixty minutes and who'd taken it all in her stride is now bordering on being a big, weepy, uncontrollable mess.

'Senator Sisk, you're needed out here, please!' shouts a loud voice from outside, to the sound of urgent rapping on the dressing room door.

'Just give us a moment!' I yell back. Then, noiselessly, I kneel down beside Katherine and slip a comforting arm around her shoulders. Emotional people, I know of old, need to be handled with kid gloves. A bit like tired, cranky children, really.

'You know what'll happen now?' Katherine sniffs, as hot, angry tears flow down her face. 'I'll get home later on tonight and I'll be catching up with the kids and organising dinners and all of that, and Philip will tell me he's going out to walk the dog, and that's when he calls her, and I'm supposed to act like I'm thick and I don't know what's going on and I want to bloody well *kill* him and I want to fire her. But I have to wait till after this bloody election and, in the meantime, I'm expected to smile and look "electable" and keep up this gruelling schedule even though I'm ready to fall over with tiredness, and then I'll collapse into bed tonight and I won't even have the luxury of sleeping because I'm so, so worried that it's only a matter of time before the media find out about

Philip and that witch who's right outside this door. And I'm *human*, Meg. And I honestly don't know how much more of this I can take.'

She finally pauses to take a breath.

But I say nothing.

Instead, I scoop my handbag up off the floor and rummage around for the kit I carry with me at all times, for emergencies precisely like this one. In a quick, practised movement, I pull out a small make-up bag and unzip it. Next, I produce a tiny bottle of Rescue Remedy, a fresh lipstick, a bottle of foundation, a packet of tissues and a travel-sized bottle of perfume.

'When the election is over,' I say soothingly, handing over a Kleenex. 'Then and only then, you can deal with Philip. I know it feels like a lifetime away, but there are only six days left and you can do it. In the meantime, this is my department and mine to deal with. So we'll have no more tears, please,' I say, taking charge. 'Open wide.'

Obediently, Katherine does as she's told, and I place a few careful drops of the Rescue Remedy directly onto her tongue.

'Good woman,' I say. 'Now close your eyes, while I patch up your make-up. You are going to go back out there and you are going to face the media and you are going to do it all with a calm, confident smile on your face. There are few enough women in public life as it is, and you are not, repeat *not* going to allow the misogynists and haters out there to see you upset and weepy. Give them no ammunition, and leave the rest to me.'

'I must be insane,' Katherine says flatly. 'To bring you into all this, and to ask so much of you, in such a short space of time. But I need you to fix this, Meg. Make it go away. For God's sake, help me.'

'It'll all be done,' I tell her, looking at Katherine's reflection in the mirror and giving her a final squirt of Jo Malone Pomegranate Noir, before I'm fully satisfied. 'Come on, then. Here we go.'

'I swear to God,' Katherine mutters, getting up to go, looking a hell of a lot better than she did a few minutes previously. 'Once I'm re-elected, you'll see a whole new me.'

'And . . . it's showtime,' I say, opening the door for her, and feeding her to the lions.

It's sheer mayhem in the corridor outside, packed and crowded, and everyone seems to be vying for Katherine's attention all at once.

'Senator, please, we need to go to the media room right away for questions!'

'Still trending on Twitter,' Jess is saying, barely looking up from her phone. 'And it's too early to say, but it now looks like you could be up as much as four percentage points in the polls.'

'If you'll all excuse me,' Katherine says, sounding a lot more composed now and back in control, 'it seems my work here still isn't done.'

She sweeps past everyone as Billy catches my eye.

'So what was all that about?' he asks straight out.

'Trust me. You don't want to know.'

*

The media room, post-interview, is about as close to a rugby scrum in a match at the Aviva as you can possibly get, without the need for actual shin guards and a gumshield. It seems like every media outlet in the country is there, all jostling for position in an overpacked, claustrophobic press room. The clamour is deafening, the flashbulbs blinding and everywhere you turn, all you can hear is, 'Over here! Senator, please just one more question!'

Katherine is instantly surrounded, then escorted up to a makeshift plinth, along with the four other candidates, to face further grilling from the print media and twenty-four-hour news channels. There's a moderator onstage who's acting as MC, and conducting the questions from the assembled room full of hacks as skilfully as you would a concert orchestra.

Meanwhile, Callaghan's older brother and election agent is leaning up against a wall, arms folded, looking worriedly over at his man. He's on his own too, with no one around him. Perfect.

I take the ball and run with it. *Fuck it*, I think, *it's worth a shot*. If this gamble pays off, then wouldn't this be a perfect way to fix this and to keep everyone happy at the same time?

I make a quick, calculated assessment, then, without any hesitation whatsoever, jump straight in. Right at the very back of the room, well away from prying eyes, where no one, absolutely no one, could see or even possibly guess at my long-term game plan.

*

At the end of a long, weary night, finally everyone is packing up and heading off to make print deadlines or, in the case of Katherine's team, going home and collapsing after yet another gruelling day.

'And just think, people, we get to do it all again tomorrow,' says Billy cheerfully, as we troop out of the TV studios together, finally free to leave. 'Starting at 7.30 a.m. sharp, when you're booked to go on *Good Morning TV*. So you'll be there, Jess? Because I have meetings for the entire day back at HQ.'

'Emm . . . yes, of course, absolutely,' Jess says distractedly, scanning the road outside the TV studio for a pre-ordered cab.

'I need you to stay in touch with me all day tomorrow,' Katherine says quietly, gripping my arm, as we walk towards the bank of waiting cars and taxis.

'Absolutely,' I say reassuringly, wishing for a minute that I could bilocate, given the number of people to meet and places I'm expected to be, all on the same day.

'Well, goodnight then everyone,' says Katherine, clambering into her government car, which is parked on the kerb waiting patiently for her. 'And thank you for all your hard work. Let's keep it up, we're almost home and dry.'

A quick, telling glance at me and she's gone.

Jess, meanwhile, hails down her own cab and is already opening the back door, when Billy ambles over to me, loosening his collar and tie.

'Well, I don't know about you,' he says lightly, 'but I could certainly do with a stiff drink after that. Don't suppose you—'

'Goodnight, Billy,' I instantly cut him off mid-sentence, before striding straight after Jess and, whether she likes it or not, jumping into the back seat of the taxi beside her.

Go for a drink. For fuck's sake. As if. Who in the real world has that kind of time?

Chapter Seventeen

Meg

'Ehh . . . this is *my* taxi. I think you probably need to order your own,' Jess says, looking up at me in rude surprise.

'Not at all, we're going the same way anyway,' I lie smoothly, strapping myself into the seat and dumping my laptop carrier down beside me, as the driver zooms off.

'How do you know where I live?'

'Your address is on the team call sheet.'

Jeez, I only wish every job came with such a handy crib sheet.

'Yeah, well, I've actually got a lot of media calls to make now,' says Jess, kicking off her high heels and starting to massage the soles of her feet. 'So if you don't mind, I think it's probably best if you make your own way home.'

'Jess,' I insist, fully prepared for roadblocks like this. 'Just listen to me for thirty seconds, will you? Something has come up and I need to talk to you urgently. In private. And, let's face it, this is as close to private as you and me are ever likely to get.'

She looks warily across at me. Knew it. I knew the whiff of a scandal or gossip would pique her interest.

'Go on,' she says, clearly interested, but unsure what this is all about.

'You may have noticed,' I say, pitching this super-carefully, 'that I was talking to Callaghan's election agent just now. When we were up in the media room for the Q&A?'

'You said this was urgent?' Jess cuts right across me.

Jesus, I think. What does Philip Sisk see in this one anyway? What does *anyone* see in her? And how does someone like this actually end up working in PR? She isn't even particularly good with people to begin with. Surely a prerequisite for a job in PR?

'Hear me out,' I smile sweetly, twisting around in the back seat to face her full on. 'Because there's actually a perfectly good reason why Callaghan's side wanted to reach out. And it might be of particular interest to you.'

Jess says nothing, just continues massaging her stockinged feet and blankly ignoring me.

'As you know, Senator Callaghan's election agent and PR is actually his older brother,' I tell her, careful to keep my tone as innocuous as possible. 'Name of Alphonsus Callaghan – short, tight grey hair, early seventies, heavy build, did you notice him?'

Because I bloody well did. And once I'd discovered exactly who he was, I was straight over to this Alphonsus Callaghan, with a pitch that I thought might just work for him. And for myself too, naturally.

'If he offered you a job on the opposition team,' says Jess, 'then I strongly suggest you go right ahead and take it. Because frankly, Meg, you were about as much use to me today as a chocolate teapot. So go on then, grab whatever money Callaghan's team are dangling in front of you and best of luck to you. I'd love to say you'll be missed, but being perfectly honest, having no assistant is better than you.'

'Oh no, you misunderstand,' I say, in a tone that I hope will charm the birds off the trees, even though she's being nothing but insulting. 'It's not me they're interested in at all. It's *you* they're after. You're the best in the business, and don't they know it!'

Now I have Jess's full attention.

'So . . . here's the thing,' I say. 'They very much want to speak to you about future projects they've got in the pipeline. Exciting things, too. You know Alphonsus Callaghan's PR reach is huge, and it seems they're going to need a young hotshot to head up their constituency offices in Brussels. Particularly if Callaghan loses the election, which looks increasingly likely, doesn't it? Well, you saw for yourself what he was like out there tonight, he was brutal. The man needs all the help he can get, you agree? Of course, I'm just a humble go-between in this,' I add. 'They wanted me to sound you out first, knowing how loyal you are to Katherine. But then, I suppose that's one of the things that attracted them to you in the first place. Everyone knows that your loyalty is legendary.'

Bit much, I wonder?

Apparently not. Jess's face is momentarily lit up by the headlamps on a passing car and I see it, clear as day. A carrot has been dangled and there's a definite spark of interest in those cold, grey eyes.

'Can you imagine the kind of money they'd be prepared to pay you?' I toss in. 'Not that someone like you is ever motivated by salary, of course.'

'Did they really mention Brussels?' Jess says, starting to look hungry now.

'They certainly did. And obviously they wouldn't sound you out like this unless it was going to be worth your while financially. So here's the business card I was asked to give you,' I say, handing over a neatly printed card which I'd tucked away into a pocket of the tailored jacket I've got on. 'They're expecting your call, Jess. And, judging by Callaghan's performance tonight, the sooner the better, I'd say. If he loses this election and has to crawl back to Brussels with his tail between his legs, can you imagine the amount of PR rehabilitation work that will need to be done?'

So I've dropped the bait and now it's your turn to say something. Come on, this is Brussels. This is Europe. This is a massive step up the ladder for you . . .

'Hmmm,' is the only response I get though. But instead of going straight back to staring at her phone, which Jess seems to spend ninety-nine per cent of her tim doing, now she's just sitting back against the seat of the car, staring blankly out of the window, lost in thought.

Gotcha, I think.

11.00 p.m.

'Drive around the block a few times, will you?' I say to the taxi driver, as soon as Jess has clambered out of the car.

We've just dropped her off at her flat, which is in a row of newish-looking town houses, all red-bricked, all identical, all neat and perfectly well maintained.

'Seriously?' says the driver, twisting around to face me.

'Don't worry, I'll pay you in cash,' I reply coolly. 'Just keep driving and, whatever you do, make sure we're not seen from the house, OK?'

I'm working on a hunch here, and I've got to make sure I'm right.

'Jaysus,' the driver grunts, turning back to the wheel. 'Up till now, I've only ever heard people come out with that kind of thing in Robert De Niro movies.'

11.10 p.m.

Well onto our fourth spin around the block, and nothing. Just a cyclist from Deliveroo pedalling furiously down the road, leaving a smell of garlic wafting after him.

Come on. Come out to play.

I'm here and I'm waiting.

11.14 p.m.

'What's the story, anyway?' the taxi driver asks, most annoyingly.

I blank him, of course, but he still insists on chatting.

'Are you stalking that young one, or what? 'Cos my guess is she's your ex-girlfriend and you're mad jealous on account of she's seeing someone else.'

Silence from me, as I stay focused on the road outside.

'Well, just as long as you're not going to torch her house or do anything stupid like that, love, all right?'

'Do you mind?' I sigh wearily. 'I'll pay extra if we can just do this in silence. Keep driving around the block and be sure to keep out of sight. And if it's all the same,' I add, 'I could really do without the running commentary.'

11.34 p.m.

And there it is.

Just like I figured it would be. A sleek, black Audi glides up to the row of town houses and pulls over. There's a minute-long delay, most likely because he's either calling or texting her. *Are you home now, is this a good time? Need to see you.* The same shite I know goes on between couples in love all the time. Gormless, easy-to-read shower of idiots that they are.

But then a woman gets out of the car. Older, wearing medical-scrub blue trousers and a white healthcare uniform on top, with a watch pinned to the side of it. She has the exhausted look of a frontline medic who's been working a late shift at a hospital and who's only getting home to bed now. She reaches into the passenger seat for a box stuffed full of thick files, then plods her weary way to the house right next door to Jess.

Bollocks, I think crossly. *Have I read this all wrong? Am I losing my touch?*

11.40 p.m.

Not as much as a leaf stirring. No cars coming down the quiet little cul-de-sac where the taxi's parked. But at least he's reclined his seat and is almost dozing off, so I'm spared from having to listen to his stream-of-consciousness babble any longer.

Using the time productively, I whip out my second phone, the vital one, the one that if I ever lost, I'd be utterly bereft without.

Nineteen missed calls and voice messages. Jesus. That's how flat-out busy I am, that's how little time I have to be loitering out of sight of a target's home late at night, hoping that a hunch I had earlier might pay dividends.

I click on my voicemail.

'Meg? Denys here,' is the first message. 'We spoke yesterday, remember? About that tosser on my team at work who I need gone, ASAP? I've sent you on as much of the information that I have, just like you asked. His Twitter handle, plus all his Instagram details. He's on Facebook too, but unfortunately you have to send him a friend request to access his page first. Anyway, I'm still waiting for you to get back to me – so ring as soon as you can. The gobshite messed up a big order on me today and, of course, he blamed everyone else around him, except himself—'

Thankfully, the voicemail cuts him short, or Denys's little rant, I know instinctively, would have turned into the equivalent of a radio play with two acts and a half-time interval.

Coolly, I click onto the next message and I know it's going to demand my urgent attention the minute I get home.

Because it's Harriet. Yet again. Sounding so breathless and overhyped, I'm hardly able to decipher her.

'Meg, where are you? I've been calling you non-stop all night, why don't you pick up? You will not *believe* what I have to tell you!'

And you will not believe what I'm seeing, I think, instantly clicking off the phone and squinting out the car window.

At first, it looks innocuous. Just a middle-aged man, out walking his dog late at night. Strolling nonchalantly down the street with a gorgeous chocolate-brown Labrador, who's straining at the leash to such an extent, you'd wonder who was walking who.

It's pitch-dark, but still, I'm pretty sure it's him. Same height, same gait, same slightly stooped walk, everything.

I run a lightning-quick Google search on my phone, and bingo. There's a photo of him in a magazine from last year, a pretty twee-looking family photo shoot that's been staged for the election campaign and clearly modelled on a Homebase ad, but where everyone involved ends up looking over-dressed, stiff and uncomfortable. The only one who looks relaxed and happy is the same chocolate-brown Labrador, to the forefront of the group shot, lying obediently across a rug in front of an overloaded log fire. Meanwhile, the rest of the family are all clustered around a Christmas tree, pretending to drape tinsel and bulbs onto it, even though it's already fully decorated. The very definition of forced cheesiness.

Senator Katherine Sisk, pictured at home with her family, including her loving husband of over twenty years, businessman Philip Sisk, runs the banner caption underneath it. *Even Mycroft, the family dog, is getting ready to join in the fun!*

Yup, there we go, I think triumphantly. Katherine's loving husband of over twenty years, who's just about to pay a sneaky little nocturnal visit to his girlfriend.

Noiselessly, so as not to wake the dozing driver, I tiptoe out of the car.

It's been a long and gruelling day. I'm used to being busy and chasing my tail, but it's next level at the moment. I'm beyond exhausted, I feel like I'm juggling seventeen balls in the air all at the same time and that's before I even get started on the stress of Harriet Waters landing on top of me at the very, very worst time possible.

And yet, and yet. This part of the day, I absolutely know, will be bloody brilliant.

This, I'm most definitely going to enjoy.

11.42 p.m.

Nimbly, filled with fresh energy and that late-night surge of adrenaline you only get when you know things are finally going your way, I hop out of the taxi and stride across the deserted road. There's a small bay window to the very front of the house, but, try as I might, it's hard to see inside, as it's in pitch darkness. Meanwhile, there's a light on in the hall and further down the hallway, I'm guessing, a living room, where it's all happening.

At least, that's what I'm counting on.

I knock on the door. Immediately, I can hear a dog barking loudly and incessantly from inside the house, followed by a man's voice shushing him back into silence.

So I wait. Knock again. Wait again. More loud barking, but still, no one's coming to answer the door. Carefully, I glance over my shoulder at the street behind, but it's a quiet residential area and most of the houses are in darkness. I strain at the hall door to hear what's going on inside the house and could swear I hear voices, but they sound too muffled for me to pick up anything clearly.

Annoying.

One last knock on the door before I take out my phone to call Jess as a last resort – but just as I'm reaching down into my bag for my work mobile, the hall light grows brighter and through the opaque glass on the door, I see two shadowy figures loom into view.

'Don't even dream of answering,' a man's voice mutters, to the background noise of a dog panting. 'Good boy! Lie down, good boy.'

'I ordered takeout food for us, that's probably who it is,' says Jess; I'd know that high-pitched, nasal whine a mile off.

So I rap on the bay window at the side of the hall door. Then, unable to resist, call out, 'Hi Jess! It's me, Meg. Can you open up, just for a quick sec?'

'Fuck, fuck, fuck,' I hear Jess whispering. Then a quick, whispered conflab seems to take place, as I wait patiently on the doorstep.

Morons. How thick are these people? Don't they realise that they can be overheard loud and clear? Idiots, I sigh deeply, almost wishing this could be a bit more of a challenge.

A tiny chink in the hall door as it's opened. And there's Jess, poking her red mane of hair out through the gap.

'What is it?' she says tersely. 'It's almost midnight! What is *wrong* with you?'

'I'm so sorry to disturb you,' I say, starting into my little pre-rehearsed speech. 'But I just remembered you saying Katherine was going on breakfast TV in the morning, and I wanted to let you know that I'm happy to go with her. You've got quite enough to get on with, and I thought this might lighten the load for you a little.'

'You couldn't have phoned?' Jess says.

'Battery died. So it was just as easy to get the taxi to come straight back here instead.'

Did I play that all right? Conscientious and embarrassed for disturbing anyone this late at night is what I'd been going for.

'Hey! Nice doggy!' I throw in, as if noticing for the first time that there's an actual dog in the house. 'Lucky you, having such a gorgeous dog. A Labrador, right?'

'Oh . . . I'm just . . . looking after him for a friend,' Jess stutters, looking, it has to be said, a bit flustered.

Meanwhile, the dog nuzzles up to the door to have a good sniff at me, so she's forced to open it a little wider.

'Good boy!' I say, as the dog slobbers all over my hands and legs, tail thumping excitedly off the door frame. 'Well, aren't you just the cutest?'

I take a tiny step inside the hall and while the dog paws at me and licks my hands, I grab the chance to run a quick scan of the place. Absolutely no sign of any company, which means Philip has to be hiding in what I can only guess is a downstairs loo under the stairs.

Unbelievable. Like I've just walked into a late-night French farce.

'I *love* Labradors,' I say, ruffling the delighted dog playfully on his ears and whisking around the name disc on his collar. 'What's your name then, boy? Well, well, well. Would you look at that. Mycroft.'

Silence as Jess and I lock eyes.

'I'll take care of breakfast TV in the morning,' she says curtly. 'So you don't need to worry about that at all. Now, if you'll excuse me, it's very late and I really need to sleep.'

'Mycroft,' I repeat, saying the name slowly, not letting it drop. 'A very unusual name for a dog. Exactly the same name as the Sisk family dog. And they have a chocolate Labrador too, don't they?'

Another tense little pause, except this time Jess starts to get a bit twitchy and uncomfortable.

'Wow, that's some coincidence, I'd say,' I smile. I can fake-smile with the best, but this one is genuine. I'm enjoying this.

Not a word out of Jess though. And that silence speaks volumes.

You know I've rumbled you, so here we are.

'Philip called over to drop off some campaign notes for me,' Jess eventually mutters, looking down at the floor, knowing she's utterly checkmated. 'That's all. He was out walking the dog, so it was on his way.'

'Of course.'

'And you'd be doing me a favour if you didn't mention this to Katherine. She's under quite enough stress as it is.'

'I wouldn't dream of it,' I smile sweetly. 'We women need to stick together. Don't we?'

11.51 p.m.

Walking away from the house and getting back into my taxi, I'm certain of a few things at this particular moment. I know that right behind me, I've unleashed full-on, full-scale panic. In fact, I almost wish I could linger outside the house for a bit longer to overhear what's being said, just for the laugh. I can only imagine the row that's broken out, and it makes me smile to think of it.

I don't, though. Instead, I flee the scene of the crime, waking up my slumbering taxi driver and crisply giving him my home address.

'Jeez,' he says sleepily, glancing down at the still-ticking meter, 'this is turning into some late-night bonanza for me. And I hope you're well prepared for it, love. Because this fare is costing you about the same as a flight from here to New York. Return.'

'Don't you worry, you'll get paid,' I say distractedly, already busy on my phone.

WHITE SMOKE, I quickly text Katherine, fingers flying. **HOPE TO HAVE SOME DEVELOPMENTS SOON.**

WE'LL DISCUSS IT IN THE MORNING, pings back the instantaneous response.

Which is probably as close as I'll ever come to an actual thank you.

But still. Sitting back against the seat of the car, I allow myself a rare moment of self-congratulation. Regarding this particular situation, I think, reaching my hand back to massage throbbing neck muscles that have been at me all day, I'm making progress. It's not over, certainly not until I've brought Philip and Jess's little dalliance to a firm end, but to paraphrase Winston Churchill, this appears to be the beginning of the end.

They know I'm on to them and that's a start. Now, of course, I need to work on Jess, and hopefully persuade her to take up that job offer in Brussels – if Callaghan loses the election. All going to plan and, with any luck, the whole affair should quickly die a natural death.

Oh, who am I kidding? This doesn't rely on luck, this is down to skill on my part and nothing else.

Then it'll be Philip Sisk's turn for a royal comeuppance he'll never forget, and all will be well in the world again. Wrongs will be righted and balance will be restored.

Soon. Very, very soon.

WEDNESDAY

Chapter Eighteen

Meg

I pay the driver and wearily plod my way inside my apartment building and on up to the penthouse floor. Yes, there's much, much work ahead to do, but at least regarding the Katherine Sisk case, I can allow myself to feel pretty bloody smug, actually.

The lovely, warm, satisfied glow doesn't last long though. Serves me right.

My hall door is opened before I've even had a chance to put the key into the lock. And standing there, brazen as you like, is my biggest headache of all.

Harriet.

Still here, acting like she owns the place, even though I made it perfectly clear to her that she couldn't stay. Looking fresh-faced and pink-cheeked and scrubbed and blonde and pretty, like something off a shampoo ad, even at this ungodly hour.

'Meg! There you are – finally!' Harriet gushes breathily. 'I've been phoning you and phoning you, and I've waited up for you all evening . . . Oh, Meg, I have something incredible to tell you . . . and you won't believe it!'

'What now?' I say exhaustedly, beyond caring if it sounds rude.

'You'll never guess who was here when you were out! Freddie de Courcey!'

For a second, I don't register this. Just stare blankly back at her, saying nothing, doing nothing.

I possibly blink, but don't breathe. Can't.

'And I think he's single and most definitely finished with that doctor ex-girlfriend of his now,' Harriet witters on, 'and . . . oh, Meg . . . he says he really missed me and thought about me a lot when I was away – isn't that so sweet? He's talking about taking me out properly . . . how amazing is that? I mean . . . isn't that just the best news you ever heard? . . . Meg? Meg? Why aren't you saying anything?'

*

Four a.m., and I actually think I might be having a mild heart attack. All those horrible, sweaty palpitations are back, and the more I think about how the whole Harriet situation is upending on me, the worse they get.

He was here. Actually here, in my home. Somehow Freddie de Courcey found his way here. So now, of course, it's only a matter of time before word leaks back to the mighty Ellen de Courcey, my landlady, benefactress, and pretty much the woman I owe my entire career to.

OK, so this is bad. This is unprecedented. This isn't just a waking nightmare, this is a full-on horror movie, with zombies and dead corpses lining the streets.

Nor is there any plausible way out of it, at least not that I can see. And if I can't see one, who can? This is what I *do*. This is my superpower. I fix things – messy, emotional situations just like this are my bread and butter. But I've never had one as challenging as this.

I try to rationalise it, to think through solutions, but I can't seem to find one. It doesn't help that it's practically dawn and it's sticky and humid. I'm tossing and turning around in a huge king-sized bed, stressing and fretting from the sheer worry of it all, while expensive Egyptian cotton high-thread-count sheets knot themselves into ropes around my ankles.

I've been a complete idiot.

Jesus Christ, how could I have let things get this far out of control?

I should have dealt with the Harriet situation from the get-go. To hell with any kind of latent friendship we once had, and to hell with guilt; I should have frogmarched her straight to the airport or the train station the minute she materialised on my doorstep, what was it, just one night ago? It feels so, *so* much longer.

Over by the floor-to-ceiling windows in my bedroom, heavy, shockingly expensive drapes gracefully black out the early-dawn light. But even through the gloom, I can still make out the silhouettes that surround me. The walk-in wardrobe, my pride and joy, that houses all my 'costumes' – every different 'look' needed to woo every different kind of client. Then there's the expensive paintings that dot the walls; artwork I chose to invest in, not only because I'd heard it was a good idea, but . . . well, because. When in my entire life did I ever have lovely, pretty things to call my own? When have I ever been able to buy something just because I felt like it? Certainly not when I was a kid growing up, that was for sure. Unlike my half-brother and -sister, who were given a beautiful painting each on their birthday. Every single year, with no expense spared.

'Art isn't just nice to look at, it's a great investment for the kids, too,' my father Charlie had proudly boasted to me on the one and only occasion when I'd been forced to visit him in his brand-new home, where he lived with his brand-new wife and his two new kids, then aged six and four, with every single luxury thrown at them that money could buy.

Expensive paintings, I'd thought. For two small kids? I was barely fifteen years of age at the time and even then, it had made me want to vomit. And that's before I got started on the neo-Georgian five-bedroomed house where Charlie and his new family were living, all thanks to a sizeable inheritance from his father – my grandfather, technically – who'd passed away not long ago. And did Mum and I even see as much as a penny of that windfall? Take a wild guess.

'Doesn't matter that your brother and sister are still too young to appreciate good art when they see it,' Charlie had bragged.

'Half-brother and -sister,' I corrected him.

'The point is, when they're older, they can flog the paint-ings and make a nice few quid for themselves. All Doreen's

idea. Good, isn't it? Better than buying the pair of them cuddly toys and dolls and all of that shite, isn't it?'

'Well, lucky them,' I said drily.

'Means a lot to them that they have their big sister back in their lives now, love. Sure they're delighted. All they want is to get to know you.'

'Yeah, but when did you ever buy me anything nice for my birthday?' I couldn't stop myself from blurting straight out. 'I'd have been doing well to get as much as a card from you.'

'Ah now, Meg, love, don't be like that,' Charlie had shuffled awkwardly. 'They were different times, weren't they? I couldn't afford anything back then, for a start. And then when your mum and me broke up . . .'

'I think you meant to say, when you first met Doreen and did the dirt on Mum and me,' I replied, coolly folding my arms.

'Meg, don't. We're having a nice day here,' said Charlie.

Did he really believe that? Wow, he really doesn't know me at all, *I thought, hating every second of this.*

I didn't answer and he started to sweat a bit and look uncomfortable.

Served him right.

'Sure, it's all in the past now, and it's great that you can be pals with Doreen and your brother and sister, isn't it?'

'Oh, would you ever fuck off!' was all I could think of firing back at him, jealousy choking me in a hot rage. I'd stormed off and it had taken me two buses before I'd cooled down again. A little.

One day, I'd thought. One day, I'll have nice things around me too, and no one can say I didn't earn them for myself, fair and bloody square.

My eye drifts out towards the balcony just outside my bedroom, with its spectacular view that never fails to soothe troubled spirits, no matter how strung out I get with all the many and varied work 'projects' I'm trying to balance.

It's been one full year since I was given the keys to this beautiful apartment. Handed them, just like that, told I'd earned it and to enjoy living there for as long as I wanted. The lease on the flat was in part payment from Ellen de Courcey, and a very handsome bargain I'd made of it at the time too. Besides, I reasoned, I earned this place fair and square, didn't I? In fact, I'd sweated blood for it. I'd fixed her situation for her good and proper – game over, job done.

From day one, I'd adored the place. It suits me down to the ground and outside of family, there's very little else in my life that I do love. I don't have a social life – it's almost impossible given the way I work. Not to mention, in this game, you soon learn no one is trustworthy and who needs friends like that? I had one friend, and look at the almighty mess that's landed me in.

And now I could lose it all, I think. *In a single heartbeat.*

This, I remind myself, is what happens when you let emotions get in the way. This is what happens when I break my own rules.

Nothing else for it. Harriet has to be dispatched. Nicely, sweetly and permanently. Now. Fast.

And I can do it too, I think, finding my resolve again as the sound of the early-morning traffic drifts up to my bedroom window.

I achieved the impossible once before and you know what? Now it's time for the final act.

Two years ago

God, when I thought back over two years ago now, it had all been so ridiculously, almost embarrassingly easy. But then that was the thing about persuading people, I knew of old. First, you found out their vulnerability, and then you went to work from there. And Harriet's weak spot was as obvious as the nose on your face. The fact that she worked in the 'vocational sector', as she misguidedly referred to that shambles of a charity shop, and had somehow, through pure, stupid, dumb luck, managed to fall in with one of the most eligible bachelors in the country. Or in most countries, for that matter.

Think Prince William, back when he was single. Now throw in Prince Harry for good measure (and looks). Combine the number of women they had throwing themselves at them, prior to each of their very grand, very royal weddings, and that would give you some idea of the number of women Freddie de Courcey had chasing him, ever since he was old enough to be chased, that is.

Back then, my streak of good fortune had continued; the mighty Ellen de Courcey had told me that one ex-girlfriend of

Freddie's stood head and shoulders above the rest, so I went to town on her, and through a very cursory online search, found out everything I possibly could about her.

Her name was Aurelia Beaulieu and she was a doctor, Parisian born, but now living in Ireland and well on her way to being a consultant neurologist, not that it mattered to me. What did matter very much was that this Aurelia seemed to really enjoy her social life, and her long, angular, beautifully French features beamed out at you from all of the gossip columns' online pages, frequently with Freddie himself looking gormlessly happy by her side. But then, that was Freddie de Courcey for you. The guy's factory default setting was joyous, bursting on euphoric. A bit like a latter-day Bertie Wooster; you could lock someone like Freddie up in prison, and he'd probably spend the whole time marvelling at how utterly wonderful the whole place was for a good detox. In the real world, in the world the rest of us operated in, there wasn't a chance in hell that someone as idiotic as Freddie would even have been allowed across the threshold of the de Courcey boardroom. It was only by the sheer good fortune of being born rich and entitled that he was even tolerated at all.

But, even I had to grudgingly admit, Freddie seemed like a perfectly nice person in every other way, on the few occasions when I'd actually met him. He seemed genuinely fond of Harriet, too. After all, she was probably the only living creature on earth who hadn't a clue who he was in the first place, and who remained stoically unimpressed by his millions. Or billions, more like.

Harriet was the type who could tell you to the nearest pound, shilling and halfpenny what everything cost, and would recoil in horror when she was out with Freddie and would see a starter on a menu that cost roughly the same amount as a flight to Paris. Had Freddie ever come across anyone like this in his life before? I often used to wonder. It was doubtful. Did he find it funny, or endearing?

After their dates, Harriet would tell me all about it and I was only too well able to picture the scene.

'Forty-two quid for a few tiny little dirty-looking mushrooms?' Harriet would say, over tea and biscuits in that poky little shop that stank of damp. 'And I'm not joking you, Meg, I was the only person at that table who was even shocked. All Freddie's pals just looked at me like they were embarrassed by me or something. "We actually call them *truffles*," one eejit said to me. And Freddie just laughed it off, but then he's such a dote like that, isn't he?'

'I don't much like the sound of those friends of his,' I said calmly.

'Oh they're awful, you've no idea!' Harriet winced. 'Magnums of champagne everywhere they go, giant bottles the size of a small child that they don't even finish – it's shocking! And the way they just toss money around like it's a head of lettuce, you wouldn't believe it. One of them is called Jamie Eynsford-Norris, and when I told him his money would be put to much better use if he gave to charity, he just laughed in my face and started calling me Mother Teresa.'

'I certainly hope Freddie stuck up for you?' I needled, sensing a chink.

'Well, yeah, sort of,' Harriet said doubtfully. 'I mean, he acted like it was a joke, if that's what you mean. But then you know Freddie, sure everything is a big joke to him.'

'Maybe next time he's out with his friends, you should just find an excuse not to go,' I'd counselled, hoping to strike at the very heart of this budding relationship. 'His friends sound so vile! Making you the butt of their jokes like that? I don't know how you put up with them at all. You're so different from that gang – thank God. And you'll never fit in with any of them, so why even bother?'

'Hmm,' Harriet said, listening intently, just like I knew she would.

'The thing you have to remember,' I gently pressed ahead, knowing that I was playing on Harriet's very weakest point here, 'is that Freddie was at public school with that gang, and then at college too. These are the people he grew up with and yes, you're dead right, they're probably the snottiest shower you could ever meet, but whether you like it or not, they're in his life for good. They all know Freddie ever since prep school, or whatever they call it, and he's never going to give them up for anyone, is he?'

'No,' Harriet said, doubtfully. 'I suppose not.'

'But you're so much better than any of them!' I'd persisted. 'So why bother trying to get on with that lot in the first place? I know I certainly wouldn't have the stomach for it. Overprivileged tossers, the lot of them. Except for Freddie, of course,' I took good care to add.

'So what do you think I should do?' Harriet asked warily, biting her lip and for the first time, looking like she was having serious doubts.

I continued to play Iago. I continued to drive a wedge.

'Well, it's obvious, isn't it?' I'd said. 'If you ask me, the next time Freddie asks you out with him and his gang, the best thing you can do is run a mile. You know how elitist his circle are. They'll never accept the likes of you or me. We weren't born into it, we didn't go to a posh private school like they did, and that's just the way it is. I wouldn't be a friend unless I said it to you out straight,' I added for good measure. 'Going out with Freddie and his gang is only upsetting you. It is a relatively new relationship and you went on a date last night, but all you've really told me is that his friends were awful to you. Dating should be fun! You should be excited and happy, and you're not. So why put yourself through all that in the first place? If I were you, I'd tell him that from now on, you want nothing to do with those arseholes. You'll be so glad you did. And you'd be doing Freddie a big favour too. If he keeps hanging around with that lot, it's only a matter of time before he ends up just like them.'

'Do you think?' Harriet said, beginning to waver.

'Seen it a thousand times,' I lied.

Harriet didn't answer, but then she didn't really need to. The look on her face told me I'd hit a home run.

And, of course, there was the fact that Freddie had been dating Dr Aurelia Beaulieu right before he met Harriet. Which was manna from heaven as far as I was concerned. Because this Aurelia one was still very much a fixture in Freddie's life – well, the de Courceys' at least. Always invited where he was, always turning up. Always, always, always with a photographer conveniently hovering around, almost as if she'd drummed up a media storm single-handedly.

So I went even further.

The de Courceys were lavish entertainers, and their donations to charity were legendary. All it took was for me to tip off a media photographer I knew well, overpaying him in cash to make bloody sure he did what I asked and kept his mouth shut. I needed a few snaps of Freddie and this Aurelia looking cosy and comfortable together at various art gallery functions hosted by his company, and the more of them, the better. Snaps which, naturally, I took care to upload to various anonymous Instagram accounts I'd set up for this very purpose, with hashtags like *#allthegossip!* All glossed up and ready to reveal to my 'good pal' Harriet.

'But Freddie denies that there's anything going on between him and Aurelia at all,' Harriet had said, at first anyway. 'She's his ex, they broke up not long after we met, and they're still friends. What's wrong with that?'

A shrug and an eye roll was all it took to cast a shadow of doubt over that.

'Has he ever asked you to meet her? Or any of his family, for that matter?' I asked, knowing full well the answer. 'Besides, once a cheater, always a cheater. My dad was a cheater and believe me, I know first-hand the pain it causes, long term. It's horrible, it's hurtful and you never get over the betrayal. I know my mum never did and probably never will.' For once, I was actually telling the truth, unfortunately.

'I'm so sorry to hear that,' Harriet said, all wide-eyed sympathy, as she leaned over to squeeze my hand warmly. 'You've never spoken about your dad before.'

'Probably because he abandoned Mum and me before I was even seven years old,' I replied stoically. 'He met someone else, who he's now married to with a second family and he never looked back. He broke Mum and me and he didn't even care. Cheaters,' I added feelingly, 'are arseholes to be avoided like the Black Death. Unless you want to have a shitty, miserable life, that is.'

'Freddie's not like that, though,' Harriet said loyally. 'I know he's not, I just *feel* it.'

'You said he was still seeing her when you met,' I threw in.

'Yes, but . . . he and I had only become friends at first . . . I mean, nothing had happened between us per se . . .'

'Does it matter? He was in a relationship when you first got together. Speaks volumes, if you ask me.'

Harriet said nothing, just looked a bit lost and confused.

'Maybe there's nothing going on with him and Doctor Aurelia,' I'd insisted, 'but can you imagine how thrilled Ellen de Courcey must be at seeing them hanging out together so much? This is exactly the kind of college-educated, high-achieving woman they want in that family. She more or less says so in this month's *Home Interiors* magazine. She says Aurelia even helped her source paintings from Paris for her new drawing room.'

'I suppose,' said Harriet thoughtfully. 'I mean, on paper, she really is so much more suited to him that I am, isn't she? This Doctor Aurelia is the kind who can perform brain

surgery on you and knows all about the world's leading artists, and still manages to have a blow-dry and a perfect mani-
cure all the time. What do I know about? How to get termites
woodworm out of second-hand furniture in the charity shop,
and how to coax homeless people into eating hot soup when
I'm out volunteering with the Samaritans.'

'She and Freddie are like a match made in heaven, I'd have
said,' I replied, sensing a breakthrough. 'And the best of luck
to them.'

'I am really out of my depth here, aren't I?' Harriet said,
sounding truly doubtful now and looking at me from under
her lashes, like a modern-day version of Princess Diana.

'Well,' I said stoutly, 'you're never out of your depth with
me, babes. I'm always here for you, through thick and thin.
You know that.'

It had been almost touching how grateful Harriet had
been.

Almost.

She'd hopped up to hug me, squeezing me tight as her eyes
welled up.

'Oh Meg, where would I be without you? I sometimes feel
you're the only person in this whole city I can actually trust.'

Chapter Nineteen

Meg

A new dawn, a new day and so I start exactly as I mean to go on. This new plan is going to take every scrap of guile I've got; this calls for a charm offensive that would seduce an army.

Bang on the dot of 7 a.m., I spring out of bed, ignoring the fact that I've got a throbbing head from lack of sleep, and get straight down to work in the kitchen. I bang pots, slam the fridge door open and shut, ask Alexa what the weather is going to be for the day – anything to make as much noise as possible and wake the still-slumbering Harriet up from where she's crashed out on the sofa.

It works like a charm.

'Hey, sleepy girl!' I smile breezily, as Harriet yawns and stretches her way into the kitchen, all swishy-haired and fresh-faced, with not a dark circle under her eyes to be seen. Which annoys me irrationally, but I let it go.

Come on, take the bait, I think, taking particular care not to show the pressure I'm under here. But then, if I say so myself, when I go into character, Meryl Streep has nothing on me. And my performance this morning is 'supportive best friend, here to do nothing more than apologise for getting off on the wrong foot'. As my nan always told me, you catch far more flies with sugar than with vinegar.

'Meg!' Harriet says, sleepily rubbing her big blue eyes. 'It's so early – what are you doing up and about?'

'Like I need an excuse to make breakfast for my best friend?' I beam back at her, flashing my very brightest smile. 'I hope you're hungry, by the way, because you want to see what I've got going on here. Fresh fruit to start, then a healthy ginger and carrot smoothie, then scrambled eggs and as much toast as you're able to eat. You got far too skinny out in Kenya, honey, we need to start piling a bit of weight back on you!'

'Wow,' Harriet says, wide-eyed, as she pulls out a stool at the granite-topped island in the middle of the kitchen, clambers up onto it and wraps her long, tanned legs around its cold chrome frame. 'You seem so different this morning. You seem much more like . . . well, much more like *you*, really.'

'Glad to hear it,' I say cheerily, tossing a tea towel over my shoulder and giving the scrambled eggs I have in a pot a good stirring.

'Because you haven't been yourself at all since I arrived,' Harriet says, looking a bit puzzled. 'I've been so worried about you. You've been so . . . so . . .'

Instinct tells me to stop with the cooking, and to go with the moment.

'I know, I know, mea culpa,' I say, turning around to face her from the opposite side of the island and spreading my hands out wide in what I hope is an 'I'm sorry' gesture. Contrite and humble is what I'm going for here. 'And I just wanted to say that I'm so sorry about that, Harriet. I really am. If I seemed a bit . . . you know . . . maybe . . . distracted?'

'Oh, no,' says Harriet innocently. 'You weren't distracted at all. You were full-on, out-and-out rude to me. You were practically shoving me out the door. As if I was being a nuisance to you. I was so upset about it. All day yesterday. I even said as much to Freddie when he called over.'

Jesus. This is far, far worse than I had thought. This calls for me at my most charming, my most sincere, my most manipulative.

'I know, love,' I say, faux apologetically. 'And I only hope that you'll forgive me. It's this new job, you see. The stress of it is killing me. The hours are horrendous, well, you've seen that for yourself, and my manager is down on me like a ton of bricks over even the tiniest little thing—'

I chance a sneaky little side-eye at Harriet, to check if she's buying into it. Bingo. Sure enough, she's looking back at me sympathetically, nodding and listening intently, just like she used to with all those aul ones in that stinking charity shop, back in the day.

'I thought it might be something like that,' she says softly.

'Now, don't get me wrong,' I hasten to add. 'The money is phenomenal. In fact, that's the one good thing about the job – it means I'm able to afford the rent on this place.'

'Oh really?' says Harriet. 'I did wonder about that, all right.'

'Anyway, I just wanted to ask for your forgiveness,' I say, praying that I've pitched it right. Harriet used to be so bloody soft-hearted, she'd believe anything, and I'm counting on that not having changed. 'You and I got off on the wrong foot,' I tell her, 'and I'm here to make amends. I was just a bit . . . surprised . . . to see you huddled up in my doorway the other night, that's all. It was so out of the blue, so unexpected. But in a good way. And now that you're here, I just wanted to say it's magic to see you again. It's wonderful. I missed you so much, Harriet, and you know you're welcome to stay here just as long as you like.'

The odd thing is that I almost believe myself. For a brief moment I allow myself to imagine having company in this apartment, not coming home to an empty place, day in, day out. I even manage to let my eyes well up as I say it. God, I sometimes think, if this line of work dries up for me, I could always turn to the stage.

It works beautifully. Next thing, Harriet hops down off her stool and comes around the island to give me a big, sloppy bear hug.

'That's OK,' she says warmly, 'you're back to being *you* again, and that's all that matters.'

'You're just the sweetest, kindest friend,' I say, blinking back a little tear, a gesture copied directly from Nicole Kidman in *Big Little Lies*. 'Now come on, sit yourself down and help yourself to scrambled eggs. Americano to have with it? White, no sugar, that right?'

'You remembered,' Harriet smiles, doing as she's told, while I plate up the eggs, sprinkle them with salt and pepper and serve them up to my guest, along with her coffee, just the way she likes it.

Course I remembered. It's my bloody job to.

'We've so much to catch up on,' I say, pulling up a stool on the island opposite her. 'So let's start with Freddie. Tell me everything, I'm dying to hear all. Omit no detail, however small!'

'But what about you and this new job of yours?' Harriet says worriedly. 'Let's talk about that first. The hours you seem to be working are insane.'

'Oh, never mind about that,' I tell her, with a dismissive flick of my wrist. 'Anyway, getting back to Freddie . . .'

'No, no, still staying with you,' Harriet insists – a trait of hers that's actually endearing. The fact that she's far happier talking about other people than herself, and always deflecting conversations towards you. 'This new job of yours. Where is it, anyway?'

'Oh, you don't want to know,' I say flippantly. 'It's so boring.'

'It's not boring to me. It's stressing you out and we really need to talk it through.'

'All right then,' I sigh, 'it's in waste management.'

'Waste management?'

'Yeah. You know, wheelie bins. Recycling. All of that.'

'And what is it that you do there?'

'I just got promoted to regional manager,' I tell the practised lie smoothly. 'Hence the crazy hours.'

'But you used to work as a stage manager in a theatre,' Harriet says, crinkling up her nose and looking puzzled.

'Why the big career change? I thought you loved working in the arts, I thought it was your passion.'

'Well, yeah, I still volunteer at the theatre whenever I can,' I improvise, thinking this is as good a cover as any for the nutty hours I'm required to be out of the apartment. 'But I was looking for a career change, and when I answered the ad for the job I'm doing now, I never in a million years thought I'd land it.'

'It's very weird all right,' says Harriet, crinkling her forehead prettily. 'You've no experience in waste management, for one thing. And for them to promote you to regional manager in such a short space of time?'

'Well, there you go,' I say airily. 'I'm passionate about . . . rubbish . . . and, you know, saving the planet and all that, and I guess that's what they saw in me. Anyway, back to Freddie de Courcey . . .'

'No, let's stay with you. So what's the name of this company?'

'Pest Be Gone,' I say, looking directly at her.

'And where are they based?'

'Ohh, you know, branches everywhere . . . you know how it is. Anyway, I'm sure you're bored stupid by all this, when we could be talking about you and your love life.'

'And who's your boss in Pest Be Gone? Have you spoken to them about the crazy pressure they're putting you under?'

'I didn't think it was really appropriate,' I reply. 'There's about ten people in the office who are snapping at my heels to get a sniff of my job.'

'You must be on a colossal salary,' Harriet insists, 'to be able to afford a place like this. I mean, just *look* at it. Even Freddie was impressed when he was here.'

She's barely back in the country a wet day and already he called to see her, I remind myself. *The pair of them could be on the brink of getting back together again. Which means I gotta work faster here. Gotta work quicker. I successfully broke the pair of them up once before, and I can do it again. Just watch me.*

'So how did you come by this flat?' Harriet persists. 'I mean, even if you were the CEO of Pest Be Gone, wouldn't somewhere like this be a bit of a stretch for you, cash-wise?'

'What can I say?' I reply, holding up my two hands as if to say, 'You got me!' 'It's actually kind of a house-sitting arrangement, really, and I just got lucky, that's all.'

'House-sitting for who?'

Fuck's sake, aren't I supposed to be the one asking the questions here?

'No one I've ever met before,' I say. 'Just stumbled across this place via Airbnb at a rent I couldn't believe. Anyway, how was Freddie when you saw him? I thought you were dying to tell me. I have twenty-four missed calls to prove it.'

At that, Harriet gives a tiny smile, cradles her coffee mug in her hand and looks particularly content with herself.

'Well?' I probe, sensing a chink. 'He must have been surprised to see you back home again, after all this time.'

'You can ask him that yourself if you like,' Harriet blushes, tucking a strand of her fair hair behind one ear and looking insanely pretty. Jesus. The woman just woke up, how is this fair? 'When you see him, that is.'

'When I . . . Sorry, *what* did you just say?'

'When you see him,' Harriet smiles. 'This weekend, actually. Turns out his grandmother is hosting some big political fundraiser at their house, because of this election that's all over the news, and Freddie is insisting that I go with him. And you too, of course,' she adds, with a little nod at me, as I sit there, frozen-faced and rooted to my stool.

'Can you believe it, Meg? After all this time? I'll finally get to meet the scary Ellen de Courcey. But the best part of all is, you, my best friend, will be there with me, right by my side. I mean, how fab is that?'

Chapter Twenty

Harriet

With Meg gone for the day, Harriet has time on her hands and the whole day stretching ahead of her, what with being 'in between contracts', as you were meant to say when you weren't working.

She can't remember the last time she had the luxury of a few days off, and now that her jet lag has worn off, she plans to do a load of things with the time. Top of the list, to go back to Dead Old Lady Dresses, and ask her ex-boss if she can have her old job back. Or she could volunteer again at the Samaritans, just like she used to. There are plenty of useful things she could be doing with herself, but before cracking on with any of it, she has decided to be a good friend and start earning her keep around Meg's gorgeous apartment.

I'll give the place a good going-over with a mop and a hoover, Harriet thinks. *And I'll rustle up a nice bit of dinner for this evening, for when Meg gets home. Be a surprise for her, and a small way of thanking her for her hospitality.* It will be a lovely goodwill gesture, too, to show that all is well again between the two pals after such a rocky start.

With a spring in her step, Harriet finds a tiny utility room off the kitchen that seems to be largely unused, because there is a mop, broom and bucket still with their shop stickers on them and a load of J-cloths in their packets. So she snaps on a pair of bright yellow Marigolds and knuckles straight down to it. The apartment is already pristine, but still, no harm in giving it a good old tidy-up, is there? For the next half-hour, she hums happily away to herself and kills time by scrubbing, polishing and even getting down on her hands and knees to wax the already shining glossy wooden floor in the living room.

Which is when she notices it. Meg's phone. Just sitting on the hall table, half hidden under a pile of post. Harriet picks it up and has a good look at it; it has been left on silent mode, but there are eighteen missed calls on it, from a whole load of people she's never heard of.

Well, poor old Meg must have been in such a frantic rush to get to that job of hers, Harriet thinks that she's accidentally left the phone behind – and she's probably going bananas in work without it.

Without a second thought, she picks up her own phone to call that place where Meg said she worked. What's the name of the company again, she wonders, *Pest Be Gone*? Something like that? To hell with it, she'll find a landline number to call and just leave a message with reception there, for Meg to get back to her as soon as she can.

Harriet googles the company on her phone, but there's absolutely nothing showing. Just a few listings for a company out in Australia that swears blind they'll get rid of all your pests for you. '100% GUARANTEED!' Their banner ad runs right across the screen that pops up at you with delightful, up-close photos of rats, bedbugs and cockroaches.

Lovely.

So this time Harriet googles all the local and national waste management companies, thinking she's got the name wrong somehow. But again, nothing. Loads of companies that will empty wheelie bins and provide skips for you, but not a sausage that even remotely sounds like the name Meg had given her.

Which is strange.

Well, I must have got it wrong, Harriet thinks. *I must have forgotten the name Meg gave me, and that's all there is to it.*

Figuring Meg will come back home for her phone as soon as she realised that's where she's left it, Harriet goes back to all her scrubbing and cleaning. This time, she works her way through Meg's living room, dusting and polishing and humming a happy little tune to herself as she goes.

Then she comes to a discreet, tiny little corner alcove, hidden out of sight of the main, sunken living area. There is a door with a lock on it but it has been left open and the door is swinging ajar. Must have been because Meg was in such a rush to get out of here, Harriet figures, wavering a bit before deciding to go inside. But sure – she's only going to give the floor a little hoover, what's wrong with that?

It's tiny inside, poky and dark, so unlike the rest of the apartment. The space is so small, it barely fits a desk and chair. But at least there's a table lamp, which Harriet clicks on, all the better to see what she is at.

Well now, that's odd, she thinks. For such a hyper-organised person like Meg, her desk is a total pigsty. There are little yellow Post-it notes scattered over every surface, and stuck to the wall right in front of you, there's a whiteboard divided into several long columns. One is headed with the name 'Nicole', the second one says 'Denys', and the third is the longest one of all, with the name 'Katherine Sisk' written in bold, black highlighter pen at the very top.

The Katherine Sisk, Harriet wonders, stopping dead in her tracks. That senator one, with the bullet-grey hair? Harriet knows who she is, but then so does just about everyone of voting age; she's been in the media and on the news for what feels like most of Harriet's life.

The Good Lady Senator, everyone calls her, because she is a feminist first and last and is always to the forefront of women's rights. The marriage equality referendum? Senator Katherine was like an engine behind the whole thing; pundits reckoned that it was her tireless support that got the vote over the finish line. Ditto the women's rights movement. She is wildly popular, too; even Harriet's dad, who's spent his whole adult life saying that politicians are a lying shower of chancers, will turn up the volume on the TV or radio if the Good Lady Senator comes on.

'A real class act,' he always says. 'If they were all like her, sure we'd have no bother.'

So what's Katherine Sisk's name doing on a whiteboard above Meg's desk? Along with a whole load of mobile phone numbers? The entries written underneath are all really weird too; there are strange, scribbled comments about someone called Jess, with a load of arrows shooting away from her name, with still more mad-looking, senseless things written underneath. The name Philip Sisk for one thing – Senator Katherine's husband, maybe?

That makes little enough sense to Harriet, but more baffling still is what's written in the column directly underneath the name 'Nicole'. It seems to be some sort of a timetable, neatly listing out all the places, and even more specifically, all of the times that this Nicole one, whoever she is, is due to be there:

'7 a.m. hatha yoga class,' it reads. Then '8 a.m.–9 a.m., @Costa on Meeting House Square, or maybe Caffeine & Co. opposite Google'. Underneath are even more dates, times and places – something to do with puppy-training classes at the weekends – it's like this Nicole one's whole life is more or less mapped out here.

Which makes no sense to Harriet whatsoever. Meg's work is in waste management – she'd said so over breakfast earlier. So all of this isn't for work, is it? Is this what the wheelie bin companies do now, if you're a bit behind with your payments? Stalk your every move till you cough up?

Because that's exactly how this noticeboard looks to Harriet.

Just like something a stalker would have.

Chapter Twenty-One

Meg

Fuck, fucking, bollocky fucking nightmare. With bells on.

I'm pounding the pavements on the way to Katherine Sisk's office, and my brain is in utter and total meltdown.

How could I have been so bloody stupid?

I'm a planner, a plotter and an organiser – I pride myself on paying meticulous attention to detail. So why didn't I plan for this? The fact that Harriet might get a bit homesick out in Kenya and would come home again? And then as soon as she was off the flight, get back in touch with Freddie bloody moronic rich boy de Courcey? And now this? Harriet planning to meet Ellen de Courcey at one of her fundraisers this weekend?

Bugger it and bugger it again, I think furiously, as I narrowly avoid being run over by a cyclist on the busy road I'm crossing; my temper so bad, I'm not even watching where I'm going.

'Are you trying to get yourself killed, or what?' a cyclist yells at me, weaving in and out of the traffic with his Lycra-clad arse held high in the air, as he gives me the finger.

No, I think, glaring crossly back at him. *Actually there's no need for me to. The de Courcey family will take care of that very nicely, thanks all the same.*

Instinctively, I fumble about in my bag for my phones, but for some reason can only find one of them.

Jesus. Just when I thought this day couldn't get any worse, now I must have left my second phone back at the flat.

I'm already running late and don't have time to go back for it, so it'll just have to stay there. It'll slow me down immeasurably though – the very last thing I need with so many work projects at such a critical stage.

A plan, I think, thundering down the pavement. I need to make a plan to scheme my wily way out of this whole dung heap Harriet has landed me in. I need to stay calm, regroup and move forward. What's utterly critical, however, is that Harriet be kept onside at all times. I've little choice in the matter, and if that means her staying on at the flat, so be it; from here on in, I'll have to be sweetness and light around the girl. I'll have to be hypocrisy itself – and no better woman.

I've done it before and now it's time for an encore.

Christmas, two years ago

As always, Ellen de Courcey was holding a huge festive champagne reception at the family home and naturally, Harriet's name did *not* appear on the guest list.

'Freddie is hopping mad about it!' Harriet had confided in me, as the two of us strolled through a Christmas market down in the dockland area on a freezing cold December evening. 'He says it's a huge oversight on his grandmother's part, and that I should be there with him. Oh Meg, it's terrifying! He wants me to meet the granny, and the grandad too, that's Freddie Senior, who's bedridden and hasn't left the house in decades, and apparently he's the grumpiest man alive. And the granny – Ellen, that's her name – sounds like the vilest woman you ever met in your life. Half of me just wants to run away and hide, but Freddie is insistent that I'm there with him. He says he's already met my brothers and now it's my turn to meet his family. And I'm petrified!'

A nearby choir was belting out 'Jingle Bells' in perfect harmony and the sound filled the air, as I stopped at a little pop-up stand that was selling home-made Christmas decorations.

'Meg?' said Harriet, stopping in her tracks and looking at me funny. 'You've gone very quiet on me all of a sudden. Come on, I really need your advice here. What would you do if you were me? Stay or go?'

'You really want to know?' I said gently, as the choir swelled to a crescendo behind us. 'Because you mightn't like what I have to say.'

'You're the only person who tells me the truth,' Harriet replied, and you know what? I almost felt guilty when I saw the trust in her eyes. Like a lost little puppy looking to its owner for guidance.

Then I remembered why I was doing all this in the first place and said exactly what I needed to, to get the right result.

'So let me get this right,' I said, turning to face Harriet, as crowds of families with kids jostled past on their way to the Ferris wheel at the back of the market. 'The formal invitations to this party would have gone out, what, a few weeks ago now?'

'I don't know,' Harriet said. 'I suppose so, yeah.'

'And you didn't get one?'

'No.'

'And it can't be an oversight on Ellen de Courcey's part, because she has Freddie in one ear banging on and on about how much he wants you there.'

'Well . . . I guess so.'

'Oh honey, it's as plain as the nose on your face,' I shrugged. 'You're not wanted, simple as that. And I don't know about you, but I certainly wouldn't dream of turning up anywhere I wasn't wanted, would you?'

'No,' said Harriet uncertainly. 'No, it would be an awful thing to do.'

'It's no better than gatecrashing.'

'Gatecrashing . . . yeah.'

'It's a snub,' I went on, really pressing it home. 'And a very deliberate one at that. So come on, Harriet, where's your pride? This Ellen de Courcey so clearly wants nothing to do with you, no matter how much Freddie badgers her.'

'So . . . what are you suggesting? That I just do nothing and tell Freddie I'm not going?'

'Tell him you can't possibly go when you haven't been formally invited,' I said, silently thanking Ellen de Courcey for playing her part so beautifully. 'Why would you put yourself through the wringer like that? Like I've told you before, that family will never accept you, no matter how hard you try. So why don't you and me just have a happy Christmas without them?'

'Best idea I've heard all day,' said Harriet, back to smiling again and linking her arm through mine as we weaved our way on through the Christmas market, all while the choir sang on.

Pitiful, I can clearly remember thinking. It was pitiful, just how easy it was to influence a mind weaker than your own. All I needed to do was play on Harriet's many, many social insecurities when it came to the de Courcey family, and I was home and dry.

There was just one tiny fly in the ointment.

Tiny. Barely even noticeable. Nothing that I was convinced would become a problem. Back then at least.

The issue was that in spite of everything, in spite of my callous determination to keep all emotions out of my work, when it came to Harriet, for some reason I found it so much harder than I'd have thought. Up till then, ninety per cent of the clients I'd worked for had wanted inconvenient third parties airbrushed out of their relationships. Cheaters, I could deal with dispassionately, almost cruelly at times. Well, would you blame me? And did anyone messing around on a partner behind their back deserve anything less?

This particular situation, however, was different. Mainly because the more I got to know Harriet, the fonder I became of her, in spite of myself. Here, I fast realised, was a good person, a genuinely open-hearted, lovely, kind woman, who wasn't cheating on anyone. And nor was Freddie de Courcey, for that matter. Did they really deserve his family, and particularly his grandmother's, machinations, just to keep him on the straight and narrow until he ended up with a partner of her choosing?

I said as much to the mighty Ellen de Courcey during one of her 'checking up on me' phone calls.

'You know, if you just gave Harriet Waters a chance . . .' I tried to say, but she cut me off mid-sentence.

'I've no doubt that's true, Miss Monroe,' she'd said, addressing me formally, as always. 'But it's quite beside the point. You must understand that, in time, Freddie is expected to spearhead the entire Connair family, which amounts to over eleven thousand employees worldwide. He needs a life partner fluent in several languages, someone well travelled,

THE FIXER

artistic and cosmopolitan, who will be able to take on the mantle I myself will one day have to relinquish. Being part of the CEO's family is an onerous job and one that requires a high degree of intelligence, ambition, business acumen and people skills. Someone who understands our world. We need the sort of woman who regularly appears on the Fortune 500 list and who's been featured in *Forbes* magazine.'

Message received loud and clear. Not someone who works for a CRAP store and who could tell you to the nearest pound, shilling and pence exactly how much you'd get for a knackered tea towel souvenir of the Pope's visit back in 1979.

By then, after a few months spent worming myself into Harriet's life, we'd grown close. She and I had become, dare I even use the word, friends. Not that I knew a whole lot about friendship. I had acquaintances before, many of them, but never an actual friend. Not since school. Not once. Not like this.

That Christmas, Harriet went 'down home' to her own family in Limerick, and I went back to my mother and Nana. Where I did nothing more than scrap with Mum and deal with all her low-level passive aggression, while trying to curtail the worst of Nan's dementia episodes. This was the Christmas when Nan started escaping from the house and warning the neighbours that if Hitler didn't come to get them, then Stalin surely would. Mum blamed me – because, of course, her having a few too many ninety per cent of the time wouldn't unsettle Nan at all, would it?

So when Harriet invited me to stay with her family for New Year's Eve, I jumped at the chance.

'The twins have gone skiing, and Mam and Dad would love to meet you. Just say yes and hop on a train!' Harriet had squealed excitedly down the phone.

Her parents, Carole and Sean, turned out to be lovely too. Carole was almost like a fifty-something version of Harriet, with poker-straight fair hair chopped into a neat, efficient bob. She dressed in outdoor, practical clothes for her job as a vet; chunky, warm jumpers along with comfortable jeans and sensible wellies. Sean, on the other hand, was hale and hearty, red-faced and florid, a retired bank manager who now lived to bake and cook and who happily told me his lifetime's goal was to represent Limerick on *The Great British Bake Off*. 'I'd love Paul Hollywood and Prue Leith to get a load of my home-made beef and ale pie – it'd knock their socks off . . . star baker, here I come!' he'd proudly boasted.

But one night sticks out clearly in my mind.

It was New Year's Day, when Carole and Sean went out to visit neighbours, and Harriet and I were left alone in front of a cosy fire in the warm, welcoming living room of their Victorian farmhouse home. A sprawling, shambling, welcoming home too, with the kids' bedrooms still exactly as they were the day they all left home, right down to Harriet's wall plastered with ancient Zane from One Direction posters and with various trophies and medals still proudly displayed on walls and mantelpieces everywhere. So unlike my own house, I thought, where every 'first in class' prize that I brought home was met with a disinterested shrug, and where you microwaved your own dinner to eat in silence in front of the telly.

The chat turned around to Freddie, as I made sure it did.

'He gave me this before I came home for Christmas,' Harriet smiled, her pretty face flushed from the warmth of the fire, as she proudly showed off a delicate filigree gold pendant that hung around her neck. 'And he says he'll see me just as soon as he's back from his holidays next week.'

'Lucky him,' I said, gazing into the flames as the fire snapped and crackled and those gorgeous turfy smells filled the room. 'I wouldn't mind being whisked off to Mustique with my grandparents for two weeks. Christmas on the beach? What's not to like?'

There was a long, telling pause before Harriet spoke again.

'You know something?' she said, looking at me and tilting her head quizzically. 'We always end up talking about my love life, don't we? Never, ever yours. So come on, Meg, what's the story with you? Any men you're interested in at the moment? Are you seeing anyone?'

'No,' I said flatly, after a pause. 'No interest, you see.'

'Oh now, come on,' she insisted. 'Look at you, you're a fabulous human being! Surely you must have fellas queuing up to ask you out? Have you ever tried online dating? Lots of my friends are on Tinder and they swear by it . . .'

'Not for me,' I said bluntly.

'I don't get it,' Harriet said, staring thoughtfully across at me.

'Because—' I told her after a lengthy pause, as I weighed up whether to confide in her or not. And decided, yeah, go for it, why the hell not? Harriet was a good soul and probably the last person on earth who'd ever judge me. 'I'm not interested in men,' I said truthfully. 'Never really was. Never will be. Fact is that ever since I was a teenager, I've pretty much identified as . . .'

'You're gay?' Harriet asked gently.

I nodded and smiled shyly – a strange, new emotion for me. 'Not that I'm seeing anyone, or even interested in anyone just now,' I replied, 'but yes. For a long time now, I've realised that I'm attracted to women.'

She got up from the armchair and walked over to where I was sitting, plonked down on the armrest beside me, slipped her arm around my shoulders and gave me a tight, supportive squeeze.

'I'm honoured you told me,' she said simply. 'That's wonderful news. She'll be a very lucky woman who gets to be with you, you know that.'

And that was it. I'd never come out to anyone before, not even my own family. That's the moment I knew that Harriet was a true, genuine friend. Possibly the first real friend I ever had.

And that's when I knew I was in trouble.

And now to the shameful part of my tale. The bit where I sold my soul.

Early in January, refreshed and invigorated from her Caribbean holiday, I had a call from Ellen de Courcey. Just to check up on me, just to see what progress was being made.

I tried to tell her that Freddie and Harriet really did seem to be falling for each other. I tried again to say that if she just gave Harriet half a chance, she might actually grow to see, over time, that here was no gold digger out for what she could get. I even tried to say that with someone as caring and warm-hearted as Harriet, from such a grounded, rock-solid, united family, Freddie might actually have a shot at happiness.

But no sooner had I formulated the words in my head than they withered on my lips.

'I have a list for you, my dear,' Ellen interrupted me, in that whispery, papery voice that I had to strain to hear from the other end of the phone. 'My private secretary is emailing it over to you as we speak.'

A list?

I raced to my laptop and refreshed my emails and, yes, there it was. Right in front of me, in bold black and white. A long list of clients, and a lot of well-known, high-profile names they were too.

'A lot of these people are close personal friends,' Ellen whispered down the phone. 'And all, I regret to say, are in need of your services. Should you succeed regarding my grandson and this . . . person he's apparently fallen for, naturally, I will be most happy to recommend you. It goes without saying that all would be prepared to pay premium prices for a discreet, speedy service.'

My head spun as I scrolled down through the list. Jesus, there were literally dozens of names here – household names, a lot of them. If I pulled this off, it would set me up for years to come. This would mean I could properly look after Mum and Nana. I could pay off Mum's mortgage, maybe even save a bit for a care home for Nana, should she get to the point where she couldn't live at home anymore. In time, I could put a bit by and maybe even get to go to college as a mature student, something I'd always dreamt of, but had never been able to.

I could do a whole lot of things.

'There's more,' Ellen whispered. 'You will recall that we discussed the apartment block currently under construction? Well, it's almost completed, I'm reliably informed, and my property agent will be more than happy to meet you at the site at your earliest convenience. Just to make sure you're quite happy with all the fixtures and fittings, my dear. I never go back on an agreement, you know. You take care of this matter for me, and it's yours.'

There comes a point in every life where two roads fork in front of you and you have to choose one. And so I chose.

Well, you don't need to be Miss Marple to work out the rest. The de Courceys would never have accepted someone like Harriet anyway, was my justification, then as now. I was actually doing Harriet a favour in the long run. Fond and all as I was of Harriet, our whole friendship had been based on a deception. Should she ever find out I'd been employed to get rid of her, what hope was there for any kind of latent friendship anyway?

Besides, you know. Morals are an expense that some of us just can't afford.

I redoubled my efforts and really knuckled down to it – then, a lucky break. After a lot of exhaustive research online and a significant amount of preliminary enquiry, I came up with the perfect solution to everyone's problem. The parent company of the CRAP store where Harriet worked coincidentally ran a clean water charity and were actively recruiting a new team, to head up a water aid project . . . all the way out in Mombasa, Kenya.

I already knew Harriet's direct boss, who was called Mona, and who Harriet said was so terrifying, she should come with the background sound of thunderclaps, dressed like the baddie out of a panto. I contacted the CRAP head office and made a point of speaking to this Mona directly.

'Now, of course, Harriet doesn't know I'm reaching out to you like this,' I'd said, 'but the thing is, I'm her best friend and I'm *sooooo* concerned about her. She's having a bit of man trouble, you know how it is.'

Yet another role play I was getting very good at. Another one for the repertoire; that of Miss Hypocritical Two Faces, Liar of the Century.

'Really?' said Mona, sounding confused. 'Because Harriet Waters always seems so chirpy to me. She's forever in good form. In fact, I can never get away from her when I call into that shop. Tell me this, does the girl ever stop chatting?'

'Puts on such a brave face,' I said, thinking fast. 'Trooper that she is. But just between us, she really could do with a distraction. A brand-new project, a challenge. Like your clean water charity out in Kenya, for instance?'

Seed sown.

Convincing Harriet was that bit more difficult, but with perseverance, I set out a case. Slowly and methodically, I went to work on Harriet, just like water wearing away at stone.

'Now, I know the last thing on your mind is an open-ended trip to Africa,' I'd said, using a combination of reverse psychology and good old-fashioned emotional blackmail.

'But that boss of yours, Mona, really seems to have earmarked you for great things in the voluntary sector and I know you'd hate to let her down. Just think what a fantastic work opportunity it would be for you. A whole year running your own NGO, Harriet, just think! You could travel anywhere in the world with that kind of experience under your belt – you'd never look back!'

We were sitting up on high bar stools in a cheap local pizzeria, where we'd been sharing a margherita pizza between us because it was as far as our budgets stretched, back in those days. But then Harriet, who had a huge appetite and who'd been horsing into her pizza up till then, suddenly stopped eating.

'Well, it's so kind of you to say so,' she said thoughtfully. 'And of course, it's flattering that Mona is even thinking of putting me up for a huge job like that . . .'

'After this, you could walk into the United Nations and get any job you like – can you imagine? They'd be fighting over you!'

'It's a wonderful job offer,' Harriet sighed. 'But you have to understand. It's not about ambition for me, and it never was. Beware anyone who works in the charity sector when they're motivated by money, because it's coming from the wrong place. I do this job because I genuinely do want to *help* people. Not because I'm after some fancy job title with a flashy salary.'

'Is it because of Freddie?' I asked her directly. Fuck it, it was what we were both thinking. Might as well be upfront about it.

'I could be away for a very long time,' Harriet said wistfully. 'And you know how close I am to my family. I'd miss everyone. The twins, even though they'd drive you nuts half the time, and my folks too. There's Freddie, of course . . . but then there's *you* too, Meg. I'd miss you.'

The guilt felt like battery acid in my throat. But I'd made my choice, so I put on my big girl pants and got on with it.

'The time away will be nothing,' I said, dismissing all her concerns with a wave of my hand. 'It'll fly! And as for me and your family? We're all here, and none of us are going anywhere, are we? We'll stay in touch via Skype and WhatsApp. What's wrong with that? Friendships like this don't fade because of distance.'

I'd deliberately omitted Freddie's name. Just to see what the reaction would be.

But none came. Instead Harriet just continued to stare out the window of the pizzeria onto the sleety, wet street outside, lost in thought.

'Look,' I said, playing my trump card, 'just think of Freddie's family and friends and that terrifying grandmother of his, who's acting more and more like the dowager on *Downton Abbey* every day, as far as I can see. You've always felt they looked down their noses on you, haven't you?'

'Since day one,' Harriet reluctantly had to agree.

'But just think. Word will get back to them, one and all, that you've landed this huge job as an NGO heading up a fantastic charity like the Clean Water Initiative. Don't you see how much they'll respect you for this? How this could change everything for you? Particularly with someone like

Ellen de Courcey, who's always in the papers banging on about how important her charity work is to her.'

'Hmm,' said Harriet, and I began to sense I was on the home stretch here. Her back straightened up and she was starting to look interested.

'Besides,' I said, really pressing my case. 'Think of what you'd be achieving out there. Bringing clean water to those who need it most. Harriet, to be perfectly honest with you, I can't understand why we're even having this discussion. In your shoes, I'd already be on my way to the airport, dying to start the work. I'd have my flights booked and I'd be off organising a load of malaria and cholera shots. It's a complete no-brainer, if you ask me.'

*

It was almost touching to see how upset Harriet and Freddie had been at this separation. There were plenty of tears and farewell dinners together, and late-night texts from Freddie along the lines of **I'LL MISS YOU SO MUCH!**

But every single time Harriet had a wobble, I was there beside her, with a sympathetic ear, a large bottle of Rescue Remedy and an industrial-size packet of Kleenex.

'You're doing the right thing,' I kept reiterating over and over. 'Wait till you see, this will be the making or the break-ing of you and Freddie.'

With the emphasis on 'the breaking' part of that sentence – though of course, I kept my mouth shut about it.

'It's just so much tougher than I thought it would be,' Harriet kept snivelling. 'Saying goodbye like this.'

'Of course it is, honey,' I'd say soothingly. 'But remember, any fella that isn't prepared to wait for you, really isn't worth the bother at all, is he? Plus I really think this is the real deal. When you think about it, time abroad won't seem all that long if you plan to spend the rest of your lives together now, will it? So come on, refocus. Regroup. Think of why you're getting on that plane in the first place. People's whole lives will change – hell, you'll save lives, because of the wonderful work you'll be doing. How many of us get to say that in their whole lifetime?'

Freddie de Courcey, for his part, seemed genuinely sorry to see Harriet leave too. Yet again, I found myself thinking that this was a real pity, actually. Here was a young couple, deeply fond of each other and who, in spite of all the odds, and the whole world seemingly stacked against them, seemed terribly upset at this forced farewell.

'He says he'll drive me right to the terminal building,' Harriet said sadly, as she clicked off her phone after yet another weepy goodbye with Freddie, even as her bags were packed and she was about to leave for the airport. Then she plonked down on her futon bed, in that grotty little studio flat she'd been living in back then, utterly wiped out from all the emotional drama. 'He says he really wants to.'

'Hey, I'm claiming best friend's rights here,' I'd said cheerily, trying to bounce her back into good spirits. 'I'm the one who gets to do that, remember?' I was taking no chances, even at this late stage, with passports and visas and antiviral shots all done and dusted. I needed to see Harriet physically walk through the departure gates – I needed to witness it with my own two eyes. Just so I could report back to HQ that all was well and that I'd done exactly what I'd been asked to do. And not least, so I could get paid.

By then, the guilt was crippling. It just seemed like a terrible shame, I remember thinking, piling Harriet's tatty-looking rucksack into the boot of an airport taxi. Because maybe this pair could have actually gone the distance, I thought, banging the boot of the car shut and going back into Harriet's flat to hurry her out the door. Maybe, in time, Harriet's charm and guileless innocence would have won over even an old termagant like Ellen de Courcey. Maybe someone like Harriet, so unmaterialistic and unspoilt, so obviously *not* out for what she could get, was actually a better bet for the Freddie de Courceys of this world than a lot of the gilt-edged, high-society heiresses who'd essentially been raised to marry someone like him.

Maybe a whole lot of things.

But then I called my thoughts to order. I'd made my deal with the devil and now I just had to live with it.

'Harriet?' I called in through the hall door. 'Taxi's outside! Come on, what's keeping you? Hurry up, would you? We need to move or you'll miss your flight!'

Anyway, I figured, striding back to the cab and strapping myself into the back seat, it was far too late in the day to start developing a conscience now.

Chapter Twenty-Two

Meg

Yes, Harriet's return is posing a major problem, no question. But I'm still a busy woman with other fish to fry and many, many other important projects on the go, all demanding urgent attention.

Plus, I remind myself, as I power down the street, aside from this unfortunate blip, my run of career success seems to be holding. I've got lots of happy, satisfied clients, for one thing. Senator Katherine Sisk's case is shaping up nicely, thanks very much. I'm on my way into her constituency office this morning, as it happens, secure in the knowledge that at least there I can hold my head up high and congratulate myself on a job that should be resolved soon. I've been hired to remove a problem person out of the Good Lady Senator's life, and aren't I very, very close to doing exactly that? Briskly and efficiently too, long before any media outlet gets wind of it.

I'm actually beginning to make pretty great progress with Denys, too, to remove a colleague from a team he project-manages in work. It's early days, of course, but I've already rushed to reassure Denys that all will be well. That I'm beginning to flex my muscles and am hopeful of having positive news for him very soon. Ditto with Nicole, my puppy-loving new 'friend', who's been seeing someone seriously off limits on the sly, and who I'm being paid handsomely to deal with.

So in spite of Harriet Waters causing major headaches, all in all, I figure, my career is in pretty good shape.

I continue to think that right up until the only phone I have now starts to ring.

I answer immediately.

'Good morning, am I speaking with Miss Meg Monroe?'

A woman's voice, crisp and efficient. Not one I've ever heard before.

'Speaking,' I answer brightly.

'This is Mrs Ellen de Courcey's private secretary speaking. Mrs de Courcey has requested a meeting with you, if you would be so kind. This morning, please.'

'Well, as a matter of fact, I'm not actually available this morning . . .' I try to say, but she barrels right over me.

'Mrs de Courcey is presently at the Marker Hotel in the city centre. She expects to see you within the hour.'

'But I'm on my way to work . . .'

'Within the hour, thank you.'

And like that, she's gone.

Shit, bugger, poo and balls. No prizes for guessing what – or rather who – this is all about. Word has filtered back to her about Harriet being back in town, and now I'm going to be held to account.

I waver on the pavement, the fine art of bilocation ever a dilemma for me. Turn up to work at Katherine Sisk's office to finish what I've started? Or bear in mind that it's only thanks to the de Courceys that I have a roof over my head and a lengthy list of clients to begin with?

It's a no-brainer. I'm playing Pip to the mighty Ellen de Courcey's Magwitch. Like it or not, she's my benefactress and when she clicks her fingers, I have to come running.

With a sizeable knot in my stomach, I hail a passing taxi, jump in and head straight for the Marker Hotel, which, by the way, is situated on Grand Canal Square, in probably the hippest part of town. It's a busy, bustling, wide-open space, with a vibrant, sprawling theatre dominating it, surrounded on all sides by coffee shops, vegan-friendly restaurants and even an organic market that caters to the armies of corporate tech workers who populate the multinational companies dotted around the area. Not for nothing is it known as 'Googleland'.

The Marker is ultra-modern when you get inside, all sharp angles, chrome surfaces, smiley staff and Instagram-ready walls of flowers you can pose for a selfie in front of. I ask for Mrs de Courcey at the hotel's reception desk and am immediately directed up to the hotel spa, which is on the top floor, right beside an outdoor rooftop lounge area. I notice a few lucky guests are already sitting out there, enjoying an early-morning coffee and the luxury of an old-fashioned newspaper in the warm summer sunshine.

Lucky them, I think, as my heart starts to palpitate and tiny beads of worry-sweat break out on my forehead. My hands are clammy, my breath is only coming in jagged bursts, and all I can think is – *fight your corner here. Defend yourself.* It's hardly my fault that Harriet came back, now is it? I can only do what I can do – and I am doing my best here.

I head straight for the spa, where I'm greeted by a stunningly attractive therapist in a neat pinafore that blends in beautifully with the decor.

'Oh yes,' she says, when I tell her who I'm here to see. 'You must be Meg Monroe? We've been expecting you. Let me show you where to go.'

She guides me straight to a private room at the very end of a long, soothingly dark corridor, raps gently at the door, listens out for a muffled response, then ushers me inside with a big bright smile, closing the door firmly behind.

So I'm trapped now, with no escape. It's dark in here, windowless and small, and the only light is from the dozens of twinkly scented candles that are dotted around the therapy room. Low, soothing music plays pan pipes, but try as I might to tune into them, they're certainly not having a relaxing effect on me.

And there she is, the mighty Ellen de Courcey herself, lying prostrate on a therapy bed, covered in towels from head to foot like an Egyptian mummy, with gloopy green paste on her face and two wobbly cucumber slices on her eyes. Odd thing though, instead of looking vulnerable as anyone else would if you found them lying semi-naked on a bed, Mrs de Courcey seems to be as much in command of the room as ever.

'What's that? Who's there?' she demands in that whisper of a voice.

'It's Meg Monroe,' I say, willing myself to stand tall and not be intimidated. And for the love of God, to stop sweating.

Gotta fight my corner. Gotta defend my case here.

'Then come closer, where I can see you,' she orders, sitting up now and slowly peeling the cucumber off her eyes.

A long pause as her eyes readjust to the gloom.

'You must forgive my appearance, Miss Monroe,' she eventually says, with a downward wave at the pile of towels that envelop her. 'My husband and I are hosting a political fundraising event this Friday, quite a large gathering too, and this is the only time I have to prepare. I must look my best, you know.'

Her wheelchair lies empty beside her and there's a spare seat, but I'm categorically not asked to sit down.

I take the bull by the horns.

'Mrs de Courcey, I can guess what this is all about, and I'd just like to reassure you—'

'Oh, but I've had all the reassurances that I can stomach from you, Miss Monroe,' she says waspishly. 'A year ago now, you took great pains to reassure me that my "people problem", as you chose to put it, had been fixed. That a certain undesirable had been removed from my grandson's life. And, most importantly of all, that she was gone for good. "You won't be troubled by this person again" – they were your exact words. I remember it distinctly – you spoke with such brazen confidence. Yet now, I find the situation quite altered. I heard it from Freddie himself. Only yesterday. Oh, it was Harriet this and Harriet that – she's all he can talk about. He's even insisting that . . . this person come with him to the fundraiser.'

'Yes, I'm fully up to speed—' I try to say, but am again interrupted.

'Miss Monroe,' she says, glaring coldly across the room at me. But even in the dim light, I can see the sharpness in her eyes. 'I am most seriously displeased. I hardly need to remind you that you owe me a great personal debt?'

'Yes, I'm well aware of that . . .'

'Not only for the lifestyle you're presently enjoying, but also for most, if not all, of the clients you're currently working with?'

'Of course . . .'

'You do realise that all it takes is a single phone call from me, and you would, quite literally, forfeit most of that client list overnight?'

I nod curtly. Course I bloody realise it, and frankly, I could do without the low-level threats, thanks all the same.

'Then you can guess the rest,' she says breathily. 'Should you wish to retain that client list, I suggest you readdress my problem yet again. Properly, this time. If you really do have the name and reputation of "The Fixer", then you'd better fix this for me, as a matter of urgency. Before this weekend, it goes without saying.'

'But you have to realise, Mrs de Courcey,' I try to say, determined to speak up for myself, 'that Harriet's coming back was as much a surprise to me as it was to you. It's just not going to be possible for me to airbrush her away again in a matter of days . . . these things take time!'

'That will be all, thank you,' Mrs de Courcey says, lying back down again, and putting the cucumber back over her eyes, our interview clearly over.

The door opens without me going near it and there's that smiley therapist, just waiting there, clearly having tuned in from the other side of the door.

'Oh, and one last thing,' Ellen de Courcey says, raising a single index finger just as I'm beating a retreat. 'You are enjoying your present living arrangements, are you not?'

'Yes,' I answer truthfully, 'yes, I am.'

'Wouldn't it be a shame if anything were to alter that cosy arrangement?'

The door shuts behind me. And that's it.

So now it's Wednesday, and I've just been handed a deadline of mere days in which to achieve the bloody impossible.

Chapter Twenty-Three

Meg

I'm striding through Grand Canal Square, my mind in panic mode, as the phone rings.

'Where are you?' a man's voice says.

'Excuse me, who is this?'

'It's Billy.'

'Who?' I repeat, momentarily caught off guard.

'Jesus, Meg, Billy Kingston, who you work with,' he sighs. 'Katherine Sisk's director of elections? Hello? We work together? We were out at *PrimeNews* just last night? Surely you can't have forgotten?'

'Oh, right,' I say, shaking my head, 'yes, *that* Billy. Of course.'

'So why aren't you at work? Remember work? Remember, the election that's happening in less than a week's time? Need I remind you? You're late, and Jess is out doing media all day with Katherine. I've got a meeting with them shortly and it's all hands to the pump here. So where the hell are you?'

'I was unavoidably detained,' I say, thinking on my feet. 'But I promise I'm on my way . . .'

Then another call comes through on my phone.

'I'll call you back, OK?'

'I'd be far happier if I just saw you walking through the door,' Billy says. 'If it's not too much to ask that you do your job? And another thing, just while I have you—'

'What?' I ask impatiently, as a third call comes through on my phone.

'How did you *know*?'

'Know what?'

'Everything you told me about myself last night? Jeez, you even knew that I was just back from holidays and that I'd been south of the equator,' he adds, sounding mystified. 'Are you some kind of part-time psychic, or something?'

'You'll have to excuse me,' I say, clicking off Billy and going straight onto the call that was waiting.

'Meg?' says another man's voice, deep, gruff and to the point. 'It's Denys here. We spoke a few days ago, remember?'

'Yes,' I say brightly. 'I was just about to contact you, actually. I've been doing a considerable amount of online searching this end and I'm very hopeful that . . .'

'I'm calling the whole thing off,' says Denys, as curtly as that.

'Excuse me?'

I have to turn into a doorway to make sure I'm hearing this right.

'You heard me. It's over. I know we arranged to meet later today, but now I'm cancelling.'

'You're cancelling . . .' I splutter, lost for words for once in my life. 'Can I ask why?'

227

'Because I changed my mind. That's why. I'm entitled to change my mind, aren't I?'

I take a second to think. Focus. Clarify my thoughts. Not panic.

'I'm so sorry to hear that,' I say coolly, 'but if there's anything I can do to turn this around, I'd love to know. I've already started to do a lot of preliminary work on your behalf, you know. If there's a problem, then I'd appreciate you telling me.'

'Right then,' Denys sighs deeply. 'You seem like a very professional person, so here it is, for what it's worth.'

I steel myself.

'As you know,' he says, 'your "services", shall we say, came very highly recommended. I won't say from whom, but let's just say I first heard about you from a friend of a friend of an old family friend. And I've just had a message from that particular person giving me some updates that they thought I should be aware of. Very timely too, I'd have said. Particularly before I hand over any money to you. Wouldn't you say?'

I stay nice and calm. I've dealt with wobbly clients before, and have found that a quick tongue and persuasive manner will always win the day.

'If I can just interject . . .' I try to say, but Denys is already ending the call.

'Gotta go. Best of luck in your . . . well, let's just say in your endeavours.'

And like that, he's gone.

Ellen de Courcey. This can only be Ellen de Courcey's doing, flexing her muscles and letting me know exactly what happens to people who cross her. So in the short space of time since I left the Marker Hotel, who else has she got to?

I call Katherine Sisk, currently my biggest client, but, of course, she's out doing media and there's no response.

And my day only gets worse. I arrive at Katherine's office, but everyone's out and I've got the whole place to myself. Getting panicky, I try Katherine's private number, the one only her immediate family and a handful of trusted confidants have, myself included. Again, no response.

Shit, shit, shit . . .

OK, so now I knuckle down to do some serious damage limitation. With no one to breathe down my neck, I text yet another high-profile client and tell her I can slip away to meet her at lunchtime, at our usual place. No choice in the matter, I've gotta keep this one sweet. She's back immediately to confirm.

So at 1 p.m. I make a dash for it while I can.

Caffeine & Co. is jammed and it's tough finding a table, with the lunchtime rush out in force. I do my usual brisk, quick scan around the place, eyes peeled for my client, but there's no sign of her.

None at all.

I check everywhere. Upstairs and downstairs, just to make sure the lady in question isn't sitting shyly in a little corner of the basement, tucked away where no one can see her, ever anxious to be discreet. This particular client is ultra-cautious and always picks this little coffee shop, as it's well away from her local neighbourhood and therefore there's minimal chance of her being spotted.

Well, she's barely even twenty minutes late, I try to console myself, but even as I perch down onto a tiny bockety table for two, there's a cold clutch of fear starting to grip me right in the chest.

I text her yet again – no response. Try calling, but the call is clicked off almost instantaneously.

Fuck. I can take a pretty accurate guess as to exactly what's going on here. This client is never late – ever. Has someone got to her, in the last hour? *Is this actually possible*, I think, beginning to get panicky, as the minutes tick on . . . *am I really being unceremoniously stood up?*

Nor do I have to dig too deep to guess at the reason why. It's yet another clear warning shot from Mrs de Courcey. *You owe your whole livelihood to me, and look! Here's how easily it can be taken away from you*, the old she-devil might as well be saying.

And still no word back from Katherine Sisk. Nada, not a sausage. Do I still have a job there or not? Who knows?

I sit back as the barista clears away the table, utterly lost in thought. When was the last time I'd actually sat still like this? Without my phone-hopping, and my daily round of places to go, people to meet and comeuppances to deliver?

But I can't relax, I can't even allow myself to focus on the bitter unfairness of it all. I'd go nuts if I did. Jesus Christ, it's hardly my fault that Harriet Waters has bounded back into all of our lives again, now is it?

I can't possibly be held responsible, I think, as my mind spins furiously. I'd done exactly what I'd been paid to do regarding Harriet – was I really expected to supply a statute of limitations along with it? It wasn't like I'd signed some class of legally binding document testifying that from here on in, Harriet would not only go away, but stay well away too? Did Ellen de Courcey not realise the skill it took to do what I'd done? The Olympic-sized levels of manipulation and gentle coercion, plus months of building up a relationship with Harriet to earn her trust in the first place.

The more I think about it, the more I'm almost ready to scream in frustration. And now, like it or not, as the café gets increasingly busier all around me, I'll have to do a major bit of damage control and spin, such as I've never done before in my entire career.

I whip the one and only phone I'm down to out of my pocket and call another high-profile client, who I'm due to meet later tonight. The phone is answered on the very first ring, so I deliberately keep my voice low and distinct, reminding myself to stay as businesslike and professional as ever.

'Good afternoon,' I say briskly, 'just to say that I'm actually running ahead of schedule, in case it might suit you to meet that bit earlier? At our usual spot? Or if it's more convenient for you, I could always call over to your house?'

Again, not a phrase I've ever had to use before. Clients come to me, not the other way around. What can I say? I've been in such high demand, that's just the way it has to be. Generally I meet clients wherever and whenever it suits me, and they're all so pleased to get a hold of me at all, they pretty much agree to anything. But this time, there's no response. Just a long-drawn-out sigh, with the noise of dogs yapping loudly in the background.

'Hello?' I say, taking care not to say her name out loud. Not in public anyway. 'Are you still on the line?'

'Oh, I'm still here all right,' comes the flat reply.

'Good, great,' I say, trying to stay bouncy and positive. 'Anyway, I have a lot of updates for you regarding that delicate situation we discussed, and I think you'll be pretty pleased with how it's all shaping up. I've made contact with Nicole via her yoga classes, and am planning to take puppy-training classes with her too. It's early days, of course, but I'm confident that I'll have good news for you imminently.'

'Please don't call me ever again,' my client says as rudely and as dismissively as that, and a second later, she's gone.

Bugger, shit and feck it anyway. This is so much worse than I'd thought. So, so much worse. Jesus Christ, what kind of a number has Ellen de Courcey done on me in the last few hours anyway?

A full twenty minutes pass, as I just sit there, thinking, and tap, tap, tapping a spoon off my coffee mug, counting out beats of frustration. I take my phone out of my pocket for about the twentieth time to check I haven't missed anything.

My phone is my lifeline. My modus operandi. I'd even been so run off my feet, I even had to invest in a second one, the one that's probably sitting on the hall table back at the apartment just now, so my most important clients could get to me immediately. These are people who most definitely do not appreciate being kept waiting. Promptness of service is my hallmark.

Over the past few years, I've become so adept at juggling both mobiles, it's like second nature to me. Frequently, I'm on one phone call, while checking out Twitter updates or fresh Instagram posts from various 'targets' on the other. Rarely do I ever go to check either phone without there being a minimum of a dozen texts, WhatsApp notifications or voice messages, and that's before you factor in all the emails that would be stacked up for me, all demanding urgent attention.

Until now. When there's precisely none. Nada. Zero.

I order another coffee. Feck it, I might as well have a panini to go with it. It's been an age since I actually had time on my hands to eat a lunch.

I sit back, breathe long and hard, and try to remember a time when I was a normal person, living a normal life and doing a normal, ordinary job.

Dear Jesus, I think. Has it come to this? That I'm actually contemplating having to go back to my old way of life again? Are things really *that* bad?

Twenty-four years ago . . .

There once was a little girl who started big school with all of the other little boys and girls her own age, but who, unlike the rest of them, found it – a bit boring, really. Spelling? The alphabet? Seriously, she thought? She was five years of age and had been reading and writing since she was three, thanks very much.

However, this particular little girl was lucky. She had a teacher who, mindful of how intelligent and gifted her young pupil was, bumped her up a class, thinking that would be more challenging for the child. Such a bright little girl, they all said in the staffroom. She'll go on to great things, wait and see.

That's all well and good, Miss Scott, the headmistress, replied crisply, but clearly she gets a lot of help from home. Because how else could a child her age possibly be reading to such an advanced level?

But it only took one family meeting for Miss Scott to correctly assess the lie of the land. Turned out this girl lived with her mother and grandparents in one of the council estates close to the school. Her mum was a separated single parent who worked selling flowers in town and her grandad worked in a butcher shop close by, while her granny stayed home and kept the show on the road. No sign of the girl's father, nor was he even referred to. All Miss Scott could glean was that he was in a new relationship and barely saw his daughter. The child's immediate family seemed loving and united, but at a glance, Miss Scott could see that there was absolutely no home-schooling going on. None of them had the time, apart from anything else.

So Miss Scott kept a special eye out for young Megan, because that was the girl's name, Megan, and when the time came for her to go to secondary school, Miss Scott pulled every string in the book to land the girl a scholarship place at The Academy, a high-end, high-achieving boarding school, where the fees were roughly equivalent to a cripplingly high interest rate mortgage, on a five-bedroomed property in the swishest part of town.

So off young Megan went, twelve years of age, in a too-big uniform that scratched and made her skin itch, to a part of the country she wasn't familiar with, to sink or swim in her scary new school. At a single glance, however, she knew she'd have to adapt or die. Her accent, for one thing, would have to go. The other kids were posh, worldly, talked about skiing trips and trust funds and winters in Antigua. Megan knew she couldn't compete, so didn't even bother trying. Instead, she kept herself to herself and learned to watch. She developed a brand-new skill: acute observation. At a glance, she'd be able to tell what her classmates had for breakfast, whether they'd heard from home recently or what they were planning to do after lessons.

There was nothing to it, really. All Megan needed to do was look a little closer, and listen carefully, not to what her classmates were saying, which, by and large, was innocuous rubbish, but to what they weren't saying, which was infinitely more interesting.

Over time, it became like her party piece. 'Megan! Megan!' the kids in her class would clamour. 'Take a look at Hugo and tell us everything!'

The whole room would go deadly quiet and all eyes would turn her way.

'Only child,' Megan would tell the room, as Hugo looked on, bemused and delighted with himself. 'Asthmatic. Plays rugby, but hates it and would far rather join the school debating team instead.'

'But . . . but how did you *know*?' Hugo asked, as Megan took a rambunctious round of applause from the common room.

Her friends were many, because Megan was a girl who was funny and quick-witted; the kind of kid who sat quietly at the back of the class, saying and doing nothing to attract attention to herself, then, at the perfect moment, would lob in a witty, insightful comment that would have the entire class in stitches.

Over time, even the posh kids, the ones with trust funds and holiday homes in Marbella, came to accept Megan as one of their own. But by then, Megan had learned one of the two most valuable lessons school had to teach her. First, it didn't matter where you came from; all that really mattered was how well you got on with people. And the best way to make friends and influence people was a doddle; all you had to do was be whomever they wanted you to be.

With the sporty gang, you were athletic. With the nerds, you carried comics around with you and quoted reams from obscure TV shows with virtually no viewers. With the drama queens, it was easier still; you just had to learn to laugh at yourself when asked to play the rear end of the panto horse in a school play. But the first time Megan got the train home for the school holidays and spotted her grandad standing proudly on the platform waiting to collect her, she quickly realised her most important role play of all.

'Listen to you, love,' her grandad said, as he picked up Megan's suitcases and walked her to the car park where his butcher's van was waiting. 'And your fancy new accent! Since when did you start talking posher than the Queen?'

In a flash, Megan knew the best thing by far was to drop her classy new accent and go back to speaking just the way her family did.

As time went on, she became expert at it, like a chameleon. No matter where you dropped her, she'd blend right in; she'd look the part, sound the part, be whoever she was required to be.

At school, Megan was popular and thriving, with just one black spot on the horizon, as far as she was concerned. One Christmas, when she was about seventeen, she came home for the holidays, as usual. But this time her grandad wasn't there to meet her off the train, as he usually was, standing tall and proud. He used to even take off his butcher's apron, so Megan wouldn't be embarrassed by him in front of her posh friends, whose parents all seemed to drive BMWs and the newest, most top-of-the-range Mercedes.

Megan eventually realised she wasn't being met at the station at all and had to take two buses home, dragging her luggage behind her.

'Grandad hasn't been too well lately,' her mum told her, when she eventually did get home. 'Nothing to worry about, but we're just keeping a careful eye on him, that's all.'

'Not too well' was a careful understatement though; Megan actually got a shock when she saw how thin and pale her grandad had got. Nor was there any sign of him getting better; he couldn't hold down food, and in a scary amount of time, he was a shadow of the formerly robust, fit, healthy man he'd always been.

His boss at the butcher's called to the house over the holiday with a hamper for the family and a bottle of whiskey for Grandad, but quietly, well out of earshot, he told Megan's mum and granny that really, the best thing for Grandad would be to take a bit of time off work, for the foreseeable future.

'He needs to see the best consultant you can afford,' he said. 'My own mother passed away from cancer, and she started just like this, you know. Early detection is so important – the sooner you get him to a good oncologist, the better. Trust me on that.'

There it was. The C-word. The one neither Megan nor any of her family had wanted to hear.

'We'll get through Christmas,' Megan's mum had said worriedly, 'then we'll get him to a good doctor and take it from there.'

But by Megan's Easter holidays, things had got so much worse. 'A particularly aggressive form of pancreatic cancer,' the consultant had diagnosed. 'We can set up a home care package for you for now, but long term, it's going to be very difficult to look after him at home. You really need to start looking at nursing home options. Which can be very costly, I know.'

'He's staying at home with us, where he's happy and where he belongs,' Megan's mum told him tartly, blinking back her tears, and that was the end of that.

But by that summer, Megan could see the toll it was taking on her mother and Nan, who, in spite of their best efforts, just weren't able to manage the full-time care of a very poorly seventy-five-year-old man who needed help with everything.

When Megan came to her final year at The Academy, she aced all of her mock exams ahead of her Leaving Cert. Great things were expected of her from her teachers, and her dream was to get the grades she needed to do law at college. Not just 'good enough' grades, though; Megan was chasing after a scholarship, so only top marks were acceptable.

'But if anyone can do it,' her school principal told her proudly, 'I'm confident that you can. And, of course, I'll be sure to write a warm letter of recommendation on your behalf. All you need do is work and study harder than you ever have in your whole life before.'

Which is exactly what Megan did, even as the whole axis of her warm, stable family life seemed to be shifting from underneath her. A nursing home now seemed like the kindest and most humane option for her grandad, who'd got to the point where he needed round-the-clock medical care.

'It costs a fortune,' Megan's mum took pains to explain to her. 'Literally, the price of a house, which we don't have. I'll have to keep working every hour I can get, but . . .'

It was all in that 'but'.

That 'but' meant that Megan had to start pulling her weight too. Which meant a job the summer after she finished school, while all her schoolmates went off celebrating to the sunny beaches of Mykonos and Magaluf.

She'd smile and grit her teeth and tell her school pals to 'have a great night, enjoy!' as they all went partying, while she stuck on a Smiley Burger apron and went to work in a cheesy 1950s diner; one of those places that played Elvis Presley and Buddy Holly on a permanent loop and that made her hair and skin stink of fried onions and garlic. To this day, Meg could still remember the acute humiliation of it. To her, onions and garlic smelt of poverty and mortification.

Worse still was when a few of her schoolmates actually came into Smiley Burger, intending nothing more than to see their pal Meg and catch up with all her news. As bad luck would have it though, Meg had been stuck on toilet duty that day and had never been so embarrassed as she was when her pals caught her in a horrible uniform with a mop and bucket, slopping Jeyes Fluid all over the gents' floor.

They'd even left a tip for her – Meg's manager handed her a crisp fifty note as soon as she was finishing up for the night.

'Must have money to burn, those pals of yours,' he'd shrugged, handing over the dosh.

Meg should have been touched; she knew her friends meant only to be kind. But this felt like charity and instead of being pleased, she felt nothing, only the deepest, acutest shame.

Her school friends all had the luxury of taking gap years to South America and Interrailing trips all across Europe, but there were no such privileges for Meg. Instead, it was straight to work for her in a job at the Sloan Curtis legal firm. It was a lowly, menial job, granted; basically, she was required to do nothing more than make coffee, answer phones, be the general office dogsbody and the butt of a lot of the senior partners' jokes – all of whom were predominately male, middle-aged and boring as shit, by the way.

But Meg needed to work, her family needed the salary she was bringing in and that was all there was to it. As her own mother often reminded her, 'Sure what have you got to complain about? Aren't you working in a nice warm office with fancy coffee machines and lunch breaks? It's an upgrade from the diner, isn't it? You try selling flowers on the street in all weathers, then you'd know all about a hard day's work, missy.'

So, Meg did what she always did. She plastered on her biggest, fakest grin, while her mind stayed ice-cold. *One day, I'll have all the money in the world*, she faithfully promised herself. *My family will be well taken care of and I'll be able to do whatever I want, whenever I want.*

She stayed at Sloan Curtis, worked hard and kept her head down and thought of her grandad. She thought of him every single time one of the legal interns, who seemed not to have a quarter of her intelligence, talked down to her or patronised her or came out with a sexist comment like, 'What's a nice-looking girl like you doing wasting away in an office like this? You could audition for *Love Island*, if you liked.'

She thought of her grandad every time she'd stand quietly at the back of the boardroom, laying out bottles of fizzy and still water, while meetings happened over her head. Frequently, she'd hear complex legal problems being discussed which she could see a way out of, clear as day, when no one else in the room could.

Every week without fail, Megan handed her pay cheque over to her mum, then went to visit her grandad, telling him that everything was hunky-dory at home, that they were all fine, thanks very much. 'We just want you to get well and come home to us,' she'd say.

But her grandad was too ill even to take in what she was saying. The cancer had spread by then, to the point where it was painful for the poor man to speak. All Megan could do was hold onto his bony, cold hand and think of her exam finals and the results that were due any day now. She knew she'd done well, but the bar was set high for her if she was to get the scholarship to college that she was counting on. So she let all the overpaid, overprivileged legal heads at Sloan Curtis talk down to her and pat her on the head and ask her what nightclub she was planning to go to when the results came in, and wouldn't it be wonderful if she got into a night course to study beauty therapy or something?

You wait, she thought, her mind focused and clear. *You just wait and see.*

She aced her exams. A phenomenal result. One of the top marks ever achieved in her school. Her principal and year head were thrilled and Megan was the envy of all her friends. A meeting was hastily set up for her with the university interview board to pitch her case for a scholarship; the only possible way that Megan could ever have afforded four years of full-time education.

But life had other plans for Megan.

'You've already got a perfectly good job at that law office,' her mum said, out of her mind with worry and exhaustion. 'Sure what use is college to you? We need you out earning – badly. You can't give up the kind of money you're making at that office to flounce off and be a student for four years. I'm sorry, Megan, but it's out of the question. Scholarship or no scholarship. Your grandad's more important than any poxy law degree, isn't he?'

She was right, of course, but still, for Megan, it was like all her hopes were instantaneously crushed and all her dreams of a better life sent clean out the window. The day of her scholarship interview, she took a rare sick day from work and spent the entire day sitting quietly on a bench by the sea, just staring out at the ships going by. Her mobile rang non-stop, with half her school, not to mention the principal, all wanting to know how the big interview went. Even the university rang, wanting to know had something happened to her? Why hadn't she turned up?

But Megan ignored every single call.

Not now, she thought. *It's not my time right now.*

But, by Jesus, one day it would be.

Chapter Twenty-Four

Harriet

'There's something very weird going on with my friend Meg. I mean, like, really, *seriously* weird.'

'Really? Is that right?'

Harriet is with Freddie. Really, actually, properly with him. Like a proper couple again. Almost. Sort of. At least, that's what she's starting to think. A bit. Maybe.

He'd called her earlier in the day and asked to meet up that same evening, and she, of course, presumed he meant for a drink or a bite to eat, as they had done so many times, back in the day. But Freddie, she knew of old, was not a man you could second-guess. Once he'd asked her to lunch and it turned out he'd meant at a fancy restaurant called Maxim's in Paris. Actual *Paris*.

'And I was only in my runners and a hoodie!' she'd wailed down the phone to her mam afterwards.

There had been a private plane and everything, with just the two of them on board and one, lone flight attendant, who Harriet had felt so sorry for, she'd spent the whole flight including him in their conversation, then of course, inviting him to join her and Freddie for the gorgeous lunch that was laid on at Maxim's. The minute she found out said flight attendant was gay, she'd even promised to set him up on a date with another guy she knew who was always in and out of Dead Old Lady Dresses, and who she knew for a fact was looking for someone to use a spare ticket he had for *Kinky Boots*.

'I love that about you,' Freddie had smiled at her at the time. 'I love that you really do care about other people. I've seen so many women, friends of my grandmother's, you know, on the old charity circuit, who don't give a fiddler's about the actual cause they're meant to be fundraising for. All they really want is to have a night out at some charity auction or other, so they can virtue-signal. You're so different, though. You can't pass someone homeless on the street without buying them a sandwich and a coffee. Never change, Harriet Waters, do you hear me? Never, ever change.'

This particular day, however, Freddie had called her out of the blue and said, 'Do you fancy going for a walk later on? Be so lovely to see you and just chat. Wouldn't it?'

While Harriet was delighted, she was a bit surprised that Freddie wanted to go out walking at seven in the evening. It was even odder still that he wanted to meet at Buckley Park, which was way out in the suburbs.

'But won't the park be closed?' she'd asked him worriedly.

'No, no, golly, no, not at all, that won't be a problem,' Freddie had said, tripping over his words, the way he did. 'You'll like it. In fact, you'll love it. See you later – can't wait to take you for a proper night out, it'll be such fun!'

Harriet dearly wished Meg had been around, so they could have picked it all over together, but there was no sign of her. *Well, she's got to be busy*, Harriet assumed. *I'll catch up with her later on*, she thought, *when she finishes up work for the evening.* Mind you, given how flat out Meg was with that new job of hers in waste management, she mightn't be back till all hours.

But then, something even stranger happened. In the middle of the afternoon, way earlier than she was usually home, Meg let herself into the apartment, looking ashen and white-faced and as quiet as a mouse. Not like her normal, high-octane self at all. Harriet could barely get two words out of her.

'Are you all right, hon?' she asked worriedly.

'Hmmm,' was the only muttered reply she got though, as Meg came into the flat, grabbed the phone she'd left behind, kicked off her shoes and padded straight into her bedroom. No hello, no how are you, nothing.

'You're home so early!' Harriet said. 'I didn't expect you back for hours.'

No response.

'Would you like to eat something? I was just going to run down for a few messages. I could rustle us up a grand little vegan curry?'

'No thanks.'

'Are you sure?' Harriet persisted. 'They have a special offer on vegan food in Aldi?'

But Meg just shook her head.

'Meg? Are you OK? You're very quiet.'

'I'm OK,' she muttered. 'Just going to lie down for a bit.'

'You feeling all right?'

'Hmm.'

'Because if you're not, I could do you one of my dad's special home punches to cure you? All I need is two paracetamol and a drop of whiskey.'

'No thanks,' said Meg. 'I just need . . . to think for a while, that's all.'

And with that, Meg had closed her bedroom door firmly behind her and pretty much stayed holed up there.

Well, the poor girl is shattered tired, Harriet thought. No harm for her to have some time out and a bit of a nap.

By the time Harriet needed to think about leaving, Meg still hadn't surfaced from her room. Not only that, but when Harriet gently rapped on her bedroom door, there was no response at all. Nothing. Not a single sound. Not even the smells of a delicious Aldi curry could rouse her out of there.

Very, very strange, she thought. I mean, who wouldn't want a lovely microwaved curry fresh out of Aldi?

But Harriet had a date to keep, so with a spring in her step, she let herself out of the apartment, glued to a Google App on her phone to help her find this Buckley Park place, wherever the hell it was.

*

Turns out, she realises a very long bus ride later, that it's actually a huge greyhound racing track, and when she gets inside, there is Freddie right inside the entrance gates waiting for her, dressed head to toe in a slightly crumpled work suit, with his red hair blowing upwards in the wind.

'Wow, this is so not what I expected!' Harriet says, as she looks around in awe. 'I've never been racing before – this is amazing!'

'Oh, it's the best fun imaginable,' says Freddie, bending down to kiss her lightly on the cheek. 'I hoped you'd like it – it's something different, anyway. Bit of fresh air, bit of a stroll, all pretty great, really, isn't it?'

Harriet smiles, but then that's one of the cutest things about Freddie, and one of his characteristics that makes him so easy to like; that boyish enthusiasm he has for absolutely anything and everything. Nothing ever seems to get jaded for Freddie, and it's just so endearing. They stroll into the arena, where it's packed to capacity, with punters jostling to get the best seat at the parade ring, while bookies cluster in another ring, all touting for business and shouting out the various odds on dogs with names like A Sky Full of Stars and Jumping Jack Flash.

It's only when Freddie hands her over a form sheet that the reality begins to dawn on Harriet.

The de Courcey Stakes, is the name of the championship race. There it is, printed in bold black and white.

'Oh, sweet Jesus, Freddie,' says Harriet, 'you never told me this was some posh work thing for you! And lookit, I'm only in my jeans and a jumper.'

'Oh, that's absolutely OK,' he insists politely, 'I promise, tonight's nothing formal at all – really, trust me. It's just some old sponsorship thingy, you know how it is. All I need do is be here, hand over some old trophy, pose for a few photos, all terribly boring. Much more interesting catching up with you, don't you think?'

Yes indeed, Harriet thinks, smiling happily. Because this is just like old times. It's as if, after a full year apart, she and Freddie have managed to pick up the threads of their relationship exactly where they'd left off. All the warmth, the friendly banter and the affection that used to be between them still seems to be there. It's wonderful, she thinks. It is a kind of little miracle, and every time Freddie shares a joke with her, or tells her a funny story about the day, or asks after her family, it really does gladden her heart.

The only time Harriet gets a teeny bit wobbly is when Freddie guides her up to a corporate hospitality suite on the very top floor of the stadium grounds. Heavy double doors lead into a private function room with a discreet sign outside that reads, 'DE COURCEY ENTERPRISES. STRICTLY BY INVITATION ONLY.'

'It's no one scary,' he rushes to assure her, clocking how uncomfortable she's suddenly become. 'None of my family are here. Just work people, all quite boring, if I'm being perfectly honest.'

One peek inside the door, however, and Harriet knows she'll be like a fish out of water in there. All the de Courcey guests are assembled inside for a huge, full-on shindig, with a free-flowing bar in full swing and a groaning buffet on offer, as wait staff discreetly circle the room with loaded champagne flutes on silver trays.

'Oh Jeez, Freddie, look at those women, would you?' she hisses at him. 'They're like some kind of Charlotte Tilbury-ed army! They're all in heels, and here's me in an old pair of hiking boots. I've never seen so many curly blow-dries under the one roof.'

'Not a problem,' Freddie smiles. 'Curly blow-dries be damned, eh? Just let me say a few lightning-quick words and I'll be straight back to you, OK?'

Harriet waits just inside the door, watching Freddie as he strides across the room, shaking a few hands en route, as every eye gravitates towards him. He beams at the room, runs his fingers through that shock of red hair and waves for a tiny bit of quiet so he can do his thing.

'So sorry to interrupt the old bun fight,' he grins cheekily. 'Just wanted to say, emm, well, thank you all for coming. Enjoy the races. And if I were you lot, I'd stock up on the free booze while you can, because the bar closes at 10 p.m.! So carry on, everyone – and if any of you have a half-decent tip for the Championship hurdle, I'd very much love to hear it.'

There is a polite ripple of applause, and Harriet notices more than a few puzzled looks. She even overhears one WAG saying, 'Is that it? Is that the sum total of his speech?'

'All right then,' says Freddie, bounding straight back over to Harriet, all beaming bonhomie and good humour. 'So that's the boring old official bit done. How about you and me go for a stroll and see if we can win a few quid while we're at it, eh?'

'Don't you need to stay?' she asks him worriedly. 'Don't you need to mingle and talk to people?'

'There's only one person I want to talk to and that's you,' he says, with a defiant shake of his head. 'Besides, as long as the free grub holds out, that lot will be happy, trust me. So, come on, what do you say we go down to the tote and stick a few of the old readies on some mutt we like the look of?'

So that's what they do. For the next hour, they wander in and out among the rest of the punters, chatting and laughing, easy and relaxed in each other's company. Just as they'd always been. They try to watch one or two races, but they're just over so fast, Harriet finds it impossible to see much more than a line of four-legged blurry shapes crossing the finishing line. Freddie even buys the two of them kebabs from a catering truck that has been set up not far from the parade ring, so they grab seats at the back of the grandstand, eating and talking and trying not to let hot chilli sauce dribble all over themselves.

'So, tell me how long you're in town for?' he asks her, in between big mouthfuls of the kebab.

'Well, Mam and Dad are still in New York,' Harriet smiles back. 'But they're home tomorrow, so we'll have a family reunion then, and the twins are having their stag night on Saturday, so that'll be brilliant fun. I'm dying to see them all again, as you can imagine.'

'And how are your brothers?' Freddie grins. 'As mad as ever?'

'Worse,' she says, with an eye roll.

'And your parents are going to the stag night too?'

Harriet nods, with her mouth full.

'Well, certainly at the dinner part before it,' she says, wiping sauce off the side of her mouth. 'The soakage bit, as the boys are calling it. Dad says the chances are good he'll end up having to bail the twins out of a prison cell the next day, so he might as well be close at hand to get it over with.'

'It'll be some wedding,' Freddie whistles. 'Golly. I hope the brides-to-be are all geared up for it too?'

'Well, according to Mam,' Harriet says, 'Sofia and Alisha are going to drive her to distraction before the big day. They're two lovely women, don't get me wrong, but there is a whole lot of talk about whether the toilet rolls at the reception exactly match the shade of peach the bridesmaids are wearing.'

'Really? Is that so?' says Freddie, looking bewildered that there were people out there who actually thought like that.

'I've just come back from Kenya,' says Harriet, 'where the toilets are basically a hole in the ground. And that's if you're lucky. I just can't wrap my head around the whole concept of coloured toilet roll. Did you ever?'

'It must be something of a culture shock for you,' Freddie nods understandingly.

'So that's why it's been great being able to stay with Meg,' Harriet adds. 'She was always such a good pal to me.'

'Yes, indeed. I remember.'

'Even though . . .'

'Even though what?'

Even though she was certainly less than welcoming when I first arrived, Harriet wants to say, except that it sounds a bit disloyal.

'Is Meg quite well?' Freddie asks.

This time Harriet just shakes her head.

'No,' she says, looking straight ahead to where punters are clustered expectantly around a trophy stand, as the results of one of the big races are announced. 'No, I don't think she is, really.'

'What's the matter with her?' Freddie asks, 'she's not ill, I hope?'

'No, nothing like that,' Harriet says, thinking aloud as she stares straight ahead at the racetrack. 'But I do think she's in way over her head with something.'

'How do you mean?'

'Well, take that ridiculous apartment, for one thing. I mean, Meg claims she has a great job and that she works all hours, but no one our age lives like that – *no* one. And her job doesn't match up, either. Do you know, I went to call her office, and it turns out the company doesn't even exist?'

'Really? So what does she do all day?'

'It's a mystery,' says Harriet. 'She's out day and night and yet she lies about her job. But then, why would she lie to me? I'm her friend, I'm on her side no matter what she's got caught up in.'

Drug, dealing, Harriet had thought at one point, but then abandoned the thought. No. Whatever is going on with Meg, it's certainly nothing like that. Harriet knows for a fact that she hates needles, for starters. The girl doesn't even smoke, for God's sake. Then there are all those weird-looking charts and Post-it notes that completely clutter up Meg's desk at the flat, which she'd stumbled across. All those names and dates and appointments – even Senator Katherine Sisk's name was there, for God's sake. What was that all about?

'Then today,' Harriet goes on, 'Meg came home early from work, which she never does, and she took straight to her bed. And that's it: I haven't had two words out of her since.'

'So Meg's job doesn't seem to exist, and yet she's living the life of Reilly?' Freddie says. 'Blimey. How strange.'

'I know,' Harriet sighs. 'My guess is that she got way in over her head with debt and now it's all piling up on top of her. She's been living well beyond her means for a long time now – for the last year, it seems. And you'd want to see some of the stuff she has – sure it's all worth a fortune.'

Harriet thinks back to all the trappings of wealth just lying around that flat, and her mind boggles at the sheer scale of it. The boxes and boxes of parcels that seem to stream into the flat for Meg on a daily basis. The designer clothes, the LK Bennett shoes, the handbags with labels and logos plastered all over them. The expensive paintings that are dotted throughout the apartment – it seem as though Meg is really living the high life and spending like there's no tomorrow.

And now it has all come crashing down on top of her.

'Well, perhaps there's something I can do to help,' Freddie says thoughtfully.

'What's that?'

'We've got a wonderful family solicitor's firm who deal in debt management and restructuring. I could set up an appointment for you to pop into them and have a chat, if you like?'

'But . . . wouldn't that be going behind Meg's back?' Harriet says doubtfully.

'It would be entirely confidential, of course,' says Freddie. 'Just tell them you're concerned about your friend and maybe get a few suggestions on how to help, that's all. You could chat to the lawyers about debt resolution and what's possible. So when Meg feels ready to tell you, you'll have a much clearer idea of what can be done to help get her out of . . . well, whatever it is that she's got herself into.'

'It's a lovely offer . . .' Harriet begins to say, but just then, right under her nose, she starts to notice something. Down at the winner's podium on the stands below, the crowd has started slow handclapping, as if they are waiting for something or someone, and are beginning to get a bit fed up. The clapping filters right the way back to where she and Freddie are sitting – when suddenly Freddie jolts straight up, as if there is something very, very important he's only just remembered.

'Oh, golly gosh!' he says, slapping his hand off his forehead. 'That's me they're waiting for. Oh, I'm such an idiot!' He's up and already on his way. 'Just got to present the old trophy to the winner, you know how it is. Stay right where you are, I'll just be a sec!'

In a couple of long, athletic bounds, he's already at the bottom of the steps that lead down from the grandstand to the parade ring. Harriet watches the top of his bright red head fondly as he works his way through the crowds and onto the winner's podium, to hand over a trophy to an owner and trainer who's been patiently waiting for him.

The whole evening has turned out to be absolutely lovely, she thinks, hugging her knees in close to her with a little smile. Freddie seems utterly unchanged; the same adorably scatty, all-over-the-place Freddie, but with an absolute heart of gold. Tim Nice-But-Dim, her brothers call him, and although it's a bit mean, she knows it's a nickname that they've bestowed affectionately.

I'm so glad I came home when I did, she thinks, pulling her jumper tightly around her, as the night grows cooler. It feels right, on every level. The only blight on an otherwise sunny horizon is the worry over Meg.

'Just want to say, well done on winning the champion-ship race,' Freddie's voice comes back to her, via the park's deafening, whistling PA system, as he hands over a trophy that is almost the same size as himself to the winner. 'And now, here's a fine bit of tin for your sideboard, so you can show off to all your friends. Right you be, well, enjoy the rest of the evening and see you later!' he says cheerily, before bounding off the winner's stand and making his way back to where Harriet sits waiting.

Harriet's mind drifts a bit, as she thinks some more about the generous offer Freddie has just made to her. Why not do as he suggested? Why not meet with this solicitor's firm and see what can be done to help Meg?

Harriet's whole career has been devoted to helping others. *But sure what use is that*, she thinks, *if I can't help my very best friend?*

Chapter Twenty-Five

Meg

6.30 p.m.

I hear the door close as Harriet *finally* leaves. Not allowing myself to worry about where she's going or who she's seeing, I slump back against the pillows, as my head starts to pound.

Look at me, I think. In bed. In the daytime. As the sunlight streams in on top of me, my temper flares. I've never been unemployed in the whole course of my life. Not once, not ever. As a teenager, I'd slogged and sweated in that stinking burger joint, and went straight from there to working at Sloan Curtis. Then of course, out of a clear blue sky, my golden chance presented itself. The opportunity to work for myself for a change, because, after all, I found I was a far fairer and more amenable boss than anyone I'd worked for up till then. Lovely, beautiful money, undreamt-of sums, had begun to roll in, and from that day to this, I was doing something I enjoyed, something I was good at. And I've never looked back. Haven't the time.

What I do is for the good of all concerned, I remind myself every single day. Like a mantra, like a form of meditation.

I'm actually performing a sort of public service. In the long run, what I do is always, always for the best.

So is it fair that with the merest click of Ellen de Courcey's fingers, I lose some of my juiciest and most high-profile clients? And she thinks she can threaten me out of this flat, where I've lived in peace for a full year now? Because if that's the way it is, then I'm not bloody well having it. Not for one second will I allow myself to be airbrushed out of existence so abruptly.

Well, certainly not without a fight.

This is just a hiccup, I tell myself, sitting bolt upright up in bed and feeling some of my energy beginning to fizz back. It's temporary and it, too, will pass.

OK, so now, Ellen is effectively blackballing me among some of her well-heeled friends and contacts. But surely there are other clients out there who'll approach me independently of Ellen de Courcey?

Her party is this Friday, so I've got a shot. If I can just sort out the Harriet situation, then I'll be back on track by Monday. Of course, it's an impossibly tight deadline to deal with, but deal with it I will. I've done the impossible before, and I will again. Watch me.

I retrieve my phones from the bedside drawer I'd shoved them in when I first got home, and my mood brightens further. The Katherine Sisk case seems to be ongoing – thankfully. Not only has the Good Lady Senator *not* called to cancel, quite the contrary. In fact, judging from the flurry of texts and voice messages I've had from her in the last hour, she actually seems pleased with the way I'm slowly steering her case towards a satisfactory resolution for all concerned.

I finally get to speak to Katherine and grab the bull by the horns.

'So . . . you and me are OK?' I ask tentatively, wondering if Ellen de Courcey has done a number on me behind my back, and if so, exactly how much damage she has done?

Katherine is both direct and to the point, speaking good and low, so there's no danger of her being overheard.

'If you're referring to our . . . mutual acquaintance – then you don't need to be concerned,' she says, which is music to my ears.

I have a pre-prepared little sound bite all ready to go.

'This particular person,' I say, 'appears to have put word out concerning an unforeseen twist in her case, which, of course, I'm working around the clock to rectify . . .'

'Yes,' says Katherine. 'She certainly did. The lady in question is one of our biggest political fundraisers, you know, and while ordinarily I would pay attention to her, in this case, I'm very happy with your progress, Meg. I'm happy for our arrangement to proceed as planned.'

Bingo. Katherine has to rush off the phone then, but here at least, I know I'm safe and my gig is secure. But still, I need more work, more clients, more, more, more.

The rug may have been pulled from under me temporarily, but that doesn't mean I don't have the street smarts to haul myself back on top again. Onwards. Like a shark, I just need to keep moving onwards.

With a spring in my step and feeling far more invigorated, I jump out of bed, stride through the living room and make straight for my desk, firing up my computer and avidly scrolling down through a clatter of emails I barely had time to glance at earlier.

It's in here somewhere, I think, furiously reading and scrolling and clicking. The solution to everything. Just a few fresh clients who can get me back on track again. Back on track and back on top.

It doesn't even take me that long, really. Scrolling down through the dozens of emails that I've been ignoring for so long is hearteningly reassuring. There's still a strong demand out there for my services. Maybe not clients who'd be able to pay the kind of fees I've been used to, but still. Work is work and money is money.

Some of the cases here I instantly dismiss as being too low-budget for me, viz: *'Help! My boyfriend is back with his ex, can you make her go away? I'm still in college, but I'm working in a supermarket part-time, and I'm afraid I can't afford to pay you very much . . .'*

Next, I think coldly, still scrolling down.

Other cases I dismiss as being too uninteresting, because being brutally honest about it, I still have my own professional standards to think of, thanks very much.

'Dear Meg, I'm seventy-nine years of age and I'm writing to you about my young next-door neighbour-from-hell, who's in the habit of having late-night parties several nights a week and whose drunken friends are constantly throwing empty beer cans and cigarette butts into my front garden. It's too disgusting for words, especially seeing as my roses have won two rosettes and one trophy in the annual parish flower show. Can you please make this neighbour go away? Now, as I'm

an old-age pensioner, I couldn't afford to pay very much, but maybe you do reductions for the over seventy-fives? I would of course include you in my daily prayers and novenas.'

Next, I think, getting up and taking a cool bottle of sparkling water from the fridge, snapping it open and gulping it back.

Something jammy is what I need here. Challenging. Lucrative. And, above all, with a client who has the power to recommend my services to their other affluent friends and colleagues. Word of mouth is my best friend. And good word of mouth is like oxygen to me.

I sit back down, scroll through some more emails – and then finally my eye falls on something that piques my interest. I go back and forth over the email to be certain, before making up my mind. Then I pick up the phone and dial the contact number that's been given.

'Hi there,' I say crisply, 'am I speaking with Raymond Sandros? Good evening to you. My name is Meg Monroe and I'm calling in connection with an email you sent me—'

I break off there, to double-check the date on the screen in front of me. 'Some two months ago,' I add. 'Forgive my tardiness in getting back to you, but, as you can appreciate, there's high demand for my services.'

'Right, I see, OK,' says this Raymond Sandros, speaking good and low, as if he's anxious not to be overheard. 'Well, thank you for responding, Meg. You were recommended to me by a close friend of my mother's, and yes, I'm at my wits' end here. So if you wanted me to talk you through the problem—'

'Not over the phone,' I reply briskly, knowing I'd get far more information in person. 'Let's meet up and you can tell me everything then. How's first thing tomorrow for you? Maybe breakfast at 8 a.m.? That good for you?'

'It certainly is,' Raymond says, sounding deeply grateful, like someone is finally listening to him. 'Name the place and I'll be there.'

A huge surge of relief washes over me. Meg Monroe is back and calling the shots.

'And one more thing . . .'

'Yes?' I ask politely.

'Thank you. I'm glad you got back to me. Hearing from you is probably the best thing that's happened to me all day.'

'Not a problem,' I smile, genuinely touched. 'And don't worry, from here on in, I can promise you, everything is going to be so much easier.'

You see, I think, closing my laptop, sitting back against the desk chair and feeling pretty pleased with myself, actually. *It'll take a lot more than Ellen de Courcey to put me out of business.*

I take another sip of water, then think, to hell with this. So I go back to the fridge, take out a snipe of champagne that's been sitting there for months, open it and treat myself to a glass.

Why the feck not? Because I'm celebrating. Tonight, I'm celebrating me.

Chapter Twenty-Six

Harriet

It has been such a magical evening, Harriet thinks, as the night's racing finally comes to a close and she and Freddie stroll out of the park grounds together, completely caught up in the swell of the crowds.

'Don't suppose you fancy a little nightcap?' Freddie asks her, with a big, boyish grin. 'I mean, the night is still but a pup. Why not, eh?'

'I'd love that,' she says. 'Because, as it happens, I'd really love to talk to you about your kind offer to help Meg. Do you think there's someone at your family solicitors who I could have a chat with tomorrow? Someone who might be able to advise me on how best to help Meg? It goes without saying, I'm not looking for any special favours here,' she adds hastily. 'All I'm trying to do is buy poor old Meg a bit of time. She's my friend and she's in trouble and she needs help.'

'Of course, dearest one, that's not a problem at all,' he says affably.

Dear God, Harriet thinks fondly. Jack and Terry would make mincemeat of him for coming out with a public schoolboy phrase like 'dearest one'. Was that really what they taught you at those schools that charged about twenty grand a term?

With that, Freddie whips out his phone and scrolls down through his contacts. 'I'm delighted to be able to help. Our solicitors will definitely be able to do something, I'll warrant. Jolly nice people too. They've got me out of more than a few scrapes in my time, I can tell you.'

He shares the contact with Harriet and she saves the number, resolving to chase it up first thing in the morning.

'Thank you so much, I really appreciate this—' she tries to say, but then Freddie slips his arm around her waist and pulls her in a little tighter to him.

'Just in case I forget to tell you, Harriet,' he says, leaning in just a little bit closer to her, 'I've had a wonderful time with you this evening. I so enjoy spending time with you.'

'Oh . . . that's so lovely . . .' she says, taken off guard a bit. But still. Pleased to hear it. More than pleased.

'You always make me feel so good about myself,' he goes on. 'And you never talk down to me. Golly, you'd be amazed at the number of people who do. Absolutely amazed.'

'Is that right?' she says and this time, there is no mistaking it. Freddie is definitely moving in closer to her.

'I've thought of you so much in the last year, you know. I often wondered how you were getting on out in Africa, working with . . . water and . . . latrines . . . and so forth.'

Harriet wants to say, so did I. She wants to say I thought about you when I was out there too. She could have done without the latrine reference, but other than that, she and Freddie are very much on the same page.

But then he kisses her lightly, and everything else that has been on the tip of her tongue goes clean out of her head.

THURSDAY

Chapter Twenty-Seven

Meg

He's punctual to the dot, I note with a tiny smile. Good. That augurs well, I invariably find. Not only that, but he's already seated at a tiny table for two, to the back of the café, where there's some degree of privacy. I grab a coffee and head straight over to join him.

'Raymond, I presume?' I say brightly, recognising him instantly from his LinkedIn profile, although he looks younger in real life. Normally, it's the other way around.

'Yes, yes, indeed, nice to meet you,' he says, sounding jittery, as he gets up to shake my hand, but ends up clumsily spilling a jug of milk over the table. 'Oh my God, oh I'm so sorry, forgive me . . .'

'Not a problem,' I smile, efficiently pulling a packet of Kleenex out of my handbag and starting to mop up a bit.

Meanwhile Raymond continues to faff and apologise, giving me the chance to really scrutinise him from top to bottom. Do my thing, in other words.

Age: Raymond is pushing forty, about thirty-eight, thirty-nine, I guess. He's got the unlined, fresh face of a teetotaller but has clearly been under a lot of strain recently. The giveaway being two bloodshot eyes and tiny cuts on his chin, where he's obviously nicked himself shaving. Only distracted men or those under intense pressure ever do this, I've always found. Any guy in control of himself can generally take care of a Gillette blade.

Appearance: fusty. A young fogey. The suit he's wearing is cheap, M&S at a guess, and immaculately well pressed and washed, but it's showing its age, judging by the sheen at the knees.

You're a civil servant, I think. Low-paid, but with high ambitions. The notes on the table look like college notes. The only possible conclusion? Raymond is studying at night, doubtless in the hope this will lead to promotion, down the line.

His email had interested me, but now that I can get a good look at him, this case is beginning to intrigue me more and more.

'Well, can I first begin by saying congratulations on your recent engagement,' I say, pulling out a chair and sitting down opposite.

'Indeed, thank you, yes, thank you very much,' Raymond says, speaking quickly and gabbling his words.

You're such a bag of nerves, I think, almost feeling the stirrings of pity for him. *So why is your fiancée straying?* Or was it her undoubted infidelity that turned Raymond into this jittery, edgy shell of a man?

'I'll come straight to the point, if I may,' I begin, taking out my phone to make notes. There's two missed calls flashing up on my screen, both from Katherine Sisk – calling from her private mobile. Well, the Good Lady Senator will just have to wait in line, I think, quickly turning my full focus straight back to Raymond. 'You're engaged and now you have some concerns of a personal nature about your fiancée,' I say, matter-of-factly. 'Is that correct?'

'Norma, that's her name,' says Raymond, checking over his shoulder, lest he be overhead, even though there's no one sitting even close.

'Tell me all about Norma,' I say encouragingly. 'Give me everything you've got. The more information I have, the faster I can get to work for you, you understand.'

With that, Raymond passes over his phone, where his screensaver is a shot of his fiancée. I take a glance and immediately see what the problem is here. Because Norma is drop-dead gorgeous, smiley and fresh-faced, a bit like Taylor Swift, with croppy blonde hair, wearing a polka dot dress and a slash of scarlet lipstick that makes her look to be one of those cool women who only ever shop in vintage clothes stores. She's a good bit younger than Raymond too; thirty, tops.

'So that's Norma,' I nod, taking it all in closely. 'She's very attractive.'

'Yes, indeed, yes, thank you,' Raymond fusses, as if he's somehow responsible for her good looks.

Meanwhile, I take a tiny sip of coffee as my mind begins to whirr away.

Norma, whoever she is, clearly settled for someone like Raymond, doubtless because he's Mr Boring but Reliable, with a good, steady, pensionable job, who'll be kind to her and who'll be there for her in her dotage. The usual ridiculous reasons why people rush into engagements in the first place.

Norma, however, is obviously now having second thoughts about her upcoming nuptials. Hence the reason she's indulging in one last final fling, before marriage to Raymond effectively puts an end to her gallop.

'Norma, works as a schoolteacher,' Raymond says. 'Third year. She teaches English, History and Drama. In a private school, you know, a fee-paying school. Norma's on an excellent pay grade too, and we've already been able to put a sizeable deposit on a house at a surprisingly low interest rate. We've been together for six years in total, and engaged for two of those.'

'I see,' I say, wondering if he was starting to bore Norma stupid, with all his talk about low interest rates and pay grades. 'Does Norma have a Twitter handle? Or is she on Instagram? Either would be of huge use to me here.'

'Neither, I'm afraid,' says Raymond, as I look sharply back up at him in shock. 'Nor does she have a Facebook thingy . . . page, or whatever you call it.'

'Really?' I ask. Because this is a first. This is uncharted waters for me. Everyone I've ever worked on under the age of forty was on some kind of social media, every single one of them. It's very strange for her not to be.

Shit. This is just going to make my job so much harder. Not insurmountable, but still. A right pain in the arse, no matter what way you look at it.

'It's because of her position in the school, you see,' says Raymond. 'Norma always says she's terrified one of her friends might post a less than judicious photo of her, when they're all out for the night and intoxicated on those revolting cocktail concoctions that seem to be all the fashion these days. She says she'd never live it down if one of her students were to see such an image on social media, so she's steered well clear of any of that old nonsense. A good, sensible decision, I must say, that I always applauded her for. But then, Norma used to be such a good, sensible girl.' He pauses. 'You'll notice I'm using the past tense here.'

'I'm guessing something happened recently that made you look at Norma in a whole new light?' I prompt. Although I really mean to say, 'I'm guessing Norma met someone much more exciting, who blindsided her and who she's now seeing on the sly?'

The coffee table we're sitting at is in bright, direct sunlight and, with much faffing and fussing, Raymond takes a handkerchief out of his side pocket and begins to dab at a few perspiration beads glistening on his forehead.

'He's an *actor*, can you believe that?' Raymond says. 'An actor, who appears to spend more time out of work than in it. Norma is a great enthusiast for the theatre and I have to say, that was always something I admired about her – her great love of culture and the arts. She goes to all the fringe theatre shows and often takes her students too. And that's where she met him,' he adds sadly.

'Never mind about how she met him,' I interrupt crisply, but then clients feeling sorry for themselves get you nowhere.

'What I need to know is this, Raymond. Are you sure Norma's been seeing this actor guy behind your back? Absolutely rock-solid certain? You appreciate that I'm not a private detective. I need to know these aren't just suspicions on your part, before I knuckle down to work.'

'These are not suspicions on my part,' he replies flatly. 'I only wish they were. Our wedding is already well into the advanced planning stages . . .'

'Booked for when, exactly?' I interrupt, noting everything down with particular care.

'August,' says Raymond, dabbing at his temples with the handkerchief again.

'This coming August?'

'No, not at all, nothing so close as that,' he replies nervously. 'August of next year.'

'Next year?' I say incredulously. Is that really how far in advance you have to plan these days? Astonishing, I think. People in love are so weird. It never fails to amaze me.

'To get the right venue,' Raymond stammers, 'that's the kind of advance booking you need to make. We've paid a full deposit and everything. Non-refundable. Norma insisted on having the whole works: the chocolate fountain, the champagne, oh nothing was too much for her. But then . . .' He stops.

'Go on,' I say.

'Well, she's completely lost all interest in the whole thing. Now she spends all night, every night at the theatre, and I know she's spending time with *him*. The whole bedrock of our relationship was trust and now, I have to say, I feel very strongly that trust has been eroded.'

I sit back, fold my arms and look at him.

'If you feel you can't rebuild your relationship,' I tell him, 'then you need to be honest about it. Pointless me getting rid of this actor guy for you, unless you and Norma intend to stick together. Otherwise, you're just wasting your money and my time.'

'Oh, but I very much do intend to move forward with Norma,' Raymond rushes to reassure me, taking his handkerchief and folding it up into nice, neat squares. 'We were happy together before this idiot came along, you see, and I desperately want us to be happy together again. And I know we can be, once he's banished from the picture. Gone for good, I fervently hope.'

'I see,' I say, already busily thinking ahead.

'Besides, we've already put down a forty per cent deposit for the wedding. Did I mention that it was non-refundable?'

'In that case, you'd better tell me more about your rival,' I say, sidestepping all this talk about deposits. 'Give me everything you've got. A jobbing actor, you said?'

'His name is Jonny Featherstone-Jones,' Raymond sniffs. 'Ridiculous name, isn't it? I suspect it's some class of a stage name. And we're hardly dealing with Laurence Olivier here. Strictly spear-carrier material and nothing more. I saw him onstage once, in the world's most boring play, in a revolting little makeshift theatre above a dingy old pub. He had about ten lines in total and still managed to fluff most of them. But, oh no, as far as Norma is concerned, he's the next Daniel Day-Lewis.'

Jonny Featherstone-Jones. Good, I think, already ahead of him and googling away on my phone. But then I hit a solid brick wall. Believe it or not, there's several Jonny Featherstone-Joneses out there. I narrow the search down to 'actor', which leaves me with one who seems to work in or around the theatre world.

'Can you identify him from this photo?' I ask Raymond, holding up an image on my phone and passing it over to him to look at.

Raymond takes out a neat little pair of reading specs and puts them on, before taking the phone from me and peering down at the screen.

'Yes, there he is,' he says, pointing to the standard-looking black and white CV photo, which I instantly begin to scrutinise when he hands the phone back.

Jonny Featherstone-Jones looks late twenties tops, with a thick head of dark hair, all carefully combed forward onto his forehead and with a doleful, miserable expression on his face, which doubtless is meant to make him look mad, bad and dangerous to know, but which in actual fact only makes him look constipated.

There's the name of an actor's agency printed above it, along with all the relevant contact details. So tracking this Jonny Featherstone-Jones down shouldn't present any major roadblocks, I think, already plotting and scheming a long-term strategy here.

'Leave it with me,' I say to Raymond, briskly getting up to leave. 'I'm on it.'

'That's it?' Raymond says, looking bewildered.

'Why?' I ask, looking back at him in surprise. 'Was there anything else?'

'Well, don't you need to know more about Norma? And more details about *him*? Surely you need more to go on than what I've just given you?'

'Trust me,' I tell him, with a small smile. 'I've got everything I need right here. Now, if you'll excuse me, I've got work to do.'

'And you're really confident you can help?' Raymond asks worriedly.

On cue, my phone rings. Katherine Sisk's private number. Yet *again*.

'You don't believe me?' I say smugly, waving the phone under his nose as some of the old confidence begins to surge back to me. 'Well, here's a satisfied client calling. Why don't you ask her for yourself?'

Chapter Twenty-Eight

Harriet

Later the same morning, Harriet wakes up on Meg's sofa, in Meg's apartment, bursting to talk to her friend. To talk about this very apartment, to chat about her plan to help her stay on there and yes, even to talk about Freddie too, she thinks, with a smile, as she springs up off the sofa and pulls a sweatshirt over her nightie.

'Meg? You there, hon?' she calls out, padding over to the bedroom door and knocking. No answer, so Harriet lets herself in, to see that the bed is empty. It is immaculately made up of course, but then that's Meg for you. Everything in this entire flat is spotless and pristine.

'Meg?' Harriet calls, checking the bathroom, and kitchen, where she finds a note waiting for her, propped up against a bottle of water on the kitchen island.

> **Good morning! Early start for me. See you later. Will cook dinner for us. Much to catch up on! Save it all for later, love Meg xxxx**

She must have left at the crack of dawn, Harriet thinks, padding back out of the kitchen and over to Meg's desk off the

278

main living area, where that weird noticeboard is covered with all those Post-its and columns about various people's movements. After such a terrible day yesterday, when she came home so early and stayed holed up in her room? She couldn't possibly have gone back into work after all that, could she? That waste management place Meg had described to Harriet, Pest Be Gone? The one that Harriet can find no earthly trace of? Even if it does exist, it sounds vile, and the people Meg works for seem horrible. Harriet has high hopes that Meg walked out of the job the previous day, told them where to shove it and that she wouldn't be back at all. She also hopes that Meg will confide in her, maybe open up about her lavish lifestyle and how she must be up to her neck in debt to finance it all.

So where has Meg gone to now? Harriet tries calling and texting her, but Meg isn't answering – which means she's up to her tonsils, doing . . . well, doing what, exactly?

Then, idly, Harriet picks up the yellow Post-it note with Senator Katherine Sisk's contact details written on it.

And she wonders.

Chapter Twenty-Nine

Meg

'Meg? Katherine Sisk here. Look, you and I need to speak privately, as soon as possible. Can you come and see me, at your earliest convenience? I'm at Government Buildings today. I've left out a lanyard pass for you at security. See you shortly, I hope.'

Well, now this just got interesting, I think, listening to the message. Getting Jess out of the picture needs my urgent attention, and then of course, there's the question of Philip. What to do with him now, and how best to deliver the Almighty Comeuppance? I'm certainly not short of suggestions for Katherine; the thought has preoccupied me day and night. I'll scare him into monogamy, wait till you see. I'll make sure Philip Sisk thinks twice before he as much as looks at another woman again.

Yet another exciting challenge I've got on my hands, as the day ahead suddenly becomes a whole lot busier. Just the way I like it.

I jump into the back of a cab, bark my destination at the driver, then do one of my routine quick costume changes in the back seat. In one practised move, I produce a neat black

Givenchy shift dress out of my giant Michael Kors bag, pull the dress over my head, and shimmy out of the T-shirt and jeans I've been wearing. The taxi driver, thankfully, is far too engrossed in navigating his way through a labyrinth of roadworks to pay the slightest bit of attention.

If they were all like you, I think, looking gratefully at the back of his baldie head, *I'd have no bother.*

*

Then I slick my hair back into a neat chignon and apply just a dab of clear lip gloss. *Perfect*, I think, double-checking myself in the compact mirror that goes everywhere with me. If a jeans and T-shirt combo makes me look like a woman who'd trawl through the streets to help out someone like Raymond, then this elegant black 60s-style shift dress might as well have 'Government Buildings' written all over it.

The traffic is horrendous, and roadworks seem to have sprouted up across the entire city centre, so, with time to spare, I whip out both my phones and start work getting a handle on this Jonny Featherstone-Jones, actor at large.

I begin with the agency who represent him.

'Hi there,' I say brightly, as soon as the phone is answered. 'I'm trying to track down an actor on your books called Jonny Featherstone-Jones . . .'

'Can I ask, in connection with what?' says a warm, interested woman's voice on the other end of the phone.

Saying 'for a movie I'm working on' would arouse too much suspicion. Same with a commercial I'm supposedly casting – another lie I could get caught out in so easily. 'I'm a playwright,' I say, literally improvising on the spot. 'And I've written a new work, which I think Jonny would be perfect for. I'd love to meet with him to discuss it, if possible. And, of course, if he were interested, that is.'

'Oh, well done you!' she says happily. 'Good on you. You know, I always think there aren't nearly enough female playwrights out there – not by half.'

'So if you had a mobile number for Jonny, or maybe his address, that would be so useful?' I ask out straight. 'It is the leading role, I should stress.'

'Hmmm, that could be a bit tricky. Thing is, Jonny's actually left our books, due to . . . well, let's just say artistic differences.'

'I understand,' I say, quickly reading the subtext and putting two and two together.

Doubtless this Jonny thought he was destined for Oscar glory, whereas the reality is that he's probably more like 'background extra' material in some class of daytime soap, where the scenery shakes every time a door bangs. Certainly according to the few – the very few – online reviews of plays he's appeared in, which I'm using my second phone to scroll down through, Jonny Featherstone-Jones's various stage performances have more or less all been panned. A good-looking guy, the critics seemed to be unanimous in saying, but don't give up the day job.

'Do you have any contact details for him at all?' I ask politely, even as I can hear tap-tapping away at a keyboard.

'Not that we can give out over the phone, I'm afraid,' she replies, which I suppose is fair enough, really. 'Although I think he's on social media – you might try him there?'

I thank this lady, whoever she is, and am then obliged to honour the big fat lie I told by promising her opening-night tickets to the fictitious play I'm supposedly working on.

Meanwhile, the taxi driver is still muttering under his breath, as the traffic is now effectively at a complete standstill.

'I mean, sweet Jaysus, roadworks? At this hour of the morning, rush hour? Are they mad in the head, or what?'

I totally ignore him and sit back, as the taxi finally begins to get moving again, while I give my tried-and-tested social media strategy a go. But he's nowhere to be found on Twitter and although I've already found someone of that name on Facebook, the account has the maximum privacy settings, so all I can do is send him a 'friend' request and hope for the best.

It's not a temporary setback, it's a challenge. And challenges are there to be overcome, I remind myself.

'Here you go, Government Buildings,' says the taxi driver, as we pull up at the kerb outside.

'Keep the change,' I say, handing over a fifty-euro note as I climb out of the car.

'Very nice of you,' the driver whistles, pocketing the cash. 'Hope someone as generous as you ends up with a bit of political influence one day. You're certainly starting in the right place.'

Are you kidding? I think, dusting myself down as I make my way towards the security hut outside the giant Palladian mansion house, where both arms of Government are in full session. *A politician's salary would actually be a comedown.*

Chapter Thirty

Harriet

Unbeknown to Meg, not much later, Harriet finds herself looking for a very different address, in a very different part of town. She is in the legal district, as it happens, which seems to be dominated by street after street of five-storey Georgian buildings, all within spitting distance of the Four Courts and the Central Criminal Courts of Justice.

Unlike Meg, however, it takes Harriet all of her phone's battery life on Google Maps before she eventually finds where she's looking for. The offices of Digby, Markby and Sellers, a very discreet firm of solicitors – at least, according to Freddie.

'They're all very old chums of my grandfather's,' Freddie had told her. 'All ancient and all looking very like Dumbledore. Minus the long beards,' he'd added, in his own clueless way. 'And the wizard's hats. Actually, come to think of it, they aren't a bit like Dumbledore in the least. They're just all terribly, terribly old.'

Eventually, Harriet stumbles on a brass plaque on the wall, with the firm's name neatly written on it, so she buzzes at the intercom and waits. And waits.

And waits some more. She's come this far though, she tells herself, and feck it anyway, the bus fare was nearly three euro, so there's no way she's leaving without getting her full money's worth.

Then, with a great deal of creaking from the other side, the front door is eventually opened, and there stands an elderly man who looks on the wrong side of about one hundred and ten, clinging to a walking stick and wheezing like a train.

'Yes?' he says, eyeing Harriet up and down warily. 'How may I help you?'

'Oh . . . em . . . I'm Harriet Waters and . . . emm . . .' *I tried to make an appointment with you but no one answered the phone* seems like a pretty rude thing to say, so instead she trails off with, 'I was hoping to have a private word, if that's OK?'

'Really? Well, it's not very convenient just now, I'm afraid.'

'But it's just for a quick chat,' Harriet blurts out, desperate to talk to him.

'Oh bugger, bugger, bugger,' he says croakily. 'You mean you want me to *work*? I don't work in the afternoons. Ever.'

'But it's barely even midday,' Harriet tries to say, thinking, can this really be the de Courcey family solicitor? For real?

'Interferes with my digestion no end,' the elderly gentleman splutters back at her. 'So if you want to come back at a more suitable time . . .'

'I really am so sorry to disturb you,' Harriet says, 'but I've come a very long way to see you and I faithfully promise, it's just a few questions and then I'll leave you in peace.'

'Hmm. Will you make me a cup of tea while you're here? You seem like a nice enough girl and unfortunately my cataracts are at me, so I can't even see where the switch is on the dratted kettle, you understand.'

'I'd be delighted to,' Harriet smiles. This, she is used to. Dealing with the elderly and looking after them was something she did every day of the week, back in Dead Old Lady Dresses. 'If I say so myself, I make a grand cup of tea,' she adds brightly.

'Right then,' he says. 'You'd better come inside, I suppose.'

'Are you one of the firm's partners?' Harriet asks, as she crosses the threshold and steps into the gloomy, dark hallway, which, as Freddie had forewarned her, did indeed stink of boiled cabbage.

'Harold Markby, at your service,' he replies, leading her down a damp, poky little corridor, with files piled almost to ceiling height and thick dust on every surface. 'But I'm not a partner, not at all. At least, not yet I'm not.'

'Really?' says Harriet, following him and dodging boxes of files that are lying about everywhere. But surely he is someone very senior in the firm, she figures, at his age?

'No, indeed I'm quite low in the pecking order here,' Harold croaks back at her. 'Just a humble junior, for my sins. It's my older brother, George, who's the real boss around here. You'll find him in his office, if you'll just step this way . . .'

Older brother? Harriet thinks she must have misheard.

Harold flings open a huge, imposing Georgian door, to reveal a musty, dusty study, with mounds of paper files piled to nuisance, fire hazard height. A heavy old mahogany desk dominates the entire room, with a giant bay window backing on to an overgrown courtyard outside.

And behind the desk? The slumbering form of George Markby, senior partner, now catching up on his forty winks as he dozes away, snoring lightly.

'You see?' Harold wheezes. 'I told you. The afternoons are the worst possible time for anyone to call. I did warn you. And you, young lady, did promise me a cup of tea.'

'That's no problem at all,' Harriet smiles, knowing exactly how elderly people need to be minded. 'Sure, I'm glad to be of service.'

Harold leads her outside and down yet another winding, snaking corridor, till they come to a tiny anteroom, now clearly used as a sort of kitchenette, with a kettle and a tiny fridge, along with a bockety table for two, with a few chipped mugs on it. Harriet immediately takes charge; insisting that Harold take a seat, so she can make a big fuss of him.

'Milk, two sugars, my dear,' he says, gently easing himself down onto one of the chairs, and looking for all the world like he might drop off into a deep sleep himself. 'And then you must sit down too, and tell me what all this is about.'

She places a fresh mug of tea down in front of him, and does as she's told, sitting down opposite.

'So tell me, what appears to be the problem?' Harold asks, gratefully taking a sip of the tea.

She has prepared for this, and launches into the little speech she's rehearsed in her head on the bus here. She thinks of Meg. Clearly in way over her head with debts. And it isn't like she's looking for special favours here, is it? All Harriet wants is to see if she can glean some advice and a few guidelines that might, just might, help Meg when the time comes. That's all.

'I only came here in the first place,' she says, 'because my friend Freddie, that's Freddie de Courcey, says you've represented his family for decades, and so I thought you might be able to help me.'

At that, Harold sits bolt upright, clattering down the mug of tea in front of him. 'De Courcey, did you say?'

'Yes, that's right.'

'Oh, well, you should have said so before! That's young Freddie you're referring to, I take it? Red-headed chap, always in the papers, not the brightest bulb on the tree, according to his grandmother? Went to my old school, you know, and failed every single exam he ever sat. Except for Home Economics, for some reason. I have a distinct memory of his grandmother telling me that young Freddie made a delightfully moist hot cross bun. Not a soggy bottom in sight.'

'Emm . . . well,' Harriet dithers, torn between wanting information and not wanting to come across as being disloyal.

But Harold is like a completely different person now, springing to his feet with the aid of his walking stick, and coming around to shake her hand warmly. 'Well, may I say, any friend of the de Courcey family is a friend of ours, my dear,' he cackles. 'My brother and I were at school with his grandfather, Frederick Senior, did you know that? Oh, long before your time. Awfully good cricketer, if I remember. And so terribly generous in the bar afterwards.'

'It's great you have such fond memories,' says Harriet, anxious to get this back on track. 'But I really did just want to ask you about debt resolution, and what can be done to help another friend of mine who's in a bit of trouble, money-wise. She's living in The Towers, which is this incredibly high-end apartment complex in the swishest part of town, she's got the penthouse flat and I know she's under huge stress at the moment and it can only be related to money and . . .'

But Harold doesn't appear to be listening. 'And are you acquainted with Frederick's good lady wife?' he asks.

'Ellen de Courcey?' Harriet says. 'You know her too?'

'Do I know her? I was a guest at her wedding, when she married Frederick Senior!' says Harold. 'A most daunting lady to deal with, let me tell you. Terrifying is the adjective I'd use, actually.'

Just then, Harriet hears the sound of footsteps shuffling right behind her. She turns around to see the older brother, George, hobbling in on a Zimmer frame, yawning and coughing and spluttering, but still, very definitely alive and kicking.

'I heard voices,' George says in a voice that is as weak as water and more like a whisper, really. 'And is that tea I see? I should very much like a strong, fresh cup, please.'

Harriet immediately gets to her feet and offers him her chair, as Harold makes the introductions.

'Let me ask my brother if he can help you any further,' he says, before raising his voice several decibels so he is almost shouting. 'GEORGE, THIS YOUNG LADY IS A FRIEND OF THE DE COURCEY FAMILY. SHE'S ASKING ABOUT DEBT RESOLUTION FOR A CHUM OF HERS WHO

LIVES AT THE TOWERS, IN THE PENTHOUSE FLAT, NO LESS . . . isn't that what you mentioned, my dear?'

'Yes, The Towers,' Harriet answers.

'THE TOWERS,' Harold shouts at George.

'The penthouse at The Towers?' George says, sounding surprisingly sharp and fully *compos mentis* now. 'Do you mean number 27A?'

'That's right.'

'In that case, you're the second person to mention that wretched property in the last twenty-four hours, as it happens.'

'I am?' says Harriet, bewildered.

'Yes, indeed,' says George, gratefully easing himself down into the chair she has helpfully pulled out for him. 'I had another young lady on the telephone only just yesterday, making all sorts of claims and counterclaims about her lease agreement on a property there. So I don't mind telling you, I gave it to her straight. I'd drawn up that lease myself, not so long ago. "Ellen de Courcey is your landlady," I told this particular young lady, "and you should be grateful to her, instead of calling me up demanding I double-check the exact terms of your lease. You live at that flat rent-free," I told her in the clearest possible terms. "And have done so for the past year. Should Mrs de Courcey now wish to revisit the terms of your arrangement, then that's her prerogative. If you have any problems with whatever terms you agreed with her," I said, "then you'd better be warned, Mrs de Courcey will gladly terminate the contract."'

Harriet says nothing. Just stands there, mug of tea frozen in her hand, trying to process what she's just heard.

'Excuse me,' she finds voice enough to ask. 'Did you just say that Ellen de Courcey is the landlady of the penthouse flat at The Towers?'

'And a most generous one too,' says George.

'We are talking about the same flat here? Number 27A?'

'Yes, yes, my dear, one and the same. It was a cashless transaction with her tenant, I distinctly recall. Who wouldn't want that, eh? A penthouse flat, entirely rent-free. I did enquire as to why, as it seemed such an usual arrangement. But all Mrs de Courcey would tell me is that the tenant had done her a particular service and that the lease on the flat was in part payment for it.'

'And do you remember . . . what exactly this "particular service" was?' Harriet asks, in a very quiet little voice.

George thinks for a moment.

'A personal matter, you understand. Although I shouldn't be in the least surprised if it involved your chum, my dear. Young Freddie de Courcey. He's forever getting himself into all manner of scrapes, with all manner of undesirable young ladies. It's happened before, many times, you know. I can only hope since then that he's changed his ways somewhat.'

'By any chance . . . do you remember who contacted you about all this yesterday?' Harriet says, as her brain frantically tries to make sense of what she is hearing.

'Emm . . .' George shuffles about on his seat and stares off into space.

'I don't suppose the name was Meg Monroe, was it?' Even as she speaks the words, she half dreads the answer.

'Bingo, that's her!' says George. 'You're a step ahead of me, my dear. That's definitely her. Very brisk and business-like on the phone yesterday. Quite a bossy sort of person. A bit like a young Lady Thatcher,' he nods over to Harold. 'She was the very same when she came in here a year ago, to sign the lease in the first place. Like a whirlwind, I recall. Had more than one of those dratted mobile telephones on the go. Wouldn't even sit down, just paced around the place. Quite rude, I thought at the time, but that's just me. Certainly didn't put the kettle on and make a nice cup of tea for us, as you did.'

Harriet wants to thank him. She wants to say a whole lot of things. But instead, she just stands rooted to the spot, mute, silenced and utterly lost for words.

Chapter Thirty-One

Meg

An usher from Government Buildings had just escorted me up
a narrow back staircase and through to a tiny anteroom on the
third floor, with the name SENATOR KATHERINE SISK printed neatly
in copperplate writing on the door. Jess is at a desk over by the
window, deep into a phone conversation, but she does at least
glance up to acknowledge me when I come in.

Can't get off this call, she mouths at me.

No problem, I smile back pleasantly.

I need to talk to you, she indicates, trying to wind up her
call, but not succeeding.

Lots to talk about, I mouth back.

Jeez, I think, *lip-reading really is a highly prized skill
around here.*

Jess is being fairly polite though, as opposed to her usual
passive-aggressive self, so I'm hopeful that the little carrot
I dangled in front of her late the other night might actually
have hit home.

Billy, on the other hand, sits at the only other desk, on
his phone, but he hangs up the minute I come in and seems
genuinely relieved to see me.

'Well, aren't you a sight for sore eyes,' he smiles.

He looks tired though and probably a bit on the skinny side, given that the election is just four days away, but still. Attractive, I suppose. If that's your thing.

'Katherine asked to see me,' I say.

'But you're here to work too, I hope?' he says, leaning back and folding his arms, as he puts his glasses back on and eyes me up and down. 'If it doesn't interfere with what no doubt is a hectic social life?'

'Social life?' I repeat. 'What's a social life?'

Nor am I being facetious either.

'Well, say, for instance,' he begins, getting up from behind the desk and coming over to perch on the edge of it, long legs stretching out in front of him. 'Oooh, just a random example from the top of my head . . . if you were asked out for a drink? That, right there, that's your first clue as to what a social life is, Meg Monroe.'

'Ah,' I nod, reading the subtext.

I study him for a moment, as you would an insect down a microscope. Is this guy actually flirting with me? For real? Is this how people behave in the real world? Should I politely inform him he's wasting his time here?

'Only you bolted the other night, didn't you?' Billy says, his tone gently mocking. 'And left me all alone at a TV studio in an industrial estate in the back arse of nowhere. Dying for a pint, and with no one to play with. Ahh well, poor old me.'

'Some other time,' I say crisply, putting a quick end to this nonsense. 'So where can I find Katherine?'

'Ehh . . . there's a pile of work to be done here first. Remember work? The inconvenience of a general election?'

'Yes, of course, but first of all, Katherine and I just need to have a very quick private conversation . . .'

'The Good Lady Senator is in session in the House,' Billy says. 'Tell you what, though. Till she gets back, you could start by helping me with this.' He ambles back around his desk to sit down again and taps a biro off a computer screen.

I look coolly back at him. 'What have you got there?'

'The Registrar of Electors,' he says. 'Jess and I have been working on it since late last night. Here, I'll show you.'

I come around to his side of the desk and peer over his shoulder.

'You see?' he says. 'You do realise that this is gold dust for us? It's all heavily classified stuff though, you understand. There's a ton of legal restrictions around how we get to use it, but the bottom line is, this doesn't leave the office. Ever. We're legally permitted to use it for canvassing in the run-up to an election and absolutely nothing more. I warned Jess and now I'm warning you. That's important.'

'So . . . what exactly is it that I'm looking at here?' I ask. For God's sake, all I can see are row after row of hundreds and thousands of names and home addresses. So far, so boring.

It takes a nanosecond for the penny to drop, as Billy stares back at me like I'm a bit slow-witted.

'What are you looking at?' he says. 'Are you kidding me? Are you for real? These are only the names and home addresses of every single person over the age of eighteen, in every single constituency – and that's nationwide, by the way.'

'I see. So you want me to . . . what? Target each voter personally with glossy fliers with Katherine's policies outlined for them?'

'Now you're getting it,' Billy nods approvingly. 'Not only that, but we've got this strictly timed so that every last one of Katherine's fliers goes into the post right before the weekend, so they'll arrive first thing on election day.'

'That way, she's fresh in voters' minds just as they're going to the polls,' I say, thinking aloud. 'Nice one.'

'Got it in one. So if you could take care of this, then I can get back to her media schedule for the rest of the week. Four major radio interviews today alone, I shit you not, and Jess and I need all the help we can get. If you take over here, then I can get back to the grindstone over at the constituency office.'

'Hmmm,' I say, staring over his shoulder, utterly absorbed by the electoral database onscreen.

Just then, Billy's phone begins to ring and he instantly hops up to answer it.

'Oh and just before I take this call,' he says, 'you still haven't told me how you did it.'

'Did what?' I say, slipping into his empty seat, bewitched by what I'm seeing on the screen in front of me.

'How you knew all that personal stuff about me, the other night. About my house move, and that I was just back from holidays? You even knew I was somewhere south of the equator – it's been driving me nuts ever since.'

'When a magician gives away his secrets . . .' I begin to say, but Billy is having none of it.

'Oh, for God's sake, just tell me will you?'

'Don't you need to take that call?'

'Not till you tell me,' he twinkles back at me. 'And till then, you'll have to listen to a ringing phone and there's nothing on earth more irritating than that.'

'Oh, all right then,' I sigh. 'You were carrying an iPad the other night, your home screen was lit up and I caught a glimpse of an app for an estate agency on it, and also an app for a mortgage provider, so I just put two and two together. Plus you had a bit of black oil wedged under your fingernails . . . oh. And you still do, I see . . . ever heard of a nail brush, by the way?'

'Ahh, go easy, will you?' he grins. 'So you were right about my car giving me trouble – but how am I supposed to afford a new car, with repayments on the new house?'

'And thirdly,' I say, giving him the most cursory glance, 'you have a mosquito bite that's healing up just at the side of your neck, right on the carotid artery. Only the yellow fever mosquito ever goes for that particular blood vessel, and you can only find yellow fever mozzies south of the equator. Latin America, is my guess.'

He whistles on his way out the door to take the call.

'Rio, actually,' he tosses back over his shoulder. 'Jeez, hope this isn't your not-too-subtle way of telling me that I might end up with malaria.'

But I don't even bother acknowledging him. I'm far, far too absorbed by the electoral database in front of me.

I glance over at Jess, who's still too engrossed on her phone call to pay much mind to me.

Jonny Featherstone-Jones, I think. *If you ever voted in any election ever, then I'm coming to track you down.*

It's all working out beautifully.

So what do I do? Oh please, what do you think? I scroll all the way down to 'f' for Featherstone which takes forever, given the sheer volume of names here, but eventually, eventually, God be praised, I find what I'm looking for.

Whipping out my phone, I check on Jess again. My luck is in; she's still not paying a blind bit of attention. In that second, I grab a lightning-quick photo of the address I need, and lucky for me I do, because next thing, Katherine bounds into the office, with Billy right at her side, spouting the day's media schedule into her ear.

Shit, shit, shit. Not enough time – or privacy – for me to shove a USB stick into the side of the desktop and make a copy of the entire database. But still, I think, smiling brightly up at them, I'll figure out some way to get back into this office, alone and unsupervised, so I can knuckle down to some *very* interesting work.

'So you've got a podcast at noon,' Billy is saying, reading from the iPad in front of him, 'then you're on lunchtime news live on Channel 1, and they need you to be in the studio a good ten minutes beforehand. We're expecting updates from the Prime Minister's climate change speech live on air, and be warned, you'll probably get roped in to give your two cents' worth . . .'

'Katherine?' Jess pipes up from her desk, where she's still stuck on that call, 'I'm just onto World News Radio here and they really want you for the Women's Show this Saturday . . .'

Katherine gives her a big thumbs up, as Billy tries to pull her attention back again.

'And then tonight . . . ehh . . . hello? Katherine? Are you even taking any of this in?'

Meanwhile, Katherine comes over to shake me warmly by the hand.

'I missed you yesterday,' she says in a low voice. 'Come on, you and me, time for a quick coffee, I think.'

'Ehh . . . hate to put a dampener on any other plans you might have,' Billy interrupts, 'but you've got about fifteen minutes before we need to leave here . . .'

'That's all I need with Meg,' says Katherine firmly. 'Come on, Billy, you're working me like a dog and you know I always function better on a few shots of caffeine.'

'All right then,' Billy says, theatrically. 'Don't mind me, and this schedule that I've worked blood, sweat and tears on. Go on off and have a nice little coffee morning for your-selves. Excuse me for getting in your way.'

'I'll be right outside in exactly fifteen minutes,' Katherine smiles at him. 'And don't worry, Billy, if you behave your-self, I might even buy you a takeaway Americano. Meg? This way, please.'

'Milk, no sugar!' Billy calls down the corridor, as the two of us leave the office and disappear.

'And one for me!' Jess calls too, which Katherine more or less ignores.

It seems to me that we're walking forever, down one high-ceilinged Georgian corridor after another, before we eventually come to the main staircase, which is, to put it mildly, breathtaking. It's almost designed like a wedding cake, the coving and plastering detail is so ornate and, as your eye is drawn upwards by another five storeys towards the overhead dome, it seems like you're standing right at the very centre of the universe. This is the epicentre of government and it's buzzing with activity, as ministers sweep up and down the stairs, some with teams of advisors trailing after them, others alone and absorbed in phones.

'Impressive, isn't it?' Katherine smiles, seeing the expression of wonder on my face. 'But follow me, there's something I very much want you to see.'

I do as I'm told, as Katherine leads me down one flight of stairs and towards a huge landing, with a giant portrait that dominates the hallway below. The painting has to be about twelve feet high and even someone like me, seldom at a loss for words, finds myself just gaping up at it in awe.

'It's Countess Constance Markievicz herself,' Katherine says, as we both drink it in. 'The very first woman ever to be elected to government. Painted by her future husband in 1919, when she was first elected. Isn't she something?'

'Yes,' I say quietly. 'Yes, she's really something.'

'Every single morning, I walk past this painting,' Katherine continues, 'and she reminds me that no matter how hard the going gets, it would have been so much tougher for her, back in the early twentieth century. Can you imagine? So even on the bad days here, and God knows there have been many of them,

I often think of Countess Markievicz. And I'm grateful that she paved the way for women like me, to do the work that I'm doing today. To carry on her legacy – hopefully.'

We turn away, and Katherine guides me down yet another staircase and on towards the Member's Dining Room, which is right on the ground floor, just beside the main entrance portico.

'Which is why I'm really more than grateful to you now, Meg,' Katherine says, keeping her voice low, even though the place is actually quiet, so there's zero chance of us being overheard. 'For working on this problem of mine and for actually hitting on a solution that might – just might – work for us all.'

'Well, there's still a few ifs, ands and buts,' I tell her, 'but if you win on Monday, and if Toby Callaghan has to go crawling back to his day job in Brussels, then put it this way. We have a shot.'

'It would certainly put a swift end to her dalliance with Philip,' says Katherine, 'as well as giving him the kick in the pants he richly deserves. So now,' she adds, leading me into the grand Dining Room, 'tell me what you think of this?'

'Nothing to do but gasp,' I say, looking all around me, even though the Dining Room is built more like a ballroom, really, with teams of wait staff moving like a carefully choreographed ballet around the room.

The floor is covered in elegant dining tables, all laid out with fine linen tablecloths and expensive-looking crystal, and as we're guided to a tiny table for two, I spot more than a few familiar faces. The Finance Minister for one and, speak of the devil, but is that Senator Callaghan in the far corner? He's in cahoots with what looks like the political correspondent on the main evening news, but glances up to acknowledge us as we pass by.

Katherine picks a quiet table, well away from anyone else, and with a view right over a neat, cobblestoned courtyard outside.

'It's astonishing,' I say. 'Wow . . . just . . . wow.'

'I know,' Katherine nods understandingly. 'I think everyone feels the same way the first time they come here. It's like the whole building is designed to impress – and to intimidate too, of course.'

A waiter comes over to take our order. We both ask for good, strong Americanos, and as soon as he's gone, Katherine sits forward, lowering her voice.

'Anyway, I wanted to see you face to face,' she says. 'I don't know what happened or what didn't happen the other night after the *PrimeNews* debate, but all I can say with certainty is this. Ever since, Philip is a newly chastened man. He's being an awful lot better around the house and he's Dad of the Year as far as my daughters are concerned.'

'I'm very glad to hear it,' I say. 'He and Jess certainly got an unexpected shock, let me tell you.'

'Now please don't get me wrong,' she hastens to add. 'The very minute this dratted election is over, Philip Sisk won't know what's hit him. But I've chosen to bottle everything up until after polling day, and I'll decide what to do then and only then.'

'And what do you think you'll decide?' I ask.

Katherine sits back and takes a moment before answering.

'I'll probably make him move out,' she says. 'For a time at least. But until then – thanks to you – I can focus on the campaign properly, without my family life getting in the way. After the election though? You just watch this space.'

I'm already ahead of her.

'I'm glad you're happy so far,' I say. 'But you know, my work here is far from finished.'

Katherine looks across the table, eyebrows raised.

'We're not letting your husband get away with this,' I tell her matter-of-factly. 'Not a chance in hell. Part of my remit is to make sure Philip knows exactly what happens to men who cheat. How cold and lonely and miserable life is for a middle-aged man who dares to stray on a wonderful woman like you. I'm already working on something and I think – I hope – you'll be pleased with the results.'

Our coffees arrive and Katherine takes a sip, listening intently. Then she exhales deeply and takes off her glasses.

'You're really something, Meg,' she says, after a pause. 'Do you know that?'

I deem it best to look modest, fake humility and keep my mouth shut. But yes, actually, I have to agree. I really am something.

'Tell me this,' Katherine says simply. 'Why?'

'Why what?'

'Why do you do this? The whole "fixing people problems" thing? It's like a personal vendetta with you. I'd really love to know what motivates you, that's all.'

I shrug and take a moment to focus out the window at the courtyard outside.

'You say you stand on a platform of equality and fairness,' I say slowly. 'It's what you've been fighting for all your political life, isn't it?'

'It certainly is,' Katherine replies. 'And it's not easy, let me tell you.'

'Snap,' I tell her. 'Because that's exactly what I stand for too. Equality and fairness in all things. If you hurt someone or cheat, or make their life difficult, you should get a taste of all the pain and humiliation you caused. It's the least you deserve, if you ask me. And I'm an equal opportunities fixer. Men or women, I don't particularly care. If you're in a relationship, be it romantic or not, and mess around, there's a price to be paid and I'll make bloody sure you pay it.'

There's a thoughtful pause, while Katherine seems to be formulating her next question.

'Did anyone ever cheat on you?' she asks gently.

'You mean like romantic partners?' I scoff. 'Not a chance. But I do have personal experience of how cheating can wreck a family. Deeply personal, as it happens.'

There once was a little girl, five years of age, who had to move out of her house, leaving behind her lovely bedroom and all of her favourite toys. 'Everything will follow on,' her mum said. But her mum was crying a lot when she said it, and didn't seem happy at all about this big move.

'But I don't want to leave,' this child insisted. 'We live here, this is our house!'

'Well, from now on we're going to be living with Gran and Grandad,' her mum said. 'We need to leave here and we need to leave right now. Stop arguing, Megan, and be a good girl.'

It took a long, long time and lots of listening at doors before the truth finally began to dawn.

'That Charlie is a roaring eejit,' her nan used to gripe to anyone who'd listen. 'Him and his new fancy woman. Doreen, the state of her, with the head bleached off her, and her fake nails and her fancy job managing apartments in Marbella. Best thing you could do was to get well away from him, love, and mark my words, he'll get what's coming to him.'

But Charlie didn't get what was coming to him at all, quite the opposite, in fact. Instead, he came into a big inheritance and splashed out on a huge house that he and Doreen moved into, with a bedroom specially earmarked for when Megan came to stay.

Which she never did. Ever.

Aged nine, she'd grown devious in ways to punish her father for what he'd put them through. She'd fake being sick to get out of seeing him and Doreen, who'd suddenly decided she was going to be stepmum of the year. Once, she even locked herself in the fridge at the butcher's where her grandad worked, to avoid a day of forced 'family fun' with her father and his girlfriend.

And all the time, she watched her mum work harder to make ends meet and grow thinner and sadder and more and more bitter, while Megan grew colder and angrier as the *whole bedrock of her belief system began to form. Once it did, it wouldn't go away.* Cheating has consequences, *she decided at a scarily young age.* And no one should get away with it – no one.

Young Megan was aged fourteen by the time Charlie and Doreen got married and although she ignored her wedding invitation, she made a point of turning up to the reception. It was held in the marquee of a five-star hotel, oh, no expense spared for Charlie this time around. Doreen looked a bit like a marquee herself, in a ludicrous billowing dress, with no fewer than six bridesmaids, and Charlie looked like a bargain basement Oliver Hardy, beaten into a suit that was a good two sizes too small for him and bursting at the seams.

Megan deliberately wore her oldest, filthiest jeans and snuck in around the back, carefully picking her moment to corner her dad in the quiet of the Portaloo toilets.

'Megan! I'm delighted you came!' Charlie beamed, thrilled to see her. 'Doreen will be so pleased. All she wants is to be friends with you. But why are you dressed like that, love?' he said, eyeing her torn jeans and sweatshirt. 'Look at you, you're a mess! You don't want anyone seeing you like that, like you were dragged through a hedge. It's our special day. Can't you go home and change into something a bit classier? Then we can find Doreen so you can congratulate your brand-new stepmother.'

'But I didn't come here to congratulate either of you,' Megan replied, folding her arms and looking her father squarely in the eye. 'I came here to tell you something, Charlie.'

'What's that, love?'

She looked at him for a long time, carefully choosing her words.

'Just remember,' she said slowly, 'that you shat on our lives from a height, just so you could marry Doreen today. All those times you were taking Doreen out to dinner in posh restaurants? And whisking her off on sun holidays? I was the one who had to sit in Nan's house with Mum, not knowing what to say to her when she cried and fell into depression and stopped eating and started smoking twenty a day. Me and Nan were the ones who had to scoop her up off the floor and convince her that life was worth living again. I was only a small kid, Charlie, and because of you, that's what I had to deal with. You ruined her life, and buggered up mine. So just you remember that. Because, mark my words, one day it'll all come back to bite you in the arse. One day soon, if I've anything to do with it.'

I'm aware of Katherine blinking back at me, waiting on an answer.

'I got into this for personal reasons,' is all I say by way of a reply, with a quick, professional smile. 'But right now, you're about to do a full day of media with Billy and Jess, so why don't I help you out a bit? I can start to tackle the list of electors who have to be targeted with your policy manifesto. It's important in the final run-up to polling day. At least it's one less thing for you to worry about.'

'You're a very hard woman to say no to,' Katherine says, getting up to leave.

I say nothing. Instead I just remember that fat, juicy database that's upstairs on Billy's computer, thinking of what that information means to me, then sit back and smile, feeling deliciously in control again.

Just the way I like it.

Chapter Thirty-Two

Harriet

'Freddie? Do you not get it? Don't you see what this means?'

'Oh, yes . . . yes, absolutely,' Freddie says, looking back at her in utter confusion.

'Do you? Do you really see what's going on here?'

'Emm . . . yes! Yes, I most certainly do. And it's dreadful. Shocking! Don't suppose you fancy a bit of lunch, do you?'

'Freddie!'

'It's just that I only had a banana first thing this morning and they've got me chained to my desk ever since. Not that what you're telling me isn't of the utmost importance, of course,' he stresses. 'But couldn't we talk and eat a nice, tasty cheese panini at the same time?'

Harriet sighs deeply. She'd practically bolted out of the offices of Digby, Markby and Sellers earlier, full of gabbled apologies to Harold and George. All she'd wanted was to see Freddie and talk this over with him and see if he thought her suspicions were right. She'd hopped straight on a bus into town, her mind in overdrive, madly trying to process what she'd just heard.

Because she had to have got it wrong. It was as simple as that. This was unthinkable, it was unfathomable.

But – no – deep down, she knew right well that there was no mistake. This was a betrayal like she'd never experienced before in the whole course of her life.

And that's what made it worse than anything.

Finally, finally, finally Harriet got a hold of Freddie on his phone, who told her he was out at the Connair offices, which were right beside the airport. It was a measure of just how shocked she was, that she hailed down a taxi in town to get there instead of jumping onto a second bus, not even caring what a ridiculous extravagance it was.

It's an emergency, she told herself, so that was the end of that.

The Connair Head Office was steely and impressive when Harriet eventually arrived. She barely even reacted when the driver told her the fare was over twenty-five euro. Numbly, she stepped out of the cab and made her way inside the huge glass and concrete structure, with the distinctive Connair logo everywhere you looked.

Flights to Toulouse for €9!

That was just one of the many giant posters that lined the walls of the huge, double-ceilinged reception area, along with dozens of others that screamed *Fly to Paris East for €20 and New York for €75!* But then, in tiny writing, said that your baggage and booking charges were approximately double that and God help you if you wanted a cup of tea on board.

Normally, Harriet would have been a bit intimidated by all of this. Normally, she'd have thought long and hard about just barging in here unannounced, when Freddie was meant to be working.

But normality could feck right off with itself.

'I'm here to see Freddie de Courcey,' she said to a bright, smiley guy at reception, who appeared to be wearing foundation and contouring like a catwalk model.

'Well, well, well, lucky you,' he purred back at her, with a sly little wink.

So Harriet followed the directions to the tenth floor, stepped out of the lift and was just about to march down a long orange-carpeted corridor that she guessed led to the boardroom, when she heard her name being called out loud.

'Harriet! Golly, what a wonderful surprise!'

She looked around to see an open office door, where Freddie sat alone at a desk in a room the approximate size of a toilet cubicle, with a computer in front of him and a clear view of the airport runway through a floor-to-ceiling window directly behind.

Out it all came, everything. She blurted her story at him, her very worst fears, everything.

And now, here he is, just blinking two bewildered blue eyes back at her.

'So . . . what are you thinking?' he asks, tentatively.

'What am I thinking?' says Harriet, pacing up and down the tiny office, so she can get her thoughts properly in order. It's a trick she's picked up from Meg and you know what? It works no end. 'I'm thinking that I've been played for a complete idiot, Freddie, that's what I'm thinking. And you too. By your own grandmother! Don't you get what's gone on here? Can't you see the bigger picture? It beggars belief!'

'Right, right,' Freddie nods along. 'Goodness, yes, it's a rotten situation. Dreadful.'

'Oh, I had it straight from the horse's mouth,' Harriet blurts out. 'From George Markby Senior himself. Apparently, Meg did your grandmother a pretty big favour a year ago and was given the use of that flat in part payment.'

'Right, right, right,' says Freddie, trying to look like he knows what's going on, but still not really grasping it.

'So now,' Harriet says, turning to face him, 'ask yourself. What can that favour possibly have been? What happened one year ago? That involved Meg? Your grandmother more or less gifted Meg the lease on that apartment. Now, Freddie, why was that? Take a wild guess as to why she'd do a thing like that.'

'Well . . . emm,' says Freddie, 'a year ago . . . let me think . . .'

'A year ago is when I left to go to Africa,' Harriet finishes the thought for him. 'Now, maybe that's an astonishing coincidence, maybe I'm way off the mark – but I have a horrible feeling that I'm not. And you want to know the worst bit of all?' she asks, walking over to the window and staring down at the runway. 'My year abroad? It was entirely her doing – sure, she's the one who put the thought into my head in the first place! I had Meg down as a friend. I really did. But the whole time, she was playing me. God, when I think about it, she was playing me like a violin!'

'Utterly incomprehensible. . .' Freddie tries to say, but Harriet is way too het up to answer.

'In fact, now that I think of it,' she says, 'it's no wonder Meg was so cold and unwelcoming when I first landed back on her doorstep the other night. You should have seen her, Freddie! It was like I was a complete stranger. I couldn't wrap my head around it at first, I even put it down to her being stressed at work. Which,' she adds ironically, 'I guess she was, in a way. But now – well, now it all makes perfect sense, doesn't it?'

'Emm . . . does it?' he says cautiously.

'Because of course, the very minute Meg saw me, she knew it was game over for her. And for her precious apartment too.'

'Right, right-i-o,' says Freddie. 'Yes. Of course. All perfectly clear now. And you're quite certain?'

'Oh, I'm certain all right,' Harriet steams. 'I had it just now, in plain English, from your family solicitors.'

But he just looks back at her, blinking stupidly.

'Come on, Freddie,' Harriet says. 'Join the dots here. That apartment was payment in kind. Meg's job was to get me out of your life, and didn't she play her part to perfection? Sweet God, someone hand that girl an Oscar.'

'Right, right, yes,' says Freddie, nodding along. 'Yes, you're quite entitled to be cross about it. I know I am, too. Livid. Dreadful carry-on.'

'But here's what kills me most of all,' Harriet says, stopping to look right at him. 'Your grandmother hasn't even met me yet! So why would she just want me out of your life, without even taking the trouble getting to know me first? Have you any idea how hurtful that is?'

At that thought, Freddie says nothing, just looks a bit bashful.

'Freddie?' Harriet says, honing in on him. 'Is there something you want to tell me?'

'No, no. Nothing at all. Good lord, nothing.'

She sees through him though, in a matter of seconds.

'Maybe . . .' she begins carefully, formulating her thoughts as she speaks, 'something like this has happened before?'

Freddie blushes, like a little boy, and right there, she has her answer.

'You have *got* to be kidding me,' she says, shaking her head furiously. 'You mean, she's actually done this kind of thing in the past?'

'Well . . . em . . .' he says, twisting his hands in a nervous gesture.

'Please, Freddie! Just tell me, will you?' Harriet rarely raises her voice, but she is at breaking point.

'A lie I cannot tell,' he says, like the good little public schoolboy that he was. 'Yes, it actually did happen before.'

'Go on,' Harriet says, folding her arms.

'You have to understand,' Freddie says apologetically, 'that my grandmother very much sees herself *in loco parentis* as far as I'm concerned. Not to mention, I'm an only child. So, lord love her, but the woman does have a terrible habit of dabbling in my private life. Sometimes . . . well, more than sometimes . . . Well, quite a fair bit, if I'm being honest about it, really.'

'So? What happened?'

'Oh . . .' he says, ruffling his hands through his thick red hair, 'well, it was such a long time ago, and she really wasn't a particularly nice ex-girlfriend. A gold digger is what Granny called her, and the thing is, I don't think she was actually wrong either, do you see. Retrospectively, of course.'

'Why would you say that?'

'Because Granny went behind my back,' he says, twisting his hands nervously. 'And she offered the young lady in question a rather sizeable sum to . . . well, just exit stage left, I suppose is the politest way of putting it.'

'You're joking,' Harriet says, in shock. 'You mean she paid off your ex, to just disappear?'

'Quite a substantial sum too, if I remember,' Freddie says, shoving both his hands deep into his pockets. 'Of course, I knew nothing about this, only that one minute I had a girlfriend and the next minute, I didn't. Couldn't fathom it. Thought it was something I'd either said or done, or that she'd just had enough of me, but no, turned out not to be my fault at all. It was ages afterwards before Granny told me what had happened, and by then of course the damage was well and truly done . . . and . . . well . . . you know . . .'

'You were probably seeing someone else by then,' Harriet says, a bit calmer now. 'Of course you were.'

'Nothing quite like this has ever happened before though,' Freddie rushes to reassure her. 'This is on a whole different level. Even for my grandmother, and this was a woman who once flew the Atlantic solo, with an aircraft engine about the size of a hairdryer. She's one tough lady. Always having political fundraisers at the house, then reducing senior ministers to tears. Does it for fun, I sometimes think.'

'I mean, what kind of a family are you?' Harriet asks, shaking her head as she tries to process it all. 'Who behaves like this?'

'I know, but look at it this way,' Freddie says, sounding softer now. 'It's a measure of just how threatened Granny is by you, that she'd go to such bother in the first place. Because she knows how much you mean to me. And she knows you're different from all the others, Harriet. So wonderfully different.'

'Really?' she says, slightly more mollified now, as Freddie comes around to where she's standing, and gently slips both arms around her waist.

'Yes, really,' he says softly. 'That year you were away? Awful! I missed you so much, and it was a nightmare trying to get a hold of you with Skype or WhatsApp, because you were always working . . . on . . . emm . . . you know, latrines, and so forth.'

'Clean water initiatives,' she prompts.

'Yes, yes, all so wonderful. Anyway, it's fine and dandy now, because here we are. Together. And it's . . . lovely. Don't you think so too?'

She nods as he pulls her in tighter, till she is snuggled up against him.

'I'm so, so sorry,' he says. 'About my family, I mean. About all of it. Getting in the way, interfering . . .'

'Freddie, it's unthinkable what your grandmother did,' Harriet says, pulling away from him. 'I was played like a pawn on a chessboard. And what kills me most of all is . . .

why? Why were your family so anxious to get rid of me in the first place? You can say a lot of things about me, but I'm certainly not a gold digger. I shop in Penneys, for God's sake. And I like it. I live out of Lidl and Aldi. I'm good with budgets. I got a taxi out here, but that's about the most extravagant thing I've done in years.'

'I know,' he says soothingly, 'I know. Don't get upset, please.'

'Is it because I didn't go to the right school?' she insists. 'Or because of my accent, or because I don't have the right connections? Would you please mind telling me why I'm so objectionable?'

'But you're not! No one could possibly think that about you, ever.'

'I mean to say,' she sniffs into his shirt, as he pulls her back into his arms again, 'if you felt that way, then that would be one thing. It would be a helluva lot of trouble for you to go to, just to break up with me, but still – I'd take the hint and you wouldn't see me for dust. But for someone who's never laid eyes on me to do this?'

'Don't be cross,' Freddie says kindly. 'Because just look at us! Here we both are, and we're together and it just goes to show the lot of them, Granny included, that we're bigger than all of them.'

'So what do you suggest?' she says.

'Here's what you do,' he says gently. 'Come to the fund-raiser at the house tomorrow, just as we'd planned, and let me introduce you to Granny – and my grandfather too, and let's have it all out in the open.'

Just then, Harriet's mobile rings, in her jacket pocket. She automatically pulls away from Freddie, so she can glance down at the screen to see who's calling.

Meg Mobile

'Well, well, well,' she says, waving the phone at Freddie. 'This just got *very* interesting.'

Chapter Thirty-Three

Meg

'Hey, hon, am I disturbing you?' I ask, hoping I sound perky and upbeat. Bright and breezy is always the best tone with someone like Harriet, I've invariably found. Gets you so much further.

'No, it's OK, I can talk,' Harriet says.

I could swear I can hear the sound of someone being shushed in the background, but dismiss it immediately.

'Lucky you, lady of leisure,' I smile. 'Wish I was!'

'So whereabouts are you?' Harriet asks calmly.

'Oh, stuck here at the company head office,' I say. Total lie, of course; I'm actually still at Government Buildings, bolting up the stairs on my way to Katherine's office. Jess is due back very shortly, but for a precious few minutes, I hope to have the run of the place, with no one to double-check what I'm up to. So the plan is to make a copy of every single name and address on that electoral database onto a spare USB stick, which by pure good fortune, I have in my bag. Now, while I can.

This information, I think, breathless after yet another flight of stairs, *will make my job so piss-easy from here on in*. This is Grade A gold dust. Talk about being in the right place, at the right time? All I need to do now is get to work on Harriet and, God knows, that shouldn't pose too many challenges, should it? Like shooting fish in a barrel.

'So, you're at the head office of Pest Be Gone?' Harriet says down the phone. 'Isn't that where you said you worked? Just wanted to make sure I got the name right.'

'Yes, that's right,' I say, a bit surprised that she'd even ask, but then there you go, that's Harriet for you. Total weirdo.

'You poor thing, working so hard on a sunny day like this,' Harriet goes on, and am I imagining it, or is there a slight edge to her voice?

'Oh never mind about me,' I say. 'What about *you*? We have so much news to get through, don't we? So how about we meet up later on this evening? Slice of pizza and a glass of wine? Just like we used to?'

'No,' Harriet says. 'No, I don't think so.'

'O-*kaay*,' I say slowly, unused to hearing Harriet say the word 'no'. She's usually so pliant and malleable. 'Well, not to worry, I'll see you tonight back at the flat. Maybe we can have a glass of wine and good old catch-up chat then?'

'Or not,' Harriet says.

'But I'm so dying to hear all about your date night with Freddie! You still have to fill me in. I had to leave the flat so early this morning . . .'

'To get to work, I suppose?' Harriet says. 'To your big, important job at Pest Be Gone?'

Her whole tone has changed. No, I'm not imagining things. There's definite toughness, a flintiness that's never been there before.

'Harriet?' I ask, sounding puzzled now. 'Are you all right?'

'Absolutely,' comes the reply. 'Why wouldn't I be?'

'You seem . . .' I break off, searching for the right word. Stronger? More assertive? 'Not like yourself,' is what I settle on.

'Oh, I'm absolutely fine,' is all Harriet says. 'I'm great, in fact. Never been better.'

'Then we'll talk later?'

But Harriet doesn't answer. Instead, the call just clicks off.

I have to double-check, to make sure my phone has a full signal.

But no, there's no mistaking it. Harriet just hung up on me.

The worm, it seems, has turned.

*

And there's more bad news to come. I slip into Katherine's office and, just as I thought, have the place entirely to myself. So I fire up Billy's computer and quickly run a search for that precious, precious database.

Shit, shit, shit.

It's here all right, but password-protected. I call Billy to get the password; his phone goes straight to voicemail. Well, he's probably in the studio with Katherine right now, I think, so of course, his phone is switched off. I leave a bright, breezy message for him; nothing to arouse suspicion.

'Hey, it's me. I'm at Government Buildings, and if you want all these fliers to be zipped out to Katherine's constituents before the weekend, then it might be an idea to give me the password?'

Return my call quickly, I silently will him, *now, while the office is empty and when I can do what I need to do.*

But he doesn't. Precious minutes tick by and I'm just about to call him again when Jess bounces in, spies me on my own and is over like a bullet.

'Meg, there you are!' she beams. 'I thought I'd never get to talk to you in private! You won't believe this, but I called the number on that business card you gave me for Callaghan, and his election agent asked for a meeting with me on Tuesday morning, right after the election. "To discuss the future," were his exact words. Can you believe it?' she gushes, eyes shining. 'This could be it for me – Brussels, here I come!'

I put on my best 'interested and pleased' face, while she rabbits, on and on. Course, this means the end of any chink of privacy I might have had to get my paws on that database.

For now.

Chapter Thirty-Four

Harriet

'Harriet! Welcome back from . . . wherever the feck you've been for the last year!'

'You look good, baby sis . . . a bit on the skinny side, but good!'

'And look who's just arrived – Tim Nice-But-Dim!'

'Good to see you, Tim!'

'Freddie!' Harriet squeals at the twins. 'His name is Freddie!!! What, are you pair thick?'

'No, we're just getting married in three months' time, what do you expect us to be anyway, sober?'

The Trocadero restaurant in Dublin's city centre is jam-packed to capacity, as Harriet's family have all gathered for dinner, to celebrate the first time the entire Waters clan has been together in over a year. Sean, Harriet's dad has even booked everyone into the Brooks hotel, close to the restaurant, for the night, 'So there's no driving back home for anyone!' as he helpfully said.

'Wicked,' says Terry delightedly. 'This way we can all stagger straight to bed after dinner and a few bottles of vino.'

'Although that's the last treat the pair of you are getting out of your mother and I for at least the next decade,' Harriet's dad had replied. 'This wedding has the two of us bankrupt!'

Meanwhile, Harriet sits beside her mam, clinging onto each other, laughing and chatting and still catching up with all the gossip and news. They'd had a blissful family reunion at the airport earlier that afternoon, where Harriet had left Freddie at the Connair offices and gone to meet her parents straight off their flight home from New York. And they'd barely stopped to draw breath since. Now they are happily ensconced at a table together, both of them loving being face to face with each other again.

Freddie de Courcey has been invited to join the family for dinner too. However Terry and Jack have immediately dragged him over to the bar with them, catching him in a rough pincer movement, gripping him by the neck and arms, ruffling his hair and generally treating him like he is one of their own.

'Boys!' Harriet's mother says sternly, putting down her gin and tonic and looking disapprovingly at all the messing that is going on. 'Behave yourselves around Freddie, will you? He's only just got here, he's our dinner guest and not everyone appreciates the way you pair carry on!'

Carole Waters is tiny in stature, with a voice that makes you drop whatever you're doing, to stop and listen. But then, the woman is a country vet, dealing with large animals, and, as she has always said, dealing with runaway heifers is not that dissimilar to dealing with her twin sons.

The boys instantly untangle poor Freddie, who laughs gamely, thanks them for inviting him, then ambles over in that dishevelled, long-legged way of his, to where Harriet and her mam are sitting.

He gives Harriet a little peck on the cheek and she immediately introduces him to her mother, thinking about how often she's fantasised about this moment, and now, here she is, actually taking Freddie into the heart of her family. Pity the twins have to be at their messiest and most rowdy, even in a fancy restaurant, but then, they're like that most of the time, and at least Freddie has met them before, so he's had a bit of forewarning about what to expect.

'It's such a pleasure to finally meet you, Mrs Waters,' Freddie says, doing a tiny little head bow and shaking her hand warmly. All very public school, and posh and gentlemanly, in total contrast to the twins, who've now moved on to some class of a drinking contest at the bar and who are yelling at Freddie to join in.

'Very nice to meet you too, Freddie,' Carole says, smiling. 'And I apologise in advance for my sons. I wish I could say they're just acting like this because it's their stag night this Saturday, but sadly, that's not the case at all. They're like this most of the time. Harriet will vouch for that.'

'It was very good of you to include me,' Freddie smiles, his blue eyes twinkling. 'Certainly been a while since I've been to a lovely family dinner like this, I can tell you.'

'Freddie?' says Jack, nabbing him from behind in what looks like a Heimlich manoeuvre. 'Come and meet Dad, he's at the bar, have a few scoops with us before dinner – we're even buying!'

'Yeah, which doesn't happen often,' quips Terry, 'so you might as well make the most of it!'

Freddie, it has to be said, looks bewildered, but delighted at the same time, and willingly allows himself to get dragged over to meet Harriet's dad with the boys.

Now that they are alone, Carole Waters turns her full attention back to her daughter.

'He's a sweetheart,' she says approvingly.

'Isn't he?' Harriet smiles. 'He's such a good soul too. And I'm delighted you invited him tonight, he'll have a great time. I know he will. From the sounds of it, his family never sit down together for dinner and a big, boisterous chat, like we do.'

'From what you've told me . . .' Carole says, as if she were pronouncing a diagnosis on a colicky racehorse, 'I think you and Freddie could be good together. I really do.'

'You do, Mam?' That means such a lot to Harriet. She is incredibly close to her mam, and her good opinion matters more to her than anyone's. Carole is as straight-talking as they come; if she didn't take to Freddie, she'd have said so, with no frills attached.

'If you want to know my two cents' worth,' Carole goes on, 'then here it is. It seems to me that, to the outside world, Freddie might have money and come from a ridiculously wealthy family, but actually, he's the one who's lucky to have you. Because you don't care about any of that. You genuinely like him for who he is and not what he comes from.'

'That's a beautiful thing to say,' Harriet smiles, really touched. 'Thanks, Mam.'

'You're good for him,' her mam says. 'And now his family need to realise that they'd actually be very lucky to have you in their lives.'

'Freddie's the kindest, sweetest man I ever met,' Harriet says truthfully. 'I love that he's so innocent and enthusiastic about everything – it's endearing. And he's good to me, Mam, so thoughtful and funny and . . . look, here's the thing. I know it's early days. We were so close before I went away, and now we need to learn to be around each other again. All I'm saying is, so far, so good.'

'But let's not forget,' Carole cautions, 'there's the small matter of his grandmother sending that malicious little viper to try to break the two of you up.' She breaks off there and takes a sip of her gin and tonic, shaking her head in disbelief. 'God Almighty. When I think of how taken in by Meg Monroe we all were? I thought she was such a lovely woman – such a good friend to you too. How deceived were we? It doesn't bear thinking about.'

'Don't remind me,' Harriet shudders. 'Meg played me, right from day one. I could kick myself for being taken in by her so easily. I'm just glad I haven't had to set foot back in her flat ever since I discovered the truth earlier today. I came straight to meet you and Dad off your flight, and it was the loveliest distraction I could have asked for. But how about this, Mam. I'm meeting Freddie's grandmother tomorrow night. What do I do? How do I handle this?'

'Let's deal with one problem at a time,' Carole says calmly. 'Meg Monroe first, I think. To think that she was the driving force behind you going away for a whole year, when we all missed you so much! The woman is dangerous and she needs to be stopped. Right now.'

'You're absolutely right,' Harriet says thoughtfully, sitting back against the banquette booth she and her mam are cosied up in, as the waiter comes to deliver menus. 'I've twisted that and turned it backwards and forwards in my mind so many times since I discovered the truth. Because the thing is, I don't think I'm alone, Mam. I think that Meg has lots of other people just like me, who she's been paid, or paid in kind, to get rid of.'

'It beggars belief,' says Carole. 'It's such a violation of any kind of moral code.'

'What's most astonishing of all is how good she is at it. You'd want to see the way Meg worked on me before I went away last year. She was even crying at the airport because I was leaving, when it was all her idea in the first place.'

'Have you any idea who these others are?' Carole asks. 'Do you have any names or any rough idea of who else Meg may be doing this to? She wasn't able to keep you and Freddie apart, but there may be people out there who aren't so lucky. You could help, Harriet. In fact, you have a duty to.'

'Well, as a matter of fact,' says Harriet slowly, 'I do. Because there was a noticeboard in Meg's flat, stuffed full with Post-it notes, with all sorts of names, dates and places scribbled all over them. Katherine Sisk for one. THE Katherine Sisk.'

'Well, well,' Carole says. 'Isn't that interesting?'

'So what'll I do, Mam?'

Carole takes another sip of her G&T before answering.

'I'll tell you exactly what you do,' she says, after a pause. 'You start with Meg Monroe herself and you do whatever it takes to make this right.'

'Whatever it takes,' Harriet says, sitting back and looking around her. Her family, all in great form, happy out and celebrating being together again. And for the first time all day, Harriet Waters feels that everything is going to be OK.

FRIDAY

Chapter Thirty-Five

Meg

A crazy day ahead, but fortunately, that's just the way I like it. It's the crack of dawn and already I'm up and about, diligently working away on this actor guy, Jonny Featherstone-Jones, whoever he is, so I can really go to town on him. How, I haven't yet decided, but that'll all come in good time. I'll do a bit more online searching about him first, before deciding what costume to wear, what character to assume and how best to approach him. It's a whole process, trust me.

Which is why the home address for him, which I managed to filch from the electoral database in Katherine Sisk's office, really is beyond prize to me. And when I get my hands on the entire database, later on today with any luck? My life will be a complete breeze, I think, beavering away at my desktop computer, zoning in on all of Jonny's past addresses via good old Google Maps. From here on in, just having access to the name and address of every registered voter in the state will speed up my work rate no end. Happy clients equals happy days.

Yawning and stretching, I get up from my desk and wander into the living area, rubbing my neck. Then I pad barefoot over to the balcony, open the doors and step outside into the fresh early-morning breeze, to take a little breather and to clear my head.

My lovely home, I think. *My lovely view of the cruise ships docked out in the harbour.* And Ellen de Courcey seriously thinks she can just turf me out of here without a by-your-leave? Good luck to her with that. Because I'm already hard at work preparing a case against the de Courceys. Or rather, against those two decrepit old codgers, in that stinking excuse for a legal office.

Honestly, how do those two function in this day and age?

I'll make mincemeat of them. I picked up an impressive amount of legal knowledge working at Sloan Curtis all those years, plus I intend to bring a bit of street smarts to the fore and God help Digby, Markby and Sellers, when faced with me across a courtroom. Maybe neither of them have ever even studied the terms of the lease I signed on the flat, but by God, I'm doing it now. Ad nauseum.

Because I've got legal rights here too, lots of them. Plus, I've already spotted at least three loopholes in the lease that might effectively get me off the hook. Worst-case scenario? Maybe I'll still end up getting turfed out of this apartment, but if it comes to that, it certainly won't be without a hefty cash settlement to soften the blow.

I plonk myself down on one of the rattan sofas on the balcony, lean my head back against one of the cushions, and breathe in the mild, humid air as my mind begins to wander.

Harriet Waters. Sooner or later, all of my problems can be quickly traced back to Harriet bloody Waters. Harriet, who, by the way, never came home last night. The sofa bed was entirely unslept in when I got up. She's not answering her phone either, which is so unlike her.

Normally, Harriet's like an eager little puppy, always trying to nail me down to a time and place when we can hang out and do things together. I can practically hear her voice ringing in my ears. *'I just want to spend time with you!'* At least, until that weird phone call yesterday, when Harriet had sounded . . . so different. Plus, Ellen de Courcey's famous fundraiser is on this evening and I know for a fact that Harriet will most definitely be there, at thick-boy Freddie's express invitation.

A challenge, I think, hauling myself back to my feet, padding back in from the balcony and sliding the glass door shut behind me. *And challenges are there to be overcome.*

I pick up both my phones and get straight back to my desk.

Back to work.

Back to what I'm best at.

Back to being The Fixer.

Chapter Thirty-Six

Meg

Government Buildings

Later on that morning, I'm tucked behind a 'hot desk' in that sweaty, claustrophobic little office, high up in the eaves of Government Buildings. Still haven't had the opportunity or the privacy to download that glorious, fat, juicy database yet, as it's busier than Grand Central Station here today. So what can I do, but wait it out and grab my chance as soon as I see it? I have a fresh pile of USB sticks beside me and am ready to go at the drop of a hat. On the plus side though, I'm making terrific headway with Jess, and feeling pretty darn smug about how this one is playing out, thanks very much.

I brought her in coffee (skinny latte, extra shot, no foam – remembered exactly how she likes it, of course) and a croissant as a sort of late brekkie for her. She lit up when she saw both me and the grub, and has actually spent the rest of the morning being fairly pleasant, as it happens.

'Good to see you,' I said to her when I got here earlier, whipping off my coat. 'I know the day ahead is crazy busy, so I brought supplies,' I added, holding up the Starbucks bag.

'That's thoughtful of you,' Jess smiled back at me. 'I really appreciate it – with three days until the election, it's going to be tough getting out of here to go to the loo, never mind grab food.'

'Wait until you're in Brussels or Strasbourg,' I stage-whispered across the office to her, with a wink. 'Can you imagine the food over there? Pains au chocolat and those divine crêpes Suzette that all the street vendors sell right outside the Conseil de l'Europe, or along Parc l'Orangerie? Lunch breaks and eating out will be very different experiences over there, I'll bet!'

I have never set foot in either Strasbourg or Brussels in my life, but what can I say? I did my research. And hit a home run. Jess's eyes instantly glistened, as she gratefully took the coffee I handed over to her.

'Can you just imagine?' she said, looking dreamy and wistful. 'I can't stop thinking about it, and how much my whole life would change if it were ever to happen.'

'Oh, it's yours for the taking,' I told her confidentially. 'All you need is for Callaghan to lose this election so he has to go back to his old EU job, and you're home and dry.'

'I know I'm supposed to be working here,' Jess said, keeping her voice good and low. 'But actually . . . strictly between you and me . . .'

Then she spun her laptop around to show me what she was really at. Googling cheap flats to rent in Brussels, no less. Bingo.

*

So now we've been working side by side for hours and all I can think is – she's hooked, and all I need is the room to myself for a few precious minutes, and I'm happy.

Just then the door bursts open and in strides Billy.

'Wow,' he says, taking us both in. 'Here you both are. The hard-working team, slaving away. No sign of Philip to give you a hand?'

I throw a quick glance over to Jess, but she doesn't react at all. Instead, she's just focused on the screen in front of her, scrolling, scrolling, scrolling.

A very good sign, methinks. Brussels clearly means more to her than he does.

'No rest for the wicked,' I smile brightly back at him, while Jess just gives a friendly little wave.

Billy dumps a pile of files down on the desk I'm sitting at, then stands up to his full height to yawn and stretch.

'What are you doing anyway, Meg? Mind if I take a look?' he says, shoving his hands into his pockets and idly ambling around to where I'm sitting, still buried deep in work.

'Oh, all very boring,' I say, 'just doing as I promised, making sure all of Katherine's constituents are targeted with her election manifesto.'

'And it's all in hand?' Billy asks. 'Looking good?'

'All in hand,' I say cheerily. 'Not a problem.'

'You remember what I told you about the electoral database? It doesn't leave this room, for any reason whatsoever.'

'Absolutely not,' I say, pretend-horrified at the very thought.

'Well, the boss will certainly be pleased,' Billy says, taking out his phone and reading a text message that's just come through. 'That's her now, in fact.'

'Katherine?' Jess says. 'Where is she, anyway? I thought you and she had a full morning of radio interviews.'

'All of which are done and dusted,' Billy smiles, 'and all of which, I'm delighted to report, went very well. Few tough questions that she managed to deal with under pressure, but otherwise, not a bad morning's work. Holding steady in the polls, if you can believe pollsters, that is. Anyway, don't either of you want to know what that text message said just now?'

'Go ahead,' Jess shrugs back at him.

'Katherine says to tell you there's a photocall happening downstairs in front of the portrait of Countess Markievicz, for all the women working in Government Buildings. She says she'd love you both to be included in the photo too.'

'Me as well?' I say, surprised.

'Yes, you as well. Now go on, what are you waiting for? Scram, the pair of you!' he grins, almost scooting us out the door. 'Bring me back a coffee if you've time!' is his parting shot.

'Ha! Weren't you the one who promised to do that for us?' I toss back over my shoulder at him, already on my way out the door and banging it shut behind me, for the first time since I got here, leaving my desk and everything on it completely unattended.

Chapter Thirty-Seven

Meg

Last thing I'd wanted to do was leave Katherine Sisk's office back at Government Buildings, but like it or not, I've no choice. Another job to do, another client to keep happy – hopefully. I told everyone I was dashing out on a last-minute bit of pre-election constituency business on Katherine's behalf and that I'd be back as fast as I could. A few texts from Billy have pinged through in the last half-hour, saying, 'Where are you? You're needed here!' But nothing that I can't handle.

Of course I'll zip back to the office just as fast as I can; well, I have to, don't I? It's already lunchtime and I still haven't had a chance to download that precious electoral database. But for now, I'm busy chasing up yet another job for yet another client and so far, so good.

'You can leave me off here, just at the street corner,' I say to the taxi driver, bossily telling him exactly where to park, before handing him over a crisp fifty-euro note and instructing him to keep the change.

'Well, thanks very much, love, pleasure doing business with you,' he replies, delighted with himself.

I climb out of the taxi and take a moment to look around; so far, so normal. I'm standing on Myrtle Street, at a tiny row of council houses, all of which look like old Victorian railway cottages to me and most of which are sadly in need of an upgrade.

The rubbish bins are overflowing, the whole place stinks to high heaven and it seems the only retailers for miles consist of a bookie's shop and a solitary chipper, with a gang of lads loitering around outside, ready to pick a fight with anyone who looks crossways at them. Anyone else would have been intimidated by these surroundings, but not me. Let's face it, I come from a lot worse, and this is nothing to me. If anyone tries to mug me for my phone, or cash, or my good Michael Kors bag, God help them.

I double-check I've got the right address. I'd only managed to take a sneaky, surreptitious screenshot of this one, single address from that database, but I still needed to be careful. Billy had spotted the stash of USB sticks on my desk earlier and surprised me by being remarkably perceptive.

'These USB sticks belong to you?' he'd asked, as soon as Jess and I got back to the office after that photocall with Katherine.

'Is there a problem?' I'd asked him politely, with a big, bright smile.

'You do remember me telling you that the electoral database is highly classified information, don't you?' he said warningly. 'And that it cannot, under any circumstances, leave this office?'

'Absolutely,' I nodded.

'Because you seem to have a hell of a lot of USB sticks lying around,' he went on, looking at me all worried and frowning and concerned.

I didn't even regard something like this as an obstacle. Thinking on my feet, thankfully, is where I shine. I eyeballed him, and instantly started acting the klutz. The new girl.

'Oh Jeez, Billy, that's nothing! I always have a stack of back-up keys with me, no matter what I'm working on. Just to be on the safe side. And that's it, that's all. Nothing to see here, I promise.'

'Meg,' he said, looking at me a bit strangely. 'GDPR rules prevent us, or anyone in this building for that matter, from ever removing a shred of this from the office. *Ever*. It's privileged information, and that's the way it has to stay. We're only allowed to use it for the purposes of canvassing door to door and absolutely nothing more. I won't say it again. Got it?'

'Gotcha loud and clear,' I said, sounding bright and breezy, while thinking, *Oh spare me the bloody lecture, you sanctimonious git.*

My own takeaway from that conversation? Don't get caught.

*

And now, thanks to that precious electoral register, here I am on Myrtle Street, pounding the pavement, checking every house that has a number until I finally get the right one. At least I fervently hope it is the right one, so I can get out of this dump as fast as possible.

It turns out to be a classic two-up, two-down corpo house that opens directly on to the street, in a row of terraced houses exactly the same and all in varying states of dilapidation.

I put on the prop glasses I have with me, scrape my hair back into a neat ponytail, take a stack of fliers out of my bag and knock on the door. The window that opens out on to the street is right beside me, and I can hear the sound of a match on TV that's in full swing. It's obviously a big and important match, because it sounds like there's a gang of lads gathered around to watch it, and every now and then I can clearly hear chants of 'Go on, it's a penalty! The referee is an arsehole, is he blind?'

Eventually, on the second ring, the door is answered by a guy about my own age, wiry and lanky, wearing a T-shirt that says *Climate Action Now* and with the thickest head of hair I think I've ever seen, arranged in a gelled-up style that's shaped like an ocean wave and that has to take a good half-hour daily.

'Yeah?' he says, eyeing me up and down suspiciously. 'You here with the pizzas?'

Do I look like I work for Dominos, I resist snapping at him. Instead, I get straight into character, and launch my little pre-prepared speech. 'Hi there,' I smile warmly. 'I'm working with the Katherine Sisk re-election campaign.'

'Are you canvassing?' Gel-Head asks me, shoving his hands deep into his jeans pockets.

'Absolutely,' I reply. 'And I wondered if I could possibly have a word with Jonny Featherstone-Jones, if this is the right address for him?'

'Ehh . . . yeah. Jonny lives here all right,' this guy shrugs. 'So you don't want to talk about Katherine Sisk's election promises then? Only I'm a bit of a political activist myself, you know. Except I'm a Green Party man. Gotta save the planet, you know. Climate change is for real. There is no Planet B.'

'Sorry, but all I really want is to have a quick work with Jonny,' I say, flashing my very fakest smile, the one I only ever use when I'm dealing with halfwits. 'If he's available, that is?'

'HEY JONESY!' the guy yells, at a decibel level that makes me wince. 'There's some woman here to see you! Get your arse out here!!!'

'Piss off!' comes the roar back from the living room, where the telly is on fully sonic blast. 'We're almost into extra time – tell whoever it is to kiss my arse!!'

'It'll just take a moment,' I say hopefully.

'JONSEY? SHE'S ACTUALLY QUITE HOT . . . YOU MIGHT WANT TO MEET THIS ONE.'

Jesus Christ. I wince, and let the casual sexism wash all over me, reminding myself that I'm here to do a job and nothing else.

'Right then, bring her in here,' this Jonny Featherstone-Jones calls back.

'You heard him,' Gel-Head says, opening the door wider to let me pass through.

I do, and instantly regret it. The stench of an overflowing toilet is what hits me first, mixed with the garlicky, oniony smell of a stale pizza, that's still in its box, lying with a load of other rubbish in the hallway. Effectively, the whole house looks and smells like a pigsty that hasn't seen a bottle of bleach in years.

I hold my breath and follow Gel-Head into the TV room, where no fewer than six lads, all virtually impossible to tell apart, sit lounging around, as the final moments of a soccer match play out.

All heads swivel my way, and a weaker character might just find this intimidating, walking into such a testosterone-heavy cesspit. The smell of feet alone would take the wind out of you.

There's a couple of wolf whistles directed my way, which I will myself not to lose my cool over.

'So which one of you is Jonny Jones?' I say to the room, schoolmarm style.

'I am!' they all say in messy unison, then, all talking at the same time, try to ask me out on a date.

'Jeez, she's not half bad . . .'

'Nice legs . . . good figure . . .'

'Reminds me of your woman from the movies . . . whats-hername . . . Audrey Tatou . . .'

Enough. That's it, I've had enough. Either I get what I came for, or I'll murder one of these Neanderthals, it's as simple as that.

'Jonny Featherstone-Jones? The registered tenant who lives here? Is that you?' I ask, taking a potshot and zoning in on the quietest guy, who's sitting in a corner, the only one who actually seems to remember that there's an actual match on.

'Hmm,' he says distractedly. He stays glued to the dying minutes of the game, as I do my thing.

Age: 27–28. Clearly a man who moisturises. Which is surprising, given the state of where he lives. Whippet-thin and undernourished-looking, with the sunken pallor of a night animal. A smoker, judging by his fingernails, and someone who lives off takeout food, if the crop of acne rosacea clustered around his jawline is anything to go by.

Dressed: in Gap, but it's clearly all years out of date. Wearing jeans that are badly frayed, and not in a designer/cool way, with battered trainers that the tongues are sticking out of in one foot. And a hoodie. In fact, hoodies seem like a uniform among this gang of lads; every single one of them is in one, like they're compulsory.

'I actually am a big fan of yours,' I begin, wishing that I could get to work on him privately, away from this gang of primates.

'Aghhhhh!' the rest of the lads fall around guffawing. 'Jonny man, you just got recognised!! For the first time in your whole pathetic acting career, you were actually recognised!'

'What have you seen him in before, love?' one of them asks me cheekily. 'Was it the commercial for incontinence pads? Where he plays the loving grandson buying knickers for his grandma?'

'Some of his finest work, right there!'

'Other actors dream of playing the Dane. But with our Jonesy, no, it's incontinence pads all the way!'

'Fuck off, you lot, will you?' Jonny says sulkily, eyes still glued to the match.

'No,' I say calmly and clearly. 'No, it was nothing like that at all, actually. As a matter of fact, I saw you onstage. And that's actually why I'm here to talk to you.'

Silence from around the room now. Just the sound of the TV blaring in the background, as the commentator announces that the match is now going into extra time.

'Come out to the hall,' Jonny says, instantly getting up to his feet. 'Where it's quieter.'

I do just that, resisting the urge to hold my nose as I step back out into that putrid hallway, taking care to avoid an empty pizza box that now seems to be doubling up as an ashtray.

'I thought you were brilliant in that play I saw you in,' I gush, acting as if I've just met Ryan Gosling. 'Except the name of the play slips my mind just now . . .'

'*Two's Company, Three's a Crowd*,' Jonny prompts, looking delighted with himself, all interested now that the conversation is about him. 'So you're one of the dozen or so people who came to see it? What did you think of it?'

'You were wonderful,' I say automatically. 'In fact, I said it on the night. I said that guy is going to be BIG. And, as it happens, I'm a playwright, with a project I'm developing that I really think you'd be perfect for.'

'That's certainly interesting all right,' Jonny nods eagerly, folding his arms and looking like this is only his due. 'In fact, you and I should talk some more. Do you want to swap numbers, so we can grab a drink? And you can tell me all about the play? And how big the part is?'

I smile. 'I'd love nothing more.'

Chapter Thirty-Eight

Harriet

7.30 p.m.

It is like a fairyland. Harriet and her family, the twins included, have just arrived at the de Courcey house, and their eyes are practically out on stilts, cartoon-style.

'Harriet, be well warned,' Terry says, 'if you don't nab Freddie, I will! Would you look at this place? It's *insane!*'

'Now, boys, on your best behaviour, please,' says Carole sternly, as they all troop up the dozen stone steps that whisk you up to the main entrance door. There, cloakroom attendants are on standby to take your coats, and the catering staff almost look like they are lying in wait for you, so fast are they to offer you a glass of champagne, served, of course, in crystal flutes, with the de Courcey crest discreetly cut into each one.

The giant stone hallway is thronged to bursting and to see the de Courcey hospitality in full swing, really is a sight to behold. Scores of beautifully dressed guests, all looking their very best, mill around, and more than a few famous faces dot the crowd. There are TV presenters, government ministers, models and actors, high-brow artists and classical musicians, several representatives from the world of literature, most of the country's championship rugby team; there's even a world-famous pop star present, but, of course, given that the de Courceys are hosting, this is no wannabe boy band member. No, this is a bona fide, 'elder statesman' rock star with a sideboard full of Emmys and a wall lined with platinum discs, widely rumoured to be a shoo-in for the next Nobel Peace Prize. And of course, because this is a pre-election political fundraiser, it seems like most of Government Buildings has decamped here too.

'Jesus Christ!' Jack blurts out, 'it's like Buckingham Palace in here!'

'Are you telling me that one family really, seriously live here?' Terry asks. 'It's the size of ten Olympic stadiums put together!'

'Boys,' Carole barks at them. 'You were warned not to act the maggot, just for this one night. Remember, we're here to support Harriet and Freddie, and if you make a holy, mortifying show of us, then I'm warning you, I won't be responsible.'

'Come on lads,' says Harriet's dad Sean, who is starting to look a little bit overwhelmed at his surroundings. 'What do you say we grab a drink and explore around the place a bit? Don't you worry, Carole,' he nods to his wife, 'I'll make sure they stay well out of trouble.'

'Can you believe that pair?' Carole mutters at Harriet, when it's just the two of them side by side, in that packed, giant entrance hall, where the chatter has risen to a crescendo. 'Thirty-three years of age, and I still have to talk to them like bold schoolboys. Honestly. It would put years on you. Your poor father is worn out – he says babysitting a pair of toddlers wouldn't be as much hassle.'

'It's such a pity that Sofia and Alisha couldn't be here this evening,' Harriet says, gaping up at the ceiling, drinking it all in. 'Wouldn't they have loved it?'

'Tonight is their hen night, love,' Carole reminds her, 'and the best of luck to them. I'm telling you, my nerves are shattered just thinking about the boys' stag night tomorrow. Although I wouldn't have missed an evening like this for the world. Wasn't it kind of Freddie to invite us?'

'Are you kidding, Mam? He was so touched to have been included in our little family dinner last night – he's been talking about how great you and Dad are all day.'

Just then, from scarily high above them, Harriet hears the sound of her own name being called out.

'Harriet! There you are – look! I'm up here!'

She and Carole automatically follow the voice upwards – and upwards – and upwards again, and there, standing in a minstrels' gallery, at least thirty feet above the melee, is Freddie. Looking so handsome tonight, Harriet thinks, in a light blue suit with a white shirt opened at the neck. His coppery red hair looks freshly washed and he's beaming happily from ear to ear, genuinely delighted to see them, and waving furiously.

'Sweet divine,' says Carole, as she and Harriet wave back up at him, 'how in the name of God did he get up there?'

'Stay right where you are!' Freddie yells back down at them. 'Don't move an inch – either of you! I'm on my way down. Incoming!'

A few minutes later, he is winding his way through the throng, full of 'hellos' and 'oh, please excuse mes', till he finds Harriet and Carole, hugging them both warmly and welcoming them profusely.

'It's so wonderful that you're here,' he's grinning broadly from ear to ear. 'I've been watching out for you all for ages. And don't you both look utterly breathtaking?'

He takes Harriet by both hands, as Carole looks on fondly. 'Love the dress,' he says to Harriet.

'Thank you,' Harriet smiles prettily, twirling around in a pale blue silk dress, with thin spaghetti straps, that clings to her tall, lean figure perfectly and is the exact match of her eyes. 'Mum very kindly took me shopping today and told me to pick out anything I wanted – money no object. It was the best fun and the biggest treat imaginable!'

'Sure I haven't seen my only girl in so long,' Carole says, 'it was the least I could do for her. The only one of my kids who gives me no hassle.'

'You look jolly gorgeous too, Carole,' Freddie smiles warmly at her. 'Love the red dress on you – stunning.'

'Thank you very much,' Carole says, delighted with the compliment.

'And your husband is here somewhere?' he asks respect-fully. 'And the twins too, I hope?'

'Oh, they're here somewhere all right,' Carole says, rolling her eyes. 'Although knowing them, they've probably found their way to the bar by now. But tell me this, Freddie,' she goes on, 'how on earth did you get up to the ceiling like that? My heart was in my mouth, just looking up at you!'

'Minstrels' gallery,' he replies. 'Old trick of mine, back to when I was little and my parents would entertain in this house. I was never allowed to go to any of their parties, but my nanny would let me sit up there out of harm's way and watch all the comings and goings. Perfect way to spy on all the guests.'

'This house . . .' Harriet says, ' is . . . just . . . well, I've never been anywhere like this before, like ever!'

'In that case, I'll have to give you both the whole tour,' Freddie says obligingly. 'Takes a bit of time though. Hope you've got good walking shoes on!'

'I'd adore to see the house,' says Carole, looking keenly all around her, drinking it all in, 'it's really out of this world. A tour would be wonderful.'

'Right-i-o. In that case, come with me, ladies,' he says, linking arms with both women and leading them on through to the ballroom, just to the left of the grand entrance hall. 'But before I show you over the old homestead, there's some-one here who I should very much like you to meet.'

Chapter Thirty-Nine

Meg

7.40 p.m.

It serves me right for actually thinking that I might snatch a rare bit of privacy. It's sheer and utter mayhem back at Katherine's office in Government Buildings, like a sweatshop more than anything else, and in spite of all my watching and waiting, I still don't get five minutes on my own to do what I need to do and make a copy of that database.

Jess is here, Billy is hovering most annoyingly, Philip Sisk is in and out, and it seems like a whole cohort of Katherine's well-wishers and supporters have been dropping by all afternoon and evening to offer any kind of support they can, in this, the final push of the campaign.

My phone rings and it's Katherine.

'Meg?'

'Katherine, how can I help you?' I ask, steeling myself. She's been doing last-minute door-to-door canvassing all evening and it sounds like she's calling me from her car. 'Are you on your way home?'

'Yes,' she says, 'I'm on my way home for a quick shower, then I'm straight back out the door again. But I'll tell you exactly how you can help. You can change into a little party dress and join me and the rest of the team at a political fundraiser in about an hour's time. Forgive the short notice, Meg, but I really need you there. And I'm afraid you'll have to rush – the party has already started by now, so we're already late.'

Shit, shit, shit. Of course I know all about this fundraiser, I know exactly when and where it's happening and more to the point, who's hosting it. Jess has been banging on about it all bloody day and wondering what she'll wear, and lamenting the fact that she doesn't have time to get her hair done.

I was just quietly hoping I could weasel out of having to be there myself. Mainly because Harriet will be there, hanging out of Freddie for the entire night. Every project I've been working on colliding together at one event on one single night. A living nightmare, in other words.

A quick, fleeting sense of panic hits me and I have to take a gulp of water from the bottle in front of me to catch my breath. Half of me wants to crawl under the desk and ignore the whole lot of them, but that's not an option. Besides, I've never been a coward before in my life and I'm certainly not going to start acting like one now. I'll face them all and I'll stand tall. Defence is the best method of attack, after all, isn't it?

'Sorry to do this to you,' Katherine adds, lowering her voice, 'but I just found out Toby Callaghan will be there too, and so it's a perfect opportunity for you to tie up all loose ends with Jess, so we can nail this. You do follow me?'

Of course I follow her, what does the woman think I am, stupid? Dispatching Jess off to Brussels to work for Callaghan was my idea in the first place, I want to remind her, but professionalism prevails. It all depends on Callaghan losing the election next Monday, but even I can't control that one.

I start to think – fast. Yes, this is a nightmare, but on the other hand, it does give me a chance to make a direct appeal to Ellen de Courcey. Ellen wants Harriet dispatched right away, and I know that's a physical impossibility. But what's to stop me pleading with her for more time? To let the dust settle a bit, and maybe even – shock, horror – allow whatever is going on between Freddie and Harriet to just run its course?

And now Callaghan will be there too, as will Jess, so this is a golden opportunity for me to at least get this one in the bag.

The only risk I run, given how weird she's been with me ever since the other night, is Harriet having a go at me in public. It's risky, very risky. But in my line of work, this is a risk I'll just have to take.

'Meg?' Katherine's voice comes down the phone again. 'You still there?'

'No need to text me the address,' I tell her crisply. 'Give me one hour and I'll see you there.'

I'll have to head home beforehand, of course, to change – and whatever I do end up wearing will have to be very carefully selected.

Givenchy, I think. A short, black, lacy, sexy killer of a dress.

Because I have a strong feeling that one way or another, this is going to be a killer of a night.

Chapter Forty

Harriet

7.45 p.m.

Moments later, Freddie de Courcey is guiding both Harriet and her mum, Carole, through the family ballroom, which is almost like a scene from a movie. Everywhere you look, catering staff are expertly gliding in and out through the mass of guests, filling up champagne glasses, tempting them with tiny, elegant-looking canapés, making sure that everyone's every need has been catered for, to perfection.

'Freddie!' Carole says, gaping in awe up at the double-height ceiling, with its elaborate coving and no fewer than four enormous crystal chandeliers, which cast everyone below in the most flattering light imaginable. 'This really is something extraordinary – the house has to be early eighteenth century, doesn't it? Not often you see Palladian mansions like this still in the hands of one single family. And kept in such exquisite condition too.'

'Mam is a total sucker for old houses,' Harriet explains to Freddie. 'She's forever going off on tours of stately homes and dragging us all along with her.'

And your family actually live in one, she could add, but doesn't.

'And have you seen this art collection?' Carole says, looking knowledgeably around her. 'Look, Harriet, two William Blakes – and don't tell me that's an actual Turner over there by the fireplace?'

'Golly,' says Freddie, looking at her, impressed. 'You really do know your stuff, don't you? You should be giving tour parties, not me – I'm afraid I'm hopeless. Granny says I wouldn't know a Doric column from a jar of Bovril.'

Freddie keeps up the friendly chat and Harriet is wondering where they are headed, although she knows it has to be to meet the famous Ellen de Courcey, that universal hater of anyone who dares to look twice at her precious Freddie.

Carole shoots her a supportive little half-wink as they move towards the perimeter of the room, which is some achievement, given how packed to the rafters the whole place is.

Just then, Harriet becomes aware of a knot of guests, all clustered around one VIP guest in particular, who appears to be in a wheelchair. This elderly lady has to be ninety if she's a day, with bullet-grey hair set in a heavily lacquered 'do' exactly the way the Queen wears hers. She is dressed from head to toe in black, and it is as if other guests are lined up to touch the hem of a religious visionary, such is the deferential mood of respect from everyone who's gathered around to greet her.

Carole shoots a significant look at Harriet, a look that says so much without saying anything at all.

So this is her, then, Harriet thinks. *The high and mighty Ellen de Courcey, sitting like a queen bee surrounded by drones, and even managing to make a wheelchair seem more like an empress's throne.*

Funny, Harriet thinks, looking at her from a distance, but in the flesh, Ellen doesn't really seem like anyone you should be afraid of at all. In fact, barring her expensive clothes and jewellery, there isn't all that much between Ellen de Courcey and poor, homeless Doris that used to pop in and out of Dead Old Lady Dresses for a cup of tea and a Jaffa Cake and a chat and to get in out of the cold.

She braces herself, full sure that Freddie is about to bring her over to make the introductions. Instead though, and to her great surprise, Freddie walks right past his grandmother, gently guiding both Harriet and Carole through the throng and into a library, stocked floor to ceiling with books, as far up as the eye can see.

Mother and daughter exchange a puzzled look. *Aren't we meeting the Granny*, Harriet tries to telegraph over to her. But no, it seems not.

'Just in here,' Freddie says, politely holding the door open for them. 'Got a bit of a surprise for you.'

'Wow!' gasps Carole, her eye drawn upwards, where the shelves almost seem to reach for the sky. 'This is even more impressive than the Long library at Trinity College, if you ask me. Wouldn't I kill to spend a few days just holed up in here, reading, reading, reading? Sheer bliss, if you ask me.'

'Then by all means, you must,' says a frail voice from directly behind them. 'All these old books are just crying out to be read, you know. And I'm afraid there's no use asking young Freddie there, he only ever came in here as a boy to play hide-and-seek.'

Harriet and Carole swing around to see an elderly gentleman sitting in a leather wing-back chair, over by the fireplace. He is rake thin and with skin so white, it is almost translucent, as if he hasn't seen a glimmer of sunshine in decades. He is wearing a plaid dressing gown in a Black Watch tartan and has a walking stick clasped in his hands, with a solid silver head on it. The only clue as to who this could be is his hair, which, barring a few extra grey streaks, is exactly the same shade of coppery red as Freddie's.

'Harriet? Carole?' says Freddie, ushering them over to the fireplace. 'I'd very much like you both to meet my grandfather, Frederick Senior. Who's got out of bed especially just to come down and say hello to you. Didn't you, Grandad?'

They all shake hands warmly as Frederick Senior apologises for not getting up.

'You ladies will forgive an old man like me,' he says, speaking very slowly and enunciating every single word carefully. 'I'm afraid the old mobility isn't what it was, you see. But young Freddie here,' he looks fondly up at his grandson, who stands proudly beside him, 'absolutely insisted I come downstairs here to greet you. My first time leaving my room in a very long time. How long has it been now, Freddie?'

'Oh golly,' says Freddie, 'not since Christmas, I think.'

'Is that so?'

'That's Christmas about fifteen years ago, Grandad.'

'In that case, it's an honour to meet you,' Harriet says, instantly sitting down on the floor beside him, all the better to chat to him properly. 'We really do appreciate it – don't we, Mam?'

'Absolutely,' Carole answers simply. 'And thank you, for all your wonderful hospitality. It's some party!'

'I understand your father and brothers are here too?' Frederick Senior says to Harriet. 'I'll send my valet to find them right away. You can get out the whiskey for Harriet's family,' he calls out to a butler, who seems to manifest from out of thin air. 'The good stuff.' Then, turning his full attention back to Harriet, he smiles. 'You've been out in Kenya, my dear,' he says, in that slow, distinct voice. 'So my grandson tells me. I was there once, you know, back in my youth. Flew over it in a single-engine Cessna aircraft – managed the entire journey in less than two days. Quite a record for those times.'

'That's amazing,' Harriet smiles up at him. 'What a life you must have lived.'

'Oh, if you'd seen the aircraft I flew back then, my dear! Barely had two feet of legroom to myself. So many would say not all that different to Connair's fleet nowadays, really.'

Harriet laughs and looks up to Freddie, who gives her a supportive little wink.

'I like her,' Frederick Senior says, turning back to his grandson. 'She's got kind eyes. Never underestimate the expression in someone's eyes. They're the window to the soul, I've so often found.'

Just then, from directly behind them, there is the sound of the library's giant double doors being flung open. Harriet automatically turns around, fully expecting to see the twins rolling in, with her dad in tow.

But it isn't though. Instead, manoeuvring her wheelchair as if she were gliding on ice, there is Ellen de Courcey, framed in the doorway, taking in the scene with an inscrutable look on her face. It isn't annoyance, it isn't coldness, it is something else entirely.

'What, may I ask,' she says, in a paper-thin voice, 'is going on in here?'

Chapter Forty-One

Meg

9.15 p.m.

By the time I arrive at the de Courcey mansion, the party is in full, glorious swing. Everywhere the eye can see, elegantly dressed people sip champagne from crystal flutes, while a whole army of catering staff waltz through the melee loaded down with silver trays of finger food, which looks divine, smells of absolutely nothing and could be made of well-crafted plastic, for all I know.

I slip in the main hall door, with my eyes peeled for anyone I know, and more importantly, anyone I want to avoid. With Harriet topping that particular list, thanks very much.

To my amazement, the butler, who has to be one hundred and seven if he's a day, greets me by name. Even though it's been well over a year since I last set foot in here, even though I'm only a last-minute addition to the guest list.

'Good evening, Miss Monroe,' he says politely into my ear, with a tiny, respectful bow. 'Welcome back. I will inform Mrs de Courcey of your presence here.'

So the lady of the house can tear strips off you in public, I mentally finish the sentence for him. But just then, there's an excited tap at my elbow and as I pivot around, there's Jess, looking flushed and pretty in a strapless black cocktail dress, with the long red hair tumbling freely around her shoulders. Dare I say it, the woman actually looks happy to see me.

'Thought you'd never get here,' she says, hugging, actually hugging me, shock horror.

'Any sign of Katherine?' I ask. 'Or Billy?'

She links arms with me and excitedly chats, as we weave our way through the crowd inside. 'Katherine is just about to make her big speech,' says Jess. 'She's right up there – look.'

I follow her gaze and, sure enough, there's Katherine with Billy by her side, at the very top of an enormous ballroom, where a lectern and microphone stand have been set up, so all the candidates can address the gathering loud and clear. I glance around, taking everything in, as I always do. Sure enough, there's Philip Sisk, oiling his way around the perimeter of the floor, schmoozing with an immaculately blow-dried group of older ladies, who are wearing the most eye-watering collection of jewellery I've ever set eyes on, and who are all cackling merrily at whatever joke he's just cracked.

'Wow,' I say, having to speak up over the noise and the racket. 'The de Courcey fundraisers certainly give good value for money, don't they?'

'But Meg, look!' Jess insists, pulling my attention to the wall at the very back of the room, just behind a grand piano, where a tuxedoed pianist is playing what sounds like a Mozart sonata, even though everyone is ignoring him. And there, deep in chat with his brother and election agent, is Toby Callaghan, Katherine's main rival for the senate seat and the very man Jess is hoping to get an 'in' with.

You already know him, don't you?' she whispers, steering me nearer him. I don't, as it happens, but I've never let a minor thing like that stand in my way. 'So come on, then!' says Jess, pulling on my arm. 'Introduce me – quick, while Katherine is distracted and while I can sell myself to him.'

So I do.

'Forgive me for interrupting you, Mr Callaghan,' I say politely, 'but this is a woman you simply must meet. Please let me introduce Jess Butler, who, as you are probably aware, is the driving force behind Senator Sisk's stunning media campaign.'

'Have we met before?' Alphonsus, the brother, says to me, all dandruff and smoked salmon breath, as he takes my hand and shakes it a tad too enthusiastically. 'Meg, isn't it?'

'Ooh . . . never mind me,' I say, deflecting attention and taking my paw right back again, wishing I'd brought hand sanitiser. Eughhh. 'You see Jess here? She's who you want at your side in Brussels – believe you me, anyone would be lucky to nab her!'

'Yes, your name has indeed come to my attention,' Toby Callaghan says to Jess, sweating profusely as he hones in on her.

Jess takes up the baton beautifully and launches into a great speech about how much she's always wanted the chance to work in Europe.

'Come with me to the bar,' says Toby Callaghan, gulping back the last of what looks like a G&T, 'and we'll talk some more.'

I nod encouragingly at her, as if to say, *Go on, off you go. Really nail this contact. Brussels, here you come.* And off they disappear, talking nineteen to the dozen.

Katherine is sitting at the podium as the warm-up speeches start, when next thing, out of the corner of my eye, I'm distracted by Billy. He's striding across the ballroom to where I'm standing, looking . . . well, tense and stressed, as it happens. Because Jess and I were deep in chat with the opposition, no doubt. Not a problem, I'll charm our way out of it.

'Billy, good evening,' I smile brightly at him. 'Loving the suit – Armani, is it? Someone's being paid well, that's for sure!'

'Meg,' he nods curtly at me, and I'm not sure if I'm imagining it or not, but is there a slight frostiness there that was never there before? Weird. I make another stab at small talk.

'Enjoying the evening?' I ask, with a big, fake smile.

'If it's OK with you,' he replies almost rudely, whipping out his phone and barely looking at me, 'I'd really like to check my emails.'

Our MC for the night is just introducing Katherine, saying the most glowing things imaginable about her, and so I focus on the podium, giving it my full attention. I'm not quite certain why Billy is being like this, but that's his problem and not mine. Possibly because he asked me out for a drink and I turned him down flat? Who knows? Who cares?

Just then, from directly behind me, there's a rough tap on my shoulder.

I turn around sharply and there's a younger guy staring at me, dressed in an ill-fitting jacket with a T-shirt on underneath it. There's something familiar about him too, but for the moment, it deserts me.

'You again,' he says to me. 'I could say "fancy meeting you here", but then you did mention that you were campaigning for Senator Sisk earlier, so I guess it stands to reason that you'd be here.'

The penny finally drops. The gelled hair, carefully shaped into a beach wave, the T-shirt that says, 'Climate Action Now!' The same guy who opened the door to me when I called to see Jonny Featherstone-Jones this afternoon.

'You two know each other?' Billy asks, turning around to join in the conversation.

'Actually,' says Gel-Head, 'we only met for the first time this afternoon. When you called to our house, to canvass for Katherine Sisk? My name's Carl, by the way. Carl James.'

'You were doing door to doors this afternoon?' Billy says, turning to me, looking confused. 'Since when?'

'Emm . . . well . . .' I try to say, but Gel-Head overrides me.

'Actually,' he says, shaking his head, 'speaking as a political activist myself, I thought it was a bit weird too. For one thing, once you got inside our house, you never even mentioned the election at all. No fliers, no pamphlets, no election manifesto speech – nothing.'

'So what were you doing there in the first place?' presses Billy, as I'm stuck in between the two of them, rooted to the floor and desperately trying to come up with a good, stout lie.

'It made no sense to me at all,' Gel-Head continues, really starting to probe now. 'In fact, you even claimed you were a playwright and that you had a project in mind for one of my housemates.'

Fuck, fuck, fuck, fuck and fuck it from a fucking height, I think, frantically trying to scheme a plausible way out of this.

'A playwright?' Billy says, looking at me.

'But then the strangest thing of all,' says Gel-Head, even though I'm avidly willing him to shut the fuck up, right NOW. 'After you left our house, I went out too 'cos I was going to buy the lads a few more tins of beer from the offie down the road. And I saw you getting into a taxi and scooting off. You told us you were canvassing, yet ours seemed to be the only door you knocked at. Bonkers carry-on, I thought.'

They're both staring at me now, and I need to come up with something feasible. Fast.

'Oh, it's all very straightforward, really . . .' I start to lie, but Gel-Head isn't letting me off any hooks.

'I know the way campaigning works,' he says. 'I've done enough of it myself, in my time. What I couldn't figure out was how did you manage to get my housemate's name and address in the first place? Our house isn't even on Google Maps.'

'Yeah,' says Billy slowly. 'How did you get the address, Meg? And why did you say you were canvassing, when you weren't?'

Frantically, palms sweating, I'm try to downplay the whole thing.

'As a matter of fact,' I'm stammer, 'I'm working on a project that I needed to speak to your housemate about, and I happened to get his address from his agent. And that's all there is to it,' I half smile at the two of them, praying they'll drop it now.

'Oh really?' says Gel-Head, folding his arms. 'Well, I for one would love to know how you managed that feat. Because Jonny doesn't have an agent anymore. He got fired, and that was long before he moved into where we're living now.'

My mouth opens as if to say something. But for once in my life, nothing comes out. Not a single word.

Gel-Head looks triumphantly at me.

'You two work together?' he asks Billy, who nods yes.

'Sounds like your playwright pal here has one or two questions to answer,' he shrugs, before drifting off. Which is when Billy rounds in on me.

'Never knew playwriting was one of your *many* talents,' he says icily, 'but there you go, you live and learn, don't you?'

From the microphone at the top of the room, Katherine Sisk is still being praised to the heights in the most glowing terms imaginable.

But I'm not listening.

All I can think is – *I've got out of tight spots before. I've done it many, many times, and you know what? I'll do it again.*

I look up at Billy, desperately trying to read his face, but it's impossible.

'Meg,' Billy says slowly, really eyeballing me. 'It's as plain as the nose on your face that you stole that address from the electoral database, so you needn't bother trying to get out of it. Just tell me this much, will you? Why? Why did you do it?'

'Do what?' My instant reaction. Buys time, if only seconds.

'Oh for God's sake, you can drop the act. You were told that we can't break the law, and you still went ahead and did anyway. Don't you get it? I don't give a toss about that bunch of guys you called to see today, or your reasons why. Nor do I care about Katherine's reasons for hiring you, although I have my suspicions. It's her private business and nothing to do with me. All I care about is that it looks suspiciously like you appropriated a private residential address using government databases and then used it to your own ends.'

'But even if I did, would that be so awful?' I stutter. 'I mean, why are you acting like this? Like I just ran rampage through the streets with a machine gun? We're talking about one address here, one lousy little address! Why are you making such a big deal about nothing? The election is on Monday – don't you have other things to worry about?'

'So that stack of USB sticks I found at your workstation was just a wild coincidence, was it?' Billy persists. 'It wasn't like you intended to download the whole database?'

'I already told you . . .' I start to say, but then I break off as my mind goes blank. *Jesus*, I think wildly. *What exactly did I say to get out of that one? Which lie did I tell?*

I start to clutch at straws.

'Look, here's the truth,' I tell him, inventing on the spot. 'Believe it or not, I actually am a huge fan of Jonny Featherstone-Jones's, I've seen him in a few shows over the years, and I suppose I just have this embarrassing little crush on him, that's all. So when I spotted his name and address on that database, I just acted on it. It was a stupid fangirl moment, and nothing more . . .'

'You're something else, you know that, Meg?' Billy says, shaking his head disgustedly. 'Like you really think there's one rule for you and an entirely different one for everyone else.'

I'm about to fight back, I'm about to say something, anything, when out of the corner of my eye, I see someone very, very familiar heading this way. The very person I've been trying to avoid ever since I got here, and the very last person I want to have to face.

Thank you, Universe, I think, as the power of speech seems to desert me. *Just what I need to turn this horrible evening into Dante's Ninth Circle of Hell.*

'Meg? I thought it was you.'

Harriet. With Freddie and her mother lagging not too far behind, all three of them glaring daggers at me.

'Just give me a minute with her alone,' I overhear her saying to her mum and Freddie, before she effectively corners me.

'Hi,' is all I can think to say to her, as just then, Katherine's introduction is done and there's a thunderous round of applause to welcome her up to the podium.

'I suppose it's hardly surprising to see you here,' Harriet says, quite assertively for her. 'Still working for Ellen de Courcey then, are you? Still hoping to break me and Freddie up? Best of luck with that.'

So she knows then, I think, in a pool of panic. *She knows everything and it's game over.*

There's loud clapping and the cheering is almost raucous and suddenly I need to get out of here. I need air. I need to think.

'I know you and I should probably talk,' I almost have to yell at Harriet to be heard over the din. 'Can we step outside?'

Harriet gives a tiny nod to her mother and Freddie, as much as to say, it's OK, I'll be fine in a one-on-one with this witch from hell. Then she follows me out onto a terrace area, through French doors that open directly from the ballroom. There's a few hardy cigarette smokers having a puff outside, but other than that, we're pretty much in private. It's cool and quiet, and all you can hear is the muffled sound of Katherine launching into her big speech inside.

Now there's silence, as Harriet glares hotly at me and I wonder who'll blink first. I eye her up and, I have to say, she really looks well tonight; she's in a pale blue dress and with the long, fair hair swishing around her shoulders and just a little make-up, the overall effect is . . . well, all in all, pretty wow, actually.

The expression on her face tells a very different story though.

'Meg,' she says, folding her arms and rounding in on me, 'I *know*. I know all about you. And about Ellen de Courcey too. And how you wrangled your way into that insane flat in return for . . . how should we put it? "Services rendered"? Too bad the service rendered was getting rid of me, wasn't it? And too bad that I found out all about it. And too bad that Freddie knows all about it now, and too bad for you that we intend to do something about it.'

Well, well, well, I think, impressed in spite of myself. *Harriet grows a spine. Finally. After all this time.*

Funnily, I actually prefer her like this. Spunkier. Feistier. There's metal in her core now that was never there before.

'Have you any idea of what you've put me through?' Harriet says, her anger levels starting to rise now that there's no risk of us being overheard.

'None whatsoever.'

'Well then, let me enlighten you. Because I trusted you, Meg. I believed you. I thought of you as a pal, a real friend. But all that time we spent together? That was just a job for you. A gig. As far as you were concerned, I was just collateral damage to be dispatched and bundled out of the country just as soon as you could!'

I look Harriet up and down and weigh up how best to handle her. Gently, I figure, is probably the best option. A bit like the way you'd treat a hysterical child.

'You want an apology,' I say soothingly. 'And, of course, you're probably entitled to one. Because yes, Harriet, I'm guilty as charged. Guilty as hell. You got me. And the killer is, I thought of you as a friend too. That, believe it or not, is actually me being truthful.'

'So this is how you treat your friends?' she says furiously.

'I did you a kindness,' I tell her. 'If you'd just cool down and think for two seconds, then you'll soon realise you should actually be thanking me.'

At that, she almost splutters. 'Did I just hear you right? You're admitting to all of this and you honestly expect me to thank you?'

'Harriet, yes. I did you a favour. When you've really given it thought, in time, you'll come to see the truth of what I'm saying. Because that's the thing about what I do. Actually, I did you the greatest service possible.'

'You're insane,' Harriet says, shaking her head. 'I almost want to drag my mam and Freddie and the rest of my family out here so they can hear this conversation for themselves. Although even then, none of them would believe it. You're a psychopath,' she insists firmly. 'An out-and-out psycho.'

'You're not seeing the bigger picture,' I reply, quite calmly. 'You're just shocked, that's all. But don't you realise that your life is so much better off because of me?'

'You manipulated me, you lied to me so many times I've lost count, and you think I'm better off? Meg, are you *hearing* yourself? Are you actually aware of what you're saying?'

I sigh. This evening has been vile enough without having to deal with histrionics, thanks very much. 'What I'm trying to explain, you silly woman, is that when I first met you, you were in a dead-end job in a shithole dump, working for buttons. You didn't even realise who Freddie de Courcey was, and you'd been seeing him for weeks at that stage! And look at you now. That job I encouraged you to take? Best thing that could possibly have happened to you. Now, you're a successful person who can hold her head up high, career-wise.

You'll walk into a far better job – oh, still in your precious charity sector – but as someone who's headed up a huge initiative in the developing world, along with the budget to go with it.'

'You're mad,' Harriet says, white-faced. 'You're completely off-your-head . . . In fact, I can't stay here for one second longer. I won't listen to this. You're toxic, you're poisonous.'

She marches back to the terrace doors, then stops abruptly and turns around to face me, as though something just struck her.

'Of course, you do know,' she says, 'that the laugh really is on you, Meg.'

'You think so?'

'Well, see for yourself,' Harriet says. 'You set out to break up a couple and you couldn't. Not even after a full year apart. Not even after all your lies and your machinations and your scheming and your deception. You couldn't do it, Meg. You failed, and now we're on to you. I'm not the only one whose life you're manipulating, I know that. And I'm going to make sure that you can't deceive anyone else the way you deceived me. So it was all for nothing.'

I let her enjoy her little 'comeuppance' speech, before following her back inside.

*

Did I really think the evening had been a nightmare up till now?

Turns out that was only the warm-up act.

I step back through the terrace doors and they're all here, like they've been standing waiting for me. Harriet's parents, Carole and Sean, those oafish twin brothers of hers, Jack and Terry. Billy's here too, along with that idiot with the gelled head of hair . . . what was his name? Carl James. But front and centre, with his arms folded and a face like thunder, is Freddie de Courcey himself. Like they've all come to witness a public stoning.

I remember the following, in no particular order. I remember hearing Katherine Sisk's voice, ringing out loud and clear over the microphone, as her speech reached its climax. She was talking about climate change when Freddie stepped forward to speak to me.

'I'd like you to leave my home,' he said, in a strong, clear, assertive voice. So completely unlike him, I remember thinking. 'To say you're not welcome here is the understatement of the year.'

I remember not being able to breathe and feeling like my face was suddenly on fire.

'Now, please,' Freddie insisted. 'Surely even you realise that your presence here is an insult?'

So many faces, all glowering at me, wanting me gone. I remember the room starting to come in and out of hazy focus, as the blood left my legs.

I remember feeling so weak, I had to grip onto the wall behind me, right at the edge of the ballroom, to try and inch my way out of there.

Shock. This was total, undiluted shock, so severe I honestly didn't know whether to throw up or pass out.

I particularly remember Carole Waters. Ordinarily, she was a perfectly friendly, warm-hearted woman, but not now.

'I don't think I'll ever forgive you,' she said furiously as I passed her, 'after what you put my daughter through. After all your lies and your deceit . . .'

But then, most surprisingly of all, I remember Harriet actually sticking up for me.

'Leave her, Mam, this isn't the time. Can't you see she's not well? Meg, Meg, can you hear me? You look like you're going to faint.'

I don't faint though. Instead, I feel a strong arm grabbing me by the elbow – a man's arm – supporting me, and steering me through the crowd in the ballroom and on out to the main hallway. Whoever this was then firmly ushered me out the main entrance door, to the cool chill of the summery night air. And I remember looking up to see that it was Freddie.

'Now leave this house,' he says firmly, as a taxi crunches up the gravel driveway. 'And if you even think about contacting my girlfriend or her family again, be well warned, I will refer this matter straight to the police.'

I remember taking one final glance back at the house, as I'm bundled into the back seat of the taxi, weak as a kitten, my mind in total and utter meltdown.

Last thing I remember of all?

Ellen de Courcey wheeling herself out to the top of the steps, sitting in her wheelchair, like a queen on a throne. And even though it was pitch-dark, there was no mistaking the look in those cold, flinty eyes as she stared haughtily down at me.

And before or since, I honestly don't think I've ever been so frightened in my entire life.

SATURDAY

Chapter Forty-Two

Meg

The morning after the night before, and it's like doors have started closing in my face. That's the only way I can describe what seems to be playing out. Literally, overnight. Nothing but a long line of doors being slammed in my face, one after the other.

I start with Katherine Sisk. Call her. Am ignored. Call her again, and again and again. Nothing. So I email and text, still nothing. So I decide to visit Government Buildings, where I don't even make it past security. Instead I'm told that my 'access all areas' lanyard pass has been revoked, and that's the end of that. It's the weekend, but the election is on Monday and I know for certain they're all there and working flat out today.

I try my best to argue it with the guard on duty.

'I'm Meg Monroe,' I tell him, 'and I'm working on a project for Senator Sisk. I'm sure she's probably out of the office just now, but could I possibly leave a message for her, please? Or better yet, could I just run up to her office for two minutes? I promise, that's all it'll take.'

'I'm afraid I don't have the authorisation to allow you inside. Security concerns, you understand.'

Yeah, but security never stopped me getting in before, I want to scream, but I know I'm wasting my time.

It gets worse. As the weekend wears on, it's just one call after another from the few clients I thought I'd managed to hold onto. Each and every one telling me that my 'services are no longer required'. Even Raymond Sandros, the client I was working for when I went to see Jonny Featherstone-Jones, and first met that Gel-Head moron who started all this, calls me to cancel.

This is Ellen de Courcey's doing, I'm sure of it. It was Ellen de Courcey pretty much deciding that enough was enough and that my number was up. Maybe because she couldn't handle seeing her precious Freddie happily reunited with Harriet at the fundraiser. Maybe because I'd caused a scene at her fancy benefit. Maybe because of a whole lot of things.

By the end of the loneliest and probably the most dismal weekend I can remember in a long, long time, all I know is this. It's over. This time, it really, truly feels like it's over.

Monday comes and goes. Election Day. The election which Katherine Sisk wins, as it happens, and by a large landslide. Which means that Jess is more or less dispatched to Brussels and my work is almost done.

Almost.

I wait a few days for the dust to settle and, indeed, for the celebrations to be over among Katherine's team, then I call to her constituency office, hoping to take advantage of the fact that things should be a little calmer there now.

I buzz on the street intercom, but this time, shock horror, I'm actually given the time of day. Someone I've never met before, a new intern, I'm guessing, opens the door. She's a glossy-looking woman about my own age who clearly has no idea who I am.

'Hi,' I say. 'I'm Meg Monroe and I really need to speak to Senator Sisk urgently. I know she's working hard, but if you could just let her know I need to see her.'

'I'm afraid the Senator is in meetings right now,' is the only response I get though.

'Yes, but will you please just give her my message?' I insist, determined not to be fobbed off again. 'It really is vitally important that I talk to her. Just for a moment. I'm working on a project for her, you see . . . and I'm having a nightmare trying to reach her on the phone.'

Glossy New Intern thinks about it for a minute, wavering.

'Come on inside,' she eventually says, 'and I'll see what I can do.'

It's a chink, and one I gratefully accept.

So I stand in that dark, gloomy hallway, still piled high with re-election posters, and I wait. Wonder what's being said about me now, in that inner office of Katherine's. I can almost imagine the conversation being played out.

What do you mean, Meg Monroe is here? That Dead Girl Walking?

What's a Good Lady Senator to do? Give an ex-employee the benefit of the doubt and hear her out for ten seconds, or freeze her out, just like everyone else? Katherine Sisk is a well-known bleeding-heart liberal though, and more than anything else, that's precisely what I'm counting on.

It works.

After an agonisingly long wait, Katherine herself appears out of the main office, stepping into the hallway all alone, and frowning worriedly, like this is the very last thing on earth she needs.

'Good to see you,' I say, pleased at least that I'll get to have my say.

'In here, please,' Katherine says, sotto voce, guiding me into a tiny, poky room that's more like a storage space, which overlooks the street outside. It's stacked with cardboard boxes, almost up to ceiling height, and is clearly a room that's never used.

Good, I think. Privacy. *Makes this a bit easier.*

'Thanks for seeing me,' I begin, launching into a little pre-prepared speech that I'd practised on the way here. 'I know I'm the last person you need to see . . .'

'You can say that again,' Katherine says quietly.

'Katherine . . . I messed up, I know that. I messed up royally. I want you to know that it was an honest mistake, made in genuine error.'

'Oh Meg,' says Katherine, rolling her eyes. 'You've had all weekend to come up with a half-decent story, is that your best effort? *Made in genuine error*? Really? Please don't treat me like an idiot. Remember, I'm a politician. I deal with professional liars every day of the week for a living. Billy told me everything, and said he strongly felt you couldn't be trusted.'

'Please, Katherine, if you'd just hear me out . . .'

'No,' Katherine says, folding her arms sternly. 'And I'll have no more of your bossiness, thank you very much. This time, you listen to me and you listen well, because it's a crazy day for me and I have absolutely zero time for this. Now, I hired you in good faith, Meg. You came highly recommended and I think we both know from whom. I asked you to help me and that's what you did. You found a way out of a potentially damaging, not to mention incredibly hurtful, personal situation for me, and for that, I am grateful.'

'Thank you,' I say, glad that she's at least acknowledging the hard work I put in for her, not to mention the great result I delivered.

'Jess has handed in her notice,' Katherine goes on, 'so you've done what I asked you to do and it's my intention to pay you in full, as per our agreement.'

'That's good to hear,' I say, hoping that this conversation might actually be starting to go my way. 'Because now it's my turn to ask you a favour. I work one hundred per cent on word of mouth and, as you can appreciate, that's entirely dried up on me now. So if you could possibly recommend me to a few friends and contacts you might know who are in need of my services, it would be wonderful. That's all I'm asking, just a quiet word of recommendation from you would get me back up and running again . . .'

Katherine sighs deeply, shaking her head. 'You really are something else, Meg,' she says. 'You know when we first met? I admired you. I really did. You helped me no end, and if there's one campaign platform I'll die by, it's that women should stop being each other's worst enemies, because we can move mountains when we actually help each other for a change. I liked your toughness, your street savvy, your obvious intelligence. And then you go and steal classified information from my office, having expressly been told not to – and you expect me to recommend you? Seriously?'

'Oh come on,' I plead, giving it one last throw of the dice before I'm asked to leave. 'Yes. Guilty as charged, what I did was deceitful, you have me there. But surely you realise that what I do for a living is entirely based on deception? How else am I supposed to get results? One or two words of recommendation, that's all I'm asking of you! Not a big ask, surely? New clients, political clients, constituents of yours even. Anyone. I'm really begging you here, Katherine, you're my last hope. Because if you don't . . . if you don't . . .'

But I can't even think of how to end that sentence. What will become of me, is what I'm trying to say. What'll I do then? How will The Fixer earn a living if no one comes calling with problems to fix?

'Quite honestly,' Katherine sighs, turning to face me one last time, 'I don't know where you'll go or what you'll do. But if it's any consolation, you'll probably end up coming out on top. People like you always do.'

*

And when sorrows come, they come in battalions.

Hot on the heels of this, comes my final notice to quit the apartment. And another one, and another one after that again. Not to mention bills. Lots of them. All racking up.

Weeks pass, and my savings dwindle fast, largely eaten up with the legal battle I have to hold onto my home. It's astonishing just how quickly my little nest egg evaporates, and trying to kick-start my career as The Fixer proves a dead end too. No one, quite literally no one, will touch me with a barge pole. I even offer to work for free, just to get back in the game again, just to feel the old thrill of manipulating people and relationships and all the vacuous crap that people who are in love fool themselves is so important in life.

Total waste of time.

Turns out there's only one person, just one, in my whole orbit, who actually shows me a bit of kindness. Probably the very last person I ever would have thought of, as it happens.

*

It's Christmas Day, and my Christmas present from the de Courcey family? I'm officially being evicted from the flat on the first of January, having well and truly lost my legal battle. I spend the day at my mother's house, as I do every year, my mind in turmoil, worried sick over what I'm to do now and, more importantly, where the hell I will live?

Nan gets out of bed for the day and is sitting at the kitchen table, merrily singing along with an ad on TV for tins of Quality Street that are on a half-price sale.

'It's not Christmas without the row over who gets the nice pink sweets out of the tin!' Nan is saying at the top of her voice, to no one in particular. 'Now hurry up and show the Queen's speech, will you? The poor woman just rang me from Sandringham to say she's dying to get it over with because she's bursting for a wee.'

Meanwhile, I'm over at the oven, helping Mum baste the turkey, peel spuds and chop up onions for the stuffing.

'You're very quiet,' she says to me. 'Almost like you've got something on your mind.'

'Oh, it's nothing,' I say, downplaying the whole thing. 'Just . . . work stuff. And a few money issues, that's all.'

There's a long pause, as Mum chops away at the onions. 'Meg, love,' she eventually says, 'I know you better than anyone, don't I? And I know you're worried, and although I don't know the ins and outs of it, I do know just how much your life seems to have changed in the past few months.'

'What do you mean?'

'Oh now, come on,' Mum says, abandoning the onions and turning to face me. 'I'm your mother and I'm not stupid. Those big envelopes of cash you used to leave your nan and me every week seem to have completely dried up, and I'm not complaining, far from it. But I do worry about what's going on with you.'

'I'm just in a bit of a rut, that's all, Mum,' I try to say, but it seems she's on to me.

'I know, love,' she says feelingly. 'Sure, I saw you all these past few years, waltzing around in your designer gear and living in a flat that must have cost millions, and I knew something was up. But I said nothing, just kept my mouth shut. None of my beeswax is what I told myself. So whatever is going on, just know this. Nan and me are your family and we'll always love you and look out for you, come what may.'

For once in my life, I'm stunned into silence.

'Come back home,' she says, putting her hand on mine. 'You supported me and your nan for so long, not to mention your poor old grandad when he got sick. You've worked hard ever since you left school and you never let any of your family want for a single thing. You've been a good daughter, love. And I'm proud of you, even though I don't say it often. So now it's our turn to look after you. Come home, Megan. You can share my room with me and you won't have to pay a single penny in rent.'

'Thanks, Mum,' I say, genuinely touched.

'And if you ever want to tell me what's wrong,' she adds, 'you know I'm here for you.'

'Well . . . I sort of lost my job, you see . . .' I start to say, which is probably the most honest I've been with her in years.

'So get another one.'

'I've been trying,' I tell her, starting to get teary now, as all the horribleness and loneliness of the past months finally catch up with me. 'I've been trying so hard to get work, any kind of work, but it's so frustrating. The Sloan Curtis legal firm replaced me long ago, and it turns out I'm not qualified enough for any of the jobs that I'd actually like to do.'

'So get qualified,' Mum says gently.

'It costs money, Mum,' I tell her, as the tears really start to flow. 'Money that I don't have. Not now, not anymore.'

'So let your mother pay. You looked after this family for long enough, didn't you? Maybe now it's our turn to look after you.'

She gives me a hug. A huge warm bear hug, and for the first time in months, I really feel like I'm not alone. And I honestly think it's the best Christmas present I could possibly have asked for.

EPILOGUE

Meg

Six months later

The staffroom is heaving, packed full of mostly women on their breaks having chats, grabbing coffees or a quick bite to eat and talking, talking, talking – absolutely anything to pass the time away. Because that's what gets you in a job like this, more than anything else. The long hours. Have I ever in my whole life felt the day drag on so much before? Doubtful.

I'm in Sally's Wonderland of Value! – yes, the exclamation mark really is part of the name – wearing the shop floor uniform of a tidy nylon black top, along with a name badge and a matching pair of nylon black trousers. What a delightful sight I am. Not.

I've been working here for a couple of months now, management seeing fit to alternate me in between working the tills, stacking shelves and folding jumpers, and occasionally dealing with the public at the customer service desk up on the fourth floor.

'You're a good worker, Meg,' my supervisor tells me, a skinny, pockmarked guy of about nineteen. He's called Jake by the way, and he has a voice that I'd swear is still breaking. 'You could have a bright future here. At Sally's Wonderland of Value! we're always on the lookout for fresh talent. Sure, would you look at me? I didn't know the first thing about retail when I started here, and now I'm in charge of ladies' knickers.'

What can I say? I needed to earn again, while taking a night course at college, and a friend of a friend of Mum's managed to get me this job. The work is every bit as boring and tedious as you'd imagine, certainly compared with the pace I was used to working at. Nor is the money much to speak of, particularly when I think of the figures I used to pull in. But hey, a job is a job, any money is better than none at all and at least I'm unlikely to bump into any of my former clients here. Best part of the day? When I get to hang out in the staffroom with the rest of the Sally's team, where, for some reason or another, I always seem to end up holding court.

Which is exactly what I'm doing now, as it happens. We're all on staggered lunch breaks, but today the shop floor is quiet, so there's at least a dozen of us crammed into the staffroom and pretty much all of them are clamouring for my attention. The vast majority are considerably younger than me and almost all of them are having 'relationship problems', shall we say.

'My fella is driving me mental, Meg,' one of the girls from the kids' department is telling me. This one is called Diane. She has an impressive collection of body art, covering what looks like approximately fifty per cent of her skin, and she's been badgering me for ages, trying to get advice.

'It's my turn to have a go of Meg!' another co-worker snaps. Bex, this particular one is called; she's worked here ever since she was sixteen and she's thin, so scarily thin that I suspect there might be an eating disorder involved. 'You've been hogging her for ages – Meg, listen to me, will you? My problem is urgent! Hers is only about bleeding fellas. *Again*.'

'Don't worry, ladies,' I say placatingly. 'If it's one thing we all have in here, it's time to kill. Diane, go on, you were saying. What's that fuckface gone and done on you now?'

Giggles and catcalls from around the room as Diane picks up her tale.

'I'm ninety-nine per cent certain he has another girlfriend on the go. Heard it from me sister and her mate, they seen him with this new one loads of times. Lying, cheating bastard. So I need her gone, Meg, and you have to help me. You're brilliant at this kind of thing.'

I suck in my cheeks, and the whole room goes quiet, waiting for a response.

'Diane,' I tell her firmly, 'you know perfectly well what I told you. This guy is a worthless arsehole and if he's cheating on you, then he doesn't deserve you. End of story.'

There's a round of applause from around the room and I say no more. But the truth is that I don't want to do personal relationships anymore. Too messy. Too liable to go wrong. Too easy to get in trouble.

'My turn now!' Bex says, loudly shouting down everyone else.

'No, me!' says Suzie, a tall, rangy, dark-haired woman exactly my own age, who, like me, is just putting in the hours here to make a few quid while she puts herself through a marketing course at night. Suzie is turning into a friend, though. A proper friend. One I seem to be growing closer and closer to by the day. To my amazement, actually, given that romance was the last thing on my mind when I started this job.

I had always thought, *I don't do relationships*. That emotion only ended in tears and that you'd be an idiot to hand your heart over to another person. But you know what? Sometimes, it's good for us to be proved wrong.

'Fuck off, Suzie, you don't get special treatment, just because Meg is your *girlfriend*.'

A quick, knowing smile passes between me and Suzie, both of us half mortified and half pretty pleased, actually. But just then, the skinny figure of Jake, our teenage supervisor, looms in the doorway, interrupting everything.

As ever, the sight of a gang of women intimidates the shite out of him and, as ever, he still has absolutely zero control over us.

'Excuse me, ladies,' he has to say about ten times, before we eventually shut up and listen to him. 'There's someone out on the shop floor asking for you, Meg. Says she needs to have a quick word with you.'

Puzzled, I get up to follow him, to a chorus of 'Meg! My go when you get back! I've been waiting ages!' as I'm led out of the room.

'And just to remind you,' Jake says to the rest of the room, 'lunch break is actually over for most of you, so if you could get back to work . . .'

There's not even a break in the chat as my colleagues completely ignore him.

The customer service department is pretty empty when I get to the top floor, except for one lone person, standing beside a discount rail of three facecloths for the price of two.

Harriet Waters.

Mother of God, the very last person I expected to see. It's an odd thing though; I should feel panicked here, I should be freaking out at the past coming back to haunt me like this, but strangely I don't. In spite of everything that's gone down between us, there's a large part of me that's actually weirdly pleased to see her.

I take a deep breath and walk towards her, quickly scanning her up and down, making rapid-fire assessments. Just like I always do.

Appearance: healthy. Robust. Well. Harriet is lightly tanned and dressed that bit more smartly than normal, in a long, khaki-green shirtdress, belted at the waist, and worn with slides, and her long, fair hair hanging loose. You're just back from a holiday, I surmise, looking at her. Tan mark at her watchstrap a total giveaway. The handbag at the floor beside Harriet is a fairly sizeable clue too. It's a Mulberry, €600–€700 at a guess, and there's just no way in hell Harriet would ever fork out that much on herself. A gift, I assume. Which means one thing and one thing only. Lover boy Freddie de Courcey is very evidently still on the scene.

Harriet looks up, spots me stepping off the escalator and gives a self-conscious little wave.

'Hi,' she says, as soon as I come over to her. 'It's good to see you. You look well. Black suits you.'

I glance down at the standard-issue black tunic and trousers I'm wearing and grimace.

'I'm hoping to start a trend,' I say wryly. 'Watch this space, in case it goes viral on Instagram.'

A pause, while both of us just look at one another, each sizing the other up.

'You're the last person I expected to see,' I eventually admit.

'I know,' Harriet replies. 'I was actually here last week doing a bit of shopping and I spotted you then. I nearly died, I couldn't believe you were working here. You were run off your feet though, so I didn't dare go near you. But you've been on my mind ever since, so that's why I called in today.'

'I mean, the last time we spoke . . .'

'I know.'

'It was awful. Horrendous.'

'I know.'

'So . . . if it's not too rude to ask . . . what made you want to see me?'

She looks everywhere except at me before replying.

'I felt awful,' she says, after a pause. 'Ever since the night of the fundraiser at the de Courceys'. Of course, I was furious with you, we all were, but now that the dust has settled, all I can think about is how lost you looked. How alone and vulnerable. I said to Freddie that you were on my conscience, and I knew I wouldn't get a minute's peace till I buried the hatchet with you.'

'So you're still seeing Freddie, I take it?' I smile. Knew it.

'Absolutely,' Harriet says, blushing very prettily. 'We've just been away together for a proper two-week holiday – to Croatia, actually. It was magic. Just wonderful.'

'That's great news, I'm really happy for you.'

Then she comes back down to earth.

'Anyway,' she says, 'the last thing you need is me here wittering on, when you're trying to do a day's work.'

'No,' I say, genuinely interested, 'tell me all your news. I really do want to know. How are all the de Courceys? Including the delightful Ellen?'

'The same as ever,' Harriet says, pulling a tiny face. 'I've met Freddie's grandmother a good few times now, and it's like the nicer I am to her, the more bolshie she is back to me. As my mam says, I can't do right for doing wrong. But it's fine, honestly. Freddie and I just giggle about it afterwards. And his grandfather seems to have got this whole new lease of life – he's a dote, we get on so well. He even offered me a job working with the de Courcey charity group, but I said thanks, but no thanks.'

'You want to stand on your own two feet,' I nod approvingly. 'Good for you.'

'I've got another job now,' Harriet chats away, 'with a government aid agency, so yes, like you say, standing on my own two feet. Freddie is well too – he and I are actually talking about moving into a flat together soon, isn't that amazing?'

'I'm delighted for you, Harriet,' I smile warmly. 'I sincerely mean that.'

'And you should see him with his grandmother these days! He's so much stronger and more assertive when he's dealing with her now, like a whole new man.'

So I was right then, I think. The night of that awful fund-raiser. Freddie de Courcey has finally developed guts.

'Anyway, the main reason I'm here,' she goes on, 'is just to tell you . . . well . . . that there's no hard feelings from me. I said a lot of harsh things to you that night, and I really did come to regret them afterwards. Because I don't think you're a bad person, Meg. In spite of everything. I just think you got in above your head – it's like you were totally seduced by the lifestyle you could afford by . . . by doing what you did.'

'Well, thank you,' I say, taking the olive branch in the spirit in which it is offered. 'That's good to know. Right now, I certainly need all the good wishes I can get.'

'So what are your plans long term?' Harriet asks, looking at me worriedly.

'I'm doing a course at night,' I fill her in. 'In theatre studies, can you believe it?'

'As a matter of fact,' she says slowly, 'I can. You'd suit the theatre world, Meg. In fact, you'd be brilliant. And if you're ever in a show, you know Freddie and I will come and support you.'

'Thank you,' I tell her, really touched, mainly because I know she means it. 'Anyway, working here is just to keep my head above water, cash-wise. You'd be amazed how much the legal action against Ellen de Courcey ended up costing me.'

'Well, good for you,' Harriet smiles. 'I know you wouldn't dream of going back to your old ways again. Back to getting rid of people for a living. You've learned your lesson there, I hope.'

I take a moment to really think about what she's just said.

I think of the long line of women back in the staffroom. Just waiting to talk to me, to pick my brains, to get my advice, to find out how unwanted people can be airbrushed from the picture.

For a moment, I think of going back to my old ways. Of a very lucrative new little client base that's actually right here, just waiting for me. All the women I've met since coming to work here, who mightn't be able to pay the kind of money I've been used to – but, what the hell, work is work, and that kind of work, I know I can do standing on my head. Even the theatre studies course I'm doing at night could only be a help to me, in this particular line of work.

The Fixer could be ready for her Act Two.

It's tempting . . . but then I pause for a moment to think. I think how high I flew and how spectacularly I fell. I think how nice it would be to go straight, as it were. To live an ordinary, normal life and forge ordinary, normal relationships with ordinary, normal people. No more ducking and diving. No more lying for a living. No more deceit.

'You don't need to worry about me,' I say to Harriet, as my name is called out over the tannoy, to get to the homewares department on the third floor urgently. 'I'll be just fine, thanks.'

We say our goodbyes, promising to stay in touch. Harriet gives me a big, warm hug and I watch after her as she jumps onto the escalator, down to the main entrance door and out of my life.

When I get to the homewares department, I'm put on the tills and Suzie is there ahead of me. 'You're smiling,' she says to me, teasingly. 'So who was it who wanted to see you? Another girlfriend, maybe?'

'Not at all,' I grin back at her. 'I'm smiling because . . . it's like a weight I didn't even know I was carrying, has lifted.'

I don't get to explain any further, as I turn to serve a hassled-looking woman with three screaming children, who's trying to buy a duvet set in our deeply discounted bed linen range.

But I know one thing. It's time for me to rebuild. Rebrand. Work my way out of here and start afresh. I think back to a year ago, when I was living in the lap of luxury, with not two seconds to myself to enjoy it. I may be back living at home now, but I'm far, far closer to my mum than I've ever been. I went from having no friends at all, to having a whole roomful of people fighting over who gets to talk to me.

And maybe, just maybe, I've actually found someone who seems to like me for me. Best of all? I think I like me, for me. I know who I am now.

The Fixer is finally getting fixed.

'You have a great day now,' I beam at this poor, stressed-looking mother, handing over her change.

And for the first time in as long as I can remember, the smile on my face is genuine.

Acknowledgements

Thank you, Marianne Gunn O'Connor. Always and for everything.

Thank you, Pat Lynch – love our movie chats!

Thank you, Vicki Satlow.

Thank you, Sarah Bauer, the kind of editor you dream about.

Thank you Katie Lumsden and Katie Meegan.

Thank you, Perminder Mann and Kate Parkin.

Thank you (and congratulations!) Francesca Russell.

Thank you Stephen Dumughn, Jenna Petts, Felice McKeown, Grace Brown, Elise Burns, Stuart Finglass, Mark Williams, Nico Poilblanc, Vincent Kelleher, Sophie Hamilton, Margaret Stead, Kelly Smith, Alex May, Laura Makela and Alexandra Schmidt. I couldn't be happier or more grateful to be a part of Team Bonnier.

Thank you, Simon Hess and his wonderful team, Helen McKean, Declan Heeney, Eamonn Phelan and Gill Hess.

Well, hello everyone!

What a joy it is to be able to write to you all. It's so wonderful to be able to chat to you all directly like this, isn't it? And what a pleasure it is to tell you all about what's been going on at this end. I am crazy excited about *The Fixer*, so I really hope that you've enjoyed it.

When I was first planning this book, I thought I'd love to write about an anti-heroine for once. A real baddie. A right piece of work. The kind of person who's all sweetness and light to your face, but who'd cut you to shreds the minute your back is turned. Did you ever come across anyone like that in your life? I certainly hope not! But there are people out there who can manipulate and lie, yet still charm the birds from the trees.

Which is very much the sort of character I wanted to write about – and so, Meg Monroe was born! She is everyone's friend, Miss Popular, the charismatic type of person. However, this is very much a woman with an agenda.

From the beginning, I knew I wanted to write about what happens when she becomes tangled in her own web of lies. I won't tell you much, in case you've skipped to the end to read this, but a blast from her past arrives and threatens to derail Meg's carefully constructed life.

Can I talk about the cover? I think it's my favourite cover yet. And that's *really* saying something. I've loved the covers for all my books, but because this story is quite different, I knew the cover would have to be, too. But my publishers pulled it out of the bag – as I knew they would – with this gorgeous cover. Isn't it just brilliant? It is so bright and vibrant, it reminds me of those old rhubarb and custard sweets – delicious!

Finally, I'd love to tell you all about my Readers' Club. We all love to read, don't we? Sure, that's why we're here! And what's even better than a great book? The inside scoop on one, the bits that only a select few dedicated readers get to read. Which is why the good folk at Bonnier Towers came up with an absolute diamond of an idea: my very own Readers' Club.

My Readers' Club is full of exclusive content that you'll love, and my job is to make sure that if you sign up, you won't regret it. Head over to www.bit.ly/ClaudiaCarroll to join, and you'll get access to a free short story by yours truly. Of course, all your information is entirely confidential.

I really do hope you'll enjoy the little extra treats I've included in My Readers' Club and until then, feel free to review the book on Amazon or Goodreads, or on social media – because it's always good to talk books, isn't it?!

Fondest wishes to you all, THANK YOU for reading this little letter, and of course, as ever, happy reading,

Claudia xxx

**If you enjoyed *The Fixer*, keep your eyes peeled for
Claudia Carroll's next book . . .**

The love. algorithm

True love is only just a swipe away? Right?

Iris is good with numbers. In fact, she's great at numbers.
Educated, cultured and career-driven, she's got it all. Well,
nearly. The only thing missing from her perfectly calibrated
life is a partner – and not for lack of trying. After almost
30 years of searching, Iris has tried it all. Now, she approaches
disappointing dates like research, gathering statistical evidence and formulating hypothesis on why she just cannot
seem to find 'the one'. But something still alludes her – that
unquantifiable spark.

Kim is too busy being the life and soul of the party to be
looking for love. Her terrible dates make great stories for her
friends and co-workers as long as she's not caught by her
strict boss, Iris.

Recently widowed Connie is single for the first time since
the 1970s. Her daughter, Kim, is determined to get her to try
online dating. But suffice to say, a lot has changed.

When Iris decides to take matters into her own hands –
using her extensive research to create the most scientifically
accurate algorithm for love. She decides to launch Analyze,
a dating app like no other. But she can't do it alone, roping
in Kim and Connie as guinea pigs, setting them up with their
scientifically-approved soulmates.

Because, after all, love is just a numbers game . . . isn't it?

Read on for an exclusive extract . . .

Chapter One

She was nervous. He was hungry. She'd had her hair done specially. He seemed far more interested in the menu than he did in her. She was wearing a brand-new dress. He was in trainers. She didn't want to drink. He ordered a full bottle.

'So, tell me all about yourself,' she said, reminding herself to smile and maintain eye contact, as all the dating websites advise you to do on a first date. *Remember to sit forward and show interest in the other person. Don't be a conversation hogger, but do ask pertinent questions. Create a strong first impression, and prepare some interesting first-date topics in advance.*

'You want to know how I am right now? Bloody starving,' was his blunt answer as he scanned up and down the menu, all eight pages of it. It was an expensive restaurant, with white linen tablecloths, cut-crystal glasses and a sommelier. And he was the one who'd chosen it, which she thought augured well. Statistically, men who were prepared to expend on a date were 72 per cent more likely to end up in a serious, committed relationship within six months. Fact.

'So tell me, whereabouts do you work?' she asked politely.

There was a lengthy silence which wore on, until eventually the penny seemed to drop with him that it was not a rhetorical question.

'Ehhh . . . sorry . . .? So . . . what were you saying there?' he stammered distractedly, looking up from the menu. 'Oh, right – OK, so I work in sports management for a big multinational. I'm pretty senior in the company, actually.'

His profile specified that he'd played rugby at club level, and he looked every inch of it: a physically huge, hulking man in every way. He must have stood at about six-four with hands the size of shovels and the thickest neck on any human being she'd ever seen.

'Sounds great! Tell me more.' She smiled agreeably, but by then she'd already lost him back to the menu.

'Tell you what,' he replied, 'the starters here look really good. How about we order a few of those, then we can share?'

Appear compliant and agreeable on any first date, she'd seen on a Ted Talk before setting out that evening, so that's what she did, she nodded and agreed. She wasn't remotely hungry, but she knew that low blood sugar driven primarily by hunger led to a 45 per cent decrease in social skills. Maybe, she hoped, this date would get off the ground properly once he'd eaten.

He ordered for both of them – an astonishing four starters in total: the chicken skewers, pork falafel, beef carpaccio and smoked salmon.

'I'm vegetarian,' she gently reminded him. This was clearly specified in line three of her dating profile – had he just forgotten?

'Oh yeah,' he said to the waiter who was scribbling down their order. 'Better throw a few greens in there for herself, OK?'

Sure enough, when the food was served, exactly 80 per cent of it was entirely inedible to her, leaving her with no option but to pick at a watery-looking garden salad. This did not seem to bother her date, who ate like a man on death row. And that was before he got started on the wine list.

The first bottle of wine he'd already milled his way through long before their starters had even been cleared. It was ferociously expensive, and she nearly choked on an asparagus spear when he called the wine waiter over and ordered the same again.

'But I'm driving,' she spluttered.

His response? 'You've got a car? Great. Maybe you can give me a lift into town when we've finished eating? A few of the lads are meeting up in the Capitol bar and I said I'd stick my head in when we're done here. Oh, and don't worry about the vino – my treat, I'll take care of it.'

Well, at least that's something, she thought.

Then he couldn't decide between entrées, so he decided to order two: a filet mignon and a tuna steak. 'This way, I can make my own DIY "surf 'n' turf",' he said. 'Hey, I'm a big guy, gotta get the old protein into me.'

Not only that, but the amount of side dishes he'd ordered filled the entire table to groaning. Food, food and more food just kept rolling out of the kitchen, and while he horsed hungrily into it, she picked at a mushroom risotto and valiantly tried to steer this date back on track.

'So tell me what you like to do when you're not working,' she asked, even though she had done her research on him thoroughly beforehand. Just like she did on everything. 'I can see that you enjoy eating out, and I know you're a sportsman, but what other hobbies and interests do you have?'

Regular theatregoers scored particularly high with her here. As did any potential partner who'd visited an art gallery or exhibition in the past six months. Extra points for raising the topic of books, particularly if any date was prepared to discuss what he was reading at the moment. Top marks if this happened to feature something on the Booker Prize list.

'Well, work takes up most of my time right now,' he shrugged, speaking with his mouth full of tuna and *pommes frites*, a sight too disgusting for words. 'Any free time I do get, I'm either at club matches, or else the big international games. Did you happen to see Ireland versus France last weekend?'

She was about to reply that no, actually, she hadn't. She wasn't particularly interested in rugby, or soccer either, for that matter. As he'd have known if he'd bothered reading her dating profile properly. But just then, as soon as he'd finished eating, abruptly and without even excusing himself, he got up to go to the gents.

She sighed deeply, taking the chance to sit back, have a sip of water and reflect on how the evening was going so far.

It was only when he'd been gone for a good ten minutes and still hadn't returned that she began to wonder where he'd got to. The probability of him having bumped into an acquaintance she gave a low 15 to 20 per cent. So what was keeping him? A binge then purge eater, she wondered, as the minutes ticked by? No; statistically, bulimic men in his age category only accounted for 0.1 per cent of the population. More than likely he'd taken a call and was outside somewhere on his phone. Rude beyond words, but then in her long and bitter experience, rudeness seemed to be a factor in approximately 67 per cent of all her first dates.

'OK if I clear away now?' their waiter asked, and she nodded yes.

He'd been gone a good fifteen minutes now, and still no sign of him. Annoyingly, she didn't have his mobile number, as they'd been direct-messaging via the dating app they'd met up on, so she tried contacting him on that instead.

Everything all right? Where did you disappear off to?

Still no response. She tried again – still nothing. Should she just pay for herself, then walk out, she wondered? But she quickly dismissed the thought. Apart from anything else, it would be a rotten thing to do to the restaurant staff. The waiter came back with dessert menus, which she waved away.

'May I bring you some tea? Coffee?' the water asked her instead.

'I think just the bill, please,' she said. Moments later, the bill arrived, elegantly secured in a leather-like wallet and discreetly placed in front of her.

She opened it up. Glanced down at the total. Took it in. Processed it. Tried not to panic. Snapped it shut again, and did her best to act as if this was not a problem for her.

Nine hundred and twenty-one euro. *Nine hundred*. Almost a month's mortgage payment on a dinner for two, and she'd hardly eaten a scrap. The wine alone was an astonishing two hundred and thirty *per bottle*. Wine that she hadn't even sipped. By her calculation, the head of lettuce and minuscule portion of risotto she'd consumed should have cost approximately seventy-five euro, even in an upmarket restaurant like this.

She willed herself to remain calm. A sudden spike in blood pressure, she knew, led to a 45 per cent increase in poor decision-making, and right now, she needed her wits about her. He'd be back, of course he would, and he'd split it with her, as she had assumed all along would be the case. It would still end up costing her considerably more than she rightfully should be paying, but still. It was better than nothing. She was a financially independent woman; she earned well; she had credit cards; she always, always paid her own way. Particularly on any first date, where dividing bills fifty-fifty was par for the course.

'May I bring you the card machine?' the waiter asked, by now hovering in a most irritating way. Did he perhaps suspect that all was not well?

She tried to remain cool and collected.

'I'll just pop to the ladies' first. May I ask if you've seen the gentleman I was dining with? I assume he's still in the bathroom? Or else taking a call outside?'

'I'm afraid I haven't, madam,' her waiter replied smoothly, tactful enough not to embarrass her. 'Also, just to remind you Madam, if I may, that your table is booked as a time limited reservation.'

It was crowded at the bar, and she was aware of multiple eyes boring into her, the middle-aged single woman hogging a precious table for two.

She went downstairs to the bathroom to splash cold water on her face and check for herself whether he was down there or not, even though she knew in her heart of hearts that the probability of the waiter lying was close to zero. She even slipped outside onto the street, to double-check that he wasn't there either, perhaps indulging in a sneaky cigarette as, she knew, 23 per cent of the population did.

It was at this point that she had to remind herself of the principle of Occam's razor, in Latin sometimes known as *lex parsimoniae*.

That the simplest explanation is usually the correct one.

Like it or not, he'd done a runner. Which made it worse, far, far worse than being stood up. In this case, clearly he'd arrived, taken one look at her, decided she wasn't for him, but figured what the hell, he'd stay for dinner anyway, consume as much as he was capable of, then stick her with the bill and vanish into thin air.

It was cruel beyond words. It beggared belief. It was unthinkable. But with the waiter hovering beside her, credit card machine in hand, she did what had to be done. Swallowing her pride, she handed over her card, paid the bill and somehow managed to leave the restaurant with her head held high.

By no scientific or mathematical law that she was aware of, she thought on the drive back home, could it possibly get any worse than this.

She had officially hit rock bottom.

Her name, by the way, was Iris Simpson, and if all her years of unsuccessfully scouring the dating coalface had taught her anything, it was this.

You wanted to meet a partner? Then you had to be optimistic. You had to trust in the triumph of hope over experience. You had to strategise, you had to be brave, you had to be prepared to make the first move and not take it too personally if you were rebuffed. You had to put real thought into writing the perfect profile – that went without saying. But above all, you absolutely had to believe in your heart of hearts that dating was purely and simply a number-crunching game. The greater the number of dates you went on, the higher your chances of securing a partner. Simple as that.

Numbers, fortunately, happened to be Iris's particular area of expertise.